Slough Library Services

Please return this book on or before the
date shown o
To renew go to
Website: **www.slough.gov.uk/libraries**
Phone: **01753 535166**

MT 101

0466

Slough
Borough Council
www.slough.gov.uk

DAUGHTERS OF PENNY LANE

In 1946, Alice Quigley returns to her childhood home on Penny Lane, having lost three sisters and her house in Bootle to the bombs that fell over Liverpool. Estranged from her husband Dan, who suffered from two strokes triggered during the Blitz, she moves in with her remaining sister, Nellie. But even though the bombs have stopped falling, tremors still rock the family when Alice's reviled mother is kicked out of Nellie's home and seeks vengeance. When visions from the past resurface, she soon uncovers a dark secret that her mother has kept hidden...

DAUGHTERS OF PENNY LANE

DAUGHTERS OF PENNY LANE

by

Ruth Hamilton

Magna Large Print Books
Long Preston, North Yorkshire,
BD23 4ND, England.

British Library Cataloguing in Publication Data.

A catalogue record of this book is
available from the British Library

ISBN   978-0-7505-4602-7

First published in Great Britain 2017 by Macmillan
an imprint of Pan Macmillan

Published in Large Print 2018 by arrangement with
Macmillan Publishers International Ltd.

Magna Large Print is an imprint of Library Magna Books Ltd.

Printed and bound in Great Britain by
T.J. (International) Ltd., Cornwall, PL28 8RW

One

1946

It was different here. Different? The houses hadn't changed – bay windows, little front gardens with paths and gates, glazed attic dormers perched on some roofs, several residences doubling as shops. 'It's me,' Alice Quigley informed her canine companion, 'it's me that's different.' Had returning to Penny Lane had an effect? 'It's stronger than ever, Frank,' she whispered.

It. The bloody it was taking over her life, and she wasn't in the mood. Muth had nominated Alice's it her 'otherness', as it separated her from ordinary people. She was special. She saw things, heard things, knew things... 'But not today, please,' she whispered. Having moved house just this morning, Alice was in need of some supplies.

The sky was splitting into small prisms, tiny shards with no glue holding them together. 'Sugar,' Alice spat. 'Clouds next, Frank. Clouds, mist, grey blotches, then action from long ago or far away. Or both,' she reminded herself. Would she ever see the future? A rainbow was trying to form right above her head, but chances were that she alone could see it. Oh, Frank sometimes saw, too. And today it was different, more powerful than ever before. She needed answers to a hundred questions.

9

As she opened the door of the ironmongery a few inches, shapes began to form in the air. It was, at first, a corner of the eye moment, a heraldic split second that warned of something momentous, and she tried to shake it off. She had no time for messing about today, because Dan was coming home soon. Did she have a choice? Had she ever had a choice? Frank, on his new red lead, was pulling slightly, trying to hold her back. He probably knew the day was out of order.

All her life, Alice had experienced visions, flashes of times past – even of the present in places far away. Why now? Ah, it was clearing … no, it lingered inside the shop, and it belonged to the woman behind one of a pair of counters that formed an L in line with two walls. Alice pushed the door to widen her view of the interior.

The shopkeeper was handsome, tall, middle-aged, with threads of white woven into severely pinned-back dark hair. The forehead was high, cheekbones well defined, and she carried herself proudly. There was an inherent elegance that defied the unremarkable clothing: a grey dress, a washed-out blue cardigan and an apron that tried hard to remember being white. This shop was not the right setting, since the keeper seemed to be a rare jewel planted in base metal.

But Alice was here for … firewood and … and…? For years, she had experienced othernesses, strange moments that were sometimes frightening and always strange. 'You're different, child,' Muth had insisted. 'You will see and know what others can't, because you are a seven, and so am I.' A seven? Alice wished she could have been a one or

10

a six or an eight, or … or anything bloody ordinary. Even bottle-bottom glasses would have been preferable to second sight.

The back wall of the shop was covered by creeping sepia smoke that only she could see. No. Once again she was all but certain that Frank could see it, too. It became a huge face with a wide-open mouth that seemed to frame a silent scream. So far, there was nothing new – she'd seen it all before.

Alice opened the weighty door as far as it would go and stepped inside. There was no choice – she always had to face whatever turned up. Running would make no difference, because things always caught up with her, damn them. 'All I want is to be normal, Frank,' she said behind gritted teeth.

The large, white dog hung back, his behind planted firmly on the outer doorstep.

'Get in,' ordered the owner of the nervous boxer. 'Do as you're told.'

He scratched an ear. It was one of the habits he employed when wishing to distract himself and others. 'In, Frank,' Alice repeated.

He abandoned his protest and followed her, parking his backside firmly between paraffin heaters and firelighters. It was going to be one of those days, and he wasn't best pleased, because moving house was enough to take on without visions and all that palaver. He scratched the other ear. He hadn't even been fed yet.

'Unusual dog,' the shopkeeper announced. 'One like that, I am never see before in my life. Sad face, but so beautiful.'

The newly arrived customer managed a tight

11

smile; this ironmonger lady was by far the most unusual item in the small shop. 'You're not English.' At least Frank was inside now, though he looked about as happy as a wet and windy weekend in Blackpool. He was doing that blowing out of his cheeks thing again.

'No,' the woman replied after a pause. 'I am Russian, from a village over to the west of Moscow. But in England now many years.' She stared hard at the customer. 'Sitting down, please. Your face is being pale.'

Alice sank onto a hard kitchen chair. 'Alicia Marguerite Quigley,' she said. 'But they call me Alice.' The shop darkened; even the street outside looked black, as if Penny Lane had acquired its very own dense cloud.

'Olga Konstantinov. In Russia I am Konstantinova, but here I find women take father's name unchanged, so I do same. Shop is called Konnie's Korner – bad English I know, but my father wanted a name to remember.' She shrugged apologetically.

Smiling became impossible for Alice, and the shopkeeper's voice faded away as her customer shifted into another dimension. The small, seated visionary accepted the inevitable, since there was little she could do to alter her environment. Frank settled, thought better of it, and moved to stretch out across Alice's feet. He would guard her; his job was to care for the woman who fed and loved him.

A door in the corner disappeared, as did all the display shelving. There was a cart. Muffled hooves seemed to beat the earth until the cart stumbled and spilled its contents onto the ground. Bodies. Adults and children tumbled down when a wheel parted company with the rest of the vehicle. The corpses fell in impossible shapes that imitated broken marionettes. It was like a silent film that kept sticking on the reel: jumpy, too fast, too slow. Alice stared into violence and chaos, and she shivered in spite of the warm weather. She was looking at the results of an unholy massacre.

'Madam?'

Alice was beyond listening to the here and now. 'Children,' she whispered. 'Clothes ripped off. Jewels sewn in the hems of girls' dresses. Children,' she repeated. 'All dead.' A lone tear trickled down a cheek. 'Sweet Jesus Christ in heaven, what am I seeing? And why am I seeing it?'

Fortunately, there was a chair behind the counter, and Olga dropped onto it, grateful for the support offered by this wooden item. Was the unknown customer another Rasputin, the creature who had tried to rule the whole of Russia through his so-called mysticism? She shivered. In her book, Rasputin was a son of Satan, and she was grateful to those who had supposedly murdered him. Hell must have claimed the man, as he had been suitable for no other destination in the afterlife.

For Alice, the picture faded, leaving just the silent, wide-open mouth, which disappeared after a few seconds. She blinked while returning to the now. 'Sorry about that. It happens. I'm the seventh child of a seventh child – I wish I wasn't. I get visions. This one was yours, though. What I just saw belongs to you and your family from

13

somewhere else, not here, not this country.'

Olga allowed a few beats of time to pass. 'I am having no family here or anywhere.'

'In Russia?' Alice asked. 'Have you nobody in Russia?'

'My grandfather and my father brought me here. My mother, she die young when I was about ten years. I have also two brothers who bled – they had bleeding disease and they die also when very young.'

'Haemophilia?'

Olga inclined her head. 'I am carrier. If I have sons, they bleed, so I not marry. If I have daughter, she carry the illness and pass it on. Is only way to stop, to be alone, have no children, make it end.'

Alice swallowed hard; this Russian lady was afraid. 'I'm sorry,' she said.

But today's show wasn't over. Frank raised his head and stared mournfully at his owner. Being a boxer meant that he always appeared puzzled or morose, but he managed a wonderful imitation of grief by displaying the whites of his eyes. He followed his mistress's gaze, which was fixed on the woman seated behind the counter.

Alice saw a younger Olga in a ball gown. Diamonds and other jewels – green ones – twinkled in a tiara and at her throat, and she was beautiful. 'Your dress was purple, but not darkest purple. Like a deep violet. Where were you when you wore that gown?'

The ironmonger shivered, but felt bound to answer. 'It was our dacha. Usually small house for summer days, but ours was big. It was ball when

14

I was almost eighteen years. Next day, we leave to other parts in Europe, and Europe was at war. Difficult, so journey took days. Romanov family dead one week after we go. We are escape revolution.'

'So you're rich?' Alice's words were delivered on a whispered breath. 'Royal, like?'

'No, not rich,' was the quick reply. She paused for a second. 'My father, Ilya Konstantinov, had farms. We had money enough, but not very rich.'

'And your mother?'

Olga sighed as if defeated. 'She was ... connected to Romanovs.'

'Romanovs?'

'Tsar Nicholas was killed with family and servants. Nicholas cousin to my mother, but we no speak of this. I have forty-seven year now, but Russia will find me out if you speak. Our lands gone, our houses gone, yet they fear return of royalty.' She smiled and shrugged. 'They think I go back with army? Just you, myself and dog? Speak not of what you know from today. As far as Russia believes, I am dead. Allow me to remain safely dead.'

Frank chose this moment to rise to his feet and yawn before pointing a wrinkled face at the ceiling and delivering his impression of a whole pack of wolves, as his howling changed key for each one. Exhausted after a minute, he collapsed.

'He's too spoilt to howl for long,' Alice said, pulling herself together determinedly. 'Give us two bundles of firewood, Olga. I need a shovel and a box of candles, too. Oh, and calm down, will you? I'll not tell nobody nothing about what

15

happened here today. Anyway, I bet Russia's not interested in you no more.'

Bearing candles and a shovel, the Russian returned to her counter. 'Me, I am being learning the English very slow. You go fast and make too many negatives. We being teached about double negatives.'

'Taught,' Alice replied promptly, a smile broadening the vowel sound. 'You a Catholic?'

'Russian Orthodox, but I go any church – don't care. Christ say where two or more gathered, he is among.'

'Not in the House of Commons or the Lords, I reckon.'

Both women laughed. 'Nor in Kremlin,' Olga chuckled. 'Stalin believe in Stalin, workers grateful for pennies they get. Idea is poor are all same, while rich bank in Swiss places. They think we not know this, but my father is understanding what was to happen. So we run and are come to here.'

'I am running too, Olga. Lived in Bootle and got wiped out. There were only two houses standing on our road when the war ended, and they looked a bit drunk, all wobbly chimneys and crooked doors, and no glass in the windows. And funnily enough, we're being resettled here, in the house where I was born.'

'No!'

'Yes. They've built an extra bit downstairs for my husband. He's had a stroke and can't do stairs. How much do I owe you?'

'Two shilling and sixpence; is good shovel.'

'It had better be – that's a day's wages for some.' Alice placed two florins on the counter

16

and took her change. 'I'll see you soon.' She picked up her purchases, and Frank followed her out of the shop.

Olga Konstantinov sat for a while, her mind busy processing the recent happenings. It was a strange world, yet she had made a friend at last. Since Batya's death, she'd been so lonely, communicating only with customers before going up to eat in the living quarters above the shop. Raising her eyes heavenward, she thanked her Maker. 'Spasibo,' she mumbled. 'Thank you, God.' And she also thanked her dad, her beloved Batya, for sending Alice Quigley to Konnie's Korner. Olga had sold a shovel, but her heart had given itself away to a large white dog with sad eyes and a face that needed ironing.

Alice's neighbour on one side was a thin yet robust woman of indeterminable age with lisle stockings (wrinkled), very white teeth (false), rusty red hair, two sons (God alone knew where the buggers were), and a laugh that sounded like water rushing to find its way down a plughole. Although Alice was a native of Liverpool and inured to the speed of its speech, she decided that keeping up with this woman was going to be difficult. She found herself fascinated by the other's eyes, because a turn in the left one grew more pronounced when she became excited.

Vera Corcoran was a character, and she worked hard to show Alice she was deserving of the title. She had delivered babies, tended the sick, laid out the dead, and seemed to know everyone's business. The Hillcrest family were all in a 'sanctimonium' with TB, Bert Warburton had been arrested for drunk and 'disorderedly', while an unfortunate woman called Philomena Lever had shingles on account of her Annie who had come down with chicken pox. 'But Jimmy won't let me do it no more,' Vera went on sadly. 'People die at night and babies are born at night, so he made me stop, cos he wants me safe.'

Alice began to feel dizzy; did this woman never shut up? On the other hand, the relentless flow gave her time to work out Vera's eye problem: sweat on the nose caused spectacles to slip, and the eye returned to its rightful place of abode only when the glasses were pushed back into the correct position.

By two o'clock, Vera had stripped and cooked the bare bones of Alice's curriculum vitae, and she intended to fill in all missing flesh at the earliest opportunity. A new neighbour was fair game and great fodder for Vera's eclectic portfolio. Dan, Alice's absent husband, had suffered two strokes. The first had struck when their Bootle house had got flattened and he'd been digging his wife out of rubble under which she'd been trapped; the second and larger event had happened on the docks, where he'd been loading munitions to be returned to arsenals at the end of the war.

'What a shame,' Vera said, head shaking. 'Was he not in the war, love? Might have been safer abroad instead of lugging all them bombs about. Why wasn't he called up?'

'Fallen arches,' Alice replied while she had the chance. 'He couldn't have got through basic training with feet as daft as his, so he specialized in loading munitions instead.'

'And he's been away for months with these strokes?' Vera asked, sliding the words in between her descriptions of nightmare births and gruesome deaths, club feet, cleft palates, bunions and a very bad case of pneumonia in the middle of June 1941. 'So I was always busy. What's the dog called?'

'Frank.'

Vera blinked and adjusted her specs. 'No, I mean what make is it?'

Tempted to say 'Rolls-Royce', Alice curbed her impatience. 'He's a boxer.'

'Oh.' The neighbour wasn't stumped for long. 'I didn't know they made them in white.'

'Neither did I. He's quite a rare specimen.'

Vera folded her arms under a non-existent bosom. 'Was his mam white?'

'No. She was a kind of blonde colour – I have a photo of her somewhere. It's black and white, but you can see that she's pale.'

'His dad?'

'No idea.'

Vera launched herself into yet another tale, this time about the disgrace of a white woman with a white husband. 'They live in Smithdown Road. She had a little lad, a darkie. She says he's a throwback, and he is – a throwback to when the Yanks were here. Her husband fought his way through the desert and up Italy while she was working under the American air force one at a time.' She patted her metal curlers. 'Well, I'm saying one at a time, though you never know with Yanks, do you? Randy buggers, the lot of them.'

Alice found no answer; she'd had enough of the surreal for one day.

'Have you got anybody round here, like? You know what I mean: family, friends and all that.'

'I had six sisters. One emigrated to Australia, and three died when a shelter got hit. Their kids are that bit older now, but it was sad when it happened, all crying and a big funeral with three coffins.' She pinned Vera with piercing blue eyes. 'Dad's dead. Muth talked him to death, cos she never learned when to shut her gob. He just hit the floor like a sack of rocks while she was moaning on about the neighbours, know what I mean?'

Vera bridled. For a small-boned woman, she bridled quite well, seeming to expand upwards and outwards while she unfolded and refolded her arms. The metal curlers shivered slightly as her head moved quickly from side to side. Her displeasure was evident, and her spectacles slid down her nose no less than three times, so overheated did her skin become.

Alice, aware that her neighbour was shifting up a gear, put out her hand and patted Vera's arm. 'Lovely to meet you, Mrs Corcoran. I must go in and start getting the place ready for my Dan. They're bringing him home soon.'

'Oh. Can I help? I'm very good with them what's not well. Our doc's always saying I should have been a nurse, cos I'm a natural.'

'Er ... no need, thank you.' She didn't want the eyes and ears of Penny Lane assessing her worth, her furniture and every word she spoke. 'I know where all the stuff is, so I'll manage better by myself.' She turned and walked into her house with

20

Frank hot on her heels. The door clicked shut, and she pressed her back against its welcome support. Getting used to Vera Corcoran wasn't going to be easy. She wondered who lived at the other side. Oh, how she hoped Vera was a one-off...

That click. She opened the door an inch or so, then closed it again. The click; she remembered it. 'I must have been no more than two or three when we left here, Frank.' The scents arrived – Dad's pipe tobacco, Muth's pan of scouse, a whiff of Derbac soap, the smell of clean, bleached sheets hanging from the pulley line. 'I do remember, Frank, I do.' She had worshipped her father, and had come to hate the woman who had given birth to her. For the first twelve years of Alice's life, she'd been Muth's favourite, the clever one, the sighted child, the angel. But as soon as Alice had begun to have opinions of her own, things had changed. 'And my sisters were jealous of me, Frank.'

The dog sat at the bottom of the stairs, his face an embodiment of misery. It was hours till feed time, and this wasn't a proper place yet, since there were boxes everywhere. Removal men had positioned larger items of furniture, but much of the Quigley household was packed in cartons. And his mistress was expecting something else to happen, though he couldn't work out what the something might be. He waited for her to move, but she'd gone into one of her quiet times, so the dog yawned, lay down and slept. If there was no food, he might as well absent himself from this new situation.

Alice grinned at him. He could sleep at the

21

drop of a hatpin, and oh, how she loved him. The Russian ironmonger promised to be interesting, too. Perhaps Penny Lane might turn out to be a good move.

As she walked towards the rear living room, the area set aside for Dan, she heard muffled voices that gradually got louder. Her dad was crying, while her mother released a wail the like of which Alice had never heard before. A newborn screamed, but the sound ceased suddenly, as if somebody had switched off a wireless. This was day one, she told herself. The othernesses connected to this house would probably get worse...

Returning to the hall, Alice stood by Frank and heard nothing apart from the dog's snoring; it was plain that he hadn't been disturbed by any of the sounds. But one thing was for certain sure: the house on Penny Lane, the place in which her life had begun, was not at ease. The trouble belonged to her parents, as had she. Well, as long as it didn't bother Dan, she would cope, she told herself firmly. Dan had always been deaf and blind when it came to his wife's visions, thank goodness.

The front door knocker hammered. It was a lion's head – now, how had she managed to remember that? Perhaps she'd noticed when following removal men in and out. She opened the door. Frank placed himself beside her. A tall, well-built man stood on the step. He gave off the odour of cement, and his facial skin was grey, as if the materials of his job had covered all exposed parts of his body. 'Yes?' she asked.

'Mrs Quigley?'

Alice inclined her head.

'I'm Harry Thompson and I live next door. The builder paid me to help with the extension and fit your new bathroom, so I thought I'd call round and see if it was right for your husband's needs. I'm really a plumber, but most of us have become jacks of all trades since the war.' He glanced down at his feet. 'I'll take my boots off if you'll let me in.'

She widened the open door while he removed his workday footwear. 'You're all sand and cement. Go on, then. I'll follow you through.' She shook her head and grinned while walking behind him – he had sizeable holes in both socks, and his clothes were filthy.

They stood in the new room, Frank between them. Like a spectator at a tennis match, he moved his head from Alice to Harry, from Harry to Alice, keeping pace with the lines they delivered.

'So all you do, Mrs Quigley, is get the temperature right and push the wheelchair in. Of course, you'll have to give him a bit of a wash first, but this will rinse the soap off him. When he gets a bit better for you, he might be able to climb in the bath.'

Alice smiled sadly. 'I don't think so. The second stroke nearly did for him, you see. He's a big chap, built on the same lines as yourself.'

Harry nodded. 'Right, I'll stick a bell in.'

'A doorbell?'

He laughed. 'An alarm. If I'm at home, I'll hear it, then I can help you with him. It'll ring in my house. Your dog's taking it all in, I see.'

'Yes, he does that. Never misses a trick, my Frank.'

23

'Frank?'

Alice nodded. 'He was already Frank when I got him. Grief-stricken, he was, because his owner had died and he'd been locked in with her body for two days. He took to me straight away, though. I lived in a bedsit in Sefton Park, but I was allowed to keep Frank as a guard dog.'

Harry chuckled. 'What a ridiculous face.'

Deadpan, Alice turned and stared at him. 'Me or the dog?'

'The dog, of course. He looks like he ran at a wall in top gear and pushed his nose in with the force of impact.'

'He's beautiful, Mr Thompson.'

'Harry. I'm Harry. And yes, he is beautiful in a crazy, mixed-up way. It's the two grey spots on his forehead – they make him look like a deep thinker.'

'Oh, he's that, all right.' She looked round the room. 'You've done a good job, but tell me why there's a grid in the floor here.'

He explained that he'd studied wet rooms when helping to fit facilities in an old people's home. 'The whole room's a shower, because you'd never get a wheelchair over the rim of a standard shower stall. I'm not just a pretty face, you know. I went up to Maryfields and spoke to Dan himself, and the staff. Matron said a wet room was a good idea. And you're right – he is about my size, so take care of yourself.'

'What did Dan say about the bathroom idea?'

'Well, he nodded when I told him, and I think he asked me to keep it as easy as possible for you. They say his speech is improving.'

24

'It is, God help us.'

He grinned. 'Why do you say that?'

'He's very left wing. He could start a war in a shopping basket. He'll be going on about it being 1946 and when will this bloody health system they keep talking about be up and running proper, and why are war widows given such poor pensions, and who does the adding up when it comes to income tax, because the soft bugger needs a new abacus. In words you might use as a plumber, he's like a tap with a washer loose, drip, drip, drip. Pick a subject, and he'll have an opinion.'

Harry's laugh was infectious. It seemed to rumble like thunder from his diaphragm before spilling out loudly enough to crack the tiles on which they stood. She found herself joining in until her stomach ached, while the dog, unamused by all the noise, left them to it. In his opinion she should have been looking for his blanket, but she seemed to think she had better things to do.

Harry stopped laughing. 'Do you want me to run a second alarm through to the other side? Vera Corcoran – she's small, but she's strong.'

Alice took a long draught of oxygen. 'No, thanks.'

Harry grinned again. 'Ah, so you've met her? We call her the Penny Lane Echo, because she knows the news before it happens, then spreads it all over the place. But she's not a bad person, Mrs Quigley.'

'Alice.'

'Alice, then. And I might be as much at fault as she is, but this is truth, not decorated gossip. Her old man's broken her jaw, her ribs and her collarbone. And I haven't told you that. If she wears long sleeves in summer, that'll be to hide the bruises. You'd use the alarm only when he's not in, of course. I'd hide the bell. He doesn't like her talking to people in case she tells somebody who'll beat him up for being such a swine.'

'No,' she whispered in disbelief.

'Yes,' was his swift response. 'When he's at work, she goes about telling everybody's business to keep her mind off her own problems. Twenty years ago, she was a grand-looking girl with a good figure and shiny hair. He soon knocked the shine out of her, and her lads have grown up thinking it's all right to beat people up and steal. I feel sorry for her.'

'So do I now. But we're private people, me and Dan. No children, which is just as well, because he'll take up all my time when I'm not working.'

'You work? How do you manage that?'

'Sewing machine upstairs. That ship's bell fastened to the wall above Dan's bed is going to be his way of summoning me. I do alterations, wedding dresses including for bridesmaids, smart suits for women, kiddies' clothes, curtains. I've a full order book. Mind, they usually have to find their own material, because it's still in short supply. But I'm never out of work.' There was pride in her tone. 'I'm a qualified tailor and dress-maker and I don't charge a fortune – tell your friends.'

'I will. And don't be frightened of asking Vera for help. She sat with my dad many an hour towards the end. I fetched him over from Everton, you see. Everybody else left and got married, but

I was the youngest, and somebody had to look after him. He had a few bob, so I retired early to look after him, and went back to plumbing and building after he died. But I don't know how I would have coped without Vera. She needs to feel important; appreciated, I suppose. Her husband's cruel and her boys are wild, so she hasn't much to live for.'

Alice was the youngest in her family, but she could never have Muth living with her. Muth ruled now in her oldest daughter's house, and no way would Alice even consider housing her unless all her remaining sisters died. And if that terrible thing should happen, Alice would still have to think very hard before opening her door. Compared to Alice's mother, Vera Corcoran was merely playful, because Elsie Stewart was a monster.

'Have you got food in for your tea?' Harry asked.

Alice failed to understand the reason, but she suddenly felt shy. He was nice. With a bit of spit and polish, he'd probably turn out to be quite handsome. 'Yes, I've got everything I need, ta. Tell you what, though. If Dan's orderly ever can't get here, you could come in for ten minutes when you get home from work. You might help me get him out of bed and sit him in the wheelchair for his tea.'

'I'll be glad to. Then I'll come back and throw him back in bed for you, eh?'

'Thank you.' She couldn't quite manage to work out why, but she trusted this man, had recognized a kindred spirit as soon as she'd opened the front door.

He smiled down at her. She was no bigger than two penn'orth of chips, but she had guts and humour. 'Let Vera do your shopping, girl. Not at weekend; not while Corcoran's there. Try to be nice to her, because she's what they call isolated. He keeps her in her place, and neighbours avoid her. Give her something to live for, Alice.' After a pause, he continued, 'Vera was a bad picker. She chose him instead of me. Be good to her, I beg you.'

'All right.' She glanced at a clock. What was the matter with her? Why did she still feel slightly shy? 'Dan'll be home any day now.' The invisible baby cried again. That would be the reason for her discomfort – perhaps she'd been waiting for it to happen. It seemed that her neighbour heard nothing.

'I'll leave you to it, then,' he said. 'By the way, I like your dog.'

Harry had definitely heard nothing. Alice sighed her relief. 'So do I. And he loves Dan, so he'll be company for him while I'm at work. Matron let me take him into the rest home a few times.'

When Harry had left, she perched on her husband's bed. Perching took effort, as the bed was hospital height; at five feet and two inches on a good day, Alice had to use a stool, a sturdy little item with two steps. This had been bought in hope, and in case Dan ever found the ability to get himself out of bed. She thought about Vera Corcoran and Olga Konstantinov. While occupying her mind in this way, she managed to avoid musing about Harry-next-door. He was a good, kind man, and she wasn't thinking about him...

28

The chaos that disturbed her nap after about twenty minutes would be ingrained forever in Alice Quigley's memory. Being psychic was all very well, but the gift was seldom useful. Why hadn't she seen what was about to happen here in this house on this day? So much joy, so much hope, both flavoured with sadness – surely the seventh child of a seventh child might have been granted a glimpse of what was about to take place?

Harry must have left the snick on the front door, because it flew inward and crashed into the wall. Frank barked. It was his greeting bark, so the door-flinger was probably not an intruder. Alice jumped down from the bed and ran into the hall.

It was Dan, her Dan, her Danny Boy. He was on crutches and swinging his legs into the hall. Oh, God, dear God, thank you!

Alice sat on the next-to-bottom stair and burst into tears. 'Why did nobody tell me?' she managed through a torrent of saline.

'S-Alice,' Dan cried. 'S-Alice!'

Dr Bloom from Maryfields Convalescent Home bustled in. 'He wanted to surprise you, Mrs Quigley. When he makes a decision, there's no stopping him. Stubborn as the proverbial mule.'

'Surprise?' she answered, a handkerchief mopping up tears. 'It's a wonder I didn't have a bloody stroke myself.'

An ambulance driver entered the fray. 'Where are we putting him?' he asked.

Alice waved a hand towards the door to Dan's room. She rose to her feet just as the rest of the cast turned up. Olga Konstantinov led the way;

she carried a lidded bowl. Vera Corcoran arrived behind Olga, and a cleaned-up version of Harry Thompson brought up the rear. He was wearing fresh clothes and a wide grin, and he winked at Alice.

'Is this what they call a cabinet meeting,' she asked, 'or have I been invaded? Where's bloody Churchill when he's needed?' She was babbling, and she knew why; she didn't want Dan or Harry Thompson to see her all red-eyed and teary. She needed to pull herself together. The man she loved, the dear man she had married, was in the rear living room waiting for her. She shouldn't be looking at another person, no matter how handsome he was. And he was definitely handsome without sand and cement decorating his features.

When she entered his room, Dan was seated in an armchair. 'S-Alice,' he said again, a frown spoiling his face. The struggle with words was proving much harder than the difficulty with limbs. 'S-nice,' he managed. 'S-room s-nice. S-garden.' Almost everything he said continued to begin with s.

She brought the two-step stool and sat on it, reaching up to hold the hands of her beloved man. 'Dan, this is Vera from next door. I think she'll help us with shopping.'

'S-Vera,' he answered.

Vera beamed. A husband was talking to her without shouting.

'And this is Olga. She has an ironmongery shop up the lane.'

'S-Olga.'

'I bring borscht,' Olga announced. 'Beetroot soup.'

30

Alice allowed herself a small grin as she imagined what disasters might be created if Dan got within a yard of beetroot soup.

Harry stepped forward. 'You know me, Dan. I've done your bathroom.'

'S-yes.'

'Come,' Olga ordered. 'This man tired – is big day for him.' She led the neighbours out of the house.

Dr Bloom stood by Dan's chair. 'We'll miss you, Dan. You've organized the workers and forced them to join unions. You've been the biggest nuisance we've seen in years, and I've found a speech therapist who will call in from time to time, because we need to be rid of your s.'

'S-yes, s-we s-do.'

The ambulance man glanced at his watch. 'I'll be off now.' He grinned at Dan. 'I need to get my s-ambulance back to base.'

'Watch it,' Dan exclaimed clearly.

The doctor's jaw moved south. 'That's the answer, Mrs Quigley. Annoy him. I think he's been having us on.'

'I daren't,' Alice said. 'He might have another troke.'

The ambulance man left chuckling.

'It all right,' she continued, 'I've wallowed it for him. Twenty-five letter in the alphabet now.'

'S-stop it.' The patient closed his eyes. At the age of thirty-three, his Alice was more beautiful than ever. Would he ever share her bed again? Or was he destined to live in this room for the rest of his days? Stairs. For him, a flight of stairs presented a problem the size of Everest. He'd been

31

away for so long, and Alice was the sort who turned heads in the street. Had she found someone else? Might she leave him?

He raised his eyelids and looked into her blue eyes. No. That wonderful, gorgeous, open face would have betrayed her. She was completely without guile, since she seemed to be almost unaware of her own attractiveness. Perhaps what her mother termed her 'otherness' made her different.

'How are you?' she asked when the doctor had left. 'Any pain?'

He shook his head.

'I missed you, Dan. Living in the bedsit in Seffy Park was no fun till I got Frank. I had to keep the wireless on and borrow library books. I never even enjoyed sewing without you.'

'S-sorry.'

'Sorry? Don't be soft, lad. You got me out of that mess, remember?'

He remembered. If she'd been any bigger, she might have lost her legs, but her neat little body had been protected by the kitchen table, a solidly made item that had covered her completely. He'd passed out afterwards, waking some hours later in a hospital bed next to which she had sat all night. 'S-thanks, s-Alice.'

'Oh, stop it. For better or worse, in sickness and health – remember?'

He nodded.

'You're my boy, Danny, my beautiful, beautiful boy.'

One side of his face smiled while the other side made an effort.

'I'll get you right. Now, I'll make us a bite to

eat, then we'll put Harry-next-door's bathroom to the test. All right? And I suppose this dog of ours will want feeding, too.'

'S-wait. S-here.' With his better hand, he took a sheet of paper from a pocket. 'S-doc wrote s-for me.'

He'd left off the s twice again! Alice scanned the page before reading aloud.

'My beloved Alice,

'The money Granddad left me has paid not just for the house and alterations, but also for a male orderly to come in morning and night seven days a week rather than just weekdays. He will stay for a while, get me out of bed, clean me up and dress me every day, and he'll get me ready for bed at night.

'All you have to do is feed me and help me with exercise for one hour each day. I will not be so much of a burden, and it will be good to give a part-time job to someone who needs the cash.

'I have missed you so much. Thanks for being mine, love.'

'Your Danny.'

Alice took a deep breath. 'You're so welcome,' she managed, eyes filling and lower lip trembling.

He nodded. It had all been explained to him, the depression that followed stroke, the lack of confidence, the physical changes that might render him unable to make love. It would be all right. At home with his Alice, he was going to be on the mend.

Frank sat with Dan while Alice went to prepare a meal. The dog knew Dan well, because he'd visited him in the other place that smelled so horrible, all sickness and other odours that made him sneeze. This man was a part of Frank's job, and he would guard him well. Ah, food. That was a good smell, but Frank was a great dog. Instead of following his nose, he lay down and placed his head on his front paws.

'S-good dog,' Dan said.

Frank emitted a friendly growl. Where he was concerned, the extra s didn't matter a jot.

Two

Everyone within walking or cycling distance of Browne's shop on Smithdown Road knew that Elsie Stewart was verbally lethal. She had a tongue sharp enough to slice bacon down the Co-op, held strong opinions on every subject from politics through religion and all the way to furniture polish, and people joked about selling her to primitives on the other side of the globe. Perhaps the natives of some faraway shore might learn to extract her poison and use it as weaponry. Her eleventh commandment – *thou shalt keep thy daughters safe* – had resulted in the Stewart house becoming a jail rather than a home, and her girls had fought for freedom.

Hers had been a far from happy family. She had been free with her tongue, free with the flat of her right hand, and on occasion she'd also used implements – a belt, a slipper, or the ruler from her husband's tool cupboard. But the youthful females had eventually fought back, while their father, a gentle soul, had shrivelled until he'd found his exit feet first in a box through the front door. Elsie, now in her seventies, continued vile and venomous.

Elsie's youngest daughter had been known to declare that curare should no longer be required – 'All they'd need would be to shove the ends of their spears in her gob.' This statement summed up perfectly the young Alicia Stewart's view of her surviving parent. 'My mother is a thing with no antidote. The School of Tropical Medicine will find no cure for the slime on her fangs, vicious old snake. Death on legs, she is.' Thus was dismissed the mother of seven girls, widow of an excellent carpenter known as Chippy Charlie Stewart, and current self-appointed boss of the Brownes' shop. Some custom had been lost to a newsagent across the road, but the shop continued to fare well enough.

Legends were myriad. She had deprived her husband of peace and quiet until he'd lost the will to live, and had dropped stone dead with a massive heart attack. One of her daughters had clouted her with an old encyclopedia; Elsie had emerged unscathed, but the tome had crumbled into confetti, or so the fairy tale announced. She was a witch who made potions, and she'd killed her old man with a noxious brew disguised as frothy cocoa. He was better off out of it, as were three girls killed by German bombs and one who had escaped to the other side of the globe.

The latest tale about her antisocial behaviour

involved a paper boy who'd pinched a bar of chocolate from the shop and ended up in hospital with scarlet fever, mumps, measles and something multisyllabic ending in itis. Along Smithdown Road and all adjoining streets, the hatred for the old bag was treasured and nurtured like a cherished child. Against all odds, the matriarch thrived, while the daughter, joint owner of her husband's business, retreated ever further into her shell. Poor Nellie had always been quieter and more timid than her siblings, so Muth was now clog-dancing all over her life.

Elsie Stewart, widow/witch/monster, lived with the eldest of her seven daughters, Helen (usually Nellie) Browne, who supposedly ran the shop selling sweets, tobacco, newspapers and fancy goods on Smithdown Road. However, having seen off Martin Browne and his offspring, Mrs Stewart called the shots, while Nellie, reputed by her mother to be a few bob short of the full quid, kept a low profile. Muth did the selling, and Nellie wrapped things while Elsie looked after details like working the till and counting change. The elderly besom was in charge of everything and everybody, so very few answered back when her harsh words cut right through to the bone marrow.

Nellie Browne wasn't happy; nor was she good at expressing her feelings. Both her daughters had left home and married young, while her husband hadn't been seen for well over eighteen months, and Nellie was sure that Muth had been the reason for all the disappearances, though she never said as much. So far, she'd been too scared

36

to speak up. But even a slowcoach has her limits, and Nellie wanted her family back. She missed her husband, and would have done almost anything to persuade him and her daughters to come home. Inside, where she kept her feelings, a little cauldron began to bubble. 'Your fault,' she told herself quietly and frequently. 'You should have thrown her out years back and made them stay.' Was it too late? Could Nellie manage the shop without her mother?

Unlike her eldest daughter, though, Muth wasn't backward at coming forward, and she often pushed Nellie to one side even when customers were in the shop. 'Born with a screw loose,' Elsie Stewart would announce loudly. 'Get out of me way – I'll find the bloody magazine. Brainless, she is, absolutely without a clue.' Many customers came along for the rather nasty entertainment value; shopping was incidental, because they all wanted to be there when Nellie finally snapped, as she surely must. Elsie was thin, Nellie wasn't, so if the latter simply sat on the former ... well, who knew what the result might be?

Just lately, Nellie had started to get a bit steamed up about life. At the age of fifty-three, she had become decidedly menopausal and slightly fractious, so she resolved to go and have a word with one of the clever girls in the family, their Alice. Alice knew stuff. Alice was good-natured and generous and all the things Muth wasn't, and she had no time – not even a split second – for Muth.

On a fine Sunday in the middle of June, Nellie left the shop at the crack of dawn without saying a word, abandoning Muth to deal with the Sun-

37

day newspapers. 'See?' Elsie asked of the customers. 'She doesn't give a half-penny damn for this bloody shop. He was the same, that Martin, always nipping out for a drink and a smoke, leaving me to cope because our Nellie's as thick as tapioca pud during a milk shortage. I'm a slave, that's what I am.' She doled out newspapers and weighed sweets. 'I've no idea where she's buggered off to, and nobody's seen her.'

A man spoke up. 'Never mind – you got the girls' big bedroom, didn't you? Oh yes, you made bloody sure you got what you wanted. Rid of me first, then your talons into my kids. Nigel's right – you should be put down like an old cat.'

The whole shop froze. A heavy silence rested on the shoulders of half a dozen customers while Martin Browne and his mother-in-law prepared for battle. This was interesting, because it looked as if neither party would give an inch.

Elsie found herself staring into the eyes of a man she loathed. She swallowed nervously; she wasn't used to being nervous. 'What the bloody hell do you want?' she snapped. She watched open-mouthed while her daughter's estranged husband led the shoppers outside. 'Go across to Miller's,' he advised them rather loudly. 'You'll get treated better there, away from the mother-in-law from hell.'

He re-entered the shop, locked the door and turned the sign to display CLOSED. 'Right, that's that,' he said, almost to himself. 'Clear coast, so I'll sort things out here and now.' He addressed her. 'Right, that's your last audience out of the way. Get your stuff together and move out. Today.'

'What the hell are you doing in this shop?' she hissed. 'Bad penny's turned up again at long last – is that it? Run out of cash, have you? Or has some woman with sense thrown you out?'

'Where's my wife?'

There was no joy in the chuckle she emitted. 'She's wandered off and left everything for me to do. She's lazy and stupid and totally incapable of managing without me.'

He nodded, lips set in a grim line for a second or two. 'Listen to me, you old bitch. Gnawing away at me till I left was one thing, but chasing my girls out's another matter altogether. And before you ask, because I know you have to be told everything, I've been in Manchester working as assistant manager in Woolworth's and saving up to pay off the mortgage on this place. But I'm back now, and I'm staying, so go and pack your bags and bugger off out of it while there's still room for you in hell. You don't belong among decent folk, so that's where you'll finally meet your match.'

Elsie sank onto a stool. 'She doesn't want you here, our Nellie. She'll not have you back; I can tell you that much for no money. And she's even stupider than she used to be.'

Martin stood motionless for several seconds before speaking again. 'She's not stupid; all she needs is encouragement. So. Let's see what's what, then.' He narrowed his eyes.

'Right.' She folded her arms and chewed thoughtfully on her lower lip.

He raised the flap at the end of the counter and marched through the storeroom and upstairs to the living quarters. 'Back in a minute,' he promised as he went.

Elsie stayed where she was for a while. Marie wouldn't have her, would she? As for Alice – there was no chance in that household, either. She thought about her 'treasure', the seventh daughter who had arrived on Elsie's fortieth birthday, a beautiful child, blonde and lively and happy. Alice had been a star.

But the other six had been jealous of the favourite, because they'd had to make do with second-hand while Alice had worn only the best, everything new and pretty. And Elsie herself had reaped no reward from Alice's 'otherness'. She'd tried to force the girl to do séances or to perform for an audience in halls and small theatres, but the answer had always been in the negative, since Alice had insisted that she owned no control over her episodes.

In spite of all she'd done for the child, Alice had turned nasty in her teens. A lot of girls did that, of course, mostly because of changes at certain times of life, but that one? Elsie blew out her cheeks. Alice had gone too far, had developed and nurtured a strong antipathy towards her mother, and that had intensified after the death of her father. Not that Chippy Charlie had ever been much use, but his youngest had adored him.

Of course, three daughters had perished in the Blitz, stupid cows. Why had she let them out? Why hadn't they used their brains and done the serving of soup and tea on different nights? That way, Elsie would now have had more options, more chances of finding somewhere to live in comfort. Marie, the other good-looking one, had married a vet who had offered to euthanize Elsie for the good of mankind – bleeding clever clogs, he was. No way would Marie's Nigel – what a soft name – allow his mother-in-law to tarnish that great big house up in Waterloo. As for Alice … well, least said, soonest mended. Australia? Oh, bugger that for a lark; Theresa probably wouldn't have her anyway.

The inner door opened and two suitcases were hurled under the raised flap. 'Your stuff, madam,' Martin Browne said, sarcasm dripping from every syllable. 'I'm not so good at folding, so some of it's a bit creased.'

'Have you been rooting in my room?' she shouted.

'No.' His tone had turned icy. 'I've been emptying cupboards in my daughters' room, because they each have a child now and we can help mind the babies. Nellie and I have two grandchildren, but we haven't seen either of them. I bet Nellie doesn't even know about them, because they're kept away from you. I found out from a sales representative who covers Liverpool and Manchester. He knows our Claire, and he recognized me from here, from this shop. Anyway, that's all by the by, isn't it? You're going. No matter what, you're going.' He retreated and slammed the door hard.

'You bugger off,' she screamed. 'You're not wanted. Our Nellie doesn't need you; we've managed without you for long enough.'

The door opened a fraction. 'Nobody knew they were married till it was in the paper, two sisters having a double wedding. I bet you made damned sure my Nellie never saw that copy of the *Echo*. I had to find that out through the salesman as well. I'm going bloody nowhere, but you are. I hope your broomstick can carry you as well as the cases.' He left the scene.

She had nowhere to run, and she suddenly felt her age. Up to now, she'd been as fit as a whippet, but fear seemed to grip her by the throat. Breathing wasn't easy. Then she remembered: the Turners had made a fortune out of their home-made ice cream, and they'd bought a house somewhere.

They'd gone mobile with the ice cream, sending out carts every day to streets all over Liverpool, and there was a flat above the empty business premises a few doors down the road. She would have to pay rent for the first time in years, would have to cook for herself. But she'd be able to keep an eye on Nellie and all the goings-on, wouldn't she? Did she want that? She didn't know what the hell she wanted.

Elsie was finally beginning to realize that this was the time to do it. Not for nothing had she stood over the deathbed of her own father in Ireland. Not for nothing had she listened to his moaning and groaning, because he'd owned two farms and some serious stock. As for her brothers and sisters, they'd all gone to America or Canada, so she'd inherited the lot, because he'd signed it over to her. The idea of sharing it out would have been silly and expensive, because nobody knew where the heck the other six were living. It was time to use the rainy day money. Bugger the Turners – Elsie didn't need to stay near Nellie, did she? No, she would get away from Smithdown Road, make a fresh start elsewhere.

Out of four remaining daughters, she had only one who was biddable – the big, daft lump who owned this shop with the fellow upstairs. Nellie, the oldest and daftest, was now a grandmother, and she would choose the babies, that much was certain. So it would have to be the bank, the money she'd hidden for years. Yes, she would be forced to use Da's legacy and hope against hope that none of her older siblings would return to claim a share in it.

What Elsie didn't recognize was her own reluctance to live alone, her fear of isolation. Nor did she understand the quickening of her heart and the flood of adrenalin that announced the imminent arrival of panic. She picked up her suitcases, walked through the stockroom and left by the back door. A house. She would buy a house.

Nellie Browne was also having serious breathing difficulties. After hanging around playing fields and cricket grounds since sunrise, she'd walked from the Smithdown Road area to Sefton Park, and she felt frazzled. The sun was already hot, she was overweight by a couple of stone, and Alice wasn't here any more. She wondered what had happened to Dan, though she didn't dare ask.

'Do you know where she's gone?' she asked the handsome young man who had answered Alice's front door. 'They were sent to this flat after their house in Bootle got bombed. Dan's her husband, but she would have been here on her own a lot, cos he got put in the ozzie for months at a time.'

'I'll find out, love,' he answered. 'There's a woman in the roof flat who used to visit Alice and her dog. Just you wait while I go and ask her if she knows.'

'Thank you.'

The young man went back inside.

Nellie sat on the outdoor steps. The merciless heat seemed to be doing its best to kill her. If her arms hadn't been so fat and flabby, she would have removed her coat. Muth was going to be livid by this time; what excuse might she offer to explain why she'd left her to struggle alone with Sunday papers and delivery boys?

The man reappeared. 'You're not her mother, are you?'

'No. I'm twenty years older than Alice, though. Muth had Alice when she was getting on, you see. I'm Nellie – Helen, really. I'm Alice's oldest sister.'

'Oh, right. Well, Miss Foster said your Alice returned to Penny Lane, and the house is the one where she was born.'

Nellie blinked. 'Really?'

'Really. They've had it altered to suit her husband's needs, or so Miss Foster said.' He shrugged. 'She was worried – Miss Foster – in case you might be Alice's mother. Good luck, then.' He returned to the hall and closed the door.

'Bugger,' Nellie muttered under her breath. In this family, everybody kept secrets because of Muth. The Stewart girls had been born to a terrible woman, and that terrible woman had damaged Nellie's life, and Martin's, and the girls'. Where were they? Where were Claire and Janet?

44

They were married; it had been in the *Echo* – a customer had told her. She'd found a copy of the paper and cut out the photo, without telling Muth, of course. Were they happy, and did they have children?

On leaden legs, she retraced her steps. But she wouldn't pass the shop, so she cut through different streets. There would be hell to pay afterwards, but it was time for the worm to turn. Alice, the prettiest and cleverest, would have an answer, wouldn't she? Or Marie, who was similarly blessed in the looks and brains department.

Happening on a little cafe, Nellie bought a glass of iced orange and swallowed it within seconds. In the tiny washroom, she splashed cold water on her face and tried to tidy dull brown hair. 'I'm ugly,' she mumbled. 'Ugly and fat because I eat too much.' Food had become her first love since the disappearance of Martin, followed by Claire and Janet. What sort of mother didn't know where her daughters were? What sort of grandmother chewed away until granddaughters sneaked out at night and never came back? What sort of mother came between a daughter and the man she loved?

'She's no sort of mother; she's a killer,' Nellie advised her reflection in the badly marked mirror. And that was when she reached her moment of clarity. Yes, she was afraid of living alone above the business and no, she wasn't really up to scratch in the shop, but Muth had to go. If Muth went, Nellie would seek out her daughters, and try to find Martin, because Muth had made all three of them leave. With Elsie Stewart gone, the girls might visit home with their husbands. 'I'll man-

45

age,' she told herself, 'because that's what women do. They have to.'

She left the cafe behind and continued the trek to Penny Lane. Alice was clever; Alice would know what to do.

Alice took a liking to Peter Atherton from day one. He had a Woollyback accent, a mop of thick, curly, silver-grey hair and a sense of humour that belied his slow, exaggerated speech. 'I were over here a few years back, watching a scrap between Liverpool and t'Wanderers,' was his answer when she asked how he had come to be living in Allerton. 'I'd no bus fare home, so I stopped.'

She dropped the tea towel she'd been folding. 'No,' she said after he'd retrieved the item for her. 'You're having me on, aren't you?'

'Am I?' He winked.

'Wanderers? Where were they wandering?'

'Back home,' he said solemnly. 'They got beat three nil. That were t' other reason why I stopped. Liverpool looked gradely compared to t'Wanderers.'

'What?'

'Eh?'

'I said what, as in what the hell are you jangling about?'

His speech slowed all the way down to first gear. 'Right, love. Bolton Wanderers football team; are you with me? They were rubbish that week, and I'd no money, so I stayed here, got a job, found a room, turned mesen into a Kopite.'

'Mesen?' Her eyebrows climbed up her forehead.

'Myself,' he explained as if talking to a child.

'Gradely?' she enquired.

'A bit good. Do you not understand English, love? Anyway, take me to your leader. I've already met the miserable bugger at Maryfields, so he's used to me. Retired, I am now, but not ready for pasture up on t' moors. So I'm your helping hand. I mean hands, because I've got two.'

'That's handy,' was her smart response.

'Another bloody clever clogs just like him,' Peter mumbled. 'Still, they might as well keep all t' sharp knives in t' same drawer. Hiya, Dan. Dan, Dan, the custard man,' he said as he followed Alice into her husband's room. 'Does this lass know you want hot custard with everything? Even ice cream?'

Dan shook his head. 'S-don't start, Pete.'

Alice left them to it. Hoots of raucous laughter followed her about the house, and she knew from the start that Peter Atherton was the right man for the job. According to Dan, the bus fare-less Peter had been a docker, a union leader, a builder, an insurance collector and an orderly in the convalescent home. At sixty-three, he remained as fit as a butcher's dog, a Liverpool supporter, leader of a darts team, an expert crown green bowler and a killer at poker, his main source of income.

She peeled vegetables and basted the Sunday roast. Peter stayed every Sunday, playing dominoes and cards with his patient. Apart from cooking a meal for three, she had Sundays to herself, so she could read, go for a walk or listen to a radio play. Frank drifted from room to room, his nose following the scent of cooking, his heart

47

sending him back to check on Dan. A responsible animal, he took his job seriously.

When the door knocker made a noise one Sunday in June, he performed his duty by barking in a restrained I'm-not-really-worried tone. Alice shoved the lamb back in the oven, removed her apron and walked down the hall. Not Vera again, please! No; the abused Vera's husband and nemesis usually stayed in until Sunday evening, so... She opened the door. 'Nellie, love?'

'Hello, Alice.'

Alice stepped back to allow her sister into the house. In her fifties, the oldest Stewart sister was red-faced, sweaty, breathless and older than her years. 'What's happened to you, Nell?' Something had stamped hard all over Nellie's features. Alice felt that she already knew the reply to her question.

'Muth. Muth's happened.' And the tears flowed.

Once settled at the kitchen table, Nellie calmed down and mopped her face with a handkerchief. 'Can she get the shop off me, Alice?'

Alice was making tea, the panacea for all ills. 'No, she can't. That shop's in your name and Martin's, so she hasn't a cat in hell's chance. Here. Let it brew for a while, then we'll have a nice cuppa.' She placed a tray in the centre of the table. 'But you'll have to go back and keep paying the mortgage. It's the bank that will take the shop off you if you don't pay up.'

'I think Martin's been paying it. But I'm scared of her.'

Alice laughed, though the sound arrived without humour. 'Everybody's frightened of her. With a gob like that, she probably scares herself when she looks in a mirror.'

Nellie shook her head. 'She makes a show of me in front of customers.'

'I'm not surprised. She made a show of our Theresa, remember? Accused her of sleeping with loads of boys. Well. Theresa showed her good and proper, got herself a grand life at the other side of the world, and I can't say I blame her, because she's better off out of it.'

'Martin left cos he couldn't stand her bossy ways. Claire and Janet are God alone knows where, married to men I've never met. They had a double wedding – did you read about it? It was in the newspapers. Muth wanted the big bedroom, you see. And I just let it all happen because she was in charge. I'm weak, that's the trouble; I'm not like you and our Marie. Alice?'

'What?'

Nellie twisted nervous hands. 'Have you ever wanted somebody dead? I mean really, really wanted them dead?'

'Oh, yes. Adolf Hitler. He obliged by topping himself in his rat hole.'

'Just him?'

The younger woman's lower lip curled. 'No – our mother as well. She drove our dad to an early grave and tried to turn me into something I'm not. Theresa travelled thousands of miles to get away. She drives people to distraction, that one.'

'Muth's the one I want to kill. She's a bad woman, isn't she?'

'Oh, yes. Sometimes I feel as if she's still here, in this house. And I get a whiff of Dad's tobacco,

49

as if he's trying to save me from her.' She gazed round the kitchen. 'This place isn't at ease with itself. There's something...'

Nellie shivered despite the heat. She couldn't smell anything apart from roasting meat. 'Muth won't come here. Ever since you clouted her on the back of her head with that cuckoo clock, she's called you mad. She calls me useless, fat and stupid. Nigel and Marie make her jealous, because they have that cracking house up Waterloo.' She paused for breath. 'I hate her.'

'When I hit her with the clock, I was just giving her some time.' Alice giggled in spite of her sister's terrible sadness. 'She tried to stop me going to see our Marie, because she decided I was thinking of moving in with her and Nigel.'

'Which you did.'

Alice nodded. 'Well, our mother gave me the idea. They were good to me, them two. They were good to Dan, too. And I loved working with the animals, you know. Especially dogs. I remember when we took turns to stay up all night to feed newborn puppies while their mum got better.'

'You like animals, don't you, our kid?'

'Yes, I do. You know where you are with them.'

Nellie patted Frank. 'This is a lovely dog,' she said. 'You got wed from their place, didn't you, love? Great wedding, not spoiled by Muth.' Nellie paused. 'Is that your Dan laughing? Is he home? Is he all right, Alice? Can I see him?'

'Drink your tea first. Dan and his so-called assistant are a comedy act. It's a Peter Atherton from Bolton, used to wander about with the Wanderers. He got converted to Liverpool, calls himself a Puddler.' She lowered her voice. 'He still supports Bolton on the sly, and he won't go to a match where the two teams are playing each other. But he's a case. He reckons to be teaching Dan the guitar, but it just sounds like a cat in pain. Pete says they're going to get spots in local pubs, and they'll be the cripple and the crooner. I take no notice. Dan's a rotten guitar player, and Pete sings like a dying frog.'

'So they're just kidding?'

'Yes. Dan can get about with crutches now. He's doing well.'

In spite of fear and bewilderment, Nellie smiled. Alice would make everything right. She found herself wondering whether her little sister might be in possession of a second cuckoo clock...

Martin Browne reopened the shop. By tradition, newsagents served customers on Sundays right up until lunchtime, and they arrived in droves once Elsie had left. No one had volunteered to help with her suitcases, and no one had offered her a room, so she had wandered off down back streets in the direction of town without a word from any of them, though gossip among the neighbours had burgeoned. She'd gone; a cancer had been removed from Smithdown Road.

They bought their cigarettes, Sunday papers, sweets and comics for the kids. Martin spoke to them. 'Does Nellie make a habit of disappearing?'

'No,' was one response. 'But she was getting fed up. We could all see she'd had enough of her mother. As you know, your Nellie's a bit on the gentle side, so Elsie rode roughshod all over her.'

'We'd all had enough as well,' a tall man said. 'She's 'orrible.'

Grunts of agreement filled the shop. From a jumble of sentences, Martin learned that Nellie wasn't looking after herself, that she'd put on weight, and that people agreed that she'd been compensating for the loss of her husband and her daughters. 'She's turned to food to fill the space,' an old woman said, 'and it's made her ill. Your mother-in-law was cruel to her. Nellie needs her girls back. I'll have a quarter of mint imperials and ten Woodbines. I've got my sweet coupons. When will they come off ration?'

'No idea, love. They need to stockpile enough sugar, you see. There weren't many ships doing sugar runs during the war, so there's catching up to be done.'

She nodded. 'And she needs you,' the old dear continued. 'Nellie. She needs you back, lad.'

'She wants looking after,' someone else added.

He closed the shop at one o'clock and waited. Where was she? Where were the girls? The salesman had said he'd met Claire in town, and she'd had a little boy in a pram. She'd told him that Janet had a boy, too, but she'd refused point blank to disclose addresses. 'It's Gran,' she had explained. 'We don't want her to find us.'

Martin ran a hand through his hair. He was back in Liverpool, yet he felt no closer to his family, because they were all missing. 'Jesus, help me,' he whispered. 'I've got rid of the dragon, but where's my Nell? What about the girls and our grandsons?' He didn't care about Nellie getting fatter – he was no plucked pullet himself. She was still his Nell, and he'd left Liverpool only to bring her to her senses. It had been her mother, of course. Even after he'd shifted the bed away from the dividing wall, his wife had refused to allow him near her. 'Old bitch,' he spat.

He peered through the glass in the door. Where had Nellie gone? Perhaps she had arrived at her senses, though he didn't know that address, either. Oh, where could she be? With Marie? With Alice at that flat down Sefton Park way?

His reason for leaving had been to force Nellie to get rid of Elsie, he reminded himself yet again. It had taken time, and he'd had to come back anyway to do the deed. Nellie usually took a while to cotton on to things. She was slow, but not stupid. 'Come back to me, Nell,' he mumbled. He wanted all three of his girls – Nellie, Claire and Janet. Nellie was the old boot's eldest. Marie was number two – she was married to Nigel, a good chap, and they lived up Waterloo in a big black-and-white house filled with stray animals.

Three daughters had copped it during the war – Constance, Judith and Sheila, which left just Nellie, Marie and Alice, because Theresa was a world away. Dashing upstairs again, Martin Browne checked on his wife's wardrobe. She'd never owned many clothes, but he felt sure that there wasn't much missing.

He rushed down again, climbed into his battered Morris and drove to Sefton Park. For the second time within hours, the handsome young man was disturbed. 'Alice doesn't live here any more,' he said, patience etched into every word. 'And there was a woman here earlier looking for her.'

'Brown hair?' Martin asked hopefully. 'A bit of weight on her?'

The young man nodded. 'I sent her to Penny Lane, because Mrs Quigley's moved back to the house she was born in.'

The young man disappeared, and it was Martin's turn to sit on the steps. Alice. Well, fancy Alice moving back into the place in which Elsie Stewart had managed to make life difficult for seven girls and one decent man. Alice was ... oh, what did they call it? She saw things, things that weren't there for ordinary people. Psychic, that was it. She'd seen through Elsie, all right. The precious seventh child of a seventh child had dealt many blows, most verbal, a couple physical, every one of them aimed at the woman known as Muth. There wasn't one good bone in Elsie Stewart's body, but she was tough. He grinned. She'd needed to be tough once Alice had got her hands on that bloody cuckoo clock. Chuckling to himself, he stood up. There was no time to waste.

He returned to the car and sat in the driver's seat. Penny Lane was nearer than Marie's place in Waterloo, so he would have gone there first anyway. He talked to himself all the way up Smithdown Road. 'Be there, Nellie. Please be there, my Nell.' He parked the Morris and popped a mint in his mouth. For his wife, he wanted his breath to smell fresh, at least.

The house door was shiny black and newly painted. The rule about green woodwork had finished after the war, and Alice liked everything spick and span. Inside would be the same, each item in its rightful place, no dust, rugs beaten halfway to death, brasses as shiny as the lion's head door knocker.

A man answered Martin's knock. 'She's just dishing up the dinner. Can I help you? I'm Peter Atherton, Dan's minder.'

'Is Nellie here?'

'She is. And you are...?'

'Martin Browne. I'm Nellie's husband.'

Peter hesitated. 'But Dan said you'd ... er ... left and ... er...'

'Well, I'm no longer erring. Are you going to let me in? Alice knows me.'

Peter stepped to one side. 'Come in. We're just about to sit down and eat.'

Martin entered the large kitchen. Dan was there, sitting in a dining chair, a carver with arms and a padded seat, crutches propped against the wall by his side. Alice was fussing about with a roasting tin, stirring frantically while adding stuff to turn meat juices into gravy. Nellie was near the back door. 'Martin!' she screamed. They ran towards each other and collided. He grinned; he needn't have worried about bad breath, because his poor wife was hot, agitated and sweaty. And he didn't care. 'I'm home, love,' he said.

'Oh, God,' she cried before bursting into tears yet again.

'No. It's just me, Nell. God's busy with it being a Sunday.'

'But ... but Muth,' she spluttered.

'Gone. I threw her out.'

Nellie took a step back. 'You got rid?'

He nodded. 'And hello, Grandma,' he announced. 'Claire and Janet have both had boys. I don't know where, and I don't know when, but we've two grandsons.'

Alice abandoned her gravy, while even Peter Atherton brushed a tear from his cheek. Dan grinned. 'S-hello,' he said.

'He's collected a pile of s's,' Alice explained, 'so we're having s-roast s-lamb. Sit down. I can stretch to five, but you all have to save a bit of lamb for him.' She pointed to Frank. 'His begging bowl's in the middle of the table next to the mint sauce.'

'Grand animal.' Martin patted the white, worried head, then kissed his sister-in-law on the forehead. 'Guard dog in Seffy Park, wasn't he?'

Dan frowned. 'That woman's mine,' he pretended to growl.

'See?' Alice asked of no one in particular. 'He can drop the s when he needs to. Does it for attention.'

Dan eyed her coolly. 'I'll s-show you some ... s-attention later,' he threatened.

She grinned at him. 'You'll have to catch me first, love.' She blinked rapidly, trying hard not to spill tears. If only he could chase her. Blackpool beach, concrete posts planted to stop German ships and weaponry landing; running and weaving between these obstacles, Dan complaining because his feet hurt. Fallen arches had saved him from combat, but not from war. Would they ever be close again? Might she produce a child at last?

When the meal was over, Nellie touched her sister's arm. 'He'll be all right, Alice.'

The younger sister managed a smile. 'Are you

56

psychic, our Nellie?'

'I hope not – one's enough for any family. No, I mean he's walking a bit, isn't he?' She pointed at the crutches. 'And I like that Peter and I love Frank. We could do with a dog at the shop. Can we have one like this?'

Alice studied Frank, her sole baby so far. 'There's only one Frank. An Alsatian would be good. But find Claire and Janet first – they may not want dogs near their babies, Grandma.'

'God, I'm old, aren't I?'

'Let's not bother about age. After clearing these pots, we'll go upstairs to my sewing room and find a pattern. I can make you some clothes that'll suit you better than what you're wearing. I'll make you young again, our kid.'

'I need a diet.'

Alice nodded. 'We'll see to that, too. No sweets, no chocolate, five-minute walk every day, then ten minutes, build up to half an hour. Do it for yourself, not for Martin. You first. Time you thought about yourself, missus. Now, what about giving me a hand with these dishes?'

Nellie nodded, a smile plastered across her homely face. 'All right, boss.' She tutted. 'Who's the oldest?'

'I am, love. By about a thousand years. It's something to do with my otherness.'

Nellie chuckled. 'My Martin's back, our kid.'

'He was always planning to come back, Nell. He wanted you to get rid of Muth, but you just wouldn't, so he's done it for you.'

The older woman's grin faded. 'She'll be on her own.'

'I know.'

'She's never been on her own.'

'I know.'

'You have to stop saying, "I know."'

'I know.'

Nellie slapped her little sister's hand. 'Let's leave the washing up till afterwards and find a pattern. I need to look nice for me feller.'

'I ... won't say I know. And you'll look nice for yourself, Nellie. That's the law.'

Three

Marie and Nigel Stanton lived in blissful chaos, in Waterloo, in a large mock Tudor house and in abiding love. When out shopping together they still held hands like the pair of teenagers they'd been over thirty years ago, and they didn't give a damn about what people thought of them. Nigel's oft-stated opinion was that he didn't see the point in growing up, since adulthood brought little but worry about bills, about the state of an unforgiving world and about run-over dogs and their chances of survival in his busy surgery. Although a vet, like a doctor, needed to distance himself from his patients for the sake of sanity, he didn't always achieve that sensible goal, and his wife loved him all the more for his attachment to animals, since she, too, was a lover of most creatures, though she wasn't terribly keen on llamas. For this attitude, she had good reason.

Marie was the second of Elsie Stewart's seven long-suffering daughters and, at the age of fifty-one, had long abandoned the idea of motherhood. In order to lavish her surfeit of maternal affection on living, warm-blooded creatures, she had filled her enormous home with animals. Dogs, cats, birds and rodents shared space amicably, since she insisted on entente cordiale. Anyone not co-operating got the message after being stuck in isolation for a day, and Marie took joy from watching birds preening cats, rats playing with dogs and rabbits cuddling kittens. This was the perfect life.

Many arrived too ill to fight, and incapacity made them accept the strange mix contained in the house known as Chesterfields. Marie Stanton welcomed them with open arms, an open mind, and a strong, loving heart. The only one she couldn't say she loved was Larry the llama; she simply understood his attitude to humankind, which species he seemed to find wanting in many areas.

Nigel Stanton, the vet who had offered to put down his wife's mother, conspired with his beloved spouse to save the young, the weak, the elderly and the neglected in Chesterfields, which was one of the few houses in Liverpool North to have acreage. Young, weak, elderly and neglected were terms that described most comers, but Elsie Stewart, though old, was banned from the list (though Nigel had offered, out of the goodness of his heart, to stable her with Larry, whose manners were questionable).

The Stantons sheltered instead of Muth a homeless Irishman in a large, heated and weather-proofed shed, kept him fed and watered like the rest of their rescued creatures, and allowed him one bottle of Irish whiskey per week. In return, he helped with the animals and cheered up the household with his attitude, which spanned amusing to curmudgeonly with many tram stops along the way. A dyed-in-the-wool itinerant, Tommy finally settled into the comparative luxury of his shed, from the vantage point of which he kept a weather eye on the outdoor animals. The war between him and Larry seemed to be permanently stuck like a game of tennis between two players of equal aptitude; it went from deuce to advantage back to deuce, and there was seldom a clear winner.

The day Larry the llama staked his claim on the house would be emblazoned forever across Marie Stanton's mind. Tombstone Tommy, the rescued Irishman, was hot on the animal's heels, and his language was interesting. The gist of the intelligence he delivered was that the llama was evil, a sneak, and had been spitting liberally at anything that moved, as well as some stationary items. He and Larry burst into the hall, and Marie was left in the kitchen with her mouth hanging open. Oh, to be in Africa, she mused. At an edge of the Serengeti from which orphaned lion cubs were plucked after watching the murder of their mothers. That was her dream, and her husband shared it. 'One day,' she whispered. When Nigel retired, they would be off to the greatest place on the earth, and Tommy, or someone of his ilk, would work here.

Nigel, currently operating on a beagle in the South Road surgery, was unavailable, so just Marie and Tommy were in charge, though Larry seemed to have other ideas when it came to management. With that arrogance etched into the face of every member of the camel family, he looked down on the two humans who were trying to control him. They really had no idea at all when it came to the negotiation of terms.

Within seconds, every creature whose proper place was inside the house dashed past Marie and made for the back garden and the stables. Tombstone Tommy returned. Clearly out of sorts, he was breathing hard through his mouth, allowing a grand display of the items that had won him the nickname. Just two teeth remained in his lower jaw; they were stained by tobacco, spaced well apart, and represented small imitations of graveyard stonemasonry. 'He's in the glass room,' he panted, referring to the conservatory, 'and he's in a mood similar to Hitler's, so he is, always spits on me when he's the wrong side of hell's doorway. God damn him, that bloody animal will be the death of me, I swear.'

'I know you swear – I heard you. Leave him to calm down, Tommy.'

'Calm down? That thing is a bloody lunatic, missus. I've seen better behaviour from a gathering of men filled to busting on Uncle Michael's poteen.'

'I know.' Marie sighed. 'He ate my best blouse. Parachute silk, with some lovely pleating. Our Alice made it for me. But Nigel won't let Larry end up in a zoo or a circus. I'll go and try to get

61

him in a better mood.'

'A better mood? He's in the son of Satan himself, and I think—'

'Tommy, wait here.'

When she reached the conservatory, she marched past the recalcitrant ruminant; eye contact might have made him worse, so she simply threw open the glass doors, stood back, and waited for him to leave. The animal stalked towards her, pausing for a moment so that this inferior two-legged creature might know its place, then left the house with his head held high. He was in charge, and they would have to live with that fact.

Everything outside that should be inside ran into the conservatory because Larry was on the loose. Marie sighed heavily. Her husband would deal with Larry when he got home from his emergency. Nigel suffered many emergencies, including the two current residents of the laundry room. Marie grinned. They were the lucky ones, God bless them. She closed the doors and did a quick headcount – yes, five cats and seven dogs, all present and correct, if slightly disturbed by a loony llama. They all scattered to beds that lined the conservatory walls.

Tommy was back. 'I wonder what llama tastes like? A few roast spuds, some parsnips, plenty of gravy ... and stuffing. Ah yes, we should be sure and have him stuffed, so. If we froze the meat, we'd get many a Sunday dinner out of that fellow, so we would.'

'Stop it,' she giggled. 'We shall never know the answer to that one, because we're not going to eat him.'

'But missus – doesn't himself threaten to turn Larry into sausages?'

'My husband says a lot of things he doesn't mean. I've been trying to work him out for well over thirty years, so don't you bother – it's a waste of time.'

Tommy grinned broadly. 'Are we fit for the job, then, Mrs Stanton?'

'We're as fit as we're ever going to be, Tommy. Let's get them fed.' She picked up the necessities, including a key, and led the way to the locked laundry room.

Within seconds, each human held a lion cub. Rejected by their very young mother, the babies had been brought home by Nigel, who was one of the vets used by Chester Zoo. Once the lioness had been sedated, Nigel had entered the enclosure to rescue the unwanted twins. Falling in love with the cubs had been easy; the idea of saying goodbye to them hurt. 'They're like our children, but,' Tommy murmured. 'It'll be like letting go of our own the day we have to lose them.'

'Don't think about it,' Marie advised. 'You know Nigel's made up his mind, and he's right. They deserve a chance to live where they belong, on the Serengeti. They're lions, and they must be allowed to be lions – not pets. You know how Nigel feels about zoos, even though he works in one.'

Marie's husband had agreed to nurse and nurture these two, but they would not return to Chester; Hercules and Jason had their future mapped out. As soon as they could feed themselves, they would be shifted to a reserve on Jersey

63

to mix with others of their kind before being shipped to specialists in Africa. They were going to be free. Suckling on very large bottles with very large teats, each animal kneaded the chest of its human as if encouraging the arrival of mother's milk. They were hungry and beautiful, and parting would not be sweet sorrow, Mr Shakespeare.

Tommy and Marie grinned at each other. 'Let's hope they learn what they need to know in order to survive,' she whispered.

'They will,' Tommy replied. 'There's wisdom born in them. Ah, they're beautiful, so. I hope no English aristocrat fires his gun at them.'

When feeding was done, the mistress of Chesterfields opened an outer door so that the babies could play in their run, which was sealed off from the rest of the property. Standing side by side, she and Tommy watched them. They had old tyres, some very solid rubber balls and an ancient blanket that was now in several pieces. They tripped repeatedly over their own disproportionately huge feet, waging war about bits of blanket and ownership of other toys, snarling and purring all the time. 'I love them,' Marie whispered. 'So beautiful.'

'And so do I, missus. Remember that first night? Me asleep on a cot on the landing, you and mister taking turns with me for the feeding?'

She smiled. 'Yes, and all that linoleum spread out to save the carpet.'

'Didn't work.' Tommy grinned. 'How to wreck a house in one night, eh?'

Noises off began to reach their ears. 'Marie? Nigel? Where are you?'

'Stay with these two, Tommy. I think we're being invaded.'

She dashed through the house. In the hall stood Alice and Nellie. Both spoke at once. Used to disentangling messages from several sisters at a time, Marie gathered that Martin was back, and that Muth had been shown the door on Smithdown Road. Alice was living back on Penny Lane, and Martin was outside helping Dan with his crutches.

As if on cue, the two men entered the house.

'Here they come,' Alice announced unnecessarily. 'We're calling them the crippled and the cruel. Martin's the cruel one, because he threw Muth out today.'

Marie clapped her hands. 'Well done, Martin. She'd better not come knocking here. I'm so glad you're back – we've all missed you.'

Nellie was worried. 'Where will she live, though? I know she's a nasty piece of work, but she shouldn't be homeless at her age.'

Marie's lips tightened. 'Dan, I'm happy to see you home with Alice where you belong.' She didn't want to think about Elsie Stewart, not even for a split second. The woman was a miserable old mare – no, that wasn't true, because a mare would have been given a home here. Muth was a demon.

'Nellie's right, though,' Alice said. 'If Muth's out there in all weathers, we'll be the worst in the world when she gets ill or something. You can just imagine the jangling in the shops and down the bagwash about us leaving a woman in her seventies to die of the pneumonia.'

Martin lowered Dan onto a monks' bench. 'She made Nell's life a misery,' he almost snarled.

65

'What was I supposed to do? Our daughters are God alone knows where, and I'm told we have grandsons.' He held up a hand against Marie's joyful exclamations. 'Don't get all executed,' he begged. 'I've enough on with my Nell. If Elsie had demonstrated the slightest improvement in attitude, I would have kept her on in the shop and found her lodgings nearby, but she showed no symptoms of humanity. I'm sorry but there it is,' he said with a finality that precluded response.

The ensuing heavy silence was broken by the clatter of claws on the parquet as Frank arrived. Even had he spoken English, he would have been unable to account for the previous five minutes of his life. He'd been chased by a thing. The thing was tall, nasty and four-legged. It spat. Breathing heavily, he sat among friends.

'Hello, gorgeous,' Marie exclaimed. 'So beautiful, he is.'

Alice scowled at her. 'You're not having him.'

Frank looked from sister to sister. What was the matter with them? Couldn't they see he needed help? There was a thing outside that needed killing. It spat. It had a long neck and evil eyes, and no, he shouldn't have worked hard to squeeze under the gate. But there'd been a scent, an exciting smell, not the reek of that article's vomit.

Marie and Alice dragged the reluctant boxer through the house to the animal bath, which was just off the laundry room. He stank of llama sick.

The dog's nose twitched excitedly. Before reaching the bathroom, Frank pulled both sisters into a right turn. The exciting scent was here! Shocked and rendered unsteady, Marie and Alice let the collar go, and Frank went off like a weapon from a crossbow. Tombstone Tommy was seated on the floor of the lion cubs' outdoor run. Frank, slightly stained by llama vomit, leapt on the two babies. Using his nose, he rolled first one then the other over on the straw and sawdust covered floor. He then rolled himself, leaving behind most of the deposit donated by Larry.

Tommy joined the sisters. 'Would you ever take a look at that, now?'

'The dog won't manage them if he comes back in a few weeks,' Marie said. 'The cubs will be gigantic very soon.'

Alice mopped her eyes. 'They're beautiful,' she managed.

Marie smiled. 'And they know it.'

A golden-and-white item with twelve legs wriggled about on the floor. It separated into three animals and began dashing round the run and the laundry room. 'Chaos with a capital K,' was Alice's opinion. Marie delivered a quiet, 'Bloody hell,' while Tommy simply shook his head.

Nellie hurried in. 'There's a thingy in the wotsname,' she gabbled.

'A what in the which?' Marie wanted to know.

But Nellie, having set eyes on the two cubs, was no longer with them. A lion was a lion whatever its size, and she flew back to the relative safety of the large hall. Changing her mind because the thingy remained in the wotsname, she backed into the kitchen and peeped out through a small gap in the slightly ajar door. 'Our Marie's got lions,' she told the two men in a stage whisper. 'Baby ones. The lions have got Frank.'

Larry the llama, in the centre of the hall, turned his attention to Nellie. She was afraid of him. He hadn't had this much fun since he'd got out at the front and frightened the milkman into dropping a full crate of bottles. That daft dog had been fun, too. Most dogs were fun when it came to chasing.

'What is that s-animal?' Dan asked. 'A s-baby camel? And how have s-lions got hold of s-Frank? Alice will go crazy. She doesn't like anything or anybody upsetting her Frank.'

'Llama,' Martin said. 'Like a camel, but smaller. The lions will be cubs, Dan, don't worry.'

'It's a s-bastard. I feel like a s-sitting duck here, can't s-run away with crutches, can I? I'd like to see the s-lions. I want to s-hold a lion. How many times in s-life does a s-bloke get the chance to s-do that?'

Nigel marched in through the open hall door. He glared at Larry. 'Out,' he snapped. 'Go on, bugger off or you'll be in next week's meat pies. You're looking well, Dan. Glad to see you're back, Martin. Clear off. Didn't you hear me, mop head? Get lost. Piss off. Do a runner or you're dead.' He'd worked for hours on the poor beagle, and he needed this kind of trouble like he needed a knife in his back.

The llama sauntered towards him. Knowing he didn't dare spit at either of the truly in-charge humans, he decided to put a stop to the hunt. Nevertheless, he awarded Nigel a hard stare before leaving gracefully through the side door.

Nigel followed the beast and called for help. 'Martin? We must mend this gate.'

'That'll be s-Frank's doing,' Dan whispered as Martin left.

A great deal of hammering and cursing ensued. Nellie came out of the kitchen to sit with Dan. 'They've got lions,' she murmured. 'What the bloody hell are they doing with lions, Dan?'

'Don't worry, s-Nell. It'll all be s-part of Nigel's plan to save the s-wild. You know how much he loves s-Africa. They'll be off again soon now the s-war's over, saving young s-elephants and what have you. How s-big are these lions?'

Nellie pondered. 'You're doing less essing now, Dan. Well done. The lions are smaller than your Frank, but there's two of them. Feet like dinner plates, they have, and they snarl.'

'Well, they would snarl, s-being lions. They must have s-no mother. Go and ask s-Nigel about them, eh? He's outside with your Martin s-mending the gate. Frank must have broken it, and that's how we got s-lumbered with the lunatic llama.'

Nellie left.

Inwardly, Dan prayed that she would stay away for a few minutes.

Still on the monks' bench, Dan plotted the building in his memory. Alice and he had been married from here, had lived at Chesterfields until they'd got the Bootle house. There was, at the back, a large kitchen. If he could get through that, he would reach the laundry room. That was likely to be the lions' place. OK.

He grabbed the crutches and heaved himself into a vertical position. But there remained the daft left leg. It didn't seem to be connected to his brain, since it tried to wander off on its own, so he seldom allowed the left foot to touch the ground, swinging it along from the hip while depending on the right leg and his crutches. He felt a bit stiff in all his limbs, probably because of the journey to north Liverpool.

Yes, the problem had worsened. His stupid left foot seemed determined to drop and trip him up, but he wanted to make it to the lions' den. This was going to be his first unsupervised journey, and he had decided to make it happen.

But Nellie found him. 'What the hell are you up to, Dan? Alice'll kill both of us if she finds out what you're doing.'

'Hold my s-left leg.'

'You what?'

'Just stop it from s-dropping. Sometimes, I can't s-feel it, and it trips me up. Grab it, s-please.'

Thus they arrived at the laundry room, Dan on crutches and Nellie bent double in charge of the offending limb. 'This wasn't my idea,' she told Alice when she and Dan reached their destination. He was placed in a lion-chewed chair. Alice shook her head and tutted, though the smile remained on her face.

Nellie turned to leave; she'd had enough exotic carryings-on, thanks.

'Don't go,' her youngest sister begged. 'How many people can brag about having held a lion? Not many.'

Tommy entered with a tired and droopy cub under each arm. Marie took one and placed it in Dan's arms before offering the other to Nellie. 'They just need love. Like any young animal, they play, eat and sleep, that's all.'

'Where's their mam?' Nellie's voice shook.

'In the zoo. She was too young. The pregnancy was an accident. She treated them like toys, like rag dolls. They're just a few weeks old.'

Nellie sighed and smiled. 'A lion,' she whispered, 'a real lion.'

Dan knew he would savour this moment for the rest of his days. The density of the fur, the little grunts and growls, warm breath at his throat, claws tapping his neck. 'You're s-beautiful,' he said, his voice heavy with emotion. Would he ever hold a child of his own? Would Alice have her longed-for baby?

Nellie burst into loud sobs. She was holding an African youngster, a cub that would grow into one of those big things like the one that growled on the cinema screen before a film started. He carried a warm, slightly oily smell, and he smiled at her. Oh, God. Where were Claire and Janet, her babies? Where were their babies? Then the rough, pink tongue made contact with her cheeks – the little fellow was drinking her tears.

'Don't cry, love,' Alice advised. 'He won't hurt you.'

'I'm not frightened any more. I just want to take him home. He'd be a great guard cat in a few months, eh? His tongue's a bit rough, bless him.'

Marie smiled and said nothing. Everyone loved the cubs.

Frank sat between the two people who had stolen these new friends. His companions were tired. Did none of these humans know about the young? Pups dashed about, made a mess, ate, and slept. Ah. It was clear that one of the two-legged

71

agreed with him. Marie unrolled a battered mattress. 'Dump them here,' she advised. Nellie
placed her burden on the mattress before reliev-
ing her brother-in-law of his. 'God bless,' Marie
whispered. 'And don't eat any more of your bed,
eh? You'll have nothing left to sleep on if you carry
on ripping it up.'

'Come on, s-Alice,' Dan said. He stared at her.
'She's gone again,' he whispered. His wife was
staring through the doorway into the cubs' empty
play run. Her expression-free face was suddenly
visited by a slight smile as she resurfaced. 'What's
mass-eye?' she asked.

Everyone stared at her.

Marie laughed. 'Masai are warriors who live on
an African plain. Some people call the plain Serengeti from the native language. I think it means land
that never ends. Nigel will know. What did you
see?'

Alice looked at the little lions. 'I saw them.
They were huge, and they had great big manes;
they were together, but apart. Lots of lionesses
and cubs. That's the future. I don't think I've
seen the future before; it's always been the past or
the present. There were elephants and zebras and
funny-looking trees with flat tops. Oh, and a
bright red sunset, too.'

'People?' Marie asked.

'No, just lots of animals.'

'The lionesses do all the work, Alice.'

'So what's new?' Alice raised her hands and
shrugged. 'Same with us, isn't it?'

'Sorry, love,' Dan whispered.

'I don't mean you, you fool. But men do one

thing at a time; a woman can iron with one hand and bring up kids with the other.'

He offered no reply. She needed a child; she'd always wanted children. It might be achievable, but she would need to do the work. As a gentleman, Dan had never introduced his wife to unusual positions in the marriage bed, but it had to be done. Alice, at thirty-three, was already past the best of her childbearing span, so the delicate subject needed to be discussed very soon. And would the activity cause him to have another stroke?

'Smile, Dan,' his wife ordered.

Removing Frank from his adopted brood proved difficult, though Marie managed to entice him eventually with a slice of boiled ham. When Dan and the three women returned to the main part of the house, they found Nigel and Martin embedded in armchairs and in a heated discussion on politics.

Once seated, Dan joined in with his usual gusto and with fewer s's in the mix. Nigel, who had still not recovered from what he termed the betrayal of Winston Churchill the previous year, now faced a dyed-in-the-wool left-winger, and voices were soon raised.

Marie led her sisters back into the kitchen where all three washed their hands. 'Nellie, you're on brewing tea and setting trays. Alice, you do the buttering while I find some innards. Nellie, why are you wriggling?'

'It's me corsets.'

The other two stared at her. 'Corsets? All that whale-bone?' Alice cried, her eyebrows raised. 'They do elastic things now, Nell. They still have the doo-dahs to hold your stockings up, but there's no need to be trapped in whalebone these days.'

Nellie actually laughed. 'Are you trying to deprive me of my moment? When I take this thing off at night and have a good scratch, it's heaven.'

The men's voices grew louder. 'He was all right and fit for purpose when it came to s-war,' Dan yelled. 'But we need a proper s-Labour lot to sort us out s-now.'

'We need Labour like we need a hole in the head,' was Nigel's reply.

Martin chipped in. 'I'm bloody sure they'll be more use when it comes to the National Health thing.'

Nigel was becoming excited. 'They know nothing–'

'Shut up,' Marie screamed. 'I've two bloody lions that make less noise than you lot. Talk about the weather or something.'

'He'll blame Labour for that as well,' Dan shouted.

'No esses on him,' Alice whispered. 'He's getting better.'

The three sisters worked together, each content in the company of the others. Most people in Liverpool ate their dinner in the middle of Sunday instead of at the end of the day, because few worked on the Sabbath, so high tea was commonplace in the late afternoon.

Three women bearing tea, sandwiches, cake, and scones with strawberry jam and cream entered the war zone. 'Stop the arguing now,' Marie chided from the doorway. 'We're having a

74

civilized Sunday tea, no Churchill, no Clement Attlee, because they weren't invited.'

Dan opened his mouth to speak, then closed it. Alice looked displeased.

Nigel rolled his eyes. 'Here we go. The boss has spoken.' He winked at his wife, picked up a sandwich and got on with life. The beagle would survive, so all was well with the world; for now, anyway.

'Take it away! Now. Get rid of–' Elsie Stewart sat bolt upright on the narrow bed. 'Get rid of it,' she whispered. She didn't want to look at it, couldn't look.

It was happening again. Someone tapped on her door. 'Mrs Stewart?'

Oh, no. Somebody had heard her; she'd been screaming out again, and she hadn't done that for years. She'd felt safe with Nellie, hadn't she?

The door opened slightly. 'Sorry,' said the woman in the bed. Unused to apologizing, she had to force the word out. 'Nightmare,' she added. 'I haven't had one for a very long time – it must be because I'm in a strange place. I don't mean you've got a strange house, but it's just that I'm not used to it. And I thought I'd grown out of these bad dreams.'

'Oh, I'm sorry, love.'

'It's not your fault, but thank you.'

'Shall I make you some cocoa, then? It might just settle you, take the heat to your stomach.' The intruder opened the door further so that Elsie's room could borrow light from the landing.

Elsie wasn't used to kindness, either. 'Please,'

she answered, her tone shaky. 'A hot drink might help me to drop off to sleep again.'

'I'll leave the landing light on for you.'

Alone once more, Elsie emitted a long sigh. Perhaps hot cocoa might make her sleep more heavily, might keep her beyond the reach of dreams and nightmares. She propped herself up on her pillows, her brain working hard to avoid dregs that lingered at the edge of her mind. God, she didn't want to go back there after all these years, to the pain, the hideous sound, the smell of death and the sight of him, his face all twisted and horrible and wrong, so wrong. No. That terrible time needed to be forgotten.

She tried to concentrate. Should she buy a house or rent one? What about a flat? With the nightmares back, she would be waking everyone in other flats, so she needed to be separate... Detached? How much did detached cost? Even in a semi, she might wake the neighbours. Why hadn't she suffered while living with Nellie? Or would this have been about to happen anyway, that terrible scene, that awful night when...? 'Stop it,' she murmured. It was in the past, and it should stay where it belonged. Chippy Charlie was dead, so it was all over and done with. Wasn't it?

The landlady entered with a tray. 'Now, I don't want you worrying,' she said, 'because you're the only guest at the moment. Mostly, I have people who live in Manchester and work in Liverpool. They sleep here Monday till Thursday nights, then they go home Friday after work and set out early from home on Monday morning. So there's only me, and I don't need as much sleep as I did.

Now, let's have a nice drink' After passing a cup to Elsie, the woman perched on the edge of the bed with a mug of her own and asked, 'What are your plans?'

'I'm not sure.'

'Hello, Not Sure. I'm Annie. Annie Meadows.'

'Elsie Stewart.'

Annie took a gingerly sip at the boiling hot cocoa. 'Elsie with two suitcases and no idea where she's going? That's a kettle of fish, as our Doe might have put it.'

'Yes, that would be me, a kettle of fish.'

Annie nodded. 'Well, while we're talking about fish, I'm in the same boat. See, I buried our Doreen last week – she went with something to do with her heart, bless her. I don't know where to turn. I'm not used to being by myself, you see.'

'Have you got kids?' Elsie asked after a sizeable pause. 'Are they grown up and gone, like?'

Annie shook her head sadly. 'No, love. A pair of spinsters, we were, never married. There was just me and our Doe, and we liked it that way. I might sell up. I can't see me running this place without Doreen. I mean, she couldn't do much for her last few months, but she was there.'

Elsie immediately thought of herself; was there anything to be gained here? 'Well, I'd stay a few days to help you out, Annie, but if I'm kicking off with these nightmares again your lodgers won't get a wink.'

Annie Meadows nodded thoughtfully. 'There's always our Doreen's room – and no, she didn't die there, because she was in hospital. It's next to the kitchen, her room. Doe couldn't manage stairs, so there's a little bathroom, too.'

Elsie wasn't sure, and she said so.

'Try it tomorrow. If you don't wake anybody up, you could stay till you make your mind up. Where've you come from?'

'Smithdown Road. Don't get on with my son-in-law, so I got thrown out.'

'That's terrible. Do you think you'll be all right for the rest of tonight?'

'I hope.'

Annie stood up. 'I'll leave your door open a bit then you won't be in darkness. The landing light will be on.'

'Thank you.'

Elsie finished her cocoa, settled down in the bed and pondered. A great believer in fate – as long as fate stayed on her side – she considered the idea of staying here with this woman who clearly needed help. It would be much better than living alone, though she would need to learn to bite her tongue.

Within minutes, she was asleep. And the nightmare paid no return visits.

It had been a difficult few weeks for Olga Konstantinov. Between spending twelve hours each day running the shop, and most Sundays searching for a dog like Frank, she was exhausted almost to the point of coma. After visiting Alice and Dan several times, she had learned that friendship was vital and that living alone would always be tedious, so had decided to get a boxer. This would mean a walk every morning and each evening; she would also close the shop for an hour on workday lunchtimes, because dogs needed exercise and contact with humans and, eventually, with other dogs.

Her patience was eventually rewarded on the Sunday when Dan and Alice were out in Waterloo with family; she finally got her hands on a white boxer. Well, he owned several black patches and a bit of brown on his chest, but he was mostly white. He was an adorable little package, silky, warm and ridiculous. She introduced him to the living quarters on the first floor, cleaned up his deposits, then thought about his name. Romanov was too near the bone, Pushkin seemed more suitable for a cat, and Konstantinov was too long. So she decided on Tolstoy. Within half an hour, Tolstoy was Tolly, and all was well in his confused little world.

He liked the shop, loved his basket bed in a corner behind the counter, but was rather less than helpful in the firewood department, because he ate it. She liked him, and he knew it. After eight long weeks in the world, he had learned a lot. Be nice to the bipeds, and they'll give you fun and food. He knew now that chewing on bundles of wood was a no-no, and he needed to find somewhere acceptable to relieve himself.

His new companion took him out again into the yard at the back of the shop. He tried to cock a leg, fell over, righted himself, and squatted like a female; soon he would get the hang of it, but for now his centre of gravity was preventing him from conforming to the behaviour expected of grown-up dogs. Stairs, too, presented a problem, but he was being carried up and down until he got the hang of things.

'I want to be showing you to my friend who is Alice. She is having a husband, Dan, who cannot walk well at this time. You will make him smile. I am believing that peoples get better if they do smiling. And now, you smiling at me, is it?' She picked him up and allowed him to lick her face. Was this healthy? Did she care? He was wonderful; Leo was her little baby, and she adored him. Would Mr Atherton be there, she wondered?

At seven o'clock precisely, she walked down to Alice's house. Peter Atherton opened the door. 'Come in,' he said, a smile plastered across his face. 'They'll be back soon, I expect. I've spent the day cleaning windows and twiddling my thumbs. Alice and her sister went upstairs to do some dressmaking after dinner, then everything changed in the blink of an eye, because they decided on a family reunion up in Waterloo. They change their minds more often than some folk change their socks. And yon's a grand little dog.'

Olga stepped into the house. Yon? He was Leo, not Yon.

'Tea?' he asked.

'Please. Russian style, no milk. I have some cube of sugar in my bag.'

She dug out the little box in which she carried hard-to-come-by cubed sugar wherever she went.

When the tea was made, Peter sat fascinated, watching his visitor as she sipped hot, black tea through the sugar lump held between her teeth. 'Well, that's a new one on me, love. I'll just let your pup out, shall I?'

'As you wish.'

Olga gazed lovingly at the little dog. 'He started off as Tolstoy, then he was Tolly. Now, I am thinking he is Leo; this was first name of the great Russian writer. Yes, he can be Leo.'

'There's a few things women are always changing,' he said. 'Sheets, pillowcases, towels, and their minds. Come on, Leo, before she gives you another name.'

Olga smiled to herself as Peter Atherton took the puppy on another small journey of discovery. She now had a partner to share the adventure, a little companion to take with her when she visited new friends. After pouring herself a second cup, she picked out another precious cube from her bag and drank tea the way she liked it, uncontaminated by the addition of dairy products.

The front door crashed inward. Startled, Olga jumped to her feet and swallowed the remains of her sugar. Who would treat a door so badly? 'Hello?' she called. 'Who is there, please?'

Vera Corcoran fell into the kitchen. 'He's going to kill me this time,' she muttered before passing out in a pool of blood. Even Olga knew about the situation in that household. She ran to the window and rapped her knuckles on the glass. 'Coming in now!' she yelled at Peter. 'Quick, quick, please!'

Peter and Leo entered the scene just in time to see Olga at her brilliant, brave, Russian best. Open-mouthed and riveted to the spot by shock, Peter held on to Leo and watched as the action played out in slow motion. What he saw was barely credible, yet he knew it was real, it was happening, and it was now. The woman was

81

absolutely bloody magnificent.

Corcoran held an axe. Olga dashed it from his hands so hard that Peter swore he could hear a bone breaking. Grabbing the front of the puny man's clothing, the shopkeeper lifted him up the wall. She bunched her other hand into a fist and smashed it against his face. When he was out for the count, she allowed him to fall in a crumpled heap where he lay motionless. 'Get police,' she ordered. 'Take Leo to phone – he should not be seeing these things.'

'Bloody hell, Olga,' Peter whispered.

She raised her chin. 'Bloody hell is true – look at her. This is going on many years. Get ambulance also. We must try save life of this poor woman.'

When Peter had left with the pup, Olga examined Vera. Bleeding had slowed, but the skull was possibly fractured. As an amateur when it came to medical matters, she simply sat on the floor and held Vera's hand. The woman was still breathing, so hope remained.

The other article on the floor opened its eyes. Olga rose to her feet, took two paces and towered over him. 'Touch her again, you dead,' she advised. 'In Russia, we are making our women strong. We are needing no axe, no gun, no knife.' She paused, remembering how her beloved Batya had employed a man to teach her self-defence, since all connected with the Romanovs were about to die.

'She's my sodding wife,' he cursed.

'My sodding customer and friend,' she spat back. 'You not own her. She belong herself.'

Two terrified boys entered the house. These

82

were wild ones, yet they were weeping. 'He done it,' said the taller of the two. 'He hit Mam with the round end of the axe.' With his right arm, he supported the sobbing younger brother. 'Is she dead?'

Olga shook her head. 'Bleeding slower now. Try not worry.'

Peter returned and took the lads and Leo into the front room.

Thankful that Corcoran had not used the cutting edge of the axe, Olga sat and waited. After ten minutes, the ambulance and police cars arrived. She nodded her head. 'Now, you go to jail,' she whispered, 'and I pray you die in there.'

Four

By the time they reached Penny Lane after their zoological adventure in Waterloo, Martin, Nellie, Dan and Alice were ready for a rest, but there appeared to be not the slightest chance of that. Neighbours milled about talking to each other, while police in uniform and plain clothes were in and out of the Quigley household in a constant stream. Alice frowned. She had new lino, a carpet in the front room, and two good rugs in the kitchen. And there they were, the heavy-footed coppers with size twelve feet and no idea of the purpose served by a doormat. She began to simmer. What the heck was going on, and was anybody hurt? Even Frank felt her tension, jump-

83

ing up from a recumbent position on the back seat of the car to look through the window.

'What the hell's been happening?' was Dan's reaction to the chaos. 'Can we not go out for a couple of hours without the place turning into a circus?' Alice made an effort to calm down before replying. She had a disabled husband who needed settling for the night, and her beautiful house was crawling with police. In the seat in front, Nellie was dumbstruck and shaky; her husband took hold of her hand. 'Try not to get upset, love. It's more than likely something and nothing.'

Alice got out of the car.

Fortunately, the ambulance had left, though two police vehicles remained. 'There's been some trouble,' Alice was informed by an officer who stood guard at their front gate. 'No one from your household was hurt, and you haven't been burgled, but you can't go in just yet, sorry. It's procedure, you see. We have to follow the guidelines.'

Alice took a step closer to the representative of law and order. Although he stood head and shoulders above her, it was clear that she considered herself to be in charge of the whole strange situation. Her eyes moved down then up, as if assessing his suitability for the job in hand. His response was to straighten his shoulders and stand tall. Liverpool women could be ... difficult.

'Ma'am?' the policeman enquired in response to her deep frown.

Refused entry to her own home, Alice was immediately on her high horse; from the invisible saddle, she had words with the uniformed person. 'We live here, by the way,' she told him sharply, 'so we've every right to go inside. It's procedure, you see. When you own a house, it's yours, and you can come and go as you please, so them's my guidelines. Right, tell me what's happened. Is Peter all right? Peter Atherton?'

'He is. But this is a crime scene, Mrs er...'

'Quigley,' she snapped. Folding her arms, she began to tap a foot.

'She's tapping,' Nellie whispered.

Dan laughed. 'We'd better pray for that poor man.'

'You're right there,' was Martin's reply.

'Listen, officer,' Alice continued, her voice dangerously quiet. 'It's them two next door again, isn't it?' She nodded vigorously. 'I've heard her screaming more than once – he should be shot at dawn for treating his wife like a slave. Well, just you listen to me, because my feller is crippled after two strokes. He was clearing up munitions to send back to the arsenal when the second one happened. The war had just finished when he copped it. So, are you going to leave a sick man out here?' She turned. 'Martin, take this one's details; I want him out of a job by tomorrow.' Alice looked the constable up and down once more. 'As much use as a concrete jelly,' was her final barb.

The front room window was pushed wide, and Peter stuck his head through the gap. 'Nay, don't report him,' he said in his best Boltonese. 'The man's only doing as he's told. Harry-next-door's just come home – go in there. Vera's in hospital; so is her owld feller. It's been a bloody shock, I can tell you that for no money. Harry will be annoyed, cos he was out while it happened, and

I've got Vera's lads and Olga in here with me. We're getting interviewed.'

'Damn,' she cursed under her breath.

'Behave,' Dan ordered from the car's open window.

Alice scratched her head. She couldn't remember when she'd last had a day out except for hanging somebody's new curtains. 'I go to our Marie's just once in a blue moon, and something happens. What's he done to her this time? And why did they end up in our house? They've no right to use my house for killing each other, not without permission.'

'I can't tell you owt yet – me and Olga and the two lads are witnesses, like I said.' Peter spotted Frank. 'And Olga's got a dog like him,' he added.

Alice was about to ask what Olga's new dog had to do with anything, but Peter closed the window. 'Go home,' she advised Nellie and Martin. 'You'll have the morning papers to deal with, so try to get some sleep. But, before you do drive off, Martin, just help Dan into next door, will you?' She pointed to Harry's house.

When her husband had been parked safely on Harry's couch in the front room with Frank in charge, Alice said goodbye to her sister and brother-in-law before seeking out the owner of the house. She found him eventually in a back bedroom. He was sitting on a wicker chair, head in hands and crying like a baby. 'Harry? What's the matter?'

'Go away, love.' He tried to dry his eyes on a sleeve.

'Why?' she asked, her tone gentle.

'Well, I should have been here, shouldn't I? There's a cop round the back, a lad I was at school with, and he told me that bastard hit Vera with an axe.' More sobs choked any further words he might have wanted to deliver.

Alice dropped onto the edge of a bed. 'No.'

'Yes. And Olga Kostalot knocked him out.'

'Konstantinov, Harry.'

'All right – Olga Russian lady.' He inhaled deeply. 'She broke his metacarpals, whatever they are. I hope they're private bits. But an axe, Alice? On her little head? I went for a pint and a game of arrows, that's all. And it kicked off while I was out, so I wasn't much use to her, was I?' His voice quietened to a whisper. 'She could die, Alice.'

'It's not your fault.'

He raised his head. 'I tried to get your house when the Carters moved out, but it had already been allocated to you.'

She crossed the room and stood next to him. 'Look, even if you'd lived next door to her, you might have been out. Nobody can be in the house all the time, Harry.' She placed a hand on his shoulder for just an instant. A shock travelled up her arm, and she stood back. They weren't alone in here. Whatever was keeping company with them belonged to neither occupant of the room, though it owned... What did it own? Both of them? Was she having a moment of otherness?

He was staring at her. 'Are you all right?'

'Yes,' she replied. 'Why do you ask?'

'I'm not sure.' He stared hard at her; she was clearly in shock. 'And I'm not sure you are all right,' he said.

Neither was she, and she decided that changing the subject might be a good idea. 'We're not allowed to go in our own house. Dan's downstairs with Frank. Olga and Peter are in our front room with Vera's kids. Peter says they're witnesses to what happened.'

He nodded. She was beautiful, and he was no longer weeping.

'So we had to come in yours, because our house and Vera's are crime scenes, I think.' She managed a smile. 'You loved her.'

He shrugged. 'I did. A long time ago. I think she's more like a sister now. We've both changed, I suppose. I feel pity for her and hatred for him.'

'They say pity's akin to love.'

'No,' he whispered. 'When love knocks at the door, I know it.'

Alice told herself to breathe. The way he was looking at her, as if she were a painting or a sculpture... 'Dan will be wondering where we are,' she mumbled.

'I'm wondering where we are,' was his answer.

So was she, but she said nothing.

'Alice, I–' He cut himself off. She had a husband downstairs, a man who had suffered two strokes, a decent bloke who probably couldn't manage the act of love. So, was Harry Thompson trying to step in and service her? Was this just physical? Was it bloody hell. Alice was delightful, lively, funny, cheeky, adorable. She was also very desirable. And he needed new curtains. 'I need new curtains.'

Alice blinked. 'Where do curtains come into it, then?'

'They cover windows, love. You make them; I need them.'

She felt the heat in her face; this was not a good time to start blushing.

For several seconds, each stood as if riveted, eyes locked somewhere in the small area that separated them. It was as if some invisible chain bonded them together. He turned to the window, and the chain slackened.

She was the first to move out to the landing. What had all that been about? Huh, as if she didn't know. A little poem entered her stupefied mind – Dan's your man; don't tarry with Harry. This was a mad situation, and she'd seen enough of mad with Muth. Anyway, happily married women didn't go about falling in love with next door neighbours, did they? Some might take a fancy to a film star, but that was different, because film stars were miles away. Harry was a danger zone, and that zone was just that little bit too close for comfort.

He followed her downstairs and spoke to Dan while Alice rattled about in the kitchen – kettle on, cups on saucers, teaspoons clattering. 'Well, this is a bloody mess,' he said. 'The one night we were all out, too. I was at the pub for a pint and a game of darts.'

Dan agreed. 'We were at Alice's sister's s-house, so we don't s-even know what happened.'

So Harry told him.

'A woman did s-that?' Dan asked. 'I know she's tall, but–'

'But she did. Knocked him spark out on the floor, or so I was told. You've met her – she visits

89

you. Olga Kan't Stand Enough,' he said, straight-faced.

'Konstantinov,' shouted the oracle from the kitchen.

Dan rolled his eyes heavenward. 'She's off,' he stated. 'Always has s-to stick her oar in, does my Alice. So Olga Konstantinov had a go at s-Jimmy Corcoran?'

Harry sat in an armchair. 'Olga Whoeverinov certainly did. But I don't care what happens to Jimmy Corcoran. He went for Vera with an axe, so he deserves a noose.'

'Bloody hell.'

'That would describe your kitchen floor, Dan. I've a mate in the force, and he told me what happened, more or less.'

'Alice'll go s-mad about Vera. There again, it might not be a s-long journey for my s-Alice. Has she told you about her s-otherness? She had one of her turns today, ended up in Africa for five minutes with s-lions and zebras. Shut your mouth, Harry, there's a bus s-coming.'

Harry allowed himself a grin. Dan was attaching fewer s's before his words. 'That speech therapy's doing you good, Dan.'

'S-sometimes. But I s-think the shock's made me s-stammer.'

Alice entered bearing tea. 'I've made us all a nice cuppa,' she said. 'Harry, stop looking at me as if I've grown another head. I'm not the only one in the world with a bit of second sight. Seventh child of a seventh child, that's me. Some bloody use it was when we got bombed, though. I can't control it. If I could, I'd have stayed at home today. Oh, Vera.' She sighed heavily. 'What gets me is the bloody law about not interfering with domestic fights. They leave it till somebody's murdered, and I can't see the sense of it.'

Harry agreed. 'This was always going to happen, Alice. Looks like she's got a fractured skull according to my friend in the force. If she survives, she might not be the full quid. And he'll be done for attempted murder if she lives; if she doesn't, he'll be on nodding terms with the hangman.'

They drank their tea in silence. Harry remembered the girl he'd loved, her humour, her naughtiness, the shine on the bouncy, curly, russet hair. That Vera didn't exist any more; Jimmy Corcoran had reduced her to a shadow of her former self. Had he killed her? Or had he dulled her sharp brain? Oh God, oh God.

Frank sniffed. It was the sort of sound that reminded Alice and Dan that there were biscuits in the room, as was a starving and neglected canine.

The boxer, presented with a bowl of milk and water, slurped greedily. When the rich tea biscuits were passed round, he won a couple just because he looked so sad. 'He'll end up with an arse the size of your s-Nellie's,' Dan mused.

'Cheeky bugger. She's my lovely big sister, so behave.'

He behaved. Although he wasn't a visionary, Dan Quigley had spent extended periods in hospital, a few weeks here, a month there, sedation for high blood pressure, broken bones setting after the second stroke, a bout of pneumonia, arrhythmia – the list was endless. His heart had been tested, and it was being tested at this very moment, because Dan had learned to be astute, had become a people-watcher. Alice and Harry weren't looking at each other.

Harry's brain was shifting like the Flying Scotsman. Two women. One was in hospital fighting for her life; the other sat here, and she was possibly fighting for her soul. The attraction was shared; he knew that instinctively. He had loved two women in his life, and both were in trouble. Perhaps he was a bringer of bad luck, though he scarcely believed in karma, destiny, or good or bad luck. Mankind had free will, though attraction seemed to come from the animal within; it was nothing to do with picking and choosing.

Alice was in a different place. There were flowers, scented blooms. Their aroma was typical of freesia, sweet peas, or something very similar, and the place had panelled walls on which paintings or framed photographs were hung. People stood in lines, though she recognized none of them. Frank was in a vestibule with another little dog, also a boxer. Olga Konstantinov wore a violet gown; in contrast, a huge green pendant nestled in the dip at the base of her throat, while matching earrings were fastened to her lobes. Purple and green together – Alice must remember how well they looked. It was a wedding. Whose wedding? Olga's? Alice's? But Alice was already married, and the scene was returning to sepia smoke...

She was whisked back to the present day; her tea was still in her hand, still hot, and not a drop had spilled during the otherness. For the second time today, she had seen the future, and she clutched at her husband's hand. If she was going to remarry, that meant that Dan had to die. He mustn't die. No woman could love two men, surely? And she continued to avoid the eyes of Harry Thompson.

Meetings of the Penny Lane Traders' Association took place on a more or less monthly basis, sometimes in a local pub, occasionally in living quarters attached to businesses, and, on dry summer evenings, the shopkeepers might meet in a park where they would take thrown-together picnics with beer for the men, sweet cider for the women and pop for the children.

This was a summer evening, but Olga decided to invite people to her flat above the shop. It was her turn, and she wanted Leo to become used to people, since he needed to learn manners as a shop dog. Still in training and leaving puddles here and there, he was doing his best to be a big, grown-up dog in order to please his kind owner.

As things turned out, Olga's Monday night meeting scarcely happened. Just the butcher and a greengrocer turned up, because the lane was buzzing with tales relating to the previous day. Vera Corcoran's life was hanging by a thread, while her husband and attacker, whose fingers had been broken, was now in plaster and in a holding cell. 'Where he belongs,' concluded Matt Gibson, who was flowers, fruit and vegetables.

Terry Openshaw, butcher, agreed whole-heartedly. 'Is it true, Olga, that you threw him across the room like a bag of bones?'

'He is bag of bones,' she answered, 'but no. I lift

93

him up with one hand and hit him with other after I make him drop axe. Bad man. He very bad man. What he did to Vera was nasty. She lost a lot of blood and her head was broken into her brain. She still asleep, I am thinking. I pray she wakes up from this sleep a mended and happy woman, and that her attacker stays in jail.'

'You broke his fingers, girl.' Terry was grinning. 'If they ever need help down the slaughterhouse, I'll tell them to come for you.'

She nodded thoughtfully. 'I can fight a person, but cannot hurt animals. This one, he is Leo. He will go to Alice's sister's husband, a dog doctor, so he not chase lady dogs. Operation. I feel terrible doing this to Leo, but too many unwanted creatures in the world. So.' She sat down. 'How are we? The Co-operative Society is taking business from us still?'

Terry the butcher sighed heavily. 'They give divi; that's short for dividends.'

Olga had been thinking about this. 'Christmas,' she began.

'What?' Matt interrupted. 'We haven't done with summer yet.'

His companion agreed. 'You're jumping the gun a bit, aren't you?'

'We think ahead – months ahead,' Olga insisted. 'Look at profit margin. Decide what you afford to give for little book belonging each customer. Little book is dividend for Christmas. When they spend, you put some pennies in Christmas book. From you, Matt, they can get some free vegetables and fruit for Christmas table. From you, Terry, some meat.'

'What about you, Olga?' Terry asked.

'Ah yes. About this I am thinking for weeks now. My dividends will be toys I buy wholesale – cars for boys, dolls for girls. Every time they buy the coal bricks, the paraffin, the pots or pans, I mark book.'

Terry whistled. 'Clever girl. So we have a chance against the Co-op.'

Olga blushed. Sometimes, just sometimes, Terry Openshaw was a little too generous with his praise for tonight's hostess. 'Well,' she concluded, 'as there are so few here, we need to carry this business over until next month. Perhaps you two gentlemen might go to the pub? Me, I am taking Leo to meet again Alice and Dan and Frank. He needs education.'

The two men stood up. Matt Gibson needed little persuasion when it came to a pie and a pint, though the butcher looked slightly crestfallen. Matt shook his head; Terry had no chance with Miss Russia. Russia was a cold, heartless country and this daughter of Russia kept herself very much to herself. Beyond these meetings and her acquaintance with the recently arrived Alice Quigley, she had no social life. They left.

Alone, Olga picked up her beloved puppy. 'I am too old for loving a man, but I have you, Leo.' She glanced at the clock. He would still be there. Standing before the mirror, she softened her hair by taking it down and tying it more loosely, allowing the usually pinned-back fringe to cover her forehead by dipping the comb into a jug of water to help the process. A few side curls were similarly encouraged, and the results were pleasing. 'I am

95

now looking younger,' she advised her reflection. Yes, he would still be there...

Leo emitted a high-pitched woof – he wanted his walk.

'Soon, soon, baby.' A little powder, coral pink lipstick, sandals, no ladders in her stockings. 'Leo?'

The little dog cocked his head to one side.

'Your mama is stupid. Who will look at me? I am too old.' She picked up her pet and whispered in his ear, 'He is older than I am. Let's take our little run first.' Terry Openshaw? Olga chuckled, because Terry hadn't a hope in hell.

After their short expedition, Olga and Leo arrived at Alice's house. The visitor tapped before admitting herself into the hall. This, she had discovered, was customary in these parts if the door was not locked. Frank immediately took over the care of Leo, leading him through the kitchen and out to the rear garden in search of mischief. Olga could hear the two men talking in Dan's room, so she went in search of Alice, who wasn't on the ground floor.

The visitor climbed stairs up to the first storey. The sewing room was empty, as was the spare room, but she finally found her friend in the room at the front of the house, the master bedroom, which would have been shared by Dan and Alice had the poor man not suffered such ill health. Olga stood in the open doorway. 'Alice?'

The mistress of the house didn't turn round. 'I was born in this room,' she said.

'Oh, yes?'

'Yes. On the day my mother turned forty. It was April, 1913. The eighth day of April.' At last, Alice swivelled and faced Olga. 'Can you hear it?'

Olga paused and listened. 'I hear nothing unusual.'

Alice nodded. 'Just me, then. Frank doesn't hear it, Dan doesn't, and Peter's said nothing. So it's just me now.'

'And you are hearing?'

'A baby. It cries, then it stops. Real babies wind down, don't they? They mutter for a while, build themselves up to a scream, then get tired, but they still moan. When they've moaned for a bit, they slow down and stop unless they're in pain. But this one goes silent right in the middle of a scream, as if a switch has been turned off. I hear it nearly every day now.'

'Not in night?'

Alice shrugged. 'Sometimes. But it's as if the baby doesn't want to disturb me. It knows me. It likes me. God, what do I sound like? Go and put the kettle on, love.'

'Yes, yes, I go down and make tea for all.'

When Olga had left the room, Alice sat on a padded stool at the dressing table. Since moving back to Penny Lane and into the house where she'd been born, her periods of otherness had become more intense, while their frequency had increased. The click of the front door, a curl of smoke from Dad's pipe, the accompanying scent of Virginia tobacco, the muted sounds of children at play – all these she heard, inhaled, almost saw. But only almost. Apart from Dad's bit of smoke, there had been no real visions so far.

'Is that me crying?' she wondered aloud. 'And why do I stop so suddenly?' This room held the answers, of that she felt certain. She wanted to see Dad, to talk to him, because he would have some answers. As for Muth – she wouldn't know the truth if it sailed up the Mersey on a Viking ship with a full crew. Am I hearing the sound of a baby not yet born, Dad? And will that child die minutes after birth? If you're here – and I know you are – please tell me.'

The crying had stopped for now. It seldom disturbed her in the night, and she slept well in this room. She slept like a baby... Like a baby.

'Are you from the past, from now, or are you unborn?'

'I am here now with tea.' Olga approached the dressing table and looked into her friend's re-flected eyes. 'You are troubled, Alice.' She placed a cup and saucer on the Utility dressing table. 'Milk no sugar is you, sugar no milk is me.'

'Am I going insane, Olga?'

The Russian removed the cube from between her teeth and placed it on her saucer. 'If you are insane, God must help the rest of us. You the sanest person I am know.'

'You don't need the "am", just the "I know".'

'I know.'

'Are you taking the wee-wee, Olga? Oh, and you look different.'

'Do I?'

Alice turned on the stool. 'Hair pretty, pink lipstick and nice sandals. Is this for Peter?'

When no reply arrived, Alice asked again, 'Is it for him?'

'Is for me. I was having traders' meeting, but everyone gone in pub talking about poor Vera. Now, this baby you are hearing – is he crying now?'

Alice shook her head before turning to face the mirror once more. She began to tremble. 'Olga?'

'Yes?'

The seated woman swallowed audibly. 'When you put my cup and saucer down on the dressing table, was this here?' She pointed to a bottle of California Poppy. 'It isn't mine.'

'There was nothing there,' Olga murmured.

Alice felt the blood draining away from her face. During the war years, perfumes had been scarce, and women had been forced to choose between lavender water, Midnight in Paris, and California Poppy. On the few occasions when Alice had seen her in that time, Muth had reeked of the last of those three options. 'But I don't think she wore it when we lived here.'

Olga remained silent.

'It's all getting a bit too ... real for me. Take it away and put it in the outside bin, please.' She didn't want to touch it. 'Olga, please take it away.'

Olga left with the offending glassware.

Right. This was all becoming rather intrusive and daft now. It made no sense. A baby, noises, some scents, fair enough, but a bottle of California Poppy? It – he or she – was growing stronger. 'If he can move things in the real world, he has true power.' How did she know the baby had done this, and that the baby had been, was, or was going to be male? Perhaps the bottle of perfume was from another source – from Dad?

99

Was Dad connected to the crying child?

A slim, blue-grey and transparent ribbon appeared in the corner of the room. Weightless, it floated towards the ceiling, and Alice could smell the rich odour of tobacco from America. Dad had brought the bottle, hadn't he? Why hadn't she seen its arrival? Why had he allowed it all to happen in the presence of Olga? Olga was possibly here as witness, and Dad was trying to tell his daughter something important. 'I know she caused your death, but did she actually kill you? Dad, did my mother murder you with poison or something? I need to know how bad she really is, and only you can tell me.'

The smoke disappeared. How she wished he could stay and talk to her. He probably had answers to questions she hadn't yet thought of.

Olga returned with her pup. 'Alice? This is Leo, named from one of Russia's greatest writers. You didn't meet him properly last time we here, because you were finishing curtains for Mrs Vernon.'

Alice held out her arms. 'He's beautiful.'

'Like Frank?'

'Yes. He's very like Frank. Is he trained?'

'Almost. Sometimes, he leaves me small gift, but we are talking about these things, and he is trying to learn. Good boy, he is.' She waited a moment. 'Would you like me to stay here with you tonight?'

'No. See, I've never been frightened of it, Olga. It's been more of a nuisance, really. Like when I came to your shop that first time and saw – well, you know what I saw on that back wall. But here, in this house, I'm nearer to something or other.'

'Nearer to start of your life, then.'

Alice stood and paced about. 'It's like I'm being prompted by somebody else, somebody stuck in this room. He's never gone through to the next level.'

'Your batya? That what I named my father. Batya is Russian for daddy.'

'I don't know. I've absolutely no bloody idea, and that's the truth. See, I don't look into the future or the past. I don't stand staring until something from Russia barges into your shop. It just arrives. There's no control; I have no say in what comes to me.' She stood still. 'It's someone else working through me, telling me stuff. And like a wireless, I get a better signal through an aerial. This room's the aerial.'

'It is all very strange, Alice.'

'Don't I know it?' She passed the puppy back to her friend. 'You go, Olga. Pop in and see Dan, but knock first to make sure he's decent.'

The daughter of Russia, a possible Tsarina, descended the flight. Leo wriggled in her arms. 'You want to try? Very well, this we do now, but be careful, baby.'

He managed two stairs, but then went into freefall until he reached the hall. Olga ran down and retrieved her precious puppy. Sitting on a step, she cuddled him until a pair of legs arrived on the scene. 'Peter?'

'Come on,' he answered. 'Leo's fine, and I'm done here for today. Let's go for a walk, eh?'

'Yes. A walk. This is good idea.' She took the first steps towards her future. A Russian aristocrat and a nursing home orderly held hands once they reached open land at the bottom of Penny Lane. Affection was, indeed, the greatest equalizer. And Leo, walking proudly at the end of his lead, seemed happy for them.

Nellie and Martin worked together as smoothly as a well-oiled machine. Perfectly capable of calculation and change-giving, Nellie realized how far Muth had hammered her into the ground.

'She undermined you.'

Nellie made a mental note; she would ask him later about that word.

When the paper boys and the on-the-way-to-work purchasers had cleared, the pair sat on stools and enjoyed a brew. Nellie grinned. 'I think if any more customers had said how pleased they were to see you back, you'd have gone mental.'

'I would, but oh, I'm glad to be home; I've missed you, Nell. You've always made me laugh. And it was great having a good old cuddle last night.'

She blushed. 'It was. Anyway, have you thought about how we're going to set about finding our Claire and our Janet?'

'We'll have to make a plan about that. But I'm sure we can get a private detective without too much trouble.'

She touched his face. 'Right, you're in charge. I'm going to put the stew on the hob. See you later.'

Martin grinned. He was home. He was back where he belonged. And Liverpool was by no means the biggest city in England. All marriages were recorded, weren't they? And all births. The girls would be found.

'Martin?'

'What, love?'

'Shall I go on a diet?'

He laughed quietly. 'No. I like all the ballast.' She would be quiet for a few minutes now while searching the dictionary for another new word. He loved her just the way she was; fat, thin or in between, she was his Nellie.

Harry Thompson didn't hesitate. With their father in prison and their mother in a coma, the Corcoran lads needed looking after. They were wild, they were out of favour in the community, but they were Vera's, and they'd seen the attack. Tony, at sixteen, was the leader. Twelve months older than his brother Neil, he was cock of the walk, and he had led his sibling into a great deal of mischief. 'We don't need to stop with you,' he told Harry. 'We've got our own house, and we've both left school, so we can see to ourselves. We can cook a bit, and–'

'And what about money, eh?' Harry asked.

Neil agreed with their host, though he kept his head down and said not a word. He didn't want to live where one of his parents had tried to kill the other. And he liked Mr Thompson.

Harry went in for the jackpot. 'Look, if you stop running about like a couple of wild apes, I can get the two of you apprenticeships. Just think – you could both be working towards a trade when your mum comes home. There'd even be a few bob in your pocket – not big money, but a wage you've earned instead of stripping lead off roofs, eh?'

103

Tony stared into the empty grate, while Neil swayed from foot to foot as he waited for his brother's decision. He glanced furtively at Tony, who shrugged. Although determined to appear hard, the older boy heard the sense in Harry's suggestion. Dad had been in prison a few times, and he'd be inside for a good few years now. He spoke for both. 'We could give it a try. What do you say, Neil?'

'We could.'

Harry made for the front door. 'Right, come on. Let's go and get your stuff, shall we?' He stopped and turned to face the pair. 'Just one more thing. Any fighting, and you'll be out. You've seen first hand what beating people can lead to. We'll get fish and chips when we're done. All right? Are we all on the same page?'

They nodded.

Wondering how long their co-operation would last, Harry led them out. Only time would tell.

The shop door opened. Martin stood up. 'Hello, Mr Turner. We thought you'd moved on and started selling from carts.'

The ice cream maker closed the door. 'We have. Hello, Mrs Browne. I've come with a message from—' The door opened, and the 'glad to see you back' business started up again. Geoff Turner moved to the closed flap at the end of the counter and began to scribble. When finished, the note was handed to Nellie, and Mr Turner left, bequeathing a wink and a broad smile.

Old Mrs Girling was in full flood. Elsie Stewart was a very nasty woman. She thought she was in charge of everything and everybody, including her oldest daughter. 'And three times she sent me the wrong magazine, and my son never got his fishing paper, that monthly one. A quarter of butter-scotch? A quarter? On my scales, she did me out of nearly an ounce, but she wouldn't admit it. Glad to see the back of her. There's nothing wrong with my scales; they were my grandma's.'

Martin winked at his wife as he weighed dolly mixtures for Mrs Girling's brood of grandchild-ren. 'There you are, love. Half a pound, but I'll charge you for the quarter.'

The customer smiled. 'You're a good one, Mar-tin.'

With the transaction completed, he joined his wife. 'You're like a cat on hot bricks, missus. Where's the fire?'

Nellie fought for breath. 'Mr Turner – he knew all along. Geoff Turner. Ice cream, home-made. They have a telephone. They're in Crosby.'

'The Turners?'

She nodded. 'And our Claire and our Janet. Waiting. Waiting for Muth to go away from here. See.' She passed the note to him.

He interpreted the message aloud. 'They've got a house, Nell. Between them, like. Our Claire and our Janet live together with their husbands and kids. In Blundellsands. Fur coat and no knickers, as they say. God's good, Nellie. He's on our side – no, don't start bloody crying, Grandma. It says here that Geoff Turner will be in his old place for an hour, and we can use the phone. Come on.'

'What?'

'We're shutting the shop, queen. This is a red-letter day.'

Vera Corcoran was in a single room. She lay as still as a marble statue in her hospital bed, head swathed in bandages, facial skin whiter than the fabric wrapped round her skull. Only the slight movements of her slender chest betrayed her status as a living person. The doctors still didn't know whether or when she would come round. And would she be right in the head if she did?

At one side of the bed, Harry Thompson and Alice Quigley sat, their eyes straying from the supine form of their neighbour to her sons, Tony and Neil, who occupied seats at the other side. 'Will she wake up?' the younger boy asked, his tone thickened by emotion.

'We don't know,' was the answer from Alice.

'Even the doctors aren't sure,' Harry added.

Tony spoke up. 'She's been coming to hospital for years with broken bones. I've heard her joking about buying a season ticket like a football supporter. She's like that, always making fun of herself. It was her way of trying to stop us worrying. We hardly ever saw her without bruises.'

Harry nodded his agreement. 'And you two went wild out of the house because you daren't tackle him, so you took it out on other people. We all know why you were out of control, but Vera wouldn't want that for you. She'd rather you got a decent trade and led decent lives.'

Tony made a sound that emerged suspiciously like a strangled sob. He rose to his feet and dived through the door.

Neil stood up. 'Shall I go after him?'

Harry shook his head. 'No, lad. Pretend you didn't notice.'

'Leave him,' Alice advised. 'He's too proud to be seen crying.' She gave her full attention to the figure in the bed. 'Come on, Vera; they need their mum.'

Harry looked at his neighbour. 'You shivered then. Are you cold?'

'No.' It was true, though she could have expanded on the single syllable had she so wished.

'Are you sure?'

'I'm sure.' She didn't tell him that she'd just seen two Veras, one in the bed and another near the door. It had been just a split second, anyway, and she didn't want to raise false hope in Vera's boys. 'Time to go home,' was all she managed.

Five

Four adults plus two babies lived in almost organized contentment in a large, four-bedroom house on St Michael's Road, Blundellsands. Claire Holden and Janet Myers, daughters of Nellie and Martin Browne, had set up home together; each had a husband and one boy child, and it was a lively household. Away from their dictatorial grandmother and their loving but weak-willed mother, Claire and Janet began to thrive. Life was fun, babies were fun, and husbands were hilarious, especially when it came to interior decoration and the cleaning of windows. Had the house merited a

107

motto, it would have been You Missed a Bit.

The babies, just a few months old, were almost exactly the same age, both precocious, both noisy, both adorable. Often mistaken for twins, the happy duo provided priceless entertainment in queues for shopping, since they had developed to a high standard a routine of synchronized crying, babbling, laughing and singing, though the singing was still under development, with many of the more delicate points in need of fine-tuning.

Mam and Dad had phoned several times. Dad had come back from Manchester to throw Gran out of the Smithdown Road shop, so there had been much rejoicing in the Holden/Myers residence. Guinness and sherry were consumed, and it was fish and chips all round for supper on the day the girls heard about the eviction of Elsie Stewart. They were a delighted group except for one important aspect of life – there wasn't much work to be found.

Having survived till the end of the war as mechanics servicing RAF fighters and bombers, two weary servicemen had come home to their women and to their dream – a business of their own. Since leaving school together, this had been their plan, and they remained determined to be their own bosses, answerable only to their wives, a strong-minded pair of sisters who shared plenty of sense seasoned by a great deal of humour. Holden and Myers formed a motor vehicle outlet; they sold cars and motorbikes, and mended broken ones. The two women took turns at working for the business one day and childminding the next, and thus the four soldiered on against odds

108

which included a shortage of car parts, teething, nappy rash, clients who needed to pay instalments for work already done, and petrol, which showed few signs of coming off rationing. A plan was necessary, because rumour had it that fuel might well be restricted until the end of the decade. In some senses, this post-war period was almost worse than the battlefield, because young men had expected to return to a land fit for heroes, but rationing continued to be harsh. Having come home, survivors of warfare and their families had slid towards the Labour Party; a coalition was fine when it came to protecting the homeland, but Labour was nearer the common man.

Often, one of the husbands expressed regret about not having served abroad. His wife's answer was always the same – 'You had to go up in the bloody planes to prove you'd fixed them properly, so stop talking soft.'

Kevin Holden and Paul Myers each had a full complement of slates on the roof, plus qualifications more than adequate for working with vehicles, and neither was backward at coming forward. We need to diversify,' Kevin said, bouncing baby Simon on his knee. 'No point hanging about till we fall off the tree, lose our home and stop putting food on the table.'

'We need a bloody miracle,' was Paul's terse reply.

'Domestic machinery, repairs of,' Kevin continued, not in the least perturbed on the surface. 'Hoover cleaners, sewing machines, wirelesses and the like. Anything that needs fixing, we fix. Cars will come back, Paul. Petrol will come back.

There'll be washing machines, too, them Hoover things with the swing-across rubber mangles – they might need repairing. We've got a key-making kit, so we can help people who need spares. And we can sole and heel shoes, too.'

Claire chipped in. 'I suppose me and Janet could take washing in.'

Janet laughed. 'Not flaming likely. We've enough with nappies and greasy, oily husbands.'

'I resemble that remark,' her husband said, using the malapropism deliberately. 'It's a mucky job, mending engines.'

The phone rang, and Claire went to answer it in the hall. 'Don't cry, Mam,' she begged, a deep frown transforming her face. She covered the mouthpiece. 'Janet, it's Mam. She's at the Turners' place again and still a bit dampish after finding us. Very weepy.'

Janet arrived at her sister's side. 'Don't worry, Mam, we'll get there. We're just worried about you-know-who following you up here. Sunday week, yes. We've got the address, and the boys know every inch of Liverpool – Waterloo's only down the road.' She handed the phone back to Claire. 'Stop her crying. Tell her they can come up here tonight. And you can dry your tears, too – you're getting on my nerves. We'd better peel more spuds.'

They returned to the front room. 'Claire?' Kevin winked at his wife. 'That shed at the back of our workshop – what do you think about second-hand furniture and household goods?'

Claire stood still, immobilized by too many thoughts. 'Mam and Dad are coming for their tea.'

'I thought we were going to your Auntie Marie's Sunday week? Have I got it wrong again?'

'No, we are going to Auntie Marie's, but Mam can't wait. And it would be nice if she and Dad could see just us first, us and the babies, as long as old Elsie doesn't follow them. I can't cope with more spuds and second-hand furniture on top. Sausage, egg and chips is all we can offer.' She took a pace towards the kitchen, stopped and swivelled. 'Furniture?'

Kevin, struggling to contain laughter, nodded at her. 'Furniture,' he repeated, grinning in reaction to his wife's expression.

'Why, Kev?'

'Why not? It's a big shed, and we need to keep going till the rationing stops. People always need furniture, and they're fed up with Utility. We could do house clearances when somebody dies.'

Claire sighed. 'That's what I love about you,' she said, 'so bloody cheerful.'

Kevin covered their son's ears. 'No swearing in front of the children, Claire.'

Claire dragged her sister into the kitchen. 'Why did we marry them?'

'Love,' was Janet's swift answer. 'Well, that or mental illness.'

They pondered the subject for seconds, then began chipping the spuds. Mam and Dad were coming.

She didn't need Frank any more. Well, she did, because she loved him, but the dog was no longer attached to the otherness. A part of Alice understood why; Frank had been an extra receiver, because the signal had to travel over some kind of immeasurable distance, but now that she was right on top of the main transmitter the boxer was no longer a necessity. Here, in this house, a baby cried, and she alone heard it. Whatever she needed to know, it would come from the house in which her life had begun thirty-three years ago. Waiting for an answer wasn't promising to be easy, but she owned no say in the matter, because the whole mess was acres beyond her control.

'Frank,' she whispered, addressing the best dog on the planet, 'you've always been a good lad, but I'm glad you're getting a rest. I think it's all down to me from now on. Whatever it is will find us, but thanks for sticking by me, beautiful boy.' She patted his head. The 'whatever' was getting closer, and she felt it in her bones.

And to top all that, there was the other thing. Dan had been reading a book, had finally made her sit and listen, and this was the day on which the deed must be done. Oh, bugger in a bucket.

'Frank, life's getting very strange.'

She cast her mind back to the start of the war. Dan had chased her all over Blackpool beach, round the house, round the bed – there'd been fun and romance and joy before the strokes. Now it was all how many days since bleeding, and she would have to be on top, because he was crippled, poor soul. It was like discussing some kind of scientific experiment or planning a list for the shops. She wanted love and laughter rather than a list of instructions which ended with her lying flat on the bed with her legs up the wall. Yes, she wanted a baby, but wasn't Dan enough when it came to nursing care? Peter wasn't here all the time... She found herself blushing. Harry was usually available in the evenings. Dan sometimes acted like a spoilt child who had to get his own way no matter what the cost to others. He'd become institutionalized. Hospital staff had indulged him, and he seemed to expect the same behaviour from his wife.

Alice pulled herself together. The mechanics of the bed business didn't quite defeat her, though she remained slightly puzzled. He would put her right if she got flustered, or so he'd said. To hell with it; she was going to make herself look good: brushed hair, a bit of make-up, a new nightie. Somebody had to make an effort in the area of romance.

Romance? When they were finished, she must lie on the floor or the bed with her legs up the wall – she'd never heard anything like it since gym class at school with those flaming medicine balls. After lugging one of those things round, a girl needed a dose of medicine. He was frightened; she was frightened. They both feared another episode in his brain, though nothing had been said.

She blew out her cheeks and huffed. Oh well, better get on with it.

Leaving Frank in the kitchen with a juicy marrowbone, she walked into Dan's bedroom.

'Turn the big light off,' he ordered quite brusquely.

She blinked before complying and moving to stand awkwardly by the bed. Just two dim lamps illuminated the room.

'Get undressed,' he said. 'The less that gets in

113

the way, the better.'

Struck almost dumb, she stripped. It was like preparing to be examined by a doctor.

'You have to straddle me,' he muttered.

Naked, she lingered at the foot of the bed, feeling safer there for a reason she didn't want to investigate. Where was the love? Where were the kisses and the whisperings and the silly words? Not even a smile – nothing. 'I don't want to do this,' she whispered on unsteady breath. 'Please, Dan, there has to be some other way, something nearer normal.'

He stared hard at her. 'We have to make the effort if we're to have a child.' He paused, his expression blank. 'Alice, I love you, but I have to concentrate. Things aren't as easy as they were before the second accident in my head. We need a child, don't we?'

'Why?'

'What do you mean?'

She swallowed hard. 'Why?' she repeated. 'Is it so that when he grows up he can look after you and push your wheelchair? I suppose that's as good a reason as any in your case.' She wished she could bite back the cruel words. 'Sorry. I just don't want to carry on like a robot. It's too ... too scientific, too medical.'

'I have to,' he almost growled. 'No choice in the matter.'

'But I have a choice, Dan. I'm supposed to climb up there and bounce about like a ball on a field – no. I'm not a machine. I want to make love.' She pondered. 'I could get the double bed down and put it in the front room. If we were sleeping together, we could have cuddles and kisses and...' Her voice faded away. 'I'm sorry.' She pulled on her nightdress. 'I'm going to bed, because I can't do this. I won't do it.'

'This is not my fault,' he roared as she reached the door. 'I didn't ask to end up like this, did I?'

Alice stopped in her tracks. 'It's not my fault, either. Or perhaps it is. If I'd died under that blooming bomb, you wouldn't have had the first stroke.'

Dan banged his head against pillows. 'Why don't you go elsewhere, then? Find yourself a man whose body works right.' There was Harry-next-door for a start. Oh yes, he'd noticed Harry glancing briefly at her with hungry eyes.

She faced him and his fury. 'I left home for you.'

He grimaced.

'What?' she asked.

'Did you leave home for me? I thought I might have been the excuse that got you away from your nightmare of a mother.'

'I loved you,' she snapped. 'You know damned well that I loved you. I married for the right reason – for love.'

'But you don't love me any longer because I'm not normal.'

Alice shook her suddenly weary head. 'Love moves in two directions, Dan. When you came home from Maryfields, your eyes shone with it whenever you looked at me, but something's changed in a matter of days. And it's all gone too...' She paused, searching for the word. 'Too clinical,' she concluded.

115

He closed his eyes. 'You're a beautiful girl, and I'm a mess. I don't want you turning to someone else, some bloke who can make love right. And I don't want you being on your own when I die. We always planned to have kids, didn't we?'

'Yes, we did. But children should come from love, not from a textbook. I can't do that thing – it's not normal.'

'But it is normal, Alice. It's one of the normal positions in the book Pete brought me–'

'What?' She approached the bed. 'You've talked to him about this, about us and our private life?'

'And Dr Bloom. Where else am I expected to go? You need a baby, and I need a new left leg, so this is the only way – you on top.' He paused. 'Well? Are we doing this or not?'

'Not. I'd rather try knitting fog. This isn't what I want from you. I want us to be us, or as nearly us as we can manage. A baby would be lovely, but we should make him in a proper bed, not a hospital one. Let me bring ours down. We could have two bedrooms down here, and I could move my sewing into the biggest one upstairs. I can make it into a sitting and work place. Please, Dan. You'll have your hospital bed for physio-therapy, and our bed for sleeping in with me.'

'All right.' Anything, he told himself inwardly; anything that would make her his, just his. Perhaps she might become capable of looking Harry Thompson in the eye again. Was he imagining the attraction between her and the neighbour? 'Get the bed down and we'll see what happens.'

'Thank you.'

'What for?'

116

'For seeing my point of view.'

'You're welcome.' His tone was terse.

She left the room and walked upstairs. The baby who wasn't there was grumbling, as if working himself up the short road to a full scream. 'Sssshhh, Callum,' she whispered without thinking. Where had that come from? Who the bread and dripping was Callum? 'Callum?' she repeated.

'Yes?' The single whispered word seemed to brush her cheek.

'Jesus, Mary and Joseph,' she muttered. 'You're not a baby. Or you're not *the* baby.'

She felt him leaving. A slight movement in otherwise still air told her that he was gone. And it came to her in a blinding flash that perhaps babies matured after they were dead; maybe they became in spirit what they might have become in life, in body. 'Who the hell is he?' she asked herself aloud, 'and where the heck did I get that name?'

She removed the best nightdress and folded it before pulling on her old summer weight cotton pyjamas. Determinedly, she worked her way through tomorrow's agenda. When Peter Atherton came in the evening, she would get him and Harry-next-door to move the bed. Vera's boys were still with Harry, so they might help as well. Poor Vera – she was still unconscious, bless her. 'They can move everything down,' she told the room. 'Wardrobe, dressing table – the lot. And they can bring the suite up here. Let them think what they like, because I'm going to sleep with my husband, and that's that.'

She brushed her hair, cleaned her teeth in the bathroom and stared in the mirror. Callum.

117

Wasn't it an Irish name?

As usual, she was halfway to sleep very soon after her head hit the pillow. It was a lovely, snuggly bed, and she drifted happily into the Land of Nod. Yes, she slept like a baby in the place where she'd been delivered as a baby...

Oh no, here he came again. It was late, far too late for visitors.

Olga stepped back from her bedroom window. Terry Openshaw, butcher, was going too far with his gifts and his attempts at courtship. She didn't want him, didn't want anyone, especially now. Half her heart had been given away to Peter and a boxer pup, while the other half hung somewhere between Penny Lane and Moscow, because she had always loved the land of her birth. 'One day,' she mumbled, 'one day, all will be well and people will visit Russia without fear.'

Picking up her beloved Leo, she descended the stairs and threw open the shop door. 'Yes?' she asked.

He stared at her. She was tall, elegant, beautiful and rumoured to be related to foreign royalty. 'I've brought you a couple of lamb chops,' he managed to say, 'and a bone for the pup.'

'Time has come for me to talk the truth, Mr Openshaw. We both are members of Penny Lane traders' group, no more than that.'

He stepped back a few inches. 'So they're right, then? You've been seen walking out with that Peter fellow who looks after Dan Quigley?'

She nodded. 'He is my friend. He helps training Leo.'

'You hold hands.' His tone was accusatory.

'And this is your concern, Mr Openshaw?'

He cleared his throat. 'I'm not without money. We'd have two shops between us. He's worth next to nothing.'

'Good night,' she spat before closing her door on him and his chops. The man was a nuisance, and she didn't need him. But Peter? She smiled. Time would tell.

Nellie finally managed to stop crying. At ten o'clock, she sat in the best room with one little boy on each knee. Simon, at five months, had as strong a spine as Keith, who was six months of age. They held their heads well, 'talked' to their newly discovered grandmother and chortled at Granddad, who sat on the floor at his wife's feet pulling funny faces. He laughed at their tooth-less, bubbly grins, and they laughed when he did.

Nellie couldn't remember being so happy. She looked up. Her girls. Yes, she did remember a happy time with her own babies.

'They should be in bed, Mam,' Claire repeated several times, but Nellie always wanted just an-other minute. Janet grinned. As the Brownes' younger daughter, she just wanted to drink in the sight of her parents together again with no Gran moaning at them.

'I remember feeling like this when you two were little. We used to play for hours – do you remember? Dollies and cots and fairy tales from a big book?'

They did. 'Come on, Mam,' Janet urged. 'Let's take them up to bed. Come with us. They each

119

have their own room. Kevin and Claire have the big front room, and Paul and I have the back one. Keith's next to us and Simon's next to his mum and dad.'

'And you don't mind sharing a house?' Nellie needed to know.

'No. We're happy.'

Downstairs, the three men were talking business. 'I'll have to speak to Nellie first,' Martin said, 'but I think she'll want to help. Leave it to me. I reckon it's time for a change, anyway.' He glanced at the clock. 'How long does it take three women to put two babies to bed?' He chuckled while answering his own question. 'My Nell's waited a while for this day, lads. She wanted me back, yes, but her girls were always top of the list. Our Claire and our Janet mean the world to her, and her heart was broken when her mother saw them off. I often wonder, you know, how Nellie turned out to be such a good mother herself, because she learned nothing from old Elsie. But Elsie kept my wife squashed, so I had to come back and get rid of the old cow.'

Paul lowered his tone. 'They're coming down. Make sure you have a good think before deciding anything. You've only just met us. Kevin and I could be crooks–'

'My girls wouldn't marry criminals. They'd see through you, son. So would I. We'll carry on with the shop for now – maybe forever – but we can give you a hand and a few bob for our girls.' His eyes were moist. 'And our grandsons and our sons-in-law.'

Nellie and the two young mothers came in

giggling. 'I've been peed on,' the grandmother announced proudly. 'With having girls, I wasn't expecting that, was I? Well, I'll know in future.'

Claire giggled. 'Boys come with a little hose-pipe, Mam.'

Nellie clung to her daughters. 'We love you. We missed you.'

Martin grabbed his wife. 'Out,' he ordered. 'We've papers to sort at half past five.'

There were no more nightmares. Elsie, having moved downstairs into Doreen's old room, didn't pay for the privilege. Instead, she worked for her room by cooking an evening meal for guests. Annie Meadows bought the ingredients, and Elsie produced a decent dinner and a pudding, which meant that the men didn't need to go out to eat after work. They paid more, of course, as they were now given two meals each day in residence, and Annie was prepared to allow Elsie a wage, but Elsie had other ideas. A few days after the commencement of this arrangement, she sat with Annie when the clearing away of dishes had been done. Guests ate in a small sitting room and sometimes stayed there to play cards or dominoes, but on Tuesday they had all gone out to see a film. 'I've got a few bob,' Elsie said without preamble. 'How about we become joint owners? Then we'll take equal shares, and we'll have my cash to smarten the place up a bit.'

'What's wrong with it?' an offended Annie wanted to know.

'Not much. You need a bit of colour, some new soft furnishings and the like. Oh no, you keep it

121

lovely and tidy – it's a credit to you. A couple of cans of paint, some cushions, a few pairs of curtains and it'll be sorted. I'll pay half if you take me on as partner. Think about it. I learned the hard way to do nothing in a hurry, believe me.' She rose from the guests' chair. 'I'll sort the pots while you pick the crumbs up.' Elsie was wise enough to know when to hold off and leave her victim to think. 'I've a good few hundred in the bank,' was her parting shot as she made her way to the kitchen.

Annie thought. She missed their Doreen. She and Doe had worked together for years – they'd even housed important people during the war, folk from the War Office, the Home Office, the Inland Revenue. A chap in charge of moving and hiding major works of art had taken a room, as had the odd merchant sea captain and two sour-faced women from the Red Cross.

She could never get Doe back. Life without her sister wasn't good.

Elsie paused, her hands resting in washing-up water, a small smile arriving on thin, mean lips. Annie was coming back through the hall. It hadn't taken her long to work out which side her bread was buttered, had it? Elsie had a way of homing in on people's weaker points in order to take advantage for her own personal gain. Annie Meadows needed a sister, and Elsie Stewart needed security – two birds, one stone, and very little effort.

Annie cleared her throat. 'I'll make an appointment with my solicitor and the accountant, see which is the best way of going about this kind of thing. My sis is only just dead, but I was already thinking about selling up. I enjoy a bit of company, and you've been good to me so far, so let's look into it, eh? Get it all done legal and proper.'

Elsie agreed.

'Shall I do us some cocoa, love?' Annie asked.

'Good idea. And I made some little fancies today – they're in the pantry, that blue tin with roses on the lid.' She knew the landlady had a sweet tooth.

While wiping down the draining board, she found herself humming under her breath. Humming? When had she last done that? Perhaps all along she'd needed to get away from her family; they'd done nothing but drag her down for over half a century. She might be seventy-three, but she was as strong as a horse most days, and she'd be useful here; she'd be needed.

They sat together in the kitchen eating cakes and sipping cocoa.

'You remind me of our Doreen. She was sometimes quiet, like you.'

'Was she?'

'Oh yes. She was deep, a great reader, forever off to the library to change her books. When she died in hospital, *A Tale of Two Cities* was on her locker top with a bookmark about halfway through. I remember thinking I was glad she'd read it years ago, or she'd never have known how it ended.'

'She would,' Elsie said, 'because they can see everything from heaven.'

'I suppose they can.' Annie wanted to ask Elsie about her family, but she held back the questions, since the would-be partner seemed unwilling to discuss her relatives. Oh, well – it took all sorts to make a world, didn't it? And the idea of running this place by herself didn't appeal, so why not have a partnership? But first, she picked up a third fancy cake. All this thinking was making her hungry.

Alice, of the tit-for-tat school of thought, was measuring Harry Thompson's front window for new curtains. He, Peter Atherton and Vera's two boys had helped with the shuffling about of furniture next door, and she was simply returning the favour. Unfortunately – or perhaps the opposite – Tony and Neil Corcoran were keeping their daily vigil by their mother's hospital bedside, while Alice was keeping half an eye on Harry, who was keeping both eyes on her legs. She didn't know what to think, what to say or what to do. 'I've got some lining material next door.' She was gabbling, and she knew it. 'Now, double the width and evenly spaced pleats would be nice with the cloth you managed to buy, so I'll just have to take it away and see if we have enough.'

'I haven't had enough,' he grumbled softly.

She found a suitable reply to that. 'Oh. Do you want a pelmet?'

'Won't you have to see if there's enough?'

She turned to stare at him, lost her footing and fell ... into his ready arms.

'Are you hurt?'

'No.'

'Are you sure?'

She was sure, and she said so. No, she wasn't hurt, though her heart was doing well over fifty miles an hour in a residential area. 'Put me down, Harry. I'm all right, so put me down.' He had beautiful eyes that twinkled with humour. Was he laughing at her?

'I don't want to put you down – ever!'

'Well, you have to!'

He placed her in an armchair, but kept her imprisoned by leaning both hands on the two padded armrests and pushing his face forward till their noses touched. 'Moving that furniture down your bloody stairs nearly crippled me, Alice, and I don't mean just physically. I can't bear the thought of anyone being with you, even Dan!'

Alice relocated her voice. 'He's my husband, in case you hadn't noticed.'

'I noticed,' he snapped, setting her free by removing his arms. 'I've fallen for you, and this hasn't happened to me since...'

'Since Vera?'

'Yes, it was Vera. But I've grown out of that one a long time ago.'

'My turn?'

'Your turn.'

'And I'm supposed to be pleased?'

Harry shrugged. 'It might help a bit.'

She didn't want to want him, but she wanted him nevertheless. It was all very confusing. Thanks to him and a few others, the front room next door was now the main bedroom, and the main bedroom was a sitting plus sewing room and Harry was ... he was lovely, and she was here about curtains, about returning the favour. 'We can't do this,' she told him as she rose to her feet.

'Do what?'

'I don't know. Whatever you're thinking of doing, we can't do it.'

His bright blue eyes shining, he waded further into the morass. 'What do you think I'm thinking, Alice?'

She squared her shoulders. 'Sex,' she stated baldly.

'Oh yes, please,' he breathed. 'But Tony and Neil will be back soon, so we'd better stay dressed, or folk might talk. When Vera recovers, she'll have our reputations spread all the way from Southport to Knotty Ash.'

The maker of clothes, curtains and other soft furnishings pulled herself together. 'Dan's my husband in sickness and in health; you're just my next door neighbour. It doesn't matter how anybody feels or what anybody wants, Dan Quigley's my other half. I won't betray him.'

'Let me know if you change your mind, Alice.'

'Yes, I'll send you a postcard!'

'Telegram would be quicker.'

'Stop this, Harry!' She took a step backward. 'You're a nice-looking man, and I think you're great. I once saw a fabulous, big diamond in a jeweller's window, and that was great, too, but I couldn't have it!'

He grinned, displaying beautiful white teeth whose brightness was forgivable due to a small corner missing from a front incisor. Alice pointed to his mouth. 'What happened?'

'I'm a hard kisser. It was a clash of personalities.'

'Liar.'

'OK, it was the butcher lad's bike. I pinched it

126

when I was twelve, had an argument with a wall.' She liked him; he could tell that she liked him.

'That's more believable. Harry?'

'What?' He chuckled.

'Are you laughing at me, Mr Thompson?'

'Me? I wouldn't dare. Don't want to lose any more bits of tooth, do I?'

She tutted. 'I think I'd better go home – don't you?'

Harry shook his head gravely. 'Well, you could go for your toothbrush, I suppose. We'd have to be quiet because of Tony and Neil, but we'd manage, eh?' He took pity on her. 'I know, love. It's just my dream, and I needed to know if you shared it!'

Alice swallowed hard. 'I might have, but there's Dan. He's been so ill, and if I had an affair it would kill him. Scared to death already, he is, what with one thing and another!' She felt heat flooding into her cheeks. 'He's had to read books about ... you know, about the personal side of marriage, because we've never ... since the second stroke...' She shrugged. 'It's not easy. I feel scared in case it doesn't work out or if it makes him ill.' She stopped short. Why was she talking about this to a man? She'd never discussed it even with a woman, so why was she being so ridiculous? 'Sorry,' she concluded. 'I didn't mean to heap all my worries on you.'

'Don't be sorry. I'm honoured because you're confiding in me.'

She thought about her sisters, Nellie and Marie. Nellie wasn't the sort to talk about private stuff, while Marie was up to her eyes in dogs, cats, llamas and lion cubs. Olga might under-

127

stand, though. In spite of being sort of royal, Olga could be very down to earth...

'Alice?'

For answer, she simply raised an eyebrow.

'I think I love you,' he said. 'It's not just sex.'

In that moment, she looked into his eyes and knew that he was speaking his very simple truth. Oh, he was handsome, bright blue irises, a square jaw with a slight cleft at its centre, wilful brown hair that appeared to disobey all laws, including the one about gravity. He was a good man and he loved her. 'The first time I saw you, you looked like the wreck of the *Hesperus,* tatty and dirty. Or perhaps you were an overgrown urchin from the Dark Side.'

'I've been to the Dark Side on the ferry,' he said. 'Birkenhead's not that bad. I wonder why we call it the Dark Side?'

'No idea. I'm going to take up my curtain material and walk.'

'Spoilsport.'

In spite of her terror, she giggled. She realized in that moment that although she didn't fear Harry, she was afraid of herself and for herself. He would probably make a delicious lover and, try as she might, she could no longer look upon Dan in that light. She loved Dan – of course she did – but as a sometimes good companion rather than as a husband. Would he stay in his hospital bed tonight, or would he come into her room? And suddenly, she didn't know what she wanted from Dan. Why?

'You're staring,' Harry accused her.

'Sorry. I've a lot on my mind.'

'I know you have. Off you go, then.'

Her feet stayed where they were, refusing point-blank to do the bidding of her brain. Hands, too, acted daft, losing purchase on yards of cloth and allowing it to tumble to the floor.

He came and scooped her up like a child, crushing her to his chest. 'Alice, oh, Alice,' he groaned. By the time he laid claim to her mouth, she was in no state to oppose him, because she ... oh, hell, not an otherness, surely? Not now. But it wasn't an otherness; it was something new, someone new – she was new. She liked this; liked it rather too well. He was tickling her lower lip with his tongue, and she liked that. He was combing her hair with his fingers – she liked that, too. When she stroked his face, he groaned deep in his throat like a contented cat, and she was reminded of the lions.

Fighting for breath, they ended the long kiss. 'Bloody hell, Alice.'

'Bloody hell, Harry.'

'What the fu – what the heck do we do now?' he asked.

'Well, we don't do the word you didn't finish. We need time to think, because I'm not leaving him.'

'I know.'

'So how will it work?'

Harry shrugged. 'No bloody idea, love. But it's not something we can just switch off, is it?'

'No, it isn't.' She stepped away and picked up the cloth. 'Peter, Olga and I are invited to that party at the weekend,' he said. 'Dan invited us.'

'Yes, I know. It's open house – their friends and

neighbours will be there.'

He ran a forefinger down her cheek. 'Silky skin,' he whispered.

'Like a cat, Harry. I bite like a cat, too. Ask Dan or my sisters.'

'Passionate, then.'

She didn't know about that, so she offered no reply. These riotous feelings were not typical of her – well, not with Dan, anyway. With her husband, it had been romantic and funny, even hilarious at times. But this was very grown-up and real and disturbing. 'He wants a baby,' she mumbled.

'Does he now?'

She nodded. 'He's turned the whole thing into a kind of laboratory experiment. I've seen no pipettes or Bunsen burners, but I wouldn't be surprised if he had some somewhere.'

'Don't forget the litmus,' he whispered into her hair. 'What does that do?'

'Goes red or blue. If it goes red, you tell him to bog off. But if it turns blue, you're in trouble.'

She was in trouble here and now, and it was nothing to do with litmus paper. Except for the odd kiss in her early teens, she'd been touched only by Dan until today. Would she be able to face him? She didn't know, and scarcely had time to care. 'I'd better go.' She picked up the curtain material and walked out of the house knowing that she had left a small piece of her heart inside with Harry.

But Dan was the one she'd fought for, the love of her life whose hand she had held for hours when he was ill in hospital, the man who waited for her now, because they were going to make a baby. Harry was lovely, though she belonged to Dan. Didn't she?

Harry shook Tony Corcoran's shoulder. 'Come on, lad – wake up.'

Tony opened his eyes. 'What?'

'There's a couple of policemen waiting for you downstairs. Put that old robe of mine on while I get Neil.'

'Is it Mam? Is she dead?'

'No idea, son. Go down while I get your brother.'

Tony Corcoran got out of bed. 'I'd rather wait for our Neil. I want us to be together.'

Something in the boy's tone sent a shiver up Harry's spine. 'What is it, Tony? Was your mother worse?' He waited. 'Tony? Answer me. Was Vera showing signs of life, death, or what? Lift your head up – there's nothing interesting on the floor.' He waited. 'All right, then, go and get Neil.'

After another two minutes, Harry followed Vera's sleep-tousled boys to the ground floor.

The policemen stood to attention in front of the fireplace. 'Tony and Neil Corcoran?' the older man asked.

Tony answered. 'Yes. He's Neil, but I'm the oldest. Is our mam all right?'

'As far as we know, yes. Sit down, boys.'

They sat.

'Now,' the officer said, 'you visited your father yesterday, didn't you? Yes, it's gone midnight. Did ... er ... did you notice anything different about him?'

Neil spoke up. 'He was crying. We've never seen

131

him cry before, have we, Tony? He shouts and hits us and Mam, but he never cries.'

'So you didn't go to see your mother?' Harry asked. 'I thought–'

'He'd been begging us to visit him.' Neil's voice quivered. 'We had a visiting order, only we didn't tell anybody, because we know you all hate him. We'll go and see Mam tomorrow.'

The constable continued. 'There's no easy way to say this, lads, but your dad's dead. He ... he did away with himself a few hours after you'd gone.'

The blood drained away from both boys' faces. 'So he wanted to see us one last time, then,' Neil whispered. 'We told him Mam hadn't come round and he said ... what did he say, Tony?'

'That even if she lived, he'd be sent down for attempted murder.'

Harry realized that he was suddenly looking at two little boys. Not that they were small, but they seemed lost, confused and frightened. Tony, apprenticed to Harry, was learning the basics of plumbing, while the younger boy was doing well under the guidance of a master plasterer. 'You carry on living with me. I'll look after you till your mum gets well.'

'We'll be good,' Tony promised.

'You will.' Harry knew they would. Vera's boys had learned the hard way that life wasn't easy, and that it ended sometimes without warning. Their mother's life hung in the balance, while their father had killed himself in a cell. But they would be OK; Harry would make sure of that.

Six

A needle in one of Vera's arms was delivering into her system something akin to nourishment, while extra oxygen pumped its way to her lungs via a mask. She looked unreal, like a wax doll or some macabre piece in a waxworks exhibition. One of her visitors noticed a change. She kept her opinion to herself in case she was wrong, but she suspected that Vera was reaching sleep and leaving the coma behind, because the eyes moved slightly under the patient's closed lids.

Alice stood by the bed and said nothing about what she had seen, each arm draped across the shoulders of one of the Corcoran boys. Their father had hanged himself in his remand cell, while their mother seemed to be clinging to life with a grim determination typical of women in this part of the world. Alice knew the lads had been labelled as irretrievably bad, but they weren't; they had been confused by a lunatic, alcohol-dependent father and a mother weakened by ill-treatment. 'She looks no worse,' she told them. 'In fact, she's not as pale as she was. See, there's a bit of colour in her face.' There was no great change apart from the slight eye movements, but Alice was doing her best to remain determinedly hopeful without making any promises.

Harry Thompson sat at the other side of the bed, both his hands enfolding one of Vera's. As her

once-upon-a-time boyfriend and long-term neighbour, he found himself willing her to live not for
his sake, but for her own, Tony's and Neil's. 'Come
on, love,' he urged, 'he'll not hurt you again, I
promise. Your lads are staying with me till you get
right, and they've both got apprenticeships. That'll
take the devil out of them. They'll not follow in his
footsteps.'

'We won't, Mam. We promise,' Neil whispered.
His brother, older and determinedly tougher, said
nothing, though fear was etched into his features.

Alice pulled Tony closer. She knew he would go
away and weep in solitude at the earliest opportunity. 'All right, lads,' she urged. 'Let's go and
warm up that cauldron, shall we?'

Both adult visitors studied the grieving boys.
Jimmy hadn't been much of a parent, but he'd
still been their dad. 'Scouse for tea, lads,' Harry
reminded them. 'She makes a good scouse, don't
you, Alice? And we're invited.'

'Where's mine?' asked a rusty voice. 'I'm bloody
starving here. Can't remember when I last had a
decent chip butty or a good cuppa.'

All four heads swung round towards the pillow
end of the bed. The oxygen mask hung at a rakish
angle over one of Vera's ears. She pulled at it, as
it was blowing air in the wrong place. 'Bloody
weather,' she cursed, 'gone windy again. I want a
cup of tea.'

Neil left the room screaming, 'Doctor! Nurse!
Me mam's woke up. And she's talking!'

For the first time since babyhood, Tony Corcoran wept while in company, and he didn't
bother to wipe the water from his cheeks. Mam

was coming back, and she might even be home soon.

A battalion of medics arrived, and all four non-essential onlookers were shunted out into the corridor.

Tony, suddenly galvanized, dashed off to compose himself in private. Neil sniffed. 'He cries in bed every night, but I don't say nothing. He wants us to think he's dead hard.'

Harry grabbed Alice's hand and squeezed it. 'She seemed to be thinking clearly, asking for some dinner and a cuppa.'

'She did. Let's hope she soon gets back into top gear, then they'll throw her out just for a bit of peace and quiet.'

Neil chuckled. 'She's our *Liverpool Echo*,' he announced, grinning broadly. 'We'll be able to look after her now, what with us working and him gone. Mrs Konstant Enough was saying she wants a bit of help so she can give her dog longer walks. Mam could work for her.'

'Konstantinov,' Alice said wearily. She looked at Harry. 'Have you trained these two to call Olga daft names?'

He shook his head before plastering an innocent grin across his face. 'No – he nearly had it, because it sounds like constant enough, doesn't it?'

She gave up – he was almost correct, anyway, but wrong enough to make her angry. No, not angry; annoyed was closer to the mark. Try though she might, she couldn't manage to be angry with Harry Thompson.

The doctor came out of Vera's room. 'Well, she's lost a few days, but that's understandable.

She says she can tell she's in hospital because of the stink, and she's not living with her husband any more because he tried to kill her. I'll leave it to you to tell her he's no longer with us. I can safely say she's on her way to full recovery. She's going to sue us for shaving her hair off.'

'That's a good sign.' Harry winked at Alice. 'She only sues folk when she's normal. If she wasn't normal, she'd just thump you with her yard brush.'

Neil gulped. 'I'd best find our kid,' he said before running off down the corridor. The doctor returned to Vera's room.

Harry took the opportunity to cuddle the woman he was beginning to love. 'She's going to make it – oh, thank God.' He kissed her hair. 'Are you OK?'

'Of course I'm OK. Stop it. Dan and I are together now, and you and I are here just for Vera and her boys, anyway, so back off.'

He released her. 'I see. Well, that's me heart-broken all over again.'

'Stop thinking about yourself, then. Concentrate on Vera and her sons – they'll still want help. And I need to look after my husband and give him the child he wants. Harry, please don't confuse me. You know I'm fond of you, but Dan comes first.'

'You're first for me, Alice. Did he manage, then?'

She glared at him, though she was really angrier with herself for confiding in him. 'Enough,' she snapped.

'Constant enough?'

'Stop it now or I'm going home.' She walked away from him and leaned against the opposite wall. Dan had managed, all right, but it had happened in a strange way, and she'd had not a moment's pleasure, because she'd been expecting him to die. Getting worked up into a lather might have caused another stroke; as for being penetrated from behind – well, she'd felt like a stray bitch.

'You sulking, Mrs Quigley?'

Alice closed her eyes. 'Shut up.'

'Here comes the other doctor and Sister Hughes with all her bridesmaids.'

Sister Hughes slapped him on the arm. 'You can go back in now, but try to keep her calm. The drip's out, and she's begging for food, so we'll find something light for her.'

They returned to the bedside; Vera was not best pleased. 'They fetch you in here to make you better, then they starve you to death.' Despite frailty, she motored on. 'Drink of water – that's all I've had – Adam's ale from a cup with a spout on it. I told them I'm that hungry I might eat the pillow, and they just laughed at me. It's not funny when your stomach thinks your throat's cut.'

'Slow down,' Alice said. 'Just shut up and listen before the boys come back. We've something to tell you.' She dug her companion in the ribs. 'Go on, then. You've known Vera for a long time.'

Harry nodded. 'Jimmy did away with himself, Vee. He was on remand for attempted murder, and he tied the sheets and well ... he's gone.'

'Did he hang himself, then?'

'He did.'

Vera blinked a few times. 'Right. Any bad news?'

Having glimpsed a split second of pain in the

137

patient's eyes, Alice smiled sadly. 'No, it's all good. Harry got apprenticeships for the boys. Tony's on plumbing, and Neil's learning plastering.'

'Jimmy was good at getting plastered.' Vera pondered for a moment. 'Why have they cut all my hair off?'

Patiently, Alice explained about the fractured skull and doctors looking for brain damage. 'But there's clearly nothing wrong with your brain, Vera.'

'Me stomach feels like it's shrunk to the size of a pea. Have you not brought me grapes?'

The boys returned and stood at the bottom of the bed grinning like a couple of fools. Neil dug in his pocket and dragged out a liquorice all-sort of uncertain vintage. 'Sorry about the bits of fluff, Mam. It's been in me pocket for a few days.' He moved to stand by her side.

'This won't be easy without me teeth.' But she managed.

Now that the mask and the feeding tube were gone, Vera looked about ninety without her teeth and with unbandaged portions of her scalp on show. Alice tried hard to imagine the woman in the bed as a young girl, pretty and lively with bouncy red curls, but she failed. This was what happened to someone who married the wrong man. Harry would have been good to Vera, and her life could have been so different, so much happier, because Harry was funny and kind and ... she pulled herself together, announcing that she needed to get home to feed her own invalid.

'I'll come with you,' Vera announced. 'Where's me clothes?'

'You can't,' Tony cried. 'You can't come home till they say so.'

'Just watch me,' she said. But sitting up made her dizzy and, when her equilibrium returned and she placed her feet on the ground, she collapsed in Harry's arms. 'Shit and derision,' she snapped, 'what the buggeration have they done with me legs? There was nothing wrong with me legs. I came in with me head, not with me lower portions. They've made me worse, and I'm not having it. Tony, go and get that bloody doctor and ask him what the pigging hell he's done with me legs.'

Harry grinned. 'Are you sure they're your legs, love? Do you think they got the legs mixed up and gave you the wrong ones?'

Vera eyed Alice. 'See? He talked tripe as a lad, and he's still doing it.'

The boys left to pretend to search for the doctor.

Vera carried on. 'It's false teeth what they get mixed up in hospitals, lad, not legs. Mind, they might lose false legs.'

A nurse came in with a sandwich on a plate. 'Here you are, Mrs Corcoran.'

'What the hell do you call that? It's not enough to keep a budgie tweeting. Where's our Tony? He can go and buy me fish and chips.'

The nurse raised her eyes heavenward. 'Look, Mrs Corcoran, you've been in a coma and off solid food, so you can't go from that to a fish dinner, because your stomach won't take it.'

Vera glared at the young woman. 'Listen, you,' she began. 'First, find me teeth. Second, get me out of this room and put me with other folk. I want me legs back, a cup of tea and a lawyer. He can sue yous lot for making me bald.' She pondered for a few seconds. 'Tell you what, I'll stay in the ozzie till their father's buried, cos I'd only show meself up spitting on his coffin.' She nodded at her visitors. 'You can go now,' she told them. 'Leave me to sort this dump out.'

When Harry and Alice had left, Vera fell back on her pillows and wept. Jimmy had been a grand-looking lad, with dark hair and dark eyes. He'd been good fun, a daredevil, an adventurer. 'I should have listened to me mam,' she told the nurse. 'Jimmy's dad was a drunk, and Mam said Jimmy would turn out the same, cos it runs in families. She was right. She was always bloody right. I didn't want to cry in front of my boys.'

'I know,' the nurse said. 'You act hard, but you're not hard.'

Vera dried her eyes on the sheet. 'Right, let's you and me sort this hospital out, then. I want to be with people while I get better. Have you got any wigs? Will you find me teeth for me? And I think I might need to learn walking again.'

The boys returned doctorless. 'Can't find the doc,' Neil announced.

'No, you won't need to learn walking. Your legs are weary, that's all.'

The older woman grinned. 'What's your name, love?'

'Irene. But they call me Nurse Shearer.'

'My lads won't be alcoholics, will they?'

'No, I'm sure they won't, Mrs Corcoran.'

'Shearer, eh? Well, that suits you. Were you the one that sheared my hair off?'

140

'Not guilty, Mrs Corcoran. That would have been done before you went into theatre, and I wasn't on duty. I've looked after you most days since, though.'

Vera spoke to her boys. 'Go and find Harry and Alice before all that scouse gets eaten. See you tomorrow. And you heard this young woman – she said you're not going to be alcoholics.'

They left.

'Well, thank you for looking after me, Nurse Shearer. I mean that.' And she did.

Peter Atherton lit the gas ring under the stew. 'Will you be coming to the table, Dan?' he shouted. Peter knew that Dan was sulking; like children, people in his position sulked sometimes when they thought they weren't the centre of attention.

'Will there be room? She's bringing her s-boy-friend and the Corcoran lads, isn't she?' Peter arrived in the bedroom doorway, and Dan lowered his tone. 'I can have my hospital trolley across my hospital bed and stay out of everybody's way in my own little s-private hospital.' He rested against the wall and folded his arms, putting Peter in mind of fights down the bagwash when somebody took somebody's soap or jumped the queue for the drying cabinets. 'He's like a bloody owld granny,' Peter whispered to himself when Dan, after hobbling on crutches towards the kitchen, turned to go back for his book.

The orderly re-entered his patient's daytime bedroom. The height of the bed made it easier to help Dan exercise his legs, though the man of the house now spent nights in the ordinary double

141

bed with his missus. 'What's up now? Boyfriend? Which boyfriend? Give me your book.'

'Him from next door.' Dan handed over *Oliver Twist*.

The orderly shook his head. 'Don't talk manifold.'

'Manifold?'

'It's part of a cow's stomach. Some of the oldies back in the day filled the folds with vinegar and ate it raw.'

Dan blew out his cheeks. 'Are you trying to s-put me off my scouse?'

'No. If by boyfriend you mean Harry Thompson, I don't think so.'

'You must be s-blind, then.'

'I'm not blind and there's nothing going on.'

'Well, I think there is. They can hardly look at each other. If their eyes do clash by accident, she goes all s-pink with getting embarrassed.'

Peter sighed and marched quickly to the door. 'You know what Dr Bloom said about strokes – depression, anxiety, impatience and physical weakness. You're making progress. We're not hearing the letter s before every word – in fact, you hardly do it now. The therapist says you're getting on great with your speech. That left leg's easier to manage – and anyway, why would Alice go to all that trouble making a bedroom for the two of you downstairs? If she didn't want anything to do with you, would she have bothered to change the house round? Would she hell as like. If you carry on like this, you'll make yourself ill for no good reason. And you'll lose her. Your jealousy will chase her off like a pack of hounds after a fox.

You're like a petulant child or a miserable old man.'

Dan blinked a few times and followed Peter into the kitchen. He sat down, rid himself of crutches and folded his arms. This had become a signal for Peter to disappear, and the man at the table closed his eyes and listened while footfalls slowed before stopping as they reached the business end of the kitchen. There would be glass bowls containing pickled beetroot and red cabbage, soda bread produced by an Irish baker, best butter, and glasses of Alice's home-made lemon and honey drink. She would be back from the hospital soon.

He sighed. Because he'd been away so much, his wife had developed a level of independence which must have been necessary during his absences, but he was back now, and they were a partnership again, so why was she still distant? It wasn't even what her family called otherness, since she seemed not to suffer many absences these days.

Frank trotted in and sat on a rug at the side of the table. 'I know you're there,' Dan mumbled without opening his eyes. 'She'll be back soon, so don't fret. I know you miss her. So do I, lad.' He missed her most when she was near, when they lay in bed together like spoons so that he could love her without too much difficulty. He didn't know how to improve matters and was hesitant when it came to discussing the problem, as Alice was ... a bit old-fashioned, he supposed. To her, sex was sex, man on top, woman underneath. Anything else was a mistake or a sin or too experimental for her. She wanted their old life back, and that was probably an impossible dream.

But he loved her with all his heart, and Harry had better watch himself. Knowing that Dan was crippled and slow, the neighbour might think Alice was unprotected, but her husband had a good imagination. 'I'll put a stop to him,' he mumbled under his breath. Where there was willpower, there was always a way.

The front door crashed inward and what sounded like an invasion arrived in the hall. Most carried straight on, but Alice broke away and turned right into her husband's room. He wasn't there, so she followed the others into the kitchen.

'Dan, she's going to be all right.' Tears tripped down her lovely face. 'She woke up and took charge, started telling everybody what she wanted, tried to get out of bed and blamed the hospital for everything. She's got very little hair, and there are still some bits of dressings on her head, and she'd no teeth. But she's herself, Danny Boy – thank God.'

'Don't cry, love.'

She dashed drops of saline from her cheeks. 'Happy tears, these are. It could have been so different, couldn't it?'

'Yes, I know. If he'd used the s-cutting side of the axe–'

'Oh, don't say it. I don't want to think about it.'

'Will she be out in time for the funeral, Alice?'

She had no idea, and she said so. 'The hospital knew she was a battered wife, but police won't interfere in domestic problems, which is stupid. It has to go as far as severe injury or death before the law gets involved. That needs changing.

Anyway, she's got plenty of energy in her tongue, as usual, but none in her legs, so they'll probably keep her for a few days to build her up. I think they might find a reason to keep her in until Jimmy's six feet under.'

Without asking, she moved his crutches out of the way and fastened his dressing gown. She smiled at him, kissed him on the forehead and, after getting him to sit up straight, went off to help Peter with the meal. She ignored Harry and returned to the table with beetroot and red cabbage. 'You're doing great,' she whispered, kissing Dan's cheek lightly before straightening cloth and cutlery. She knew Harry was watching; hoped he was looking and learning.

He was watching, but he suddenly remembered an appointment. An old friend of his father's had died and, having been mentioned in the will, Harry had been invited to meet the older of two sons. Of course, it didn't have to be done today, but he wanted to get out of here. Alice was standing by her husband, and he admired her for it, yet he wanted her.

'Going?' Dan asked, eyebrows raised.

'Yes. If you'll just feed these two lads, I'll be grateful. I should be back before seven.' He went off to find out what the poor old chap had left for him.

The front door closed. Alice served up her famous scouse and handed out soda bread. 'How's Olga?' she asked mischievously.

'Fine,' was Peter's sparse answer.

'And Leo Tolstoy?'

'Fine.'

She sighed pseudo-dramatically. 'Isn't it lovely having visitors, Dan? All this stimulating conversation's great.'

Tony put down his spoon. 'If you're going to make the best scouse ever, it's your fault that we'd rather eat than talk, isn't it, Neil?'

Neil, his mouth full, just nodded.

'Shall I tell them about the arsenic?' Dan asked.

'No, love. Another spoonful?' And she ladled out more of Liverpool's famous dish.

Harry drove back home, because old Joe Foley had left him a rather nice Austin, a set of encyclopedias and... Oh, God. What the blood, guts and Southport sand was he supposed to do with two dozen pigeons, one of them a prizewinner named Blue Lady with squabs? Were the squabs old enough to be moved? 'I should never have shown an interest I didn't feel,' he told the windscreen, 'but his sons couldn't be bothered, and here I am – lumbered with a blue lady and all her babies.'

The birds could stay where they were for now; he would drive down, let them out, feed them – but how might they be settled in Penny Lane? He needed to build a loft in the back garden and... He parked outside his house and, just before leaving the car, noticed an envelope pinned inside the driver's door.

He opened it and found detailed instructions, with a note just for him. 'God love him – Joe knew he was dying.' A second sheet held information regarding the movement of pigeons from one loft to another. 'So I leave them where they are for now ... pick up the mesh-fronted transfer cages from Joe's shed, bring them here and clean them ... let the birds out while they're still living in Joe's loft, feed them ... blah, blah ... build a loft here.'

Right. The birds would be carried to Penny Lane, a few at a time, in Joe's old bird basket. They would live here in the wire-fronted cages for a few days without being allowed out to fly. The cages were to be placed so that the pigeons could see their new loft. On release from said new loft after transfer, they should not be fed when returning to the old place. He must carry on bringing them home till they realized which side their pigeon feed was buttered. It promised to be complicated and time-consuming, because he had to build one loft and destroy another.

He had jobs on. He was training Tony Corcoran in the art of plumbing. He didn't want the bloody birds, but he'd been left this car, and he must play fair. 'You trusted me, Joe, and my dad trusted you right through thick and thin, so I'll see to your birds, don't worry.'

As he entered his house, it occurred to Harry that he hadn't thought once about Alice since arriving at the Foley house. Was he about to break free? He had a car. When Vera got out of hospital and bucked up, he would take her somewhere for a rest and a holiday, and the boys, too, deserved a break. Peter Atherton would need some training in caring for pigeons, but that should present no real problem. Everything was sortable, and he could go back to living his normal, lonely life. But she would still be next door... To hell with it; he needed an early night, and the lads could see to themselves.

It wasn't far to Dudley Street. Alice picked up her tape measure and yardstick before bidding her husband goodbye for now. 'I won't be long,' she promised, 'just a couple of windows to measure – oh, and I'll have to look at the material, see if there's a repeat pattern. I should be back before Peter shows up.' She made sure he had his books, his newspaper and the reading glasses he had needed since the second stroke. 'Are you all right?' she asked.

'I am. Are you?'

She nodded.

'You're blushing,' Dan accused her. 'It's not a sin to start enjoying being in bed with your husband. We had our first really good night, didn't we? There's nothing wrong with that.'

'I know.'

He took pity on her and changed the subject. 'Where are you off to?'

'Just Dudley Street. I replied to a letter and said I would measure today.' She didn't tell him that Harry had offered to run her there in his car because he was finishing early, and the lads were at college learning paperwork. There was still awkwardness between her and Harry, and she wished she could come to terms with it. Could a woman love two men? It wasn't about the word 'could' – it was more about 'should', wasn't it? Was it right for her to love her husband to bits and desire the bloke next door? The situation was ridiculous, and she was staying with Dan, because she'd made promises before God, and–

And there was Harry standing next to the car

148

he'd inherited yesterday. 'How's Dan?' he asked while polishing a headlamp.

'He's quite well, thanks.'

'Are you sure you don't want a lift?'

'I'm sure.'

'Are you sure you're sure?'

She nodded. 'I've been stuck in the house all day, and the walk will do me good. It's not too far away from here, so I won't be gone long. Go in and sit with Dan – I've left the snick on. Peter won't be here till nearer bedtime.'

He couldn't work her out. Until a few days earlier, she'd seemed uneasy, almost unhappy, and restless, but she suddenly appeared to be settled and less needful. Anyway, he wasn't thinking about her, was he? What with apprentices and pigeons, he had enough on his plate – or in Joe Foley's back garden. Ah, she was smiling. 'What?' he asked.

'Take him out, Harry. Take Dan for a ride round the city – Pier Head, Liver Birds, cup of coffee, whatever he wants. Drive past St George's Hall – Dan thinks it's the most beautiful building in the world, and he likes to see Victoria and Albert and the horses. Make him important; just make him special, please. As long as you have enough petrol.'

'All right.' He shrugged. 'See you later, then.'

As she walked away, she could feel his eyes boring into her back. Oh, if he and Dan would be friends, how much easier life might become. They could play cards with Peter, though Peter seemed to prefer the company of Olga these days – and who could blame him? She wore prettier clothes lately, and her hair was often looser –

149

such a handsome woman, she was. Would there be a wedding in the near future?

It was further than she'd imagined, and she took wrong turnings twice, because she seemed not to be concentrating. All these streets round Wavertree looked the same, so she stopped and sat on a garden wall while she re-thought the route. Yes, it was two streets away from the main road, and she was nearly there. Her feet seemed reluctant, as if they wanted to go somewhere else, but she was a professional woman, and a job was a job.

At last she arrived – Dudley Street. The bed and breakfast place was on a corner, and it looked well cared for: newly painted and with nice potted plants here and there under the front bay window. Alice closed the gate and walked up the short pathway to the front door. As she raised a hand to the knocker, she felt a breath on her neck, so she turned and found no one near. Oh, God, not now, please. Her heart slowed, and she lowered herself until she was seated on the step. An outside otherness? Had she ever experienced one before? Perhaps that day at Olga's shop things had begun outside, but why here?

And somewhere, nowhere, everywhere, a baby cried.

Negotiations were over. Martin dashed into the shop, lifted the flap and picked up his wife. 'Nellie,' he joked, 'you'll have to get some weight off before I do myself a mischief.' He put her down. 'I've done it. Not a mischief – I mean I've done what I set out to do.'

'Have you, now? Anyway, I thought you liked me cuddly.'

'Yes, and I like picking you up. Anyway, we've got it. Turner's is ours.'

'That's great news.'

The idea was that their daughters' husbands could use the place for storage or as a shop when they started their new business. The garage was paying its rent, just about, but petrol was as scarce as hens' teeth, as were some car parts. 'We'll go and tell them.'

Nellie frowned. 'Are we becoming a pair of nuisances, Martin? We're all due at Marie's in a couple of days, so won't it keep till then?'

'Let's give them the news in private, Nellie. They'll need to get their heads round it and talk about what they're going to do. Will they let the garage go till petrol comes off ration and car parts are easier to come by? Or should they keep both businesses ticking over? It's not the sort of subject you'd discuss at a big do, is it? We need to get phones, I think.'

She agreed. 'There again, Martin, they might want to use that big shed as storage and run the shop from here. That would be great.'

Over lunch, they discussed the possibilities. They, as elders and as well-known shopkeepers on Smithdown Road, might run the business belonging to their sons-in-law part time; Kevin and Paul could take it over, or one might run the garage while the other collected, sold and delivered second-hand goods. Nellie got excited. 'If the girls run it, I could have Simon and Keith upstairs.' Another thought visited her. 'What about the flat

151

above the Turners' shop?' she asked.

Martin pondered. 'There may not be one, love. Instead of letting it as a flat, they might use it to store smaller stuff, things that are easy to carry. It might turn out to be the answer for them until we've all got through these post-war years. Depends how successful the business turns out to be, I suppose. I know they're thinking about restoring furniture. I reckon them two could turn their hands to just about anything.'

'It'll be a success, whatever they decide.' Nellie's mind was made up. 'All right, we'll go and tell them tonight.' She went to make a brew.

Olga closed the shop, locked the door and hung up a BACK IN ONE HOUR notice. He was standing behind her, and she knew what to expect after she pulled down the door blind. 'Peter,' she chided. 'This is all being new for me...'

'It's OK. I've had some experience in these matters, though I've never been engaged before. Don't worry, I've told nobody.'

'This is good, because a virgin of forty-seven does not advertise.'

'I'm sixty-three,' Peter grumbled.

She nodded sagely. 'So I marry soon a very old man.'

'With no money and no royal blood, princess.'

She took his hand. 'Come. I must learn these things. Leo will stay here.' And she led her man upstairs.

Peter grinned to himself. Whatever happened, his Olga would always be the same – sensible, pragmatic, intelligent, in charge and just lovely.

'Er ... no danger of pregnancy, is there?'

She turned and looked at him as if he'd developed a second head. 'None. I am see doctor in England after Batya die. In family, we have haemophilia, so I was getting tied up in the baby parts. Also, I think I am now too old. Come.'

His jaw dropped little by little as he watched her undressing. She had managed, by some miracle, to retain the body of a woman in her thirties. 'You're lovely.' His voice was hoarse. 'Olga?'

'Yes, Peter?'

'I'm not lovely.'

She took her hair down, allowing it to fall over her breasts. 'Then I close eyes.'

When she was under the covers with her eyes closed, he tore off his trousers and shirt before joining her. He was about to deflower a princess of Russia. God, what would his mother have said about this? But he was given no opportunity to think any further, because that same Russian princess was very, very hungry.

'Are you all right, love?' Annie Meadows leaned over the young woman who sat on her doorstep. 'God, you look as if you've seen a ghost. Come on, girl, get yourself up and I'll put the kettle on. Go through the first door on the left – that's been turned into the lodgers' dining room since we started doing evening meals as well as breakfasts. They have their breakfasts in their rooms on trays.' She tutted to herself. 'Listen to me going on when you're not feeling well.'

'I'm all right now, thanks,' Alice said, though she wasn't.

'Just give me a minute while I make some tea.' Annie left the visitor alone.

The day was warm, but Alice began to shiver. Why had she heard the baby here, in Dudley Road, the baby who had possibly grown up to be Callum? This was a mile or more away from Penny Lane, and the baby belonged there in that front bedroom. Even Frank no longer heard him, because the baby was there for Alice, just Alice. Something was going on. Things were developing, changing, becoming more intense. Soon, she would know the truth, and she sensed that she wouldn't like it.

Old Joe had bequeathed to Harry not just books, pigeons and car, but plenty of petrol in the tank. Even so, Harry used it sparingly. After a quick trip through Liverpool's centre, he drove the Austin to the Pier Head where the two men sat and gazed at a scene that had been the focus of many during Liverpool's long-term relationship with the Mersey. 'My grandma used to stand here waiting for Granddad's ship,' he commented in an effort to fracture a silence that had developed during the ride.

'Merchant?' Dan asked.

'Captain, yes. He used to say he'd climbed all the way to the crows' nest – he meant it was hard work overseeing a crew. Sailors can be a bit wild, or so I'm told.' This was a daft situation. What the hell was he doing in the middle of Liverpool with the husband of a woman he loved?

'I'm sure they can be wild; I met a fair few when I was working on the docks. We handled munitions. The services wouldn't have me because of flat feet, so I was civilian, but it was an essential job. That's where I had the second stroke.'

'I'm sorry.'

'So am I. The first happened when I was digging Alice out of our bombed kitchen. Still, never mind – I'm getting there now. Well, I hope I am, for her sake.'

'And for your own sake, Dan.'

'Well, yes.' He paused. 'We're trying for a baby.'

Harry knew that this was his neighbour's way of delivering a warning, because the undercurrent was doing its best to rise to the surface. Dan knew. He knew that Harry had feelings for Alice. 'Shall we get back?' Harry asked.

'Yes. Alice will be home soon.'

Thus ended a conversation that never happened. It never happened at a city's edge guarded by a pair of mythical birds atop a beautiful building.

Harry drove home. 'Do you like living on Penny Lane?' he asked.

'I'm happy wherever Alice is.'

The message was loud and clear; Alice was untouchable. Probably...

Peter's tsarina was tousled. Tousled suited her, but everything suited Olga Konstantinov. 'You're beautiful,' he whispered.

She smiled. 'So this is what I was missing. It is good. Now we must marry. I am citizen, so we can. Just register office, me, you and for witness we bring Alice and Dan. Is good?'

'Is good.'

And that was that.

Outside, the man in black clothing watched the shop. He had found her.

Alice measured windows in the lodgers' dining room and in one upstairs bedroom. She checked the material and found no pattern to match, picked up her bundle and made for the front door. 'This will easily do both rooms,' she said. 'Do you want them lining?'

'No, they'll do as they are.'

'Fine. I'll be off, then.' She still felt uneasy in this house, and could scarcely wait to be on her way home.

'Are you sure you're all right?' Annie asked.

'Yes.'

'I'll want another two bedrooms done when I can get my hands on some more material.' The landlady shook her head. 'How long will we have to be paying for that war?'

'The people who really paid are buried abroad, Miss Meadows.'

Annie sighed. 'I know. I wasn't thinking. Isn't that a bit heavy for you to carry all the way to Penny Lane?'

'No, no, it's not too bad.' Compared to the weight of whatever lingered in this building, the physical burden was as light as air.

'You still don't look right to me.'

She smiled as broadly as she could manage before escaping the concern of Miss Annie Meadows. Turning the corner, she stopped, placed her package on the ground, and entered another otherness. She was aware of the landlady going

156

into one of the rooms – ah, it was a kitchen. Sepia smoke eliminated the only source of light by covering a small window. Water ran. Gas popped as it gave birth to flame. Crockery and cutlery rattled. 'Callum?' she whispered.

'Yes.' The single syllable drifted past her face in a breath of air.

'Where is she?'

'Here.'

The otherness abandoned her as swiftly as it had arrived. Turning her head to the left, Alice saw a familiar figure walking towards her. 'Oh, my God,' she mouthed. So this was why she had felt so disturbed. Callum was here, and Muth was approaching.

Elsie Stewart continued down the empty road and turned right. She didn't speak to Alice, nor did she look at her. Alice abandoned her parcel and walked to the corner. 'Muth?' she called.

But the woman who had given birth to Alice entered the bed and breakfast house without making any response.

Picking up the curtain material, Alice allowed the light to dawn. Elsie hadn't seen her because ... I wasn't there. Callum hid me. Such power, that baby had. But he wasn't a baby now, was he? He sent his baby self to announce his presence, but he had become in death whatever he might have been in life. How suddenly that crying stopped, as if ... as if he had been silenced.

Hurriedly, she made her way homeward, her sense of direction unerring this time. Had Callum tried to prevent her from going to Miss Meadows's house? Had he made her lose her way? When had

157

he died and why? She needed to talk to someone, and that someone needed to be a woman.

She would talk to Olga...

Seven

Alice could hear voices from Dan's ground-floor bedroom, so he wasn't alone, and wasn't ready to move into the marital bed for the night. Olga's laughter drifted up the hall and Alice, grateful for the presence of her friend, crept upstairs, because she needed to be alone. Was she ever alone? Did Callum follow her everywhere, and how had she managed to know his name without ever being told? Who the hell was he, anyway?

She stood in the doorway clutching at the curtain material as if her life depended on its presence. Although her world had always been what some might describe as slightly mad, she had never expected it to descend into such chaos. Muth walking past her? Muth not seeing her? Muth never missed a thing, so what kind of lunacy was this? 'She must have gone blind. Or maybe I was seeing her when she wasn't really there. For all I know, I might have imagined all of it, cos I'm sure this seventh child thingy is a load of baloney.' Yet she had felt Muth's presence at the front door before entering the house...

She placed Miss Meadows's parcel on a chair and stretched out on the sofa whose position in the world had been altered by the move up to the

158

first floor. Dan and Peter were laughing. Harry let out one of his growling hoots, so Dan had three companions. All was well for now. Was all well, though? Was it normal to sleep with one man and dream about the bloke next door? Whichever way she looked at her life, she named herself a lunatic.

'Are you here?' she whispered. 'Callum? Was that going to be your name? Were you born here?' She swallowed. 'Did you die here?'

Nothing. 'He probably thinks I've had enough for one day.' Perhaps part of his brief was to protect her, since she felt almost sure that Callum had arrived to warn her or to pass on information. She wondered why he hadn't just come out with it, whatever it was. Because it was going to be a shock, she supposed. He was building up to some kind of climax, and she wasn't sure she'd want to know about whatever that was.

Today's invisibility had thrown her. A person from the other side, sometimes a baby, sometimes a man, had performed a cheap magic trick, one that might have been better placed in a theatre rather than on a street corner. 'Muth walked within inches of me...' But what worried Alice more was the thought of poor Miss Annie Meadows being within reach of Elsie Stewart's razor-sharp tentacles. The woman was a menace, and–

'Alice!'

She looked up. 'Hello, Olga.'

'We thought you were out. I am come to steal some thread to make my wedding dress right. I am going thinner these days.'

Alice's jaw dropped, but she snapped it closed and smiled. 'Peter? You and Peter? When did you decide? And when's the wedding?'

'Very soon, yes. You and Dan will be witnesses, I hope.'

'Of course we will.'

The shopkeeper sat next to her friend. 'Not a party, just bride, groom and two friends. No fuss. We went in the bed, and all was good.' She smiled at her companion's blush. 'Alice, would you buy a coat or a pair of shoes without trying on for fit? I have forty-seven years and no idea about man, and this was necessary.'

'So you tried him on?'

Both women curled into balls of near-hysteria. 'Are all Russians like you?' the younger woman finally managed.

'I not know. See, I am many, many years living in England now, so I am forgetting the land of my birth. I should be speaking better English, too. When my father and grandfather lived, we spoke Russian in the house. When they both are dead, I continue to think in my own language, and I speak English to customers only. Peter will teach me.'

Alice snorted. 'He doesn't speak English – he's a Woollyback.'

'So English is what King George is speaking?'

'Well, when he's not stammering, yes. He's a nervous man, Olga. His dad was one hard-faced bugger, and his mam looks as if her face would split if she smiled. So don't copy the king. Look, Peter's English will have to do. Mine's not great, because–'

'Because you are Scouser.'

'I am. What are you wearing for the wedding?'

160

'Red. A happy colour. Or I have a pretty blue dress with coat to match.'

Alice remembered one of her many dreams. 'Not purple?'

Olga shrugged. 'I have purple, yes.'

'And green jewellery?'

The Russian froze. 'No one ever saw the jewellery.'

'I did. It was in a kind of dream, and you were wearing a purple dress with green stones in a necklace. In another dream, you were in violet with a diamond tiara. That was an almost-awake dream in your shop the first time I met you. Just a silly otherness of mine. But you'd look great in purple and green.'

'Alice?'

'What?'

Olga got up, closed the door and returned to sit next to her friend. 'I have Romanov emeralds. They are in strong place underneath Liverpool bank. We bring them when we run. They were wedding gifts to my mother. This was a long, long time ago, when the family was safe.'

'Wear them,' Alice said, when she could speak again. 'Don't tell people they're real, but I know that with your colouring purple and emerald green will be perfect. Very dramatic. Then after the wedding, get them to a London auction house and sell them. You could buy a lovely house–'

'I am not wanting lovely house. Just Peter is what I want, and we live above shop until–'

'Until you die with no children, and the government takes the emeralds and spends your money on rubbish.'

161

It was Olga's turn to have a loose jaw moment. 'No!'

'Yes. Get rid and use the money to enjoy life. Spend it. Buy a little house at the seaside or in the country and have the best clothes, a good car, everything you want. That's better than leaving it to the state.'

'I was never consider this. You are right, of course – of this I must think. Thank you.'

'You're welcome. You said you needed thread.'

'Tomorrow. Now, I think about purple and take my Peter home if Dan has had his shower. You good friend, Alice.'

Alice, who had wanted to talk to Olga about the day's events, went down to feed first her dog, then her husband. After all, Frank was always top priority. She stood over the boxer while he inhaled his food. Dan's cottage pie was in the oven, so all she had to do was brown the top under the grill.

Harry came out of Dan's room. 'I took your young man for a ride, and he seemed to enjoy it.'

She turned. 'Good. And thank you.' He showed no sign of leaving. 'What?' she asked. 'What's up with you now?'

'My curtains, Alice.'

'I'll get Olga to come in and help me with them.'

He smiled. 'I'll help you.'

'No, you won't. Your idea of help is miles away from mine. Where's Dan?'

'In the shower. Olga's tidying up, and Peter's helping Dan.' He paused. 'Don't you trust me?'

She didn't trust herself, either, but she couldn't

162

say that. 'Leave me alone, Harry; I've had a terrible day.'

He looked more closely at her. The skin under her eyes looked slightly bruised, and she was paler than normal. In that moment, he realized that what he felt was more than simple desire; he was definitely falling in love with this delicious, tiny girl. He'd nursed strong suspicions, but he now felt completely sure that what he was enduring went beyond the merely physical. She must not become ill, because he would not be able to live in a world that didn't have Alice in it. That was a selfish attitude, but he was unable to correct it. And the thought of her suffering cut through him like a sharp, hot knife.

'What?' she snapped.

'Have you had one of your moments today?'

She felt affronted, almost furious. Why? How did he manage to get under her skin so easily? 'That is none of your business,' she hissed under her breath. Oh no, he looked so hurt. 'Sorry,' she whispered, 'but I'm very tired. I met a lovely lady who needed new curtains, and I discovered that my mother is a guest of hers. It's a bed and breakfast place. Think Hitler, multiply him by ten, and that's my mother. She's a witch.'

'Oh.'

'She's a seventh child, but with her it's a curse rather than a blessing. All her brothers and sisters emigrated, and I bet it was to get away from her. I'm told she stood over her dying father until he signed everything over to her before he died. She's shown no sign of having money, but the farm and the animals must have been worth

163

something. And now she's living with some poor old woman who deserves better.'

Harry shook his head. 'What are you going to do?'

'What can I do? Kill her? I don't think so.'

He pondered for a moment. 'Write an anonymous letter. Warn the woman she's living with.'

'Now you're talking daft.'

'Am I? I'll do it. Tell me what you want to say, and I'll do it.'

'Fingerprints, Harry.'

He grinned. 'I didn't arrive on one of last Tuesday's Fleetwood boats, Alice. I can see you're troubled, and I want to help you.' He would do anything for her – surely she knew that?

She felt the heat in her face. 'All right, I'll bring your curtains tomorrow evening.' Vera's boys would be there, she hoped. 'And thank you.'

'Alice–'

'Don't. I know what you're going to say, because it's written all over your face – and not anonymously. I even understand, because if I didn't have Dan ... well, I like you. But I can't betray him. He lives for me and almost died for me when we were bombed.'

He understood only too well. Alice Quigley was devoted to her husband. She had a strong sense of duty, and was an honourable woman with a firm moral code and ... and skin so beautiful that the marks under her eyes imitated the slight bruising on an almost perfect peach. 'It won't be easy,' he said, his voice soft and somewhat unsteady. 'I never felt like this about Vera – about anybody. I'll take her and the boys away for a while when she gets out of hospital, give myself a chance to get my head straight. Or my heart.'

Something akin to disappointment occupied Alice's chest. Why? She knew she belonged with Dan, yet this man disturbed her so thoroughly – was she in love, or was this lust? And how might she find the answer to such an impossible question? 'What are you doing to me?' her mouth said, though her brain felt disengaged from the whole scene.

Harry's eyebrows shot north. 'I'm doing nothing. You're doing nothing. Stuff like this just happens, and nobody can control it. We can ignore it, but it will build and build like pressure in a steam engine, and we'll need to scream.'

She almost smiled. 'The train now letting steam off at platform seven is the ten fifteen to hell. We have platform tickets only, Harry. We daren't board that train. It's an express, isn't it?'

He nodded. 'No stopping, no chance to have a change of mind. You can't hide in the ladies' waiting room reading some soft magazine.'

'I know. See you tomorrow, then. Oh, and forget anonymous letters.'

'OK.' He winked, turned his back on her and went home.

Annie Meadows could not account for her sudden uneasiness. The curtain girl left, and Elsie returned from shopping, and things were different for the rest of the afternoon and evening. It was something to do with the curtain girl. Things had stopped being all right and were suddenly all wrong. Life had turned seriously weird, and she

165

couldn't account for any of it. Any of what? What the hell was up with her? Was she going senile?

Elsie was cooking lamb chops in the kitchen. Normally, Annie would have sat with her new friend drinking tea or peeling vegetables, but she remained in the lodgers' little dining room, rubbing imaginary streaks off cutlery before arranging place mats in their usual order. Mr Stone had Buckingham Palace and Mr Clinton the Houses of Parliament, while Mr Timpson's mat carried a photograph of Trafalgar Square.

She placed linen napkins alongside the knives and set water glasses for the three guests. The fourth was at a business meeting – he was Marble Arch, which remained for now on the sideboard. When the table was up to scratch, Annie sat in a small easy chair and stared out into the street. As she thought about her current malaise, she decided that it had begun with the arrival of Mrs Quigley, who had been discovered having a funny turn on the front doorstep. It was as if the poor young woman had left a bit of herself behind, because the house felt ... it felt sad. Never a fanciful woman, Annie shook herself, stood up and walked down the hall to the kitchen. 'Table's ready,' she said. 'Just three of them tonight.'

'You're quiet.' Elsie turned the chops. 'Are you feeling all right?'

'Just a bit tired. I had one of my heads earlier on and took two Aspros.'

'Go and have a lie down. Oh, by the way, when's the meeting about our partnership?'

Annie felt nervous, though she'd no idea why. 'Erm – next week. They said they'd get back to

166

me when they could, because they need to find a time when they're both available.'

Elsie, always alert and tuned into whatever went on around her, was immediately on her guard. Annie Meadows was having reservations about the plan to enter an agreement regarding the business, but why? What had gone wrong? 'Are you having second thoughts, Annie?'

She was, and she had better say so. 'I may decide to retire altogether.'

'Oh.' Elsie sat in the chair opposite Annie's. 'So you'll sell the business?'

'More than likely – if I do retire. I'm not as young as I used to be.'

'Neither am I, but I'm willing to work. We could manage between us.'

Annie wasn't sure. She wasn't sure that she wanted to spend the rest of her life in the company of a woman who was so different from Doreen. Doe had owned a quiet side, but she'd also been amusing, a chatterbox with an opinion on most subjects, especially those about which she knew little. Elsie was ... well, she was sour. Her face was usually frowning, and she often looked as if she'd come across something unpleasantly smelly or ugly – or both. 'I know we could probably manage, but I'm fed up with managing. I think I'll give three months' notice, to my regulars, and put the house up for sale in the next few weeks. Sorry.'

Could Elsie afford the guest house? Did she want to afford it? There were people here during the week, but from Friday morning until Monday night she would be alone in the large house. Right, she had better start looking round for something a bit more promising. Annie could play silly buggers, but her not-to-be partner was already out of here in her head. And the chops were slightly burnt.

Vera Corcoran became the cabaret on Women's Surgical. People with stitches had to keep hands on scars, because laughter threatened to undo the careful embroidery bequeathed by theatre staff. She told jokes, few of which would have been suitable for delivery to a clergyman.

Vera was a menace, and she knew it. Her specialities were food, snorers, visitors who brought the wrong reading matter, and doctors who thought they were gods. 'See him? His nose is that far up his own arse, he can smell his breakfast.' Another of her favourites was 'How many mistakes have you buried, son?' This one she used on younger doctors. While the staff expressed delight at her speed of recovery, they were concerned for others in the ward, and Vera refused point-blank to return to what she called solitary conferment.

'Have you seen the state of this?' she asked loudly of no one in particular. 'Porridge? It looks like the stuff what sticks wallpaper up. You'll be all right if your stitches come undone, girls, cos this'll glue you back together, no danger. Me spoon's riverted to the plate.'

Her fight to remain upright when walking had almost caused a riot, since she played to the gallery by exaggerating her difficulties. Staggering along singing 'I Belong to Glasgow' had been one of her favourite tricks until the ward sister had put a stop to it. Undaunted, Vera had made her way through 'Underneath the Arches', 'Burlington Bertie', 'Me and My Shadow' and 'Abide with Me' which was reserved for evensong on the Sabbath.

On the Sunday of the Stantons' party in Waterloo, Vera got her marching orders. 'She's been nothing but trouble,' the sister told her sons and Harry. 'Keep her away from your dad's funeral and make sure she walks every day. She's a nuisance.'

'I know,' chorused the two boys.

'The funeral's done with,' Harry told the sister. 'Under the circumstances, we were allowed a rush job, even though there had to be an inquest.'

Vera looked at Tony, at Neil, and finally at Harry. 'I hope you didn't bury him in his good clothes, that three-piece suite with waistcoat included.'

'I'm afraid we did,' Harry replied. 'It was the only decent stuff we could find.'

'Then you can bloody well dig him up and put him in one of them long frocks – a shrewd.'

'Shroud, Mam.'

Vera glared at her son. 'Shrewds were good enough for our fallen soldiers, so they'd do for that bugger. I could get a few quid for his good suite. On top of all that, you got me hysterical novels from the library again.'

'Historical, Mam.'

'Depends on how you look at them.' Vera's tone was dry. 'Hey, I just read how they cut Anne Boleyn's head off and she never done nothing. Dirty old bastard, that fat King Henry was. She had six fingers on one of her hands.'

'Behave yourself,' Harry said, though he was

used to her non sequiturs. 'And nobody's being dug up. Come on, I've got a car. We're going to have a bit of a holiday in a few weeks to help build you up, Vera.'

'Good,' she snapped. 'Because these nurses have been trying to poison me, I swear. And this lot here – they all snore.'

'So do you,' accused the nursing sister. 'Oh, take her away, will you?'

'Charming.' Vera dragged the bag of clothing from her son's hands. 'Thanks, Tony.'

Sister puffed out her cheeks. 'Mrs Corcoran, please get dressed and go home. If you don't, we're going to park you down the side of the hospital with the rest of the stuff we don't want. Refuse is shifted every Monday morning, so think about that. You'll be taken away with the bins tomorrow.'

Vera grumbled under her breath.

'She's chunnering.' Harry dragged a hand across his face. 'I've found it's best to avoid women when the chunnering kicks off. Sorry, lads – I learned that one off Peter Atherton. He's a Lanky.'

Once dressed, Vera made a meal of saying good-bye to each individual on the ward. They were given advice on post-operative 'infestions', instructions on how to dispose of inedible food without the staff noticing, and a pile of magazines. 'They're not much good, but they're better than nothing.'

'Vera!' Harry called.

She turned. 'Come on, then. What are you three doing stood there holding me up? Get a move on.' She winked at the nearest patient. 'Always keep them on their toes, and always make them know everything is their fault.' She swept out of the ward with three males at her heels.

As they walked to the car, Harry found himself grinning and shaking his head. Vera, her almost bald scalp covered by a scarf, walked with her head held so high that she might have been at a Buckingham Palace garden party. She was finally free of a brutal drunk, and she even begrudged him the suit he was buried in.

'Ooh, get you,' she exclaimed when she reached the Austin. 'Come into some money, have we?'

He told her about old Joe, the car, the books and the pigeons.

'Then I'm getting a gun. I don't want pigeon shit on me tablecloths.'

Harry chuckled to himself. She would always be contentious, amusing, irreverent and outspoken, but the girl he had once known had been buried alongside a feckless drunk who had tried to kill her.

She sat in the passenger seat. 'What about petrol?' she asked. 'Is there any petrol?'

'I'll get a bit of an allowance because of my job, and I have my sources. Don't ask.'

'I won't. But where are we going?'

'Home.'

'Somebody mentioned a holiday, soft lad. Where?'

'No idea. It'll be in a few weeks, anyway. I'll drive till I stop, and that'll be our holiday.'

She muttered a few words that were scarcely audible before taking an interest in the life of Liverpool. It bustled. Soon, she could become a

171

bustler, because her enemy was dead. 'It might be spoilt now,' she announced as they pulled into Penny Lane.

'What might?' Harry asked.

'The three-piece suite,' Vera snapped. 'If he's started to rot in it, then it–'

'Mam!' Neil shouted.

'Behave yourself,' ordered their driver. 'We're here.'

'We're not here – we're there.'

He sighed. 'All right, then, we're there.'

'But we should be here.'

'We are here.'

She muttered under her breath, though all could hear her complaining that she was neither here nor there, and some people with no sense of direction shouldn't be allowed to drive cars when they didn't even know where they were going.

Harry alighted from the car and walked round to the passenger side. 'Madam?' He crooked his right arm. 'If you'd kindly accompany me...' He led her to Alice's house.

'I told you we should be there, not here,' she grumbled. 'This is not our house – it's Dan and Alice's.'

'We're here and we're there.' He turned. 'Come on, lads.'

In Dan Quigley's bedroom, people waited. The French door was open so that the party could spill out into a sunlit garden. On a table with the leaves up sat a WELCOME HOME VERA cake, and she was overcome.

'Hello,' she said softly, 'Alice and Dan, Peter, Olga, my lads and Harry.' She beamed through tears. 'I've got a big family,' she whispered. 'I've got yous lot as well as my sons.' She looked at Tony and Neil. 'Sorry I couldn't stop him; sorry you had to lose your dad, but he couldn't live without the drink.'

Tony surprised the whole company by putting an arm across his mother's shoulders. 'We'll be all right,' he said, 'so don't cry.'

Dan, the constant observer of life, knew that Tony was near the truth. Without Jimmy Corcoran, Vera would thrive and improve herself, while her sons were already showing promise in their designated areas of work. Harry was glancing sideways at Alice, but Alice's eyes were fixed on the cake whose ingredients had been acquired by begging the length and breadth of Penny Lane and all adjoining streets.

Dan made a decision. As from tomorrow, Peter Atherton could dress his client each day – shirt and trousers like everybody else. Dan looked at Vera as she sat on the floor, the huge, kindly Frank at one side of her, a ridiculously playful Leo Tolstoy at the other. In spite of her injury and the hair loss, she seemed so happy. She'd been through hell yet was keeping up as best she could, so the least Dan could do was to wear normal clothes all the time and start walking up and down outside. And he would make a friend of Harry. Surely a friend wouldn't try a move on Alice?

Alice stood in the doorway. 'Right, anybody who wants to come to our Marie's – we'll be leaving in about half an hour, so get yourself ready because our Marie's got a posh house.'

Vera touched her scarf. 'I don't think I want to

173

go without my hair,' she said. 'I feel a bit naked like this. And is it not just family?'

'Open house,' Dan answered, 'and my Alice has got you a wig. It's a kind of dark blonde, but it'll do the job. Keep your hair on, get your face done and enjoy yourself, love.'

The two women ascended the stairs. Vera looked round the main bedroom. 'What happened?' she asked.

'What do you mean?'

'I mean your house is arse over tip, Alice.'

Alice explained about the new arrangement. 'So this is my sitting and work room, and I've made you a dress. Olga had this nice piece of pale green taffeta – come on, let's get you sorted, missus.'

Fifteen minutes later, Vera stared at the stranger in the mirror. 'Are you sure this is me?' She blinked quickly. 'Is that massacara?'

'Mascara, yes. And the green dress suits you lovely. Here, try my black patents on – I've a bag to match. As for the wig, nobody would know it wasn't real.'

Vera slipped her feet into her neighbour's shoes. 'I feel like a millionaire,' she said. 'What are they celebrating tonight?'

'Our Nellie's liberation. She's got rid of Mam and found two daughters, two sons-in-law and two grandsons. Marie's friends and neighbours will be there, too.'

'Sounds a fair swap,' Vera said. 'Seems as if you don't like your mam much. Bit of a tartar?'

'She's horrible. I might tell you more tomorrow, when we've got time. But Vera, this is dead serious, so keep your gob shut, all right? My

174

mother is the nastiest woman I know, so don't gossip about her.'

Vera had the good grace to blush. 'I know what folk think of me round here, Alice. I was... I had a bad life, and talking about other people took my mind off ... off him. Things are different now, and I have to make sure them two lads grow up decent. Trust me. I won't say a word.'

'All right. Now, we're off to the zoo.'

'You what?'

'Nigel's a vet, so the house is full of orphans.'

'Orphans?'

'Yep. And two of them are lions. He works for Chester Zoo, and a young lioness got pregnant before she should have, God love her. So when she had the two cubs, she didn't know what to do with them. Nigel and Marie are rearing them, then sending them to be wild in Africa.'

Vera swallowed hard. 'Er ... are they danger-ous?'

Alice giggled.

'I'm serious, girl. Are they dangerous?'

'Not yet.' Alice put her arms round her neigh-bour, a woman she had sought to avoid after their first encounter. 'Don't be frightened any more, Vera. He's gone. He will never, ever hurt you again. When you meet people – or even animals – take them at face value. Oh, Larry the llama spits.'

'Llama?'

Alice nodded. 'Spits vomit.'

Vera shivered. 'Can my boys come?' She would feel safer if Tony and Neil were nearby.

'Course they can. The three of you can go in

Harry's car. Dan and I will go with Nellie and Martin; Olga and Peter are getting a taxi. You're free, love. This is what freedom tastes like. And Harry says he's taking you and the boys away for a week.' She reclaimed her arms. 'Never start out afraid. You're as good as anybody, and that wig suits you. Come on.'

It was party time.

Olga was waiting for Peter. Across the street, a man in black stood staring at her shop, at her home. Who was he? Didn't she have enough to contend with while Terry Openshaw sulked his way through meetings? Whenever the chance arrived, the butcher cornered her, begged her to reconsider his proposal. Peter wasn't good enough. If she married himself, their meat would be at cost, and they could live well. Now a second man was watching her place of business and her home. Should she tell Peter? She would think about it.

Peter might react and get into trouble. She studied the man who lingered on the opposite pavement. He looked Russian – well, she thought he did.

Peter came in. 'Ready, love?' he asked.

'Yes. Come along. I shall throw you to the lions.'

It all happened in the blink of an eye, or so it seemed when Elsie thought about it. A phone number in the *Echo*, a swift interview via the telephone lines, the ordering of a taxi, the packing of clothes and, by eight o'clock in the evening, Elsie was on her way to Brighton-le-Sands.

Brighton-le-Sands was a tiny village on a

minute slice of land strangled almost to death by Blundellsands on one side and Waterloo on the other. One of Elsie's daughters lived in Waterloo, so she got the driver to take her past the house, a huge black-and-white affair built in the good old mock-Tudor style with balconies, solid front door and leaded windows. 'Stop,' she ordered.

The driver applied the brakes.

'Reverse a bit,' she suggested, her tone gentler. 'I think I know the people who live there.'

He applied the handbrake. Some of these elderly lady fares could be a pain in the backside.

They were all there. Elsie saw Nellie and Marie immediately, straightening her spine when her seventh daughter put in an appearance.

'They must have a bob or two,' the driver remarked.

'Oh, they have. He's a vet, with his own practice as well as working for Chester Zoo.' She was staring at Alice, her lastborn, the one whose birth had caused Elsie so much pain. Childbirth was supposed to get easier, though Elsie's experiences had been quite the reverse. Nellie and Marie, numbers one and two, had been nothing to write home about; the final birth had been hell on wheels.

'Shall we go?' the driver asked. 'I've more fares soon.'

They carried on for about half a mile, and Elsie was finally deposited with her luggage near a large, grey house outside which her new employer waited. She was to have a small ground-floor flat, and she would be responsible for tenants in five bed-sitting rooms.

177

'Sorry for the rush, Mrs Stewart,' he gushed. 'Only like I said, Mrs Murphy's in the hospital, and she's not going to be well enough to come back as caretaker. Her daughter will take care of her.' He looked Elsie up and down. 'Are you sure you're fit enough for this month's trial? If there's any trouble, use the pay phone in your room and I'll have somebody here in minutes. The lodgers can use the phone, too, as long as they ask you and if they have the money.' He paused. 'How old are you?'

'Sixty-two,' she lied, 'and as tough as old boots. No need to worry about me, Mr Blake. I'll collect your rents, and there'll be no trouble. If I can't get you, we always have the police if anything gets out of hand. Now, you just go and enjoy your holiday with your family.'

'Collect rents on Fridays,' the owner of the property said. 'Catch them on their way back from work and before they've had time or chance to spend money. One week's non-payment and you give them a talking-to. Two weeks, send for me and I'll get them out, or somebody will. All right?'

'Fair enough.'

Elsie stepped into new territory with her employer, who carried her bags. 'You're better off than the rest,' he told her. 'You have the separate kitchen and a little bathroom; the rest have everything in just one room, and they have to share when it comes to bathrooms.' He glanced at his watch. 'I'd best be off, or the wife will have my guts for garters.'

Alone, she dropped into a seat. She had three easy chairs, a bed, a wardrobe built into a recess

178

next to the chimney, a bookcase and a small dressing table. At the end of the bed stood a chest of six drawers, so Elsie Stewart considered herself amply provided for. But the main factor was that there were other people in the building. In spite of her determined attitude to life, she feared being completely alone; she dreaded the nightmares.

Deciding to unpack later, she tidied her hair and took herself off to meet her five new neighbours. She had managed to calm down in Annie's house, and she must do her best to settle here quickly. Standing for a few moments in the doorway to her own domain, she remembered what her employer had said. Her predecessor would be looked after by her daughter. 'And I won't,' she mouthed silently. God help her if she ever became seriously ill. For now, she was in good health, and her little flat came free. She would need to use some of her inheritance for food and bills, but she was sheltered here. It was half past eight – time to face her fellows.

Alice was getting just a bit fed up with all her otherness occasions. Quite early on at the party in Marie's house, she suffered a rather prolonged one. It was centred round Muth. Muth was sneaking out through a rear doorway, and Alice felt sure that the property in question belonged to Miss Meadows, the lady who wanted new curtains. Elsie Stewart was carrying cases. A taxi was parked in a rear street. What was Muth up to? Had she informed that poor woman that she was leaving? Perhaps Miss Meadows needed to be told about how lucky she was to be rid of Elsie Stewart.

Marie joined her sister in the hall. 'Bugger,' she muttered as she led her practically catatonic sibling outside. Opening the garage door, she pulled Alice inside. 'I remember getting you tested while you were living with us,' she mumbled. 'The docs said you had petit mal, a mild sort of epilepsy, but we knew different, eh?' She expected no reply, and she got none.

There was a car. Alice, in her otherness, was seated with a second passenger in the rear seat; she believed it to be a taxi. 'Callum?' she whispered. Turning, she saw her mother sitting next to her. She was staring. Following the direction of Elsie's gaze, she looked through the window across the road and saw herself, Marie, Nellie, Harry, plus many people she didn't know. She wondered how she could be here and there at the same time, almost smiling when she remembered Harry's account of Vera's statements when she'd returned from hospital. But thinking about reality didn't help her to escape the otherness. She wasn't really with Muth; no, that was the otherness, because she was in Marie's house, wasn't she?

Marie had heard the single whispered word and wondered who the hell Callum was, but she knew that this pretty little sister of hers had stopped hearing anything real minutes ago. Yet she tried once more, just as she always had years earlier. 'Alice? Can you hear me?'

Inside the otherness, although aware that she was with Marie, Alice saw Muth, and she concentrated hard. Mother and youngest daughter were parked together in the back seat of a cab outside Marie's house. Impossible? So was invisibility.

'Alice?' Marie said again.

Very slowly, Alice's right hand rose, the index finger pointing towards the road. 'There,' she announced clearly.

Marie opened the garage door a fraction. A black hansom taxi cab sat on the opposite side of the road. Plastered against its offside window was a face she knew only too well. It was Muth. 'Oh, God,' she muttered.

'We can go back now,' Alice told her companion. 'It's finished. I'm here.'

'Do you always know where she is?'

As reply, the younger woman shook her head. 'But Callum does.'

Marie bit her lip. 'You said his name when you were gone. Who is he?'

'I believe he's a crying baby who turns into a grown-up man. I've no bloody idea, but he lives ... exists in the front bedroom in Penny Lane, the one I've turned into a sewing and sitting room. The baby cries, then he comes as a man. Dad's with him; I can smell his pipe tobacco.'

'Bloody hell.'

'It's a comfort. She killed him, you know.'

'What? She actually killed– Surely even she isn't capable of the cold-blooded murder of our dad?'

'I'd put nothing past her, but no. She mithered. Then something happened, something I'm not sure of yet. Callum's the messenger. He's leading me to Muth and warning me that she's danger-

181

ous. In the end, he'll tell me everything.'

'How do you know?'

Alice shrugged. 'I don't know how I know, do I? But I know he's here to take me back to a place he's dreading visiting, which is probably the only way he can.'

'What does he look like?'

A grin spread across the smaller woman's face. 'So far, a long streak of piss in a corner – or a long streak of Dad's smoke, more like. He'll get clearer when he's ready, and I don't mind waiting, except the otherness gets me down. It'll stop when he's told me – and don't bother asking me how I know again, because I just know.'

'I know you know.'

'Don't start taking the wee-wee, our Marie. Come on, we'd best get back.'

Vera lay fast asleep in the run now named the lions' den. Two tawny heads rested on her belly, and each cub had its own dog. Both boxers slept, too. Peter whispered to Olga, 'Well, I'll go to the foot of our stairs.'

'Why?' she asked. 'Why stairs?'

He groaned. 'It's a Lancashire saying. Sorry, I keep forgetting you're a foreigner.'

'You not forget in the bed. You tell me I have all passion of Russia in me.'

'Behave yourself. Let's go and see how Dan's getting on.'

They found Dan with Alice, Marie, Nigel and Harry. 'Are you sure?' Harry was asking.

Alice, paler than usual, simply nodded her head and sighed.

'Marie?' Harry asked.

'We're certain.' Marie lowered herself onto a sofa. 'She was outside in a taxi cab staring in at us. Alice has a feeling that Muth's left the bed and breakfast where she was staying and has come to live near us.'

'That's exactly what we don't want to hear.' Nigel closed his eyes for a second. 'Maybe I can train Hercules and Jason to attack.'

'Near Claire and Janet, too,' Marie mused. 'We'll have to warn them, but I'm not too sure about telling Nellie. She's bad enough with her nerves as it is, after living for years with that bloody woman.'

'Knowledge is important,' Alice stated. 'Be prepared, and all that.'

'Were you a boy scout?' Harry asked.

'I got thrown out for being too rough for them.' Alice looked across the room to where the oldest of the sisters chatted happily with her husband and their daughters. 'We have to warn Claire and Janet. They left home because of Muth, just like I did.' She squared her shoulders. 'Marie, go and look after your guests. Tomorrow, I am going to find our mother.'

Dan approached her on his crutches. 'Where've you been?'

'Just looking round our Marie's house. Anyway, Daniel – shouldn't you visit the lions' den like the bloke in the Bible did?'

He laughed. 'Too clever for your own good, you are.'

Eight

Olga and Peter, having left the taxi to help Dan into his house, walked the final hundred yards to the shop. As they neared the place, little Leo began to growl deep in his young, inexperienced throat. A happy animal, he seldom complained, so Olga was not surprised to discover that she could not open the door. 'There is things piled up behind here,' she announced. 'Someone is being inside and shutting us out of our own home. I have been interfered with, Peter.'

Under different circumstances, Peter might have pleaded guilty to interfering with his beloved himself, but this was serious business.

'Peter?'

He took over, pushing hard at the door, but he seemed to be out of luck and energy, as he couldn't shift the weight. 'I think you're right – we've been burgled, love. Come on, let's walk up to the phone box.' He held on to his 'girl' because she trembled, and her walk was unsteady. 'It'll be all right, sweetheart.' His tall and beautiful Russian noblewoman was not as tough as she chose to appear, but oh, how he loved her. He should be planning for retirement at his age, yet here he was like a bloody teenager... 'Who would do this, Olga?'

She shook her head. 'I am thinking is square, pale man with black clothes,' she muttered. 'I try not notice him with his grey skin. I see him, but I not speak, because I think I am being foolish and imagining.'

'What?'

She told him about the dark-clad person who had been walking up and down the lane for a few minutes every day. 'Russian, I believe from how he look,' she mouthed. 'From far up to north. We always say people from that part of Russia are short because weather so cold they do not grow; no sunshine. Prisoners in Siberia are sometimes short, too.' She glanced at the opposite pavement. 'He stands there, just there, and stares at my shop. What is he wanting from me, Peter?'

'How the hell would I know, love?'

Olga shrugged. 'He looks for something.'

'Well, it's not likely to be firewood or paraffin, is it? I mean, who's going to break in for a few gas mantles or a bucket and mop? You've nothing of real value for sale, have you?'

She shook her head. 'Upstairs, too, is ordinary. We have lived simple lives since we arrive at England. You have seen table old, chairs old, and not many of my clothes are new. The little jewellery I have here is cheap, from market.' She stopped. 'But I have a Romanov Bible, given to my mother for her confirmation. Nothing else. In Bible is signatures of tsar and tsarina and some others, but who would want to have that?'

'A collector of historical stuff might think it's valuable, Olga. Come on, let's get the police. Don't cry.'

She took his proffered handkerchief and dried her eyes. 'I am in fear. My stomach tumble about

185

like clown in circus.'

'No need to be frightened – I'm here.'

'My daddy, my beloved Batya, he read Bible aloud in Russian. It was comfort for my grandfather, you see. He was old, and he missed the country of his youth.' She shook herself. Now was not the time for nostalgia; a crime had been committed. 'But this is not someone looking for Bible, Peter.'

He took hold of her hands and folded them in his. 'We'll let the police in, then we'll go and sleep at Alice's or Harry's house. Or we could go to my flat – it isn't far. Please, love. The sooner we make the call, the sooner they'll be here. See, Leo's stopped growling, so the burglars have probably gone by now.'

'I think I not want police, Peter. If Russian communists find out I am here and I am related to the royal people, this may go in newspaper. Is frightening being a Russian exile from family so hated.'

Peter ran a hand through his thatch of white hair. 'But there's other Romanovs here, love. Nobody cares about that stuff any more. I looked it up in the Picton Reading Room. And you're no threat. You're past child-bearing, so what interest would anybody take in you?'

She lifted her chin in a way that spoke volumes about her provenance. Olga looked regal; even in working clothes, she managed to be a cut above. Now, dressed for a party, she was every inch the princess. 'Hatred is not from sense, you see. Hatred is from the animal inside us, the small creature that screams for milk, for attention, for

186

sleep. Hatred asks no question; it just kills.'

He didn't know what to say, and he told her so.

'The pogroms on Jews showed how bad Russia can be – men slaughtered, women used, and some children, too. When we are normal, the super ego, mostly taught from parents, quietens the id. Russians?' She shrugged. 'Wild. Two men made the same mistake – Napoleon Bonaparte and Adolf Hitler. Never invade Russia. She will kill you without a second glance at your face, then someone will write overture about it with bells and cannon. I come from fierce peoples. So no invasions. Except here in my little shop.'

'I won't invade Russia, love. I must write a reminder in me diary.' He didn't know what to suggest. It was dusk, they couldn't get into the shop or the flat, she didn't want the police, he didn't know whether she would accept help from the neighbours. 'Do you want me to try to get in through the back gate?' he asked.

'You think they gone?'

'Yes. Definitely, otherwise Leo Tolstoy would be spitting daggers.'

'You try, then. But if you see any sign of trouble, you come out again. Take Leo. I wait here.'

He didn't want to leave her, but she insisted. Olga in a stubborn mood did not negotiate, and she refused to knock on doors to seek shelter. Peter followed the hurrying pup and walked round the corner.

The back gate was hanging crookedly like a drunk after a night on the tiles. Buckets, bowls, candles and kindling were all scattered about, and there was blood on the flags, so the criminal had probably suffered an accident. The rear door had been jemmied, and Peter stepped gingerly into the stockroom, but it wasn't too bad except for lids spread about hither and yon. Whatever the intruder had sought must be small and containable, then. But Peter wanted to be quick, because his Olga was by herself outside a crime scene. What if...? Oh, God, he had better get a move on.

He switched on lights and made his way into the shop. Again, lids were lifted off boxes and tins, but the place wasn't wrecked or messy apart from stuff piled up inside the door. He shifted dolly tubs, galvanized baths and some very large paraffin heaters. 'Come in, Olga,' he shouted after opening the front door, 'there's no one here.' Leo was young, but the boxer would have signalled had there been an alien present.

She squeezed in and followed Peter to the back yard. 'This is mess,' she stated unnecessarily as she looked at the state of her own little realm. 'Well, we can deal with this in a few ways. Let me think.'

This was one of the many things he loved about the tall, superb woman. She got to the point quickly and seldom minced words, though she didn't deliver them too clearly. 'And?' he asked.

'My home has been ... raped? It must be cleaned. Bearing in mind that upstairs may be a mess, we can stay up and clean the place all night and work tomorrow in shop, probably to die from exhaustion before bedtime, or we can close tomorrow and put a notice to say we are restocking.'

'That sentence was in nearly perfect English.'

'Oh, shutting up.'

'That wasn't perfect English. What's the other option? Is there one?'

'Half and half. We make straight the shop, close off stockroom, and tomorrow, when you finish with Dan, you go and make straight everywhere while I help you. I am sure they went up the stairs. This square man, I am knowing two things about. He may not have been alone. But I am thinking he was leader of this crime.'

'Oh?'

'Well, even if he not political lunatic, he is still knowing who I am. He look for Romanov emeralds. Emeralds difficult stones to cut and set. They shatter. Strong emerald worth more than diamond. I am having these jewels best in world, but they not here. They in secret room under bank in Liverpool. See how he take off lids? He look for small things like jewels. About these we shall talk, Peter. Romanov emeralds give us good life. Right, which of these things we do?'

'Before we decide, let's go and have a dekko upstairs.'

In spite of the situation, Olga grinned. Dekko was a Lancastrian word; she was learning dialect rather than English. She followed man and dog to the upper floor. The Bible remained, though the lid of the box in which it was kept had been removed, while the holy book itself was on the table, unharmed. Cupboard doors had been thrown open, as had drawers. A canteen of cutlery was a tangled heap on the floor, and Leo was growling.

There was no one in the bathroom, nor in either of the bedrooms. The kitchen was messy, but empty, yet the pup continued to grumble.

'What he saying?' Olga asked.

'Whoever did this is nearby. He can sense that. I'm going to follow him; you'd better come too. I'm not leaving you here to start trouble on your own.'

Leo made short work of the hundred or so yards between his house and Frank's. Frank was his hero, and Frank would sort out this mess. Outside Alice and Dan's house, he howled magnificently and almost professionally for so young a dog. When the door opened, Alice was pushed to one side, though not quite knocked over, because Frank was very eager to get to Leo, his best friend.

Alice spoke. 'What's happened?' But she was talking to fresh air.

Galvanized by a pair of over-excited boxers, Olga and Peter chased the dogs into a small garden across the way, where they discovered Olga's square, grey man crumpled on the ground, both hands clutching his right leg. Russian poured from his lips like water over Niagara's steep drop. He seemed to be in pain, and angry, though slightly apologetic.

Alice arrived, followed by Vera, wigless, but in a headscarf and floor-length dressing gown. 'What the buggery's going on now?' she demanded to know. 'Have your dogs gone menthol? We've had enough excitement round here with my Jimmy, God rest him.' Now that Jimmy had departed, even in his 'three-piece suite', he had become a 'God rest' which was usual in these parts.

Harry ran across the lane. 'Alice?'

'What?'

'What the hell's happening, is what,' he snapped.

'Vera says our dogs have gone menthol, but I think they've caught a burglar. Go and tell Dan I'm all right, will you? He'll be in there struggling with his crutches, and he's very tired.'

Harry left, crossed the street and sat on his own garden wall. When madam was in a mood, she needed space to breathe in. He folded his arms and watched the pantomime. Dan could do as he liked; Alice needed watching over.

The incomprehensible torrent of language continued to flow, this time from Olga's mouth. She turned to her lover. 'Peter, he hurt falling over things stacked outside in my yard. Alice, can we bring him to your house? Is closer.'

Everyone was staring at a pair of beautiful, gentle boxers. No member of the group had ever before seen these snarling, angry monsters, teeth bared, jowls quivering and dripping saliva, dreadful sounds emerging from their throats. The man cowered when the boxers threatened. Frank, the older and more threatening of the pair, placed a paw on the culprit's sleeve.

'He won't attack,' Alice said uncertainly.

'Leo, stop,' Olga ordered. She turned, looked at Frank, and he backed away from her steady eye contact and lay in an almost peaceful manner at the burglar's side. 'Good boys. We go now to Frank's house, and we are all being good.'

Harry returned. Between them, he and Peter helped the injured man across the lane to Alice's house. Dan's hospital bed was empty, so they placed him on that. 'Olga and I will see to him,' Peter advised the company. He led them out of the room, dogs included, returning immediately and closing the door firmly. 'Right, Olga from the Volga–'

'Not from Volga,' she stated. 'I am coming from a few miles away from–'

'Shut up.'

She shut up.

'What the blood and sand is going on, soon-to-be Mrs Atherton?'

'Is complicated.'

Peter sighed heavily. 'The day you tell me summat about Russia that isn't complicated, I'll have a blue fit in the cut.'

Her eyes twinkled dangerously. 'Cut?' she snapped.

'Canal. Like a river, but man-made by cutting into the earth.'

'Pfff. And you think Russia complicated. He is Yuri. His daddy was looking after our lands at summer house and was shot dead because he not tell where we are gone to. Yuri's daddy was not sure where we were gone to.' She spoke a few Russian words. 'Help him take off trouser, Peter. Looking at leg, see if you can fix.'

While Peter looked to see if he could 'fix', the two Russians spoke quietly.

'How is leg?' she asked her beloved.

'I can fix,' he answered.

'Are you take mickey out of me?' she asked, poker-faced.

'I wouldn't dare. You'd have me guts for garters.' Peter pretended not to notice her eyebrows disappearing into her fringe while she processed guts and garters. He went to the bathroom, brought water and dressings, and concentrated on the injury while his better-by-far half rattled on in what might as well have been Martian as far as he was concerned.

'This man my second or maybe third cousin,' she explained when the patient's eyelids closed. 'His name is being Ivanovski. He a poor relation from my father's side of family. We thought they would be safe, classed as peasants, but we were wrong. His mother, she was dead already, but his dad was murdered and Yuri hid in forest. He had heard my daddy speaking of England, and now Yuri has come to find me. Not bad man. Frightened man, he is. He was afraid to talk to me, but yes, he was search for Romanov jewels. Desperate men do desperate things. We look after him now.'

Peter blinked. 'Where's he been all these years?'

'Prison,' she replied without hesitation. 'Siberian gulag. Come.' She led her fiancé through to Dan's bathroom while Yuri slept. 'Before revolution, they work to death millions of people mining lead, salt, silver in Siberia. Was katorga – hard labour. They dig even when legs broke, or they locked in dark holes to punish. In Nertchinsk hundreds of thousands die. Then these prisons close.'

'Who closed them?'

'Stalin. But he re-open as gulag. Fifty million in total are dying in Siberia. Communism is the people's party.' She laughed mirthlessly. 'It is a party that kills people. That man in there who look for emeralds is broken in spirit. I sell. I give him money to find life, a home, food, a bed. Batya would say this my duty.'

'Aye, I reckon he would. Come on, let's go home.'

'You go. I stay here with Yuri and sleep in armchair. Send home Vera and Harry. All they need know is that Yuri is my cousin. Will he walk tomorrow?'

'Yes.'

'Why you standing there?'

'Because I don't want to leave you.' Peter knew he had to go, since Olga's back door and the gate had been damaged by a man who now slept like an untroubled baby. Comforting himself with the knowledge that the shop carried all the tools he might need, Peter kissed his fiancée goodnight.

In the next room, he found Harry, Vera, Alice and Dan sitting round the edges of the double bed, while two dogs stretched out in the centre, both fast asleep. When fully extended, even Leo seemed unnecessarily long for a pup. 'Olga knows the man,' Peter explained. 'He's been in prison for years.'

'And he needs to go back to jail,' Vera snapped.

'He's not a criminal. Siberia is where they put him, and he's lucky to be alive. Russia has killed more people in mines and prison camps than were lost in a world war. Yuri is not a communist, and that was his crime.' Having managed to silence Vera, he allowed himself a slight smile. 'Right. He's asleep on your hospital bed, Dan, and Olga's in the chair. Alice, take the dogs through to their beds in Dan's room. Come on, Vera – I'll see you through your front door.'

With Harry acting as conductor and Alice playing leader of the orchestra, the emptying of the bedroom was achieved in minutes. She returned to collect the dogs and led them into Dan's day room. There was no more growling. Leo occupied Frank's outgrown puppy bed, while the larger boxer took the adult version. Alice brought a straight-backed chair and sat next to her friend. 'Who is he?' she whispered.

Olga retold the story from start to finish.

'So you will be rich when you sell them?'

'Yes. Peter and I could buy all Penny Lane and half Liverpool with change to spare.'

'Well, don't.'

Olga smiled.

'Don't you dare.' Alice, too, was grinning.

Olga chuckled quietly. 'We won't.' She looked at the man in the bed. 'He younger than I am,' she mouthed softly. 'But see all lines on face. This is what happen when someone like Stalin has knife in your back. Nearly twenty years, Yuri was in Siberia. He was never warm, even in sleep. All he wants is one small jewel stone to get place to live, food to eat. This I do for him, and I keep him near. He is my family. My daddy would want me to do this for him.'

'I understand.'

Olga studied her friend closely. 'Things have been happening to you, I think. You have been rather quiet and shaky for some days.'

It was Alice's turn to begin her story about Muth and Miss Meadows, the otherness, Muth watching Marie's house during the party, the power belonging to Callum. 'I don't know what he wants, Olga, but I think when he has accomplished whatever it is, my otherness will stop.'

'He guides you, then?'

'Yes. There's a story. I think it belongs to him

195

and my dad, but I can't be sure. Callum leads me gently, even though he's so powerful. It's as if he loves me, but he doesn't think much of my mother, because he hid me from her when she returned to Miss Meadows's house.'

'Good taste? Not liking your mother, I mean.'

'Yes, he agrees with all of us.'

Olga nodded wisely. 'You had no brother?'

Alice shook her head. 'Seven girls. I'm the seventh. But whatever Callum is, he works through me, and my coming back to Penny Lane is part of his plan. Frank sees nothing; he's seen nothing since that first day in your shop.'

'What next, Alice?'

'I find my mother. She is the enemy, and a person needs to know where enemies are, just to keep a step ahead. I think she's near Marie. If she's near Marie, she'll be within walking distance of our Nellie's daughters. She's not right in her head, you see. My mother is the most important person in her own life. There's no love in her except for herself.'

'Not good.'

'No. I'd better go to bed. Are you going to sit there all night?'

'Of course. He found me, now I find him and I keep him. He is my friend from when we were children together, and I can help him now.'

Alice jumped up and wrapped her arms round her friend. 'We'll be all right, love. We have to be.'

Leaving Olga to her vigil, Alice returned to her ground-floor bedroom. Dan was fast asleep, his mouth slightly open and his breathing more laboured than usual. 'How many whiskies did you have, lad?' she whispered. 'And how many bottles of Guinness?' Feeling too alert for sleep, she closed the door quietly and went upstairs to work on Nellie's new wardrobe. It was time to get Big Sis out of her old-fashioned, drab clothes and into something decent. Oh, and the corsets had to go.

Dad was there. As soon as she entered the sewing room, she saw the ribbon of smoke and breathed in the scent of her father. 'Hello, Dad,' she whispered. 'I don't half miss you. I hope the smoke from your pipe doesn't make our Nellie's cloth smell. Remember how Muth went on about your pipe? And your Friday night pint and the darts team? There's been no improvement.'

She sat down near her sewing machine. And at that very moment, a piece of tailor's chalk floated up and hung in the air. Without a shadow of a doubt, Alice knew that this was Callum's doing. Dad was just a watcher, a supervisor; Callum was the one with the power and the childlike humour. For a start, he made folk disappear in broad daylight.

The chalk floated downward until it touched some grey jersey material that was pinned together to make a skirt for Nellie. It wrote *Mersey Road East* followed by the number 57. So Muth was in Brighton-le-Sands, within easy reach of Marie and close to Nellie's two daughters.

Alice scribbled the address on an envelope and watched, almost mesmerized, as the chalked words and numbers disappeared. He was doing his magic tricks again, just like some cheap warm-up act down at the old Rotunda on Scotland

Road. 'You're showing off, Callum.' And for the first time, the baby who always cried burst into loud, gleeful laughter.

'It's lovely to hear you happy,' she whispered.

A breath caressed her face. 'Alice.'

'Yes, that's me. You're the grown-up baby.'

'Am I?'

She felt him leave, and was lonely without him.

It wasn't a difficult job. Once Elsie had introduced herself to the five residents, she found she had plenty of time on her hands during weekdays. Her brief from the boss was to make sure noise was kept down, especially at weekends, to check randomly for damage, and to keep hall, stairs and landings clean. Saturday and Sunday nights after nine she had to stay in and make sure nothing unsavoury walked into the house, but that was not a hardship. She had no nightmares, and that was the main thing.

With time on her hands, she put it to good use by walking. The expeditions included cinema visits, a search for library books, shopping, and what she termed the march-past. Her pace increased every time she approached Marie's house. Marie had been a difficult child, an impossible teenager, and had become a nasty, opinionated adult. She had run away from home before her twenty-first birthday, had married well, and Elsie had not been invited to the wedding.

After the emigration of Theresa, with Constance, Judith and Sheila killed in the war, Elsie had been left with only Nellie, Marie and Alice. Why did she still need them? What did she want or expect from them? Bunting and a brass band? More like boiling oil, she mused.

In Coronation Park, she sat on a bench in the rose garden. Was it all her own fault? She'd been firm, yes, but children needed to know the rules. Girls especially wanted training, or they brought trouble to the door, the sort of trouble that wore little bonnets and shawls. Her three prettiest, Alice, Theresa and Marie, had been kept in the house when not at school or work. Nellie, a dull soul, had stayed in voluntarily until the appearance of Martin Browne, who had seemed a fair enough catch at the time, as he had been another dull soul. But even Martin had his limits, as did his girls. It was only a matter of learning to keep her mouth shut, she advised herself.

'Yes, keep your gob shut, Elsie. And then there was Alice,' she muttered under her breath after dismissing from her mind the three dead girls. Oh yes, then there was Alice, a tiny, shining star with looks, brains and the gift of second sight, a gift she refused to use. The girl could have made a fortune if she'd listened and put in a bit of effort. She'd wasted the sight.

Elsie stood up and began the walk down Coronation Road towards Brighton-le-Sands. All mothers had been fierce back in those days, and she'd been no worse than any of the others. Chippy, her carpenter husband, had been taken in so easily by his daughters that Elsie had needed to keep an eye on him, too. Well, if she hadn't supervised him, he would have let the girls get away with... She shivered; she didn't want to even think that word. It was time to get back, because the stairs needed a lick and a promise, and she intended to keep her job. Some of the tenants were quite interesting; one was biddable...

It was serious business, yet it was hilarious. A woman from the Moscow region of the Volga basin, plus a man from an inland Lancashire cotton town, were trying to do business with a Scottish bank manager. Behind the bank manager stood two heavies who looked as if they'd been poured from Sheffield furnaces into crucible moulds, because neither of them moved or blinked. In front of the bank manager, a desk wore a velvet skirt that touched the ground on all sides.

'Why is the big peoples here with us?' Olga whispered to Peter.

'Security,' he replied from the corner of his mouth that was nearer to her.

'What?'

'Security,' he repeated.

Olga studied the bank manager. A small man, he was blessed with an unruly tangle of ginger hair that seemed to obey no order to conform, as it shifted and resettled each time he moved his head. Small green eyes did little to improve his appearance, while overlarge ears stuck out at right angles like two carrying handles on a jug. But the main item of interest on his face was a bristly moustache on an upper lip too shallow for so abundant a display, and he curled the lip from time to time as if trying to rid himself of the carrot-coloured shrubbery. Olga must not giggle; repeatedly, she ordered her face to remain straight and in good order.

With great reverence, the manager opened the lid of a box placed on the table by one of the iron men. He lifted out the suite of jewels and placed them carefully on the velvet. There were earrings, a bracelet, a huge necklace and a tiara that boasted glaring white diamonds among the vivid emeralds. Last to take the stage was a brooch made from one almost impossibly large emerald surrounded again by sizeable diamonds.

Olga picked up an earring. 'My mother was wear these when I was small. They are beautiful. She was beautiful woman, tall, elegant.'

The bank manager said something. Olga stared at him blankly. 'Sorry. I am not understanding you.'

'Och well, let's ask your man here.'

Her man fixed his eyes on the moustache. 'Yes, they must be worth a fortune, I suppose,' Peter said.

'Is this what he say? Worth fortune?'

'Yes, love, I think so.'

The manager dragged a hand through his hair, which now stood tall.

Olga gave the manager a brilliant smile. 'Putting back in box; I take home with me now and keep them next to my bed.'

The red-haired miniature Scot shuddered. 'Ye'll dae nae such thing, Miss Konstantinov.'

'What he say now, Peter?'

'He says you can't take them home.' He looked at her; the right eyebrow was arched, so this little bank manager had better watch himself. When Olga arched a brow, it was time to head for the hills. She turned slightly and faced her intended target.

'Take it easy, love,' Peter begged.

'Is these emeralds my property?' she asked. 'Also the diamonds what is with them?'

'Yes, but–'

'No yes butting with me, Mr McLeish. I take to London to sell.'

'Nae such thing; London will come here to you, madam.'

'Why?' At last, she was getting the gist of his statements.

Mr McLeish appealed to one of his unappealing guards. 'Sid – explain, will you? Tell the lady how we go about things as important as this.'

Sid was quite handsome when he switched his face on. 'Miss Konstantinov?' He bowed.

'Mr Sid?' She inclined her head in a dignified fashion.

'There's a lot of expensive jewellery on this table here.'

'This I am know.'

Peter suddenly found something interesting on the ceiling and raised his eyes to study it. One more minute of staring at the ginger-nut clown with standing-to-attention hair might have had him doubled up with laughter.

'And you might lose it. Somebody could steal it. So Mr McLeish will put it back in the strong room and he will telephone a few people in Hatton Garden.'

'Not in London?'

Peter stopped studying cracked plaster. 'Hatton Garden is part of London, love.'

Sid plodded on. 'They will buy them here. We sell only if they reach the reserve price. It'll be like an auction, but with just jewellers here. Then, when somebody buys, they will own them, and it's up to them to keep them safe. Your money will be here in the bank whenever you need it.'

At last, she understood. 'Just ring, then?'

Mr McLeish passed a small leather box across the velvet. 'There you are, Miss Konstantinov.'

She stood up, so Peter and McLeish did the same.

'Come, Peter, we go to see Leo Tolstoy, then to become engaged!' She pinned her gaze to the bank manager. 'Put those things of mine away now. Mr Sid, good man for explaining what foreign person said. Thanking you.' She swept out.

Peter winked at Sid. 'She's not bad, is she? For a Russian princess.' He went to get engaged in a Liverpool pub to a noblewoman from Moscow with a diamond and emerald ring that had belonged to a tsar. Oh well. Just another day in the life of Peter Atherton, Olga Konstantinov and Leo Tolstoy. At least it wasn't raining.

'Stop it, Harry.'

'I can't. You're driving me crazy.'

Wearing her least attractive clothes with a headscarf as a turban, Alice was fitting Harry's curtains. Vera's lads were not here; they were living at home again with their mother. 'Look, I can't work if you keep interrupting and messing about. Keep your hands to yourself, please.'

Alice had already climbed the ladder. He was making much of keeping her safe by steadying her legs, all the while stroking them and making small circles on her shins. What the hell was going to happen next? Rape? Would it be rape? She wanted him; she loved two men. No, she couldn't say that she loved Harry, because the word wanted would be nearer the truth. What if she bore a child? How would she know which man had fathered the baby? No, no, she must get home.

Dan had ceased to make her feel like this; she was eighteen again, excited, afraid of Harry, but mostly of herself.

'Beautiful legs for a short-arse,' he chuckled.

When she had finished with the second curtain, she descended the steps with determination written into every line of her body. Oh, sugar – what sort of time was this to start going into an otherness? She shook it off and picked up her box of hooks. Was Harry part of some evil plot contained within the otherness? 'I don't feel well,' she said, 'so don't take advantage.'

'You look well to me – good enough to eat. I'm in love with you, Alice.' He removed the scarf and gently re-arranged the blonde curls it had been concealing. 'Never felt like this before.' Her hair was like satin; he was the original lovelorn loon, a rare animal with no sense and no control, native of south Liverpool, England. She was gorgeous.

Her vocal cords and every muscle in her body had gone on strike, and she had to remind herself to take in some oxygen. 'Please let me go home,' she managed when the ability to make sound returned to her. 'I'm confused. I love Dan, and we're trying for a baby. I can't do this, Harry.'

He shunted her against a wall. 'You want me,

Alice Quigley.'

Her last sensible thought was that the curtains were closed.

Harry wasn't like Dan; Harry worshipped her, treated her as if she were a queen. Like a programmed automaton or someone drugged, she simply responded with every ounce of animal in her body and her psyche. This wasn't an otherness; she was simply a bad person having a wonderful experience. It was bliss, it was bad, it was wonderful, and she was a wicked woman. He covered her mouth with his own to muffle her moans. Would she shout for mercy or cry with joy when ... when he...? Dragging her mouth away, she ordered him to stop. 'I don't want this, Harry. I'm not doing it, I'm not, I'm not!' She was going to be his within seconds if she didn't put the brakes on. He was about to win the battle, and that couldn't happen.

When she finally managed to breathe properly, she looked into his eyes. 'I feel like a bloody whore. Stop. I mean it, Harry. Go any further and I'll scream rape – that's a promise.' She straightened her clothes hurriedly. 'No, not a whore,' she muttered, 'I feel more like an animal.'

'Do you, now?'

'Yes.'

'An animal? Well, I've a couple of lamb chops doing not much in the kitchen. I can cook them medium rare if you want bloody animal.'

'That's not what I mean. Oh, God, how am I going to face Dan?'

'You'll manage,' he whispered into her hair, 'and you'll be back for more. I knew we'd be great

205

together. Have you ever felt like that before?'

'No.'

'Do you hate me?'

'No.'

'But you hate yourself?'

Close to tears, Alice simply nodded.

'You know I'd marry you tomorrow, don't you, girl?'

'Yes,' she whispered. 'But I love him, Harry. He's been so ill and so patient and uncomplaining – he's a one-off. The thought of hurting him – well, I'd sooner cut my own throat.' Things in the bed department had improved, too, but now, after Harry, she owned a clearer understanding of how wonderful physical love might become if ... if she ever allowed the process to reach its conclusion.

Harry smiled. 'I'm taking him to the match on Saturday. What he doesn't know can't hurt him, and we just have to be careful. See, what's happened here's a rare thing, and I knew how it would be the minute I took my mucky work boots off and stepped into your life. Don't be frightened by this kind of love. It's real.'

Alice studied the floor. 'But I am afraid.'

'You'll get used to it.'

'We haven't done it,' she snapped.

'It will be all right.'

'Will it?' Alice picked up the tools of her trade and ran out of the room, down the hall and out of the house. She could never get used to betrayal. In her own hall, she closed the door and rested against it for a moment. Did she love her husband? Was he patient and uncomplaining, or had he become slightly demanding and spoilt of late?

'You all right, love?' Dan shouted.

'Yes.' She swallowed. 'I'm just going to get changed. Harry's house was a bit dusty.' She fled up to the first floor and turned on the bath taps. The tiniest bedroom was now her dressing room, and she knew that she could not approach her husband until she had rid herself of these clothes and scrubbed clean every pore on her skin. She picked out a pretty nightdress with a matching negligee.

In the bath, she faced the seriousness of her almost-sin and vowed that it would never be repeated. She loved Dan. Harry was probably the better lover, but there was more to life than that. Wasn't there? She needed to talk to Olga tomorrow.

Olga made sure that Yuri was asleep in the spare bedroom. She'd sent Peter down to play cards with Dan, and Alice was coming here for a chat.

From the doorway, Olga smiled at her sleeping childhood friend. It seemed like only yesterday when they'd played in the orchard together and chased each other through the fields. The grin remained on her face. He used to pull her hair; she couldn't begin to count the number of ribbons she'd lost to him. For almost thirty years she had lived in this country, yet her English remained appalling. Yuri, after spending just a few months looking for her, spoke the language almost perfectly; she really must try harder.

The shop door rattled, and Olga ran down to admit another friend. It was wonderful to have a confidante at last, someone to talk to about the wedding, about a solution for Yuri, about clothes, shoes, perfumes and make-up. She opened the door, and Alice almost fell in, tears streaming down her face.

'Alice, Alice ... what is problem?'

'I'm bad. I'm a bad woman, Olga.'

'Come here.' The Russian towered over the tiny Scouser and hugged her close. 'You not bad person. Let's go upstairs. We talk quiet, because Yuri in bed, tired after searching for me. Don't cry.' She closed the door, then led the way up to the first floor.

They sat together on the sofa. 'Now, tell me what you do that is so bad it makes you cry hard.'

'Last night. Harry,' Alice whispered.

'No!'

'Yes. Not all the way; not the – you know what I mean.'

Olga shook her head. 'You not try him on for size like me with Peter?'

'No.'

'Sorry, I should not make joke. Tell me what this about, Alice.'

'I don't know. It just happened. He says he loves me and he wants more, and we just have to be careful.' She dabbed at her eyes with a damp handkerchief. 'He's taking Dan to the match as if nothing's happened. I scrubbed and scrubbed and scrubbed myself afterwards.' She swallowed hard. 'Then I went to bed with Dan. I promised...' a sob bubbled to the surface and fractured her voice, 'I promised till death us do part.'

Olga was old enough to know that she could

offer little beyond physical contact, so she simply held her friend close. Life was a difficult journey, and this tiny woman had reached a crossroads with NO ENTRY signs everywhere. She wept like a child, felt like a child, so small were her bones. Anger burrowed its way into Olga's brain. It had risen from her chest, and it was hot. 'I make tea,' she announced before leaving Alice's side for a few minutes.

In the kitchen, she arranged a tray, prepared the tea and stood for a few moments at the window. She would deal with Harry. Oh yes, a Russian woman filled with righteous anger was more than a match for a wayward plumber. Harry Thompson was going to wish he'd never been born.

Nine

Olga Konstantinov's head pushed its impertinent way into Harry Thompson's back garden. She wore a new shoulder-length hairstyle and a very deep frown. Her hands clung to the gate while her mouth stretched fully open in order to take in enough oxygen to complete her mission. 'Stop!' she screamed. He was making a din fit to rattle slates. 'Sick man next door,' she reminded him. 'Dan needs rest and quiet, not building site in next garden. You must begin to think of others, Mr Thompson.'

'And who put you in charge? The Archbishop of bloody Canterbury?' Harry knocked the plug home. This female might have been related to Russian nobility, but she was now an ironmonger on the brink of marriage to a Woollyback who was too good for her by a mile.

He ceased hammering. 'I have to screw into this wall,' he told her, exasperation embroidering his words. 'It's going to be wood fastened to brick, so I need plugs. Plugs want hammering, and I'm hammering.' What did the blooming woman expect? A vow of silence? The rein on his temper was loosening slightly, and he wasn't used to running out of patience. She looked extraordinarily angry – this was about more than a hammer on brickwork, he suspected. It was about Alice; Alice had spilled her tale of woe to Olga Wotsit.

'For what reason is this to happen?' she asked as she entered the garden and stood near the gate, arms folded, disdain in her expression. Olga, taller than many males, always managed to make him feel inferior. How could a woman who sold firewood cause a bloke to be ... stupid? She had closed her shop in order to talk to him about whatever, because Peter was at work looking after Dan and ... and what business of Olga's was anything? Had Alice sent her? Alice had already said her piece about the racket he was creating. In truth, Alice had produced more noise than a hammer against a plug, so he suddenly felt like a victim, as if the entire female population of Liverpool had decided to attack him.

'Why you do this?' asked the intruder once more.

'Pigeons,' he snapped. 'You've seen them before – medium-sized birds, racers. They make a brrr-

brrr noise.'

'Pigeons? Birds will be fastened to kitchen wall?' She waved her left hand, causing the large emerald and its surrounding diamonds to answer the sun's rays angrily. Even her jewellery was in a bad mood.

He nodded, then blinked. Reflections from Miss Russia's engagement ring might well strike a man blind. Already irritated after yet another lengthy telling-off from Alice, he was in no mood for the Eastern European in one of her elevated furies. 'It's a loft,' he said, the words emerging slowly, as if being delivered to a child. 'The loft will be fastened to the wall – if you'll let me get on with it. At this rate, I'll be at it till Christmas, and the birds will be homeless.'

Olga glanced at the roof. 'Loft? You have attic room already in loft. I see it up there, window on roof at front of house.'

Harry was running out of patience, humour and the will to inhale. 'This is a different kind of loft; it's for racing pigeons.' Women. Which idiot had died and left females in charge, and how many more would be aiming barbs at him today? He felt like telling her to sod off, but he was not going to make a show of himself. She was tapping her nails against the gate – a definite indication regarding diminishing patience.

Aristocratic eyebrows crept up aristocratic forehead, returning quickly to their rightful place in order to create a deep frown. 'They cannot race if screwed to wall,' she said.

'No. They race when I let them out. When they're not racing, they live in this loft, a different

211

kind of loft that doesn't sit on a roof.'

'And go to where when they race?'

'How the hell should I know? I'm just an amateur. Their owner died and left them to me. But I'm told I could release them as far away as Brighton and they'd find their way back. Even from France. They were used during the war to carry messages back and forth.' He watched her mouth as it hardened into a straight line – here came the real reason for the unscheduled visit.

Olga drew herself to a full height which, for a woman, was impressive. She marched towards him. 'You, Mr Pigeon-Keeper, will stay away from my friend who is Alice,' she whispered. 'She have husband what is ill to be looking after, and you are interfere with it.'

'With what?'

'With the looking after. She and Peter are doing the special education to bad leg, trying make it stronger. Alice is work hard. You distract.'

'Do I?'

She nodded. 'This you are already knowing. She like you. But Alice give word in marriage ceremony, and you have gone far with trying to make her sin. She belong with Dan.' Olga's eyes travelled the length of Harry's body. 'You handsome and strong, but Dan only handsome. She respond to you like bitch with dog, no more than that. Leave alone.' Turning on a heel, she marched out of the garden, slamming the gate as if placing a full stop at the end of her lecture.

Harry sat on the doorstep, a heavy sigh escaping his lips. What a bloody day – and it was only about ten in the morning. Alice had been magnificent,

212

flashing eyes, balled fists, temper glowing along fine cheekbones. The Russian army had marched in Alice's footsteps, and the Russian army was not best pleased. Now, Bolton was glaring at him over the low wall that separated two small gardens which had once been paved yards. 'Don't you start,' Harry snapped.

Peter grinned.

'What's funny?' Harry asked.

'I've said nowt,' was Peter Atherton's reply. 'I'm here because Dan wants to know why you're making such a din. He gets headaches.'

'Pigeons.' Harry placed his hammer on the ground.

Peter shook his head. 'Alice and Vera will kill you.'

Alice was already killing him. 'Look, Pete – this is a matter of honour. My dad's old mate left me the car and the pigeons. I can't take the Austin without the birds – it wouldn't be fair.'

'They'll kill you,' Pete repeated. 'And I don't mean the pigeons.'

'I know.'

'There'll be bird shite all over their washing. They don't take kindly to a sheet covered in bird droppings. You'll be strung up, drawn and quartered with your head on a pike down the Pier Head. Alice has a right temper on her if she's riled, and Vera takes nowt lying down since her owld feller topped himself. I'd not want to be in your clogs, lad.'

'Shut up, Pete.'

Peter shut up.

'Look, I can't do right for doing bloody wrong

213

these days. I just listened, nodded, and asked a few questions when Mr Foley went on about his birds. Now I'm landed with them.'

'Or flying with the buggers. Sorry. I was supposed to shut up.' He paused. 'Harry?'

'What?'

'There's an answer. There's always an answer.'

Harry stared at the floor. 'Go on, then.'

'Sell them on to other pigeon fanciers.'

'I can't.'

'Why not?'

'Old Joe wouldn't like it.'

Peter rolled his eyes skyward.

'It's called loyalty, Pete. Loyalty means doing right by one another.'

Peter delivered a speech about old Joe being no longer among the living and about Vera's and Alice's washing. 'Be sensible, lad,' he pleaded. 'You've no experience with pigeons.'

Harry lifted the hammer and jumped to his feet. 'Vera and Alice?' he yelled. 'Vera and bloody Alice? Does the whole world have to revolve round sheets and towels and tablecloths? Just bugger off and leave me alone, Pete. I'm not shaping my life to fit in with two neurotic women and their laundry. Tell them to put a bill through my door, or if they'd rather I'll take their stained treasures to the Chinese wash house.' He marched into the kitchen. It was twenty past ten, and the day was getting no brighter. Bugger them. He was keeping Joe's birds, and that was an end to it. No, he didn't really want them, but he wasn't about to take orders from Vera Corcoran, Alice Quigley and Olga the ironmonger.

Somewhere in the darker recesses of Harry's mind lurked the vague suspicion that he was taking his revenge, and he caged the thought where it belonged, behind rain clouds and several compartments in his pigeon loft. He needed bigger plugs, but he wasn't going to buy them from Olga Komplain Enough. Oh no, he would go to town for his shopping. He might go to town again tonight. Somewhere in a city famous for its pretty women, there was a match for Alice. Harry would find her. No, he wouldn't; he was damned sure he wouldn't. Oh, bugger it. He put the kettle on.

Alice Quigley, in outwardly hard-as-iron mode, moved very quickly after jumping off the bus. Completely dedicated to her mission, she looked neither right nor left except when crossing the road. Today, nothing could touch her. Today, she would take the bull – no, the cow – by the horns. Even so, her palms were moist and her heart seemed to beat a little faster than usual. She was going to see Muth, the parent who had never been a mother, the cruel, cold woman with eyes like glass and that thin, disapproving mouth. 'I will not be afraid,' Alice breathed softly.

Opposite the house in which Elsie Stewart now lived, Alice sat on a low wall. The huge buildings that made up the terrace on the other side were the ugliest she had ever seen, with yellow brickwork, hideous windows and crumbling attic dormers on the roofs. Muth would fit in well here, because her soul was as miserable as mortal sin, and this was a sad, dark setting.

Her mind skipped back an hour or so. She'd told Harry Thompson to go to hell on a fast train, no stops between here and there. She was a bad woman. The telling-off of her neighbour hadn't made her so; she was bad because she wanted him. She wanted two men, while a third one, a man she couldn't even see, brushed past her. He placed himself beside her on the wall. 'Oh, no,' she breathed. Callum was with her. Who the bloody hell was he?

'Alice?'

She made no reply until she heard her name repeated.

'Alice?' Callum said for the second time.

'Yes?' God, here she was, talking in broad day-light to a man who was sometimes a baby and always invisible.

'She's in.'

'I prefer you as a baby,' she whispered. 'I don't always need to answer back when you cry.' She'd be locked up if this carried on. She'd get put away for talking to herself in a decent suburb of Liverpool. Brighton-le-Sands wasn't as snobbish as Blundellsands, which boasted large houses and people with big ideas and old money struggling to do the job of new. Brighton-le-Sands was like Waterloo and most of Crosby: working people from many walks of life, decent shops and some pleasant avenues. The sad terrace of huge houses opposite was not typical of the area, but it was Elsie Stewart's home for the time being.

Alice rose to her feet. The sooner today's un-scheduled meeting began, the sooner it would be over and done with.

'She's watching you,' Callum whispered. 'She's worried.'

Hoping he would stay outside, Alice crossed the road. By the time she reached the door, Muth was standing there, grey skirt, cream blouse, expression uncertain, arms folded. 'What an honour,' she sneered. 'How did you find me?'

The visitor raised an eyebrow.

'Well? How did you know I lived here? I've not told anybody where I am.'

'I was told by a friend.' Alice pushed past her mother and turned left into a room whose door stood wide open. So this was the dragon's den. It was a sizeable space with bedroom and living room furniture, and with two further doors leading off the wall opposite the bay window.

Elsie followed her daughter. Why the hell was she here?

'Not bad inside,' was the younger woman's spoken opinion. 'The outside's ugly, though.'

'My own bathroom and kitchen,' Elsie boasted smugly. 'The rest of the tenants have to share facilities, but I don't.'

'How nice.'

'I'm the caretaker. It's a lot of responsibility.'

The two women stood facing each other across a small, circular dining table with just two chairs. Elsie sat. Alice sat. 'You look well,' she said, deciding to open fire with blanks instead of live ammunition. Softening up a woman like Elsie Stewart was nigh impossible, though lending her a false sense of security might prove to be a good idea.

'I am very well for my age.' What was little Miss Know-It-All up to this time? Alicia Marguerite

217

was no Nellie, no walkover. This youngest one, the blessed, the gifted, the beautiful, was a little snake under spectacular skin. Was she venomous or a constrictor? Elsie stood up and stared for a moment at her unexpected visitor. 'I'll make a pot of tea.' In the kitchen, she pondered the reason for this intrusion from the self-elected representative of her family. What was she after? What plans were circulating in her head? Was the she-wolf dressed as a ewe while about to strike out with her tongue? She set a tray, poured milk into a small jug and filled the sugar bowl. She had better get back to her room and see what happened.

Alice stared through the window while awaiting her return. 'Say my name and watch her face.' She stiffened. Callum had followed her in, then. Well, there was no show without Punch, she supposed. When Elsie had returned and the tea had been poured, Alice continued in conversational mode. She spoke in general terms about Martin's return, about Nellie and the grandchildren. 'Of course, they don't want to see you again.' There was no malice in her delivery. 'Just thought I'd let you know we're all right, so you won't worry.' The words wore a dressing of sarcasm along their syllables.

'Staying away from them suits me.' Elsie stirred more sugar into her cup. Alice was in charge; ownership of the china tea set and tenancy of the flat meant nothing, because this youngest daughter had been in charge of just about any situation since her late teens. Except for her otherness, of course, because she'd always sworn that was out of her hands.

'None of us wants to see you.'

'Suits me,' the older woman repeated. She dipped a ginger biscuit into her tea.

'Dan's home, staggering about with crutches, or sometimes just one. A man comes in and helps him and we work on exercises. He gets dressed every day now, so he must be feeling a bit better.'

'That's good. Dan's a big fellow, and he might be a bit much for you to manage on your own, so I'm glad you've got help.'

Alice took a long draught of tea. 'Muth, me and Dan are back in the old place on Penny Lane.'

'So I've been told.'

'And my second sight's plugged into that front bedroom.' She watched her mother's body as it stiffened. 'It's not a bedroom any more, because Dan can't do stairs, so it's our living room. Visitors go up to the first floor now unless they want to talk to Dan.'

'I see.'

'And not all our guests are visible. Dad comes – well, his tobacco does, and a bit of smoke some-times. I've heard children playing, heard you screaming.' She paused. 'I do all my sewing up there. Made some curtains for Miss Meadows. I believe you stayed with her for a while.'

Elsie's spine became ramrod straight. 'So you put her off going into partnership with me?'

'No. No, I didn't.'

The mother, knowing that this daughter rarely lied, accepted her answer.

Alice continued. 'It's loud and strong in that Penny Lane house. A baby cries. Not all the time, but it screams. It upset me at first, but I'm getting used to it now – no choice, really.'

'Really?' The word was almost snarled.

'Yes, then it stops crying suddenly, like a wireless being turned off. And a man talks.'

Elsie swallowed audibly. 'Your dad?'

'Dad makes no noise. He just comes and goes without a word.'

Muth nodded her agreement. 'Charlie never had much to say for himself at the best of times. It was like living with a wax dummy!'

Alice nodded. 'He didn't get the chance. He lived in a house filled by females.' The second sentence made Elsie relax slightly, Alice thought. Now was the time to strike. 'Who's Callum?' she asked, her tone wiped clean of any guile. 'It's a name I picked up a few weeks ago.'

The cup rattled in its saucer when Elsie placed it down. 'Erm ... your dad had a brother called Callum. He died in Ireland years ago. Older than Charlie, he was.'

'There's a Callum in that upstairs room.'

Elsie shrugged as nonchalantly as she could. 'He must be keeping his little brother company, then. Their mother wasn't well, you see, after Charlie was born, so Callum helped to bring him up. Your granddad turned to drink. He was a feckless tramp. Callum was like him.' A headache threatened; she stopped speaking.

Alice could see that her mother had arrived at a state worse than Olga's Russia had been in about thirty years ago. 'I suppose things will get clearer the longer I live there.' She stood up. 'Right, Callum – time to go.'

Colour drained from Elsie's face until her skin

became a sick shade that resembled putty. 'He's here?' she managed eventually. 'In my home? You brought him?'

'No, he followed me. I think of him as being everywhere and nowhere at the same time. He pops up unexpectedly and makes silly magic happen – even gave me this address. Perhaps he'll stay here with you for a while – who can say?' She glanced to her left. 'What?' she asked before facing her mother again. 'He says he doesn't enjoy your company. So I suppose he feels like the rest of us. Oh, and he just told me he can be in more than one place at a time. No boundaries where he comes from, or so he reckons.'

'Go,' Elsie breathed.

'Don't worry, Muth – I'm going. Before I do, take this as a warning. Leave us alone, especially our Nellie. I'm working on her, getting her to lose weight and smarten up. Marie's fine. Claire and Janet are fine; so are their husbands and babies. Stay away from them, or I'll post Callum through your letter box and leave him here.'

Alice's invisible companion chose this moment to spill Elsie's paperwork from behind an ornament on the mantelpiece. 'Stop it,' Alice chided. 'Leave things alone for once.'

'Take him away,' Elsie begged.

'Sorry, Muth. I have no control over him. You know I've never had control over any of it. He's a show-off, like an amateur magician. My uncle Callum's more of a child than a man, I'd say.'

'Go away,' Elsie shrieked.

'He's gone, Mother.'

'How do you know?'

221

'Sometimes he lets me know.' Daughter stared at mother. Never before had Alice seen Elsie so withered, so terrified. There was something very wrong here. In spite of her strong antipathy for the woman, Alice didn't know what to do. Should she go or stay? Was Muth going to have a heart attack or a fit of some kind?

'Go,' Elsie begged. 'Go, and don't ever come near me again, especially if you have that ... that thing hanging about with you. Go on – get out.'

Alice left. Well, what else could she have done?

Outside, she spoke from a corner of her mouth. 'Who are you?'

He'd buggered off, of course. She'd asked the question before on a couple of occasions at least, but he always insisted that it wasn't time yet, that Alice must be ready before he 'showed' her who he was. Now it seemed he was her uncle, her dad's big brother.

Inside Elsie Stewart's ground-floor flat, the new tenant sat rigidly on the edge of her bed. Tricks. Alice had said he did silly magic, and here he was doing just that. He had clearly returned after his earthbound companion had left. On the over-mantel mirror a breath-like mist appeared, and an invisible finger wrote in it. LEAVE THEM ALONE AND I'LL LEAVE YOU ALONE.

The old woman blinked. In that fraction of a second, the ominous message disappeared. Was she imagining things? No. The air in the room was suddenly chilled, and she felt certain that it was his doing. After two or three beats of time, she suspected that he was gone, as the temperature returned quickly to normal. But the fear remained; her sole companion was a bleak, black terror. Control was slipping from her grasp, and Alice was the one who had removed it.

So the seventh child really had no choice when it came to her otherness. Alicia Stewart might have been a difficult teenager, but her refusal to share her gift had not been deliberately rebellious. 'The times I tried to force her to...' For the first occasion in her adult life, Elsie wept copiously. Was this grief, regret about the way in which she had treated her daughters? Did she mourn, at last, the three who had died while doing war work? Perhaps it was worry caused by her ghostly visitor.

She dried her eyes. Crying achieved nothing. She had stairs and landings to think about, and Alice's companion had promised not to come again as long as... No. It had been no promise; it was a threat wrapped in a bribe. And Elsie felt empty and alone. How might she dodge a spirit, especially one who reckoned to have the ability to be in several places at any given time? What might he do to her?

On the lower deck of a bus, Alice sat near a window. He arrived and told her Elsie shouldn't bother the family again, and she wondered what the hell he'd done now. At a bus stop, a large woman bearing heavy shopping took the place next to Alice. The new arrival was sitting on Uncle Callum. But she didn't stay. 'That seat's bloody uncomfortable,' the newcomer complained before finding a different one nearer to the front of the vehicle. Alice grinned. Callum's sense of humour was alive and well, though he wasn't. Still, he'd got rid of Muth. Hadn't he?

She alighted from the bus partway down College Road and made her way to the Stanton house. Nigel would be at work, but Marie should be in, buried in animals, of course. The lion cubs had reached the age of nine weeks and would soon be shipped off to Jersey. Marie was sad. With no children, she had always concentrated her maternal love on her ever-increasing family of pets, and now the cubs, newest yet nearest to her heart, were growing fast and needed to move on.

No one answered the door, so Alice walked down the side of the house to the rear. Larry the llama offered her a filthy look, while horses and ponies whinnied and donkeys brayed. A car pulled into the driveway. Alice retraced her steps and stood, mesmerized, while her sister and brother-in-law tried to drag something out of the back seat. The something was proving difficult to shift.

For a reason she failed for a split second to fathom, Alice started to laugh, doubling over with the pain of it, realizing suddenly that the something had just two feet. And shoes.

Marie glanced at her sister. 'It's all right for you, curled up giggling at us. We told him we were taking him to the pub for pie and chips, but we turned left at the dentist's. Without telling him, of course.'

Nigel Stanton chipped in. 'The tombstones were rotted and affecting his stomach. They had to go. He's had gas, so his legs have gone from under him, and he says they don't belong to him any more. Get your corpse over here, Alice Quigley. And watch he doesn't bleed on your clothes.'

'Like Larry the llama, he spits,' Marie added.

After a struggle and a lot of cursing from Tommy, they managed to drag him into his shed. Alice helped to dump the poor fellow on his bed before having a look round. 'It's a palace,' she exclaimed.

Marie grinned. 'Our wandering minstrel got house-proud,' she said. 'He showers where the animals get cleaned, and he has his own outside lav heated in winter by oil lamps.'

'You look after him.'

'We do,' Nigel says, 'and he looks after us and the menagerie.'

Tommy's home was pretty, but the same could not be said for the man himself. With the famous tombstones missing, his nose and his chin almost met. Further distorted by pain, his mouth took on some humorous shapes while he tried to curse the eejits who had forced him into the slaughterhouse. He intended to sue them. He needed a blood transfusion, painkillers, and an extra bottle of whiskey to compensate for what he'd been through. Throughout the tirade, Alice concentrated on her sister, because she didn't know where else to look.

Nigel was translating, since he was the only one who understood fully the gist of Tommy's ramblings. 'We should just leave him,' he said. 'Let him sleep it off and hope he comes to his senses in a few hours.'

Marie chuckled. 'Has he got senses? He's great with animals, but he's not what you might call sociable when it comes to people.'

Tommy sat up with remarkable ease for a man in so much physical trouble. He glared at her. He was annoyed. They'd dragged him to the dentist's, where a man in a white coat had pushed him into a chair and lectured him about poison in his stomach because of his two remaining teeth. He'd been gassed until unconscious, then assaulted. 'Lost me teeth, so I have,' he told Alice.

His speech was becoming clearer.

'You'll have new ones in a fortnight,' Marie said reassuringly.

Alice turned away, because she couldn't trust her face to remain in order. There was a brand new electric cooker, very modern, very clean, a sink that was probably connected to the house's water and drains, and all Tommy's dishes and bowls were arranged on a Welsh dresser.

She paced about. Tommy had carpet, rugs, sofa, chairs and a very neat sleeping area with wardrobe and tallboy. Walls were covered in photographs of dogs, cats, horses, donkeys, hamsters, rabbits, Larry the llama and two lion cubs. 'It's lovely,' she said.

'They've took me teeth and they're taking me lions away from me to some godforsaken place called Jersey,' he grumbled.

'And they've given you a roof and a job, so shut up,' was Alice's advice.

Taken aback, Tommy turned to face the wall, stretching his legs down the bed. Cursing and moaning about life, he drifted towards sleep.

'Moaning's his hobby,' Nigel said. 'He needs to moan or there'd be steam coming out of his ears,

226

and that might upset the animals. I'm going to work.' He kissed his wife, winked at Alice, and left.

Marie poured a double Irish into a glass and thrust it at Tommy. 'Drink that,' she ordered. His answer was a snore, so she set the glass on a small table. Dragging her little sister out of Tommy's famous shed and into the back of the house, she set the kettle to boil and poured some biscuits on to a plate. 'Right,' she said, 'what's happened?'

Alice shrugged. 'I went to visit Muth and had no otherness, just a companion. Callum, he's called. I can't see him, but I hear him and sometimes feel him brushing past me. I think he's our dead uncle – Dad's older brother. Muth went crazy when I said his name, and she threw me out.'

The older sister grinned. 'Can't blame her for that, because you are a bit spooky, you know. So, what's the score?'

Alice bit into a brandy snap and spoke through the pieces. 'Two nil in favour of me and Callum.' She chewed. 'He went daft, started chucking bits of paper down from the mantelpiece. She was bloody terrified, Marie. And I've got a strong feeling that he went back in after I got ordered to leave. He was on the bus with me, though.'

Marie blinked rapidly. 'Is he here?'

'No. You've never harmed me. He doesn't need to follow me here.' She paused, chewing thoughtfully. 'Why pick on me, though? He seems very protective where I'm concerned but why would Dad's brother protect me over the rest of you?'

'Because you're on the telepathic telephone and we're not. He knows you're receptive.'

227

Alice told her sister the full story, beginning with the day she and Frank had moved back to Penny Lane. 'Frank used to see and hear stuff with me, but not any more. It's all about something that happened in that house. Dan hears nothing, and neither do my neighbours.'

Marie grinned. 'That Harry couldn't take his eyes off you at the party.' She waited. 'Alice?'

The visitor raised her shoulders in a gesture of nonchalance. 'He thinks the sun shines out of my back door.'

'Has he tried anything?'

'Yes, and nearly got there. I almost ... let him.'

'So there's chemistry.'

Alice puffed up her cheeks and blew. 'More like algebra, because it makes no sense to me. I love Dan. We're trying for a baby, but Harry...'

'Chemistry.'

'If you say so.' The baby of the family poured more tea. 'Something's going to happen,' she announced. 'Something big. And no, it's nothing to do with Harry Thompson. It's tied to that bedroom we were all born in. Dad comes with his filthy old pipe. I see smoke. Callum whispers to me, writes with tailor's chalk, moves things. He doesn't like Muth. If she doesn't leave us alone, he'll haunt her, I'm sure, and she's scared stiff. In our house, a baby cries and stops suddenly. I think the baby's Callum, but I don't understand why I think that.' She sighed. 'It's all very confusing, Marie. See, that baby grows up and becomes a man ghost – no idea why he needs to do that changing about stuff.'

Marie swallowed some tea. 'What makes you

think the baby's Callum and the man, too, is Callum? He might not be changing – you could have two ghosts.'

'It's something I just know. Why he has to go right back to childhood, I've no idea, but it must be part of his message. See, where he is, there's no past, present or future – it's all one, like a continuous straight line. Maybe the little one is our dad crying, because Uncle Callum brought him up – their mother was ill, and their dad hit the bottle.' She paused. 'It's dimensions. He's in a different one.'

'What do you mean?'

'No idea.'

For a reason that was understood by neither of them, both sisters burst into loud laughter. 'You could be...' Marie fought to regain her voice, 'crazy.'

'True.'

'Or a witch.'

'Make a bonfire. Or drown me. Oh, God.'

Marie pulled herself together. 'Hey, listen to this one. Tombstone Tommy – well Gummy Tommy – is training Larry the llama to be a visitor at Mary-fields.'

Alice, suddenly as sober as a dead judge, stopped laughing. 'But he spits.'

'Exactly. We've opened a book. The odds on him spitting are varying from day to day, but if you want to back him not to spit, you'd need to put a ton of tranquillizers down his throat. His first scheduled appearance is at a garden party, so it'll be outside, at least.'

'Wouldn't Tommy be better off with dogs?'

'He already takes dogs. I've told him it's going to be a spitfest, but he won't listen.'

'And Nigel?'

'Daft as a bald brush; he says he has faith in Tommy's ability to train Larry.'

Alice, her face suddenly solemn, shook her head slowly. 'So you have one crazy bloke in a shed, and another in the house.'

Marie grunted. 'No, the one in the house isn't in the house at the moment. He's down the road with a twelve-foot python in a fridge.'

The younger sister swallowed audibly. 'And you think I'm mad with an invisible baby, Dad's pipe and Uncle Callum? Why the fridge?'

'To calm him down, of course.'

A few ticks of time strolled by. 'Nigel calming down in a fridge?' Alice almost shrieked the question.

'No, the bloody snake, soft girl. Nigel has to force-feed him.'

'Why?'

'I don't have the bloody details, do I? All I know is that a Burmese python is cousin to a boa constrictor, so it squeezes its prey to death. It needs to be as cold as possible to get it dozy and stop it killing a vet. And don't worry – there's another daft man with him.'

Alice stood up. 'Well, that's me done, our Marie. It's been a weird day.'

'You can say that again. Ta-ra, love.'

'Ta-ra, Marie. See you soon. As long as he doesn't bring the snake home.' She stopped in the doorway. 'Hey, our kid.'

'What?'

'Tell him to put the snake with Muth. They should suit each other.'

'It might kill her.'

'Yes.' Alice grinned. 'That as well. Good point, Mrs Stanton.' She left.

If Harry handled another length of two by four, he would use it to smash something. He'd made fourteen compartments, plus a large, full-length one at the top, and he'd smoothed most of it down, and–

And here she came, probably to deliver yet another lecture. Although the walls were low, she had to stand on a chair to look into his garden. 'Pigeons,' she snapped.

'Don't you kick off again,' he answered tersely. 'I've had the Empress of Moscow, Peter and you going on at me since the crack of dawn.'

'But I wasn't telling you off about pigeons before,' she whispered.

He shrugged and picked up a new sheet of sandpaper. 'How's Dan's headache?' he asked.

'I don't know, because he's emigrated.'

Harry blinked stupidly.

'They left me a note,' she explained.

'And?'

'He's emigrated to Olga's to get away from your noise. They've taken the wheelchair, and Peter will carry him upstairs with the help of Yuri.' She grinned. 'Mind you, Yuri looks like a stiff breeze could knock him over.'

Harry dropped the sandpaper. 'Come and look at my work,' he said.

'No.'

'You know you want to.' He winked at her.

She did want to. She knew she almost needed to… 'I'm off to Olga's. There's a row brewing with her and the bank in town.' Olga had gone totally royal and was listening to no advice.

'Why?' Harry asked.

'I can't say.'

'Can't or won't?'

'Both. You've got your curtains and that's that.'

Another head joined Alice's at the great divide between two houses. 'Hey, you,' Vera began. 'What the Carter's Little Liver Pills has got into you? Pigeons? I thought we were going away on holiday, but I'm not travelling with no pigeons.'

He repeated yet again, 'I was left them in an old man's will. He left me the car, too. If the birds go back, so does the car, and your holiday won't happen, so you'd better shut up.'

'I don't care.' She stuck out her chin. 'I've got a lodger ready to move in, so there's stuff to be done. No time for holidays.'

'A lodger? Who?' Harry asked.

Vera wiggled her glasses about. 'Just a minute while I think. It's that Russian feller – I remember. He's called Urine.'

Alice stared into Harry's eyes while he stared into hers. They exploded simultaneously, as if their reactions had been choreographed. Tears poured down Alice's cheeks, while Harry dragged a rather disgraceful handkerchief from a pocket, covering his mouth when laughter turned to coughing.

'What the bloody hell's up with you two?' Vera demanded to know. She stared at Alice. 'Pull yourself together,' was her suggestion.

Harry won the fight for oxygen. 'Is she taking the pi – the pickle out of us, Alice?'

Alice continued to weep her way through a mixture of pain and glee.

'What's going on?' The glasses were slipping again, so Vera's wonky eye made a move towards her nose.

'Urine is wee,' Harry announced eventually.

'Is he incompetent as well as Russian?' Vera asked.

This extra malapropism caused near-hysteria, so Vera huffed her way out of Alice's back garden, slamming the gate furiously.

'Poor Yuri,' Alice murmured. 'And they've taken my Frank. Yes, the dog's emigrated, too.'

He nodded. 'He's only gone as far as Olga's.'

Their eyes remained locked long after the laughter had ended. She tried to break the connection, but failed completely. The lightest of touches smoothed her cheek, and Callum whispered to her. 'I promise you everything will be all right. After the sadness of loss, there will be great joy.'

'Alice?' There was worry in Harry's voice.

She looked at Harry. 'Sorry, I was just thinking.' And in that thin slice of time, the possibility that Dan was going to die hit her hard. Was he? She jumped down, turned on her heel and fled into the house. Now sobbing because of fear and confusion, she blamed Callum.

'I'm here,' he whispered.

'Oh, good.' Her tone was sharp. 'You told me.'

'I had to.'

'Really?'

'Yes,' Callum said. 'And yes, I read your thoughts. Nothing you can do, my love. He won't feel a thing. This one next door will look after you better than the king gets looked after. Bide your time, and be as good as possible to Dan when he gets difficult.'

Harry entered the house. 'Are you all right?'

She nodded before using a tea towel to dry her face. 'Don't say anything to anybody,' she begged, 'because he doesn't know and mustn't know.' She would leave her otherness out of this; it was time for quick thinking and fast talking. 'Dan's not quite as well as he pretends to be. It ... it might not be long, Harry. He's had no life, anyway, since he dug me out from under that table.'

He sagged against the sink. 'How do you know you're going to lose him?'

'Doctor,' she lied. 'And I don't want to talk about it.'

'I'll be here for you – both of you. Does Dan know what's going on, that he's not going to make old bones?'

She shrugged; she knew Harry would be there for her. Oh, Dan. Poor Dan. 'He has no idea. But you have to leave me alone.'

'Yes. I'll do my best.'

'Go on, then. I'm off to get my husband and my dog.'

For two or three seconds, Harry Thompson indulged himself by drinking in the sight of the woman he loved. Then he left to carry on with the job. He had pigeons to cater for.

Ten

Well, this was a cabinet meeting in more than one sense.

Alice, having entered the shop from the back yard, walked through the storeroom and up the stairs, but that was as far as she got before encountering difficulties. Olga's flat was packed to bursting. Alice compared it to government business because it looked like a cupboard – a cabinet filled with people and raised voices. The two dogs threaded their way through and around several pairs of legs and shot past the latest arrival, scurrying their way down the stairs. They would be OK because the back gate was now bolted. There was nothing else for it, so Alice emitted a shrill whistle.

The talking stopped while people steadied themselves after being shifted by two escaping boxers. One man wriggled a finger inside an ear, since the sound made by the newcomer was enough to loosen wax. Alice took a small step and studied the scene. Dan was wedged in a corner near the window, his chair filling a small space. Oh, Dan. She swallowed hard. Was Callum right? When would Dan die? She shouldn't have been in such a hurry to see the future.

Olga, feet planted firmly apart, arms folded, expression stern, stood her ground in front of the fireplace. She had borrowed the attitude of a president on the brink of declaring war. Peter, who was slouched in an armchair, appeared bored, sleepy and slightly grumpy. Judging from his appearance, Alice decided that his beloved had indeed taken up weapons; he was thrumming his fingers slowly on an arm of the chair in which he sat. Peter was clearly not best pleased.

The rest of the area was filled by four large men, plus one small one who boasted orange hair and a strong Scots accent. He was speaking quietly to himself; it was clear that this strange creature was agitated. He glanced at Alice. 'You're the other witness for this wedding?'

'Alice Quigley, yes.'

'Och, will you get the lady to see some sense?' the bank manager begged.

Olga spoke to the girl who had become her best friend in a matter of weeks. 'All I ask is to wear tiara. Earrings, brooch, necklace and bracelet, no – is too much. I have ring to match tiara, and everyone will think this is green glass. I will wear. Auction will be after wedding.'

'But–' McLeish said no more, because Olga's stern expression shouted him down. He backed off and collided with a member of his security team.

'These jewels are Romanov. In my blood, from my mother, I am Romanov. I am last in family to wear the emeralds, and I am no longer afraid of being caught and shot. Mr McLeish, what is my bank manager, knows we want small wedding, just me, Peter, and you with Dan for witness. But no, we are to have these big men and Mr McLeish because I will wear my mother's tiara. He brings them now to introduce to me and Peter.'

She turned on the Scot. 'Now, you will go. All your men, too.'

At last, Peter spoke. 'Olga?' There was an edge to his tone.

'What?'

'Shut up. I can't be doing with all this mawping and moaning. You are getting on me nerves and on everybody else's, too. You can't wear it.'

'But I—'

'He's right,' pronounced one of the huge men. 'It's too dangerous.'

'And we've all had enough, love. Dan's sitting there because he has no choice, and Alice has only just got here. I'm betting she wishes she'd stopped at home. Listen to me, flower. I'm sick to death of your bloody emeralds and your Romanovs, God rest them. Mr McLeish?'

'Yes, sir?'

'That room in your bank where you showed us the jewellery.'

'Aye?'

'Do it up a bit. Hang like satin curtains on one wall and buy the contents of a florist shop. White or cream satin – I'll pay for that, and for all the flowers. We'll have wedding photos done in the bank, so she can wear everything in turn, ear-rings, brooch – the flaming lot.' He turned once more to his wife-to-be. 'And that's the end of it; we want to hear no more on the subject.'

Olga took umbrage; she was good at umbrage. 'Peter, I want to be married in tiara what was worn by my mother.'

'Tough. It's not happening. You listen to me, young lady.' He glanced at the four large guards.

'This is not personal, but say one of these big chaps needed money. No offence, boys. What if their families know where they are going next Saturday? What if somebody has a gun? Use your loaf for once.'

The bride blinked. 'Loaf is for sandwich.'

'Yes, and some of us are bloody starving.'

She glared at him.

'Me stomach thinks me throat's been cut,' he complained before turning back to Mr McLeish. 'I'll come and see you tomorrow. If she behaves, I might bring her with me. I'll try to talk to her before she lets her gob go roaming off. That's where her family name comes from – Romanov means Roamingoff.'

Alice might have smiled at this point. Here was another who went creative when it came to Olga's surname. But she couldn't manage even a flicker, because all she could think about was the predicted death of her husband, the man who loved her, who had saved her life before suffering a stroke that might become partially responsible for his own demise.

The bank manager and his four well-built companions left the scene. Olga followed them in order to make sure that Frank and Leo didn't get out of the yard.

Peter spoke to Dan and Alice. 'My Olga is a lot of woman to manage. She's tall, strong, mouthy and proud. I couldn't do without her now, but she's been a nightmare about this tiara. She has to learn to compromise.'

Dan chuckled. 'It's nothing to do with her being Russian or royal, Peter. This little wife of mine puts her foot down in cement, and there's no shifting her.'

Alice blinked hard. 'I love you, Dan Quigley, but shut your mouth before I change my mind. Where's Yuri?'

It was Peter's turn to laugh. 'Urine? He's with Vera, looking at the room he's going to rent from her. Olga will make sure his rent's paid, because he's had it rough these twenty-five years or so, poor bloke. Childhood friends, you see. He's setting himself up as a gardener and window cleaner, so he's not feared of graft. Mind, he looks as if he might collapse under the weight of a big ladder.'

Olga re-entered the room. 'Yuri is doing exercises each day, so he will get stronger. Peter, please go and bring back Harry the noise maker. He will help you get Dan down the stairs.'

Peter stood. 'See? Her Royal Doodah-ness plans everything. Don't be fooled by the humble lady ironmonger who escaped the revolution with her dad and her granddad.' Grinning broadly and shaking his head, he left the scene. 'It's called hiding in plain sight,' he called over his shoulder.

Olga smiled at last. 'To hide me in sight was our only choice. I am like sore thumb. See, I do know some of your crazy sayings. A woman nearly six feet from heel to head not easy to hide. Russia produced many good things; I am one and vodka is another.'

Alice stared hard at her tall friend. 'Are you going to do as you're told, then? Because I might hang a few flags out if you start obeying orders.'

'Yes. Piotr will be my husband, and I do as he wishes. I was being not sensible again. We have the ring, therefore I have my mother. See.' She opened a drawer and picked out a framed photograph. 'Mama. In last century they wore every piece they had.'

Alice took the photograph so that she and Dan could look at it. Olga was right; her mother wore a wedding dress and the full suite of Romanov jewellery. 'She looks every inch the princess,' Dan said, 'and you're very like her.'

Olga nodded sadly. 'Yes. She lose her boys from bleeding disease, and I carry that, so no children for me. This made me grieve. Now is too late for having baby, so I can marry my Piotr and we will be happy.'

'She's made her mind up. If she says they'll be happy, Peter will have no choice – he'll be happy, won't he, Dan?' Alice smiled. 'Won't he?'

Dan laughed. 'If you say so, sweetheart.' He studied her. She seemed troubled and tense. 'What's wrong?' he asked.

'Muth. Need I say more?'

'Well, at least you found her.'

She nodded. 'I just followed my nose and told her to leave everybody alone. She's afraid of me, scared of my otherness. I think she's finally realized that I'm not a medium.' Placing a hand on her belly, she grinned. 'I'm more of a small.'

'Titch,' Dan teased.

Alice stiffened. He was here. She felt movement in the air, but managed to hold on to her smile. 'It's a boy,' she heard. 'Call him Callum.' And he left on a breeze felt only by Alice.

'Well,' she managed, 'I believe I put Muth in her place at last.' She was pregnant. O God, let

240

him live until this child arrives. 'As long as she stays away from Nellie, I'll be satisfied. She has too big a heart, our Nellie.'

On their way home, Harry pushed Dan's chair. An uncomfortable silence hung over the trio until Alice broke it. 'Is anybody speaking to you, Harry?'

'No. I'm in Coventry with two dozen pigeons and everybody's washing. I've never been to Coventry before; don't much fancy the Midlands.'

'Can't you sell the birds?' Dan asked.

'No.'

'I'll get a gun,' Alice announced.

'I'll warn the neighbours and tell the police,' was Harry's reply.

Dan decided to change the subject. 'Where's Frank?' he asked.

'On a sleepover with Leo.' Alice laughed. 'I forgot to pack his pyjamas.'

As they reached their two homes, Vera emerged from her house with Yuri. She glared at her neighbours. 'He's Yuri, not Urine,' she snapped. 'Why didn't you tell me?'

'We did,' they chorused.

But Vera motored on. 'I've been calling him a rude word, a lavvy word.'

'We know,' Dan said. 'And we told you a few times.'

'It is fine,' Yuri chuckled. 'She knows now.' He tipped his hat and walked homeward to Olga and Peter. Life had dealt him a good hand at last. After more than two decades in Siberia, he was finally home. Liverpool had a quality that almost defied description. It was ... happy; it was welcoming, and few people commented on his accent. Was this because of all the comings and goings of ships from many nations? That seemed a fair enough assumption. They didn't judge; they joked and laughed a lot, but he never felt like a victim. Yes, he was home.

Now there was Vera. He liked her. She was an ordinary, if rather amusing woman, and her house was comfortable. Her sons, noisy but hardworking, brought life into the place, and Vera cooked well. Although he wasn't looking for a partner in the conventional sense, he believed that he and she would do very well together. She was kind; like himself, she had endured a cruel and difficult adulthood. For all of this, he was thankful to Olga, the girl who had grown into a tall, elegant woman. She hadn't even chided him for breaking into her house when he'd been penniless and desperate. He would live out his life here, on Penny Lane, he hoped.

Alice watched the little Russian as he walked away towards the ironmongery shop; there was an ounce or two of pride in his stance, a modicum of self-assuredness in his stride. It seemed that Yuri was going to be all right, and that idea pleased her.

'Tell Dan about the baby,' Callum whispered. 'It'll cheer him up.'

She ignored him; she would talk to her husband later. In recent days, her uncle had become a more or less permanent fixture in her life. Dan was ... she blinked rapidly ... Dan was temporary. Was he going to die soon – tonight, or tomorrow, or next week? Could a ghost be mistaken?

Harry pushed the chair into the house.

'Peter will be back to help Dan in a little while,' Alice said. 'Just stay till I find that article for you – the one on pigeon fanciers. It's upstairs in a magazine.' She fled.

The two men sat at the kitchen table, Dan in his wheelchair, Harry on a more conventional seat. Dan was the first to speak. 'You can tell me to bugger off if you like, but do you fancy that little wife of mine?'

Harry grinned deliberately. 'She makes me laugh.' What else might he say to a man whose doctor believed that his patient would die sooner rather than later? 'Vera was the same when we were young. Don't be worrying, cos there's nothing going on. All I get from her is abuse about poor Joe Foley's pigeons.'

Dan's eyes narrowed as he studied his companion. Harry continued to blink at a normal rate, no rush of blood appeared in his cheeks, and his body made no defensive moves. Oh yes, Dan Quigley was an expert people watcher. 'Harry?'

'What?'

'Alice has a lovely family except for her mother, but keep a neighbourly eye on her if ... if anything happens to me, right?'

'Right. Don't worry. There's Vera, too. And Olga, Peter and Yuri. Anyway, you're going nowhere.'

Dan smiled. He hadn't felt well for a while, and repeated attempts at baby-making were taking their toll. Even so, his mind was fixed on Alice.

'Come on,' Harry said, 'don't start talking yourself into your grave. You need to be positive.'

Upstairs, Alice was talking to her invisible

uncle. 'Will Dan see this child?' she whispered.

'Yes.'

'Callum?' There was no response. 'Callum?'

She sat on the sofa with her copy of a women's magazine. It contained an article about a female pigeon fancier who was considered strange by family and friends, since the keeping of pigeons was thought to be the exclusive province of men. This was her reason for being up here. She rose quickly to her feet. The last thing she remembered before collapsing was that the magazine was for Harry...

Peter was patting her hands. Alice found herself in the downstairs used-to-be living room. Her eyes fluttered open. 'Dan?' she asked.

'He's fine. The doctor's on his way.'

'Oh. Is Dan ill?'

'No, love – he's all right. You fainted.'

She frowned. 'I never faint. Fainting's for soft rich women who flop about moaning and having vapours.'

Dr Booth popped his head through the doorway. 'Hello, Mrs Quigley. What have you been up to?'

Almost fully returned to normal, she glared at the handsome young doctor. 'I've been climbing mountains in Wales.' Dan staggered in on his crutches, Harry behind him. The woman on the marital bed continued to look displeased. 'What's this? Have they paid to see the show? How many tickets did you sell?'

The medic sat on the edge of the bed.

'Go away,' Alice advised her audience.

They left in slow motion, Peter supporting Dan, Harry staring hard at the woman he loved.

'Right, Mrs Quigley. Forget the mountains. What happened?'

She bit her lip before answering. 'I'm pregnant,' she whispered.

'I see. When and where did you have the test?'

The blood rushed to her cheeks. 'I just know.'

He did all the checks: heartbeat, temperature, blood pressure. This wasn't his first I-just-know patient. A small percentage of women knew within twenty-four hours, and Alice Quigley was possibly one of that number. 'Have you told anyone?'

She shook her head.

'Then don't, or they'll think you're daft if you're mistaken. When was your last period?'

'Two weeks ago, but it never turned up.'

'You missed just one, then.'

'Yes. I'm usually regular unless there's stuff going on. I thought it might be because there's been a few problems, but...' she shrugged, 'I just feel different.'

He studied her. She was a sensible woman, a hardworking seamstress with a sick husband and a very pretty face. Alice Quigley, in spite of all the rumours about her sixth sense, was wise for her age, had been made wise by a mother who, according to local gossip, had been a nightmare. 'Miss another period, then come to my surgery.' He paused. 'Why are you blushing?'

She sighed. 'We've been trying hard to make a baby. Dan gets breathless, so I want to stop trying. I'm going to tell him that you think I might be pregnant, but it's a bit early for the test.'

'I'll agree to that. Doctors have been wrong before. Eat well – liver, eggs, fruit and vegetables. Good luck.' He picked up his accoutrements and left.

Someone was stroking her hair. 'Sleep,' Uncle Callum ordered.

She slept.

When Alice woke, it was pitch dark. Her husband snored quietly at her side. She didn't remember him getting into bed, didn't remember much apart from her conversation with Dr Booth. Callum was still here. He was getting closer and closer to her and to something else – she had no idea what the latter might be.

Feeling like a naughty and desperately hungry child, she slid out of bed. In the hall, she spoke to him, her voice low. 'You don't have to pretend to surprise me now; I can sense you here.'

'That's good. What's coming will be hard for you, and you will need to be strong. And I don't mean Dan – he's not due on my side just yet.'

She thought about that as she buttered some bread and slathered plum jam all over it. 'Can I be pregnant and strong?'

'You can, yes, because I'm here for you. Many people wouldn't be able to tolerate me, but you will.'

Alice chewed thoughtfully. 'Will I see you, Callum?'

'Yes.'

'And my dad?'

'He's always with me. You will see him.'

'You were close.'

'He loved me. No one else did. Get some cocoa and clean those teeth before going back to bed.'

'Yes, sir. And Callum?'

'What?'

'I've decided something, and I want you to leave Muth alone. She's in her seventies and terrified.'

'But—'

'You heard me. I know things, my dear uncle. For a kick-off, whatever's going to happen belongs to this house, and I'll move out if you don't leave old Elsie alone. I mean it.' She waited. While brushing her teeth in Dan's bathroom, she waited; while changing into pyjamas, she waited.

'You don't know what she did,' Callum said.

Alice sat in Dan's easy chair. She knew Muth had pestered Dad until death had been his only escape. Elsie Stewart was a cruel woman and had been an unforgiving, selfish parent. But she was over seventy years of age.

'I'm reading your thoughts,' Callum said.

'Read *Gone with the Wind* instead – that's more exciting. Look, I was glad in a way when you warned her, but I don't think an old-age pensioner should be persecuted by anyone, let alone a bloody ghost.'

He chuckled. 'Right, I'll leave her alone. But when she does wrong, you must take some responsibility for that.'

'Nellie worries about Muth. I love Nellie.'

'Which is why I need to keep the old witch at bay.'

Alice shook her head. 'No. I'm here and I'm real and you're not even visible.' A thought shot into her head. 'I have the power to make you go away.'

'Yes. I just sent you that knowledge. Do you want me to go before business is concluded?'

What the heck did he mean by business?

'Look at me.' His voice was soft.

And there he was. Her breath caught in her throat as she stared at the wall, still visible through a perfectly outlined figure that shone with rainbow colours. She could even see the four Stubbs prints hanging behind him. It was a tall man with an arm reaching out for her. 'Remember to breathe,' Callum said. 'Touch my hand.'

She complied, almost shrinking back when a gentle thrill shot up her arm like static electricity. And she saw. And she heard a baby crying. And she felt anger, fear and sadness while children played and Muth screamed. She remembered seeing bits of rainbow during many periods of otherness, and those shards had represented or been a part of Callum.

'You will forget this terrible noise, Alice, but you'll remember its importance.'

'Will I remember your beauty?' she asked when the colourful tableau had faded.

He chuckled. 'I'm vain enough to allow that if God is willing.'

'Who are you?' she asked.

'For now, I am whoever you allow me to be. Look after yourself and little Callum, and take good care of Dan.'

'When will he die?'

'Not yet.'

'That's not good enough...' She was talking to

thin air. Lord, whoever Callum was, Nuisance was his middle name. What had she seen, felt, heard? He was a rainbow. For some silly reason, she smiled because Dad's brother was a rainbow. Those coloured arcs in the sky marked the end of a storm and the beginning of sunshine. She had no memory of whatever he'd just shown her, yet she knew the experience had been horrible. But she also realized that at the end of everything there would be prisms of light birthed by moisture and sunlight. She returned to bed.

'Where've you been, love?' Dan asked sleepily.

She stretched out beside him. 'I've been talking to myself, but we're not alone.'

'Otherness?'

Alice swallowed. 'No. I fainted earlier on – remember?'

'Yes. You have to take iron pills.'

'There's a chance I might be pregnant. If I am, we're not alone, because there'll be a passenger on board.' She heard him gulping back happiness, laughter mixed with tears. 'Too early for a test, Dan, but a lot of women faint right at the beginning. And...' she placed an arm round him, 'I've missed. If I miss again, it'll be a certainty.'

She heard him swallow once more; he was digesting his rainbow. 'Dan?'

'What?'

'We can slow down a bit now. After all, we don't want to lose him, do we?'

'So it's a boy?'

She giggled. 'Callum Daniel Quigley. Dad's older brother was a Callum.'

'Right.' He dried his eyes on the sheet. 'What if

it's a girl?'

'Caroline's nearest to Callum. Caroline Alice. It's not a girl.'

'But–'

'But shut up and go to sleep. Women just know these things, only don't start knitting until we're sure.'

Dan laughed. He didn't know his knit from his purl, let alone pass the slipped stitch over. 'Good night, love.'

'Good night, Dan.' She was having a baby; she was losing her husband. Alice didn't know whether to laugh or cry, so she fell asleep instead.

The wedding took on a life of its own, due chiefly to the indiscretion of the Penny Lane Traders' Association. The meetings, no longer attended by the bride-to-be, concentrated on subject matter far removed from plans to fight the Co-op's divi, and recent agendas had moved on to the forthcoming wedding of Olga and Peter.

Terry Openshaw, master butcher, failed to hide his disappointment, while the rest of the retailers expressed an interest in seeing the wedding. But the register office was not the largest of buildings, and they wouldn't all fit, especially now that the whole neighbourhood knew. No one had been invited, but many intended to wait outside the office to see Russian bride and Lancastrian groom after the wedding ceremony.

On top of that large problem, Alice's family wanted to attend, as did Vera, Yuri and Harry. Marie and Nigel might not be there, as they had taken Jason and Hercules to Jersey, which was to be the cubs' halfway house between babyhood and Africa. Nellie, deprived of whalebone and slightly thinner, had a new two-piece suit and a hat, all of which needed an airing, while her elasticated roll-on would keep her in shape, more or less. Claire, Janet, husbands and babies would arrive, no doubt, while Dan and Alice had already been roped in as witnesses.

Peter found the solution. 'It's sorted,' he told his fiancée. 'There's been a cancellation. Some poor bugger's appendix exploded, so he won't be getting wed tomorrow, but we will. I must tell the bank and the photographer.'

Olga's jaw dropped. 'But everyone thinks Saturday.'

'They can think what they like. There'd be a traffic jam or a bloody riot on Saturday. This was what we wanted – a quiet ceremony. We get wed at Brougham Terrace Registry at two o'clock tomorrow. Before that, we go to the bank for photos with all your emeralds. Alice and Dan know, so we have witnesses, and they're sworn to secrecy. Best kick off sorting your clothes out, love.' He held up a hand in the manner of a policeman stopping traffic. 'Don't start. Gummy Tommy's going to open up the big house for us on Saturday. Marie and Nigel wouldn't mind, and there'll be a buffet.'

Olga was still struggling with the Gummy Tommy title. 'He was Tombstone,' she managed to squeeze out. 'Two teeth like grave markers.'

'He had them taken out. Last time I saw him, he had no teeth at all.'

'Sad,' she said absently. 'Go now, Peter, and tell

Harry he must help Dan tomorrow. I need wash hair and do nails. This is shock for me. But as you say, we cannot have rioting or traffic jam.' She stared at him. 'Jam is for toast.'

'Eh?'

'Why would traffic have jam?'

'You what? Oh, right – it's just a saying when cars or horses block a road and can't move.'

'Stuck like jam on bread?'

He grinned. 'I suppose so.'

'English is silly language,' was the remark Olga threw over her shoulder as she went to prepare for the occasion. This was farewell to spinsterhood. Spinster? She'd never in her life spun thread. Crazy language, crazy country, crazy Liverpool. This was happiness; this was home.

The overture celebrating the forthcoming marriage between Olga Konstantinov-Romanov, who had double-barrelled herself just prior to marriage, would go down in Liverpool's already colourful history as the Second War of the Roses. In a safe room behind the bank's normal working area, one of the longer walls was covered in pleated ivory satin, while the full extent of said wall was festooned in plants and flowers of many hues.

The wedding was to take place in an hour, though the chances of getting out of the bank in time were looking slim. Olga, resplendent in purple, glared at the bank manager. 'Photographer have Kodachrome,' she pronounced.

'I beg your pardon, madam?' the orange-haired boss enquired.

Olga turned to her groom. 'What he say?'

'He doesn't know about photography, love.'

'Why they have foreigner in job so important?'

'You're a foreigner, sweetheart.'

Sweetheart glowered. 'Yes, but I not bank manager.'

'Olga?'

"What?'

'Shut your cakehole.' He was grinning while delivering this order.

Countess Olga Kristina Konstantinov-Romanov tightened her lips and began to walk the length of the room, removing from display anything peach-coloured or bright blue. This was her day, her last day as a countess – or whatever she might have become had Russian royalty endured – and some of the photographs were going to be in colour, so nothing in the world should be allowed to clash with her ball gown.

The photographer arrived. Seeing the bride at work, he went to help her. 'Leave it to me, Miss Konstantinov,' he said. 'I know what you want.'

'I am glad you know. Never trust foreign bank manager with anything important or artistic.'

The heavies bearing the Romanov jewels entered the arena. So sacred were their burdens that the four men walked slowly and carefully, rather like altar boys preparing to serve at Mass. The watching bride nodded; they were right to treat the property of the Romanov dynasty with respect.

While the photographer moved flowers, arranged his equipment and fiddled about with something designed to measure light, Olga spoke to her beloved. 'Why you let them choose flowers my dress does not like?'

He shrugged. 'I'm a Lanky bloke, so I know nowt.'

She waved a hand towards the photographer. 'He knows. Look, he putting up big lights.'

'Aye, well, he's probably a Scouser. They can be on the creative side.'

Bride and groom were posed together and separately. Peter stood and watched while Olga became the aristocrat she truly was, with her tiara and bracelet, then necklace and earrings, followed by the gargantuan brooch high in solitary splendour on a shoulder. He attempted to swallow an emotion he scarcely understood, but there was pride in his heart and a lump in his throat that wouldn't shift. Was it humility? Did he feel inadequate in the presence of this tall, Russian royal?

Then she winked at him. 'They have made conglomerate,' she said.

'Eh?' was all he managed.

'Hatton Gardens have held hands together to pay for our emeralds. Americans interested, too.'

It was the word 'our' that helped him swallow his confusion. She was his and he was hers, and the emeralds didn't matter. Countess Olga Kristina Konstantinov-Romanov, soon to be plain Mrs Atherton, suspected that the suite of jewels might be broken up, planted in gold or platinum and re-sold as smaller items, so she was giving them their final celebration as a set. Or was she? Did the smile on her regal face disguise a secret?

When the happy couple had left the bank, an unusual sight was enjoyed by Liverpool's shoppers. Four huge men stood on the pavement, offering flowers and plants to passers-by. War broke out when two women argued over a potted fuchsia, while one of the guards broke ranks in order to chase a few scallies who had stolen several dozen cream roses.

Olga walked to the taxi. 'What is scallies?' she asked.

Her fiancé helped her into the hansom. 'Naughty Scousers, usually young.'

The burly guard returned with the roses and doled them out.

Olga grinned broadly. 'When Yuri and me young, we were Russian scallies stealing fruit from other people's orchard. Also flowers. So simple then, life was.'

'We're late, my love.'

She tutted. 'Children are never late. You and I are rich, we are happy, we are in love. Together, Mr Atherton, we journey towards our second childhood, never late, but sometimes delayed.' She chuckled as she placed herself on the leather seat. 'Now, the fun begins.' Out on the street, women carrying flowers waved at the couple in the taxi.

'See?' Peter chuckled. 'We're spreading the love already.'

At Brougham Terrace Registry, love was thin on the ground.

'We've never had dogs at a wedding before,' the registrar grumbled.

Alice blew a strand of hair out of her eyes. 'You've never married Russian royalty before, either, have you?'

'Royalty?' he blustered.

'That's what I said. Her mother was a cousin of the king of Russia.'

Vera dug Yuri in his ribs. 'You tell him, love.'

'This is true,' Yuri announced. 'My father worked for them. Olga and I played together, and Olga was second cousin to the tsar.'

The registrar's spine straightened and, after rearranging his tie, the man returned to his desk to wait for the latecomers; royalty or commoners, they were still late, and he had another wedding in just over half an hour. He glared at the dogs. Both wore golden collars, and each collar had a small, red purse attached to it. The younger boxer belonged to the bride, and his purse contained a ring for the groom. The bigger fellow, named Frank, had a purse that held the bride's ring, and the registrar thought the whole idea was like something out of a bloody pantomime.

Then they arrived, and he all but jumped to his feet. Almost as tall as her husband-to-be, Olga owned the office. She probably owned the building, the street, half of England and the crown of a tsarina. This bride, no longer a youngster, retained an undeniable beauty. It was in the structure of her face, in the long, proud neck, in the definition of the collar bones. The official wished he'd worn a newer suit, but his best was in the cleaner's.

During the short ceremony, he stuttered slightly until Olga placed a hand on his. 'My friend,' she said kindly, 'worry not about the stammer, because your King George has same.'

Peter swallowed a laugh and disguised it as a cough.

'Are you ill?' she asked.

'No.'

'Are you sure?'

'Yes.'

She returned her attention to the registrar. 'Continue, young man,' she suggested sweetly. They reached the giving of rings part. At this juncture the situation deteriorated slightly. Leo, owned by Olga, was supposed to be carrying Peter's band of gold, while Frank, borrowed by Peter, should have had Olga's in his red purse. Alice, who was beautifully clad in pale yellow silk, sorted out the mistakenly swapped bands of gold, while the small congregation exploded with laughter. At last, the bride held the groom's ring, while he claimed hers, and Alice threw herself into the seat next to her husband. 'Bloody circus,' she muttered as the rings were exchanged.

For the final time, Olga Konstantinov-Romanov signed her name. From now on, she would be Mrs Atherton. The witnesses signed, then the photographer took the usual pictures outside the registry. Several Penny Laners had gathered to watch, since news of the changed date had floated round the area like an invisible gas, though Vera was thought by most to have been the origin of the leak.

That night, their first together as a married couple, Peter and Olga sat at the kitchen table with their fish supper. 'In days, we will be millionaires,' Olga stated. 'And with this money, we should do some good.'

'Like what?'

She raised her shoulders. 'We talk, you and I. Together, we make decision. I have no children, and you have no children. We have no brother, no sister, no anybody, so we think hard to stop government taking our money when we are dead.'

'Millionaires, though?' He raised an eyebrow.

Olga looked over her shoulder, as if expecting to find eavesdroppers. 'I have proof of provenance, so the whole collection going to an American who wants to keep the jewellery like it is now. He will be paid for lending to museums the property of the tsar.'

'Why, love?'

'Because he can do this. Because he American. They like to be showing off. Young country, no long history yet, so they buy ours. He offer much more than what London wants to pay. And my mother's pieces might stay as they are. Like me, buyer is born of escaped Russians.' She impaled a chip with her fork. 'We are rich, so we can now buy vinegar. I like more vinegar.'

Peter studied his bride. Her English was easily as poor as his, and she was a wreck in the mornings until she'd had two cuppas sipped through cubes of sugar. Awkward customers made her stamp about like a two-year-old in a tantrum, and she was unreasonable when it came to foreigners of the Scottish persuasion. She made him laugh several times a day, had a huge heart and a loving soul, and fewer grey hairs now that harvest time had arrived; she plucked out the front ones, while he was responsible for greys that dared to encroach at the back. Olga Atherton was wonderful. 'Eh, I love you, girl,' he whispered. 'We'll be legal in bed now.'

'This I am know already. Leo, go into your basket.' She waited until the dog had performed about a dozen circles before settling. 'Husband, we go to our bed. Yuri now with Vera, so no need to worry about does he hear us.'

Peter grinned. That was another thing – Olga laboured under the delusion that she was always in charge. He chortled. She probably was.

Downstairs, Dan and Harry were trying to be friends over a game of cards. Alice was in the first floor sitting/sewing room and seemed to be whispering to herself. She wasn't, of course.

'Just being dead doesn't make me clever or special.'

Alice sniffed.

'What?' Callum asked.

'I noticed your lack of brain,' was her terse reply. 'You know I'm the one making sense. According to you, there'll be a showdown and she will need to be here. After your bit of palaver, she'll not set foot within a mile of Penny Lane.'

A few prisms of fractured light danced round the room.

'What's that about?' she demanded to know.

'I'm thinking.'

'Must be hard work, because you're coming to pieces all over my wallpaper.'

The invisible man laughed. 'It will happen on the eighth of April next year at about seven o'clock in the evening.'

'My birthday. Muth's birthday, too.'

'Quite. Your dad will be here.'

Alice chewed her lower lip. 'Is he made of stained glass like you?'

'No. He's a pipe with a man on the end of it. Alice?'

'What?'

'It will not be pleasant, so choose your witnesses carefully.'

Silence reigned for a few minutes. She broke the quiet. 'We're going to visit her and let her know you've removed the curse. But she still has to stay away from my sisters and my nieces and their kids. It'll take me months to persuade her to visit this house, anyway. So polish your leaded lights, because we're visiting Brighton-le-Sands.'

'Do I have to? She frightens me to death.'

'You're already dead, you soft sod.'

'Mmmm. I forget sometimes.'

Another quiet spell was shattered by a question she scarcely dared to ask. 'Callum?'

'Yes?'

She swallowed hard. 'My baby will be born before April.'

'True.'

'Will my Danny Boy be alive?'

'He will.'

'Thank God.' Alice slumped in her seat.

'All right. I'll thank Him when I see Him.'

'Is He stained glass?'

'No. Only angels are rainbows, my love.'

'Are you an angel?'

No reply was forthcoming: he had exited the stage.

Eleven

'If it makes no difference to you, why do I have to wait for my birthday? And why does it make no difference, Callum? You don't half talk a load of ear'ole.' This accusation had been stolen from Peter, the local Boltonian who had imported his vernacular to Liverpool, together with the flat, broad and slow speech birthed at mules and looms in deafening, overheated and damp cotton mills.

Alice, not in the best of moods these days, glared at the small prism of light that hovered over one of the chairs. Callum talked in riddles sometimes, and Alice's temper was on a very short tether, especially where her uncle was concerned. Turning, she gazed at a ribbon of smoke near the window. 'You, too, Dad. You're as bad as him, hanging about like what Peter might call cheese at fourpence, never a word out of you – so why are you here?'

'He's with me,' said the shard of splintered, mobile light.

'I'd worked that out, thanks, Uncle. After all, I'm only half Irish, so the other half can think in straight lines if the wind's in the right direction.' She gritted her teeth momentarily before continuing, 'Why does it not matter to you when this whatever it is happens?'

'Because time means nothing at this side, but it

261

does where you are. We have no clocks, no walls, no restrictions. Well, except one; we need a good reason to come back into your sphere.'

'And you have good reason to be here?'

'Yes, I do.'

'And Dad?'

'Is an important link. And he wants his girls to know he loves them.'

For want of some kind of occupation, Alice paced about for a while, her complaints continuing to pour forth. 'Why does that baby cry? Who is the baby? I used to think you were the grown-up version, but I'm not so sure now.' She stopped pacing. 'I adopted my Frank, a lovely dog with a heart of gold, and he got pulled into this second bloody sight I'm cursed with, then I moved here and watched the tsar of Russia and his family being slaughtered, and–'

Callum interrupted. 'Frank is a link that was used until you got here, on Penny Lane. As for the Russian scene, Olga needed a friend, and so did you. Frank's no longer involved, so he can be just a dog with his little boxer friend. You're here now; you're where we need you to be. Your expected bundle of joy will be born shortly before your birthday. Until then, you do the waiting and we'll do the existing. Oh, and you're right. Court your mother, because she'll need to be here next April. Please bear with me. There's something I need to do, you see. Don't be afraid, as I will not hurt you, though I will expose what happened. Get witnesses and bring your mother.'

Alice sighed heavily. 'And all this goes off on my birthday, right? She has the same birthday as me, and she's terrified of you. Frightened to death at the thought of you haunting her. And another thing – you were trying to keep her away from me, and now you've changed your mind. How come?'

'I gave you a short rest from her, didn't I? Visit her. I shall wipe her mind before you get there.'

She sat down and swallowed hard. 'Will I see my dad?'

'Yes. He was very troubled until I brought him back to you.'

'Troubled?'

'Wait until April. Then I shall give you a truth that will hurt, but it will also bring you answers. The crying baby will go forever and this house will be at peace.'

'Oh.' She paused. 'You and Dad? Will you leave forever?'

'We will always watch over you. You're our girl. Alice?'

'What?'

'I love you.'

The prism and the smoke disappeared simultaneously, leaving a bemused young woman in her first floor sitting/workroom. She felt lonely. Downstairs, the husband who had saved her life lay sleeping in their double bed, happily unaware that his time on earth was sorely limited. The guilt Alice felt rested heavily on her shoulders, because she believed she had already chosen Dan's replacement. 'No,' she whispered, 'he picked me.' She had to deal with him, too, because two dozen pigeons still wanted shifting.

Once again, from somewhere that defied all

dimensions, came Callum's answer. 'I chose you both for each other!

'Bloody Mr Clever Clogs,' she hissed. He was getting on her nerves. 'If you weren't already dead, I'd kill you. You're too high-handed.'

He hooted with laughter.

'I would. I'd separate you from your voice box, believe me.'

This time, he was almost inside her head. 'No, you wouldn't. Murder isn't in you. To commit that crime, you'd need a bit of yourself to be twisted. You'd need not to care about anyone except yourself.'

'I don't care when it comes to pigeons. Now, bugger off again, will you?'

She'd done some investigating about pigeons and was ready to approach Harry with what she believed was a sensible solution, but would he listen? She'd make bloody sure he listened, be-cause– 'Stop it.' Callum was making affectionate billing and cooing sounds down her right ear, producing his very good imitation of a pigeon. 'Go away,' she commanded.

He left, but his chuckle faded very slowly, accompanying her all the way downstairs to the marital bedroom. She switched on a small lamp. Dan looked well, she thought, hoping he felt as well as he appeared to be. He would see his child, and that was important. Yes, he would meet the second Callum. 'I'll look after you as best I can,' she whispered before joining him in the bed. Within minutes, she was fast asleep. Her dreams were of Muth chasing her with a frying pan, a man made of stained glass stopping Muth in her

264

tracks, and another man with teeth so bright that they blinded everyone. She stirred, turned over and cuddled up to her husband. Once deeper sleep claimed her, all dreaming stopped.

The rain was gaining momentum as Alice alighted from the bus.

Harry's car drifted to the pavement's edge and the passenger door flew outwards. 'Get in,' he commanded.

She had no umbrella. Black cloud was moving from the Mersey to cover the land. It was Harry's Austin, and Harry would never hurt her. Bending down, she spoke to him. 'I'm going to visit the wicked witch of the west,' she told him.

'Get in,' he repeated.

She got in. 'Go right at the end of the road, and I'll tell you when to stop.'

'Like you always do,' he complained.

'Don't start with the daft stuff, Harry. Apart from anything else, the doc says I might be pregnant, so just take me near enough to Muth's, and go home.'

'I'll wait for you.'

'No need,' was her answer.

He spaced his words emphatically. 'I ... will ... wait ... for ... you.'

Alice stared at the man who loved her. 'All ... right,' she said, copying his strange pattern. 'But stop at the blue door – she's higher up behind a red one. Believe me, the fact that I arrived there with a man would be in Tuesday's papers.'

'Another Vera, then?'

'I wish, Harry. No. We don't want to be seen by

Muth – no way.'

He grinned broadly. 'Ask your mother where she stands on pigeons.'

'Across their throats, I shouldn't wonder. She nagged my dad to death, chased our Theresa to the other side of the globe, never shed a tear when three of us were killed in the Blitz, and made life a total misery for our Nellie.' She inhaled deeply. 'Now I'm going to be nice to her.'

'Why?'

'Because it suits my purpose.'

He watched as she walked away. Pregnant or not, she had to understand that he would wait for her. Forever.

The business started like a mixed-up jigsaw with thousands of pieces, but with no corners and no edges to the picture. Martin Browne, Kevin Holden and Paul Myers were now the owners of a flatbed truck for which fuel was scarce. Because of poor petrol supplies, they had also acquired a cart with shafts and a carthorse named Nelson. Nelson lodged with the disparate collection of animal life housed by Marie and Nigel, whose permission had been sought before they'd left for Jersey with the cubs. It had been a confusing time, and the roles of various people were under discussion for several days. Who would do what, where and when was the main topic.

One person was in her element: Nellie had two babies. When she thought about her life, she realized that she'd been at her happiest when Janet and Claire had been infants. Proudly, she wheeled a second-hand twin pram up and down the road, stopping to chat to anyone who showed the slightest interest in its two small passengers.

Since Nellie had the ability to buy wholesale, babies Simon and Keith had every toy on the market. Their mothers complained daily, because Nellie was spoiling her grandchildren, but she was good at turning a deaf ear – she'd practised doing just that for years when Elsie had been around.

Things began to settle. Janet and Claire ran their parents' shop, while their dad fronted the furniture business in the old ice cream parlour and milk bar that had once belonged to the Turners. Thus, after a few hit-and-miss days, a pattern formed almost of its own accord. Kevin and Paul were busy, mostly in the reclaiming of war-damaged furniture and household goods, for which they used the large shed at the rear of their garage on the fringes of Blundellsands and Brighton-le-Sands. From two or three wrecked tables they produced a single good one, which would be sold from the Smithdown Road shop. Nothing was wasted, and within a short space of time they accumulated enough spare components to make stuff from scratch.

Nellie often brought the little ones to visit Granddad but, one Thursday lunch hour, she arrived in a state worse than Paddy's Market just after closing time. 'Martin,' she gasped. 'Oh, Martin. I don't know whether I'm coming or going.'

'What's up, love? Sit yourself down before you start bloody crying and flood the area.' He placed a hand on her shoulder. 'Come on, tell me all about it. Deep breaths, now.'

She parked the pram before dropping onto a stool and inhaling a welcome draught of oxygen. 'I met our Alice outside that shoe shop next to the bank. She's gone round to see Muth. You could have knocked me over with a feather duster, I was that shocked. But she was in a hurry so I got no time to say anything much.'

'Oh? Why would she do that? She can't stand the old witch.' Martin scratched his head. 'Sometimes, I find your Alice a bit difficult to work out, because she's always changing her mind. Saying that, though, I have to admit she's clever. There must be a damned good reason for her to go and see your mother.'

Nellie inhaled deeply. 'Well, I think the mind-changing's part of her otherness. She said that with Muth being over seventy, we should let her back into our lives, but on our terms. I thought I was the only one who worried about our mother being so old and on her own...'

Martin shook his head. 'Well, I reckon you should slow down and think. There's enough of us to stand up to her if she kicks off – when she kicks off. She's just a little old ... battleaxe. I've never met anybody like her, mean-spirited old cow.'

Nellie's spine straightened itself. 'I don't want to let her near Simon and Keith.' The grandmother's knuckles whitened as she made firmer her grip on the pram's handle. 'She's like a disease – or a weapon. It'll be world war all over again, right down to sirens and gas masks. Our Alice and Muth are a dangerous ... what's that word? Combination – like fire and brimstone, or whatever they call that stuff.'

'There'll be no war on my watch.' Martin smiled at his wife. 'Nellie, I'm back. The first thing I did was get rid of her. When I found out that we were granddad and grandma, I knew I'd had enough. If she'd been halfway decent, it would have looked terrible, me throwing out a poor old woman. But everybody along this road congratulated me.' He waved a hand towards the door. 'We'll manage.'

'I hope so, love.'

He grinned again. 'Listen, Nell. Remember last August when America dropped atom bombs on Hiroshima and Nagasaki?'

She nodded. 'Terrible, that was.'

'Your Alice is the human version of those weapons. I know she's the size of two penn'orth of chips, but she has some special power, as you know only too well. She's the one who can overcome your mother. Alice has a way of making things happen, and Marie has confidence in herself, too.'

'But I haven't any of that, have I?'

Martin chuckled. 'You're getting there. These two kiddies are helping you along. Look at you – bright eyes, shiny hair, and nearly a stone lost. I'm proud of you, girl.'

The 'girl', more than fifty-three years of age, simpered. She knew she looked well, knew she was stronger and happier than she'd been for ages, years that had been stolen by her mother. 'I want Claire and Janet and their husbands and babies kept out of it. We'll go to the meeting and I'll say then it's only the two of us. Just as well, because I might speak my mind at long last. And it's not before time – I'm the oldest.'

'Meeting?'

'Up at Alice's tonight. Just us, no Claire, no Janet, because I haven't told them about it, and I'm not going to. Marie and Nigel will be back in time for Olga and Peter's reception on Saturday – I suppose Alice will talk to them then. All right?'

'I don't know,' Martin said quietly. He tried another tack. 'You've got me, two daughters, two strapping sons-in-law and two babies. Are you better now?'

Nellie knew she had no choice. 'I suppose so,' she agreed reluctantly. After all, Alice and Marie were both cleverer than she was, weren't they? She would do her best. Nobody could do better than their best.

'We'll be fine, sweetheart.'

'Muth won't be fine if she comes near these two, because I'll crack her one across the gob,' was Nellie's reply.

They each picked up a baby and a bottle. Where babies were concerned, food mattered most.

Alice marched up to the front door of the ugly, grey house. She shivered. She had to be nice; no matter what, she would be nice.

'She won't remember anything about your last visit,' said Callum.

'Are you still hanging around like a bad smell in the public lavs?'

'Yes, I am.'

'Stay out of it,' she snapped. If this was pregnancy, it didn't suit her one bit. What with sickness in the mornings, a temper that was unpredictable, a compulsion to eat fruit and a strong dislike for meat, she was falling to bits like most of the bombed houses down Bootle way. 'Don't talk to me, don't move anything, and leave her alone. This is your last warning. And I've got a headache.' A cool breeze stroked her forehead, and the pain was gone. Oh yes, Uncle Callum was one clever ghost. An angel? One of these days he'd disappear up his own halo, taking his harp with him. Alice pressed the doorbell and rapped on the door. Perhaps Muth was out shopping – wishful thinking.

It opened after a few seconds. Elsie's jaw dropped. 'Hello,' she said sarcastically, 'what brings you here?' She looked her daughter up and down.

'A bus and my feet brought me,' was the reply.

'And how did you know where to find me?'

'A friend told me she'd seen you coming out of here. I just wondered if you were all right.' Mr Magic had kept his word, then; Muth clearly had no memory of her previous encounter with her youngest daughter.

'Come in.'

The doorway widened.

This place was exactly as Alice remembered it, except for new wallpaper and the smell of paint. 'Lovely,' she said. 'Is the rent OK?'

'I don't pay rent, because I'm the caretaker. I feed just me, and the gas and electric meters – they take pennies. So I do very well, thanks to my bit of savings. A woman my age doesn't eat much.'

271

Alice sat where she had placed herself on the earlier occasion, on one of two dining chairs at a small table in the bay window. She waited while Muth made a pot of tea. With her speech well rehearsed and lodged at the front of her mind, she was managing to squash her nerves. Well, she was nearly managing.

Mother and daughter sat opposite each other drinking the cup that cheers, though neither found anything to smile about. 'I've come to invite you to ours for Sunday dinner,' Alice said. 'Not this Sunday coming – the one after.' Following the reception on Saturday, Dan would be tired, so Muth's visit needed to be postponed for a week. 'We eat at about half past two. Will you come?'

Elsie's cup clattered on to its saucer. 'You what?'

Unfazed, the younger woman continued. 'Dinner with me and Dan a week on Sunday.'

'Why?'

'Because you're my mother, and because none of us gets any younger.'

'We don't get on, you and me,' Elsie said.

'Leave the past where it belongs, Muth; bury it in yesterday's bad news.'

'I will if you will,' was Elsie's answer after a long pause.

'I already have. I know you haven't had an easy life, with seven kids and then Dad dying young. What's the point of bearing grudges?'

Muth smiled, though her eyes remained chilled. 'I'll be there.'

Alice shivered. This woman might as well be a fridge. Wondering obliquely whether Nellie's sons-in-law might be able to find a use for Elsie's coldness in the shop's kitchen, the visitor picked up a rich tea biscuit.

Elsie's eyes narrowed. 'You look different. Have you been ill?'

'No. I'm all right.'

'You're pale.'

Alice shrugged.

'How's our Nellie?'

'OK. Thinner. Happier, too, because Martin's back.' She would be seeing Nellie and Martin tonight, but she wasn't going to tell Muth that.

'And Marie?'

'In Jersey. She'll be back soon.'

The older woman sniffed. 'It must be nice to have the money for gadding about on holiday.'

'They're not on holiday, Muth; they're doing something for Chester Zoo.'

A second sharp inhalation was followed by, 'Well, I suppose with her being barren, the animals are a substitute.'

Alice drained her cup. Muth's tongue remained as sharp as a rapier. 'Our Marie is the kindest, sweetest woman on the planet, and our Nellie's wonderful. I want you to start thinking before you open your gob, Mother. I can't and won't speak for my sisters, but I'm asking you to come back into my life, not theirs. If they drop in while you're at my house, be nice.'

Whenever Alice awarded her the title 'Mother,' Elsie knew it was a warning. 'I'll bear that in mind,' she announced carefully.

'Good.' The daughter rose to her feet and gazed at the woman who had birthed her. 'And be polite to Dan. He's not in the best of health after two strokes.'

Elsie held back a smile. The sooner Alice's cripple died, the sooner she'd be free to find somebody who could walk and work.

The air round Alice's face moved. Callum was here.

'I'm thought-streaming,' he whispered.

Elsie's unspoken words walked through Alice's mind. 'I love him, Mother,' she said.

'What?'

'I know what you're thinking.'

'Do you, now?'

'It's in your eyes. Be nice to my Dan.'

'I will.' She followed her daughter to the door. 'See you a week on Sunday, then.'

'Yes,' Alice replied. 'And keep that sharp tongue still when you get there.' She left, accepted Harry's offer of another lift, and began the journey to Marie's, where she would be checking on preparations for the reception which would take place this weekend.

'Thank you,' she said when they reached her sister's house. He had managed to keep his hands to himself, and for that fact she felt half relieved and half disappointed. She left the car and waved off the man who confused her. After finishing at Marie's, she had a bone or three to pick with Mr Harry Thompson, pigeon fancier, and it would have been rude to attack him in his own car. But something had to be done, and she was the only one who seemed prepared to tackle it. She walked up Marie's path and into the house via the rear door. Tommy had been hard at work.

Having progressed from two incisors in the lower jaw to total toothlessness, he had now become Toothy Tommy. The reason for the newest name hit any visitor immediately, because Tommy didn't own teeth – they owned him. Brilliant white and large, they seemed to guide him along like headlights on a vehicle navigating a dark road. He smiled a great deal, probably because he hadn't a great deal of choice, since the dentures seemed unnecessarily huge.

Alice stopped staring at him; staring was rude. She remembered the bright, white teeth in her dream. 'You've done well,' she managed, trying hard not to laugh.

'I've got new teeth,' he announced unnecessarily. 'They were fitted specially, just last week.'

'Er ... yes, very nice,' was her careful answer. Did he think the falsies had helped in his labours? 'I see you borrowed two trestle tables.'

'From the Methodist hall. For heathens, they seem quite friendly folk.'

At last, she allowed herself to release a giggle. 'They're not heathens, Tommy. They're Christians like us.'

'Are they?'

'Yes. They just dress plain and speak plain.'

'Right.' The teeth clattered together when he reached the end of the word.

'And the fairy lights look nice. When are Marie and Nigel back?'

'Tonight. Special arrangements had to be made, because they're bringing two more animals. I asked what they are, but they said I should wait and see. Their mammy died. So we've the whole rigmarole starting over again.'

'Good.'

'That's what I said, so. Did you know Larry has a friend?'

'Not another bloody llama, Tommy.'

'Ah no; it's Nelson. So I took them both to the nursing home last Sunday when Nelson wasn't needed, and we brought out all the old dears in wheelchairs. He never spat. Good as gold, he was, but. See, if anyone tells you there's no such thing as a miracle, you know the truth of it.'

Mesmerized by teeth and the Irish brogue, Alice went to look at the rest of the house. It was spotless. She realized now why Marie and Nigel had never employed a housekeeper, because they already had one. A local woman came in a couple of mornings every week, but Tommy was the star turn. Or perhaps his teeth were...

'When's the cake coming?' she shouted.

'Tonight,' came the reply from downstairs. 'And the rest of the catering comes Saturday morning before ten. I think we ordered enough to feed the five thousand.'

'What? Five loaves and two fishes?'

Alice sat on the end of Marie's double bed. She could hear Tommy laughing downstairs. Saturday would be a long day, and she hoped nobody would notice that she was eating salad butties and no meat. 'I am definitely expecting,' she whispered to herself.

'Crates of champagne, too,' Tommy shouted.

In spite of discomfort in the digestive department, Alice giggled quietly. Tommy's face had grown taller. With teeth, he was probably close to five feet and ten inches in height if measured at the front. And there was a twinkle in his eye. Alice the matchmaker grinned. She knew a woman who would be perfect for the Irishman. Mind, would Vera want to live in a shed...? Then there was poor Urine to think about. 'I'd better go home,' she told herself. Yes, it was time to stop the billing and cooing of two dozen birds. With the mood she was in, Harry had better not get affectionate, either.

'You're beautiful,' he whispered. 'You look like you've just walked out of the pages of a fashion magazine.'

'Don't talk tripe, Harry. I know what I look like, thanks. I'm pale. We do have mirrors in our house.' She glanced round the room; for a man, he wasn't too bad at cleaning, though the skirting boards needed a wipe down with a damp cloth. And while he was at it, he could have a go at the picture rail and that windowsill.

Harry, after watching her wandering gaze, invited her to sit. She was a fanatic when it came to housework, so this was going to be about washing and pigeons, of that he felt certain.

'I'm not stopping; too much to do today.' She perched on the edge of a large, over-stuffed armchair near the window. 'Dan will be back soon – he's gone to the park with Neil, who came home early when his job finished.'

'Can Dan get that far?'

'In a wheelchair, yes. Have you been working today?'

'Yes. I was with Vera's Tony. We finished early too.' He stood as if intending to approach her.

'Stay where you are. I'm here on business.'

Sighing heavily, he sat down again. He knew what was coming. 'Bird business?' He would behave himself, had to behave himself, because madam here took no prisoners, and her poor husband was going to die before his time. Even so, Harry's need for Alice tormented him, though he fought it as hard as was humanly possible.

'Bird business?' he repeated. He could see that she, too, was fighting to maintain her composure, though her main problem was not desire for him. She was looking to clean up, as usual. She'd had her eyes all over his paintwork, and was now ready to start on the occupants of the back garden loft.

'Bird business on my washing, yes, Harry. And Vera's, and Nancy Sugden's, and that big woman higher up who takes in laundry for a living. As if the bird dirt isn't bad enough, they start twitting about at the crack of dawn. We sleep at the front of our house, as you very well know, but we can hear the buggers. Six o'clock, they kicked off today. And they all talk at once. My husband's a sick man, and he needs his sleep. So do I. The birds are a pain, and you know it.'

Harry ran the fingers of one hand through his hair. She hated the pigeons, and he wasn't exactly thrilled with them. 'Alice, the old man left me the car, and when you think about it–'

'And a load of bird poo, but he left that for all of us. Anyway, you've these fanciers knocking at your door to buy Blue Lady. Why don't you have a bit of sense for a change and sell them on? What's stopping you?' She knew the answer, though she wanted to know whether he'd changed his mind.

'I'd be betraying my dad's best mate.'

She sighed – it was the same excuse as last time. 'Let's look at this another way, then. Are you a born pigeon fancier? And have you come from a long line of pigeon racers?'

'No I'm not and no I haven't.'

'Do you think you know what you're doing, then?'

Harry shrugged. 'Do I hell as like. I'm picking it up as I go along, borrowing books from the library. I'm doing my bloody best, feeding them, keeping the loft as clean as possible.'

'But is your best good enough for Blue Lady? I mean, she's royalty, isn't she? She's the pigeon world's version of our Olga.'

He decided yet again that Alice was a right little besom, and he loved the bones of her. She argued. She always stood her ground, even when she was wrong. She was a sight for sore eyes, daft, clever, alluring, perfect and married. She lit up the darkest corner of the grimmest room with no need for electricity.

'I know somebody who knows somebody,' she said.

He raised an eyebrow. 'We can all say that. Everybody knows somebody, and every somebody knows another somebody.'

Alice shook her head in near-despair. 'Listen, you. In the First World War Cher Ami got hundreds of starving soldiers fed. Red Cock saved a ship and its crew. They got medals for what they did. Pigeons helped turn the last war in our favour too. I mean, we couldn't send a postman to France, could we?'

'And you moan because heroes shit on your sheets.'

'Shut up.'

He glued his lips together in a thin line. Alicia Marguerite Quigley was 'on one'. In Liverpool 'on one' meant ranting, lecturing, having a tantrum, or going for some poor sod's jugular. On this occasion, he was the poor sod. He waited.

'This bloke I know lives up near St Anthony's on Scotland Road. He knows another man who was in charge of a pigeon corps or whatever in the war. The birds carried messages in little tubes, sometimes even cameras. The cameras slowed them down and made them fly lower, so a lot got shot. They died for England.'

Harry nodded. She'd gone dramatic. Alice did a very good dramatic, and if Lady Macbeth could have had a Liverpool accent, this little bundle of mischief would have done Shakespeare proud. 'Or Ophelia,' he said.

'You what?'

'I was thinking aloud about *Hamlet*.'

'That's a village with no church.' She pulled herself together. 'Yes, yes, I do read. Look, will you try and stay on the same road as the rest of the traffic? Or on the same page as other children in the class. I sometimes wonder whether you listen at all. Are you going to behave?'

'Yes, ma'am. Though I wouldn't mind being in detention with you.'

Ma'am glared at him. 'Anyway, as I was saying before you went all Shakespeare, this pigeon personnel person is interested in your birds, particularly Blue Lady and her squabs. Give them all to

280

him. It's for the birds' own good, before some-body round here puts out poisoned seed. If you want to live the long and healthy life, never come between a Lancashire woman and her dolly blued sheets. Take no money. If you take no money, you aren't betraying your dad's old pal, and the pigeons will be in excellent hands.'

He stared hungrily at her. He wanted to disturb a few sheets with her under them and him next to her. And she should be a Member of flaming Par-liament, in her spare time, too. Alice was Churchill minus cigar, male bits and about twenty stone of fat. She was gorgeous, mouthy and stubborn as a mule. 'All right, then. Talk to your man on Scotty Road and tell him to bring the other fellow with him.'

She blinked. 'You gave in easily. Thank you.'

'It's only because I love you.'

'Don't talk soft.'

A few seconds ticked away. 'Dan asked me to look after you if he dies.'

Her jaw dropped.

'Shut your mouth, love – there's a pigeon com-ing.'

'Did he really?'

Harry nodded. 'And I promised him I would.'

Alice rose to her feet. 'I wonder if I'll get a say in the matter?'

'When don't you have your say? Words pour out of your gob like water from a fireman's hose. You don't even stop to breathe.'

She grinned. 'Then how can you love a mither-ing woman?'

'Easy. Dead easy. Peter calls it chunnering – his

Olga's a chunnerer. If she doesn't shut up, he stops her with a big kiss. That gets her all flustered, and she forgets what she was going on about.'

'So that's the plan? If I talk too much I get assaulted and restrained?'

He nodded.

'It would never work on me, cos I'm dead hard.'

He wondered how she might react if he made a feeble joke about male anatomy, but she wasn't in the best of moods, so he didn't bother. 'What's happened?' he asked. 'You look a bit harassed, and it's not my fault, because you arrived in that state.'

She shrugged. 'I've been to see Muth. You know that, because you took me.'

Harry blessed himself. 'Yes, but did you carry garlic and a crucifix?'

Alice rolled her eyes ceilingward.

'Did you?'

'Like most people, you've got that wrong. For vampires, you need garlic flowers, not garlic. And I always wear a crucifix. I have to let her back in my life and in our house. Not my idea of fun, as you probably realize already, but it has to be done.'

It was her otherness, he realized immediately. 'Did the spirits tell you to go and see her?'

She nodded. 'I'm under orders from the other side.' Harry was one of the few who didn't take the salt and pepper out of her when it came to second sight. He'd made the odd remark when they'd first met, but had come to understand that Alice must never play poker, especially with

Peter, because she didn't have the face for it; she was simply too honest. 'There's some sort of plot on,' she explained. 'Thanks for not making fun of me, Harry.'

'I can tell you're not a liar. You've a very open expression, like your Nellie. Hey, she's changing for the better, isn't she?'

Alice smiled. 'She has babies. Nellie's at her happiest among nappies and National Dried. She minds her two grandsons while everybody else runs the businesses. I don't know how many miles a day she does with that pram, but she's losing weight. Muth drove Nellie not to drink, but to food. She used it like a drug. I'd better go.'

'Stuff to do?'

She nodded. 'Nellie and Martin are coming for a meeting, and I'll feed them while they're here. They're probably not bringing anyone else, because Nellie's scared of Muth, and she doesn't want the old bat anywhere near the rest of her immediate family – you know, daughters and sons-in-law and babies. But I'm under instructions, so I'm doing as I'm told.' She paused. 'He's here now.'

Something cold travelled the length of Harry's spine. 'Who is?'

'Callum. I think he's my dad's older brother, and he's mischievous. Not destructive like a poltergeist, just daft.'

Both visible occupants of the room sat mesmerized while Harry's clock struck thirteen. It was quarter past four.

'I see what you mean,' Harry managed eventually.

'He can also make you forget what you just heard, but I don't think he will, because he'll want you as a witness next April.'

'Oh?'

'On my thirty-fourth birthday – Muth's seventy-fourth. He'll show us what he wants us to know, and after that I'll be free.'

'Free?'

'From the otherness and from him.'

The clock struck quarter past, but out of tune.

'Bugger off,' Alice snapped. 'Go and play somewhere else, Uncle Callum.' She winked at Harry. 'He's gone.' She gazed round the room. Skirting boards, windowsill and picture rails were sparkling clean.

'How do you know he's gone?'

'He strokes my face or moves the air round me, thinks he's a clever magician.' She sat on the sofa deep in thought for a few seconds. 'It's something that happened in or near our house. Remember they used to have yards here, not back gardens, and I have a row of flags still there near the wall I share with you?'

'So?'

'There's one particular flag in the corner near the old lavvy shed. I don't like it. It's different from all the others.'

He nodded, waiting for more, but she was pondering again. 'How's it different?' he asked. 'Shape, size or colour?'

Alice snapped out of her reverie. 'I never noticed it till last week when I was sweeping and swilling. It looks just like all the rest, but it feels different, makes me uneasy. I got Peter to put a

284

big heavy flower pot on it and he filled it with bedding plants and greenery.'

'You think there's something buried?'

'No idea, Harry. But I've a feeling it will all come out on my birthday next April. I want you, Dan, Martin and Peter there. I think it would be too much for our Nellie.'

'What about Marie and Nigel? Will they be coming to your strange birthday party?'

'They can come if they want.' She walked towards the door and away from the man who would probably be her second husband. Poor Dan. Did he know, did he sense that he wasn't going to live for much longer? In the doorway, she paused and turned. 'Wait for me,' she whispered.

'Oh, I will. Till hell freezes over.' He grinned. 'Do you love me?'

Seconds strolled away. 'Yes, but I feel awkward about it.'

'You wouldn't be normal if you didn't feel awkward.' Harry's tone was gentle. 'Go on, now. Go and look after your old man.'

She left, missing Harry before she'd closed the outer door. Only once or twice he'd held her in his arms; only once had they started to make something approaching physical love, yet she wanted him. But she was married to a man who loved and needed her, and was carrying his child.

'He'll wait for you.'

'Get lost, Uncle Callum.'

Nellie was in a mood.

Nobody had ever seen her in a mood, so this was something of a novelty for the Quigleys –

even for Martin, her husband. 'I'm not having anything to do with it,' she said the moment she stepped into her youngest sister's kitchen.

'You didn't say that when I spoke to you earlier on.' Alice's tone was accusatory.

'I never got the chance, did I? You beggared off as soon as you'd told me. You're not the one who had her living with you, are you? I lost my husband and my daughters because I'm that scared of her. No bloody way. She goes nowhere near our girls, their husbands and their babies. We lost the first few months of them little lads' lives, too.'

Alice felt mesmerized. Nellie, the most placid of the seven, had built a wall, a defence system, and Muth was the enemy. 'You don't need to have her visiting you, Nell. You could call here for a cuppa after Sunday dinner, and–'

'And nothing. She'd take that as an open invitation to the shops, our flat, the house where our Claire and Janet live – you know she would.'

Alice folded her arms. 'You were the one who was worried about her.'

'I got over that. No. We won't come here on any Sunday, and you can tell her why, because you're the one trying to drag us into hell.'

Dan strengthened his hold on the arms of the carver in which he sat waiting for his dinner. 'Leave it, Alice,' he warned.

Martin held his wife's arm. 'Slow down, love.'

Nellie turned and looked at him. 'You weren't there,' she hissed. 'You weren't the one who came back from town to find a letter in the girls' room. *Sorry, Mam, but we can't live here any more till she goes.*'

286

'I know. I'm sorry.'

Nellie shook her head. With her mouth down-turned and eyes wet, she moved to face her small audience. 'You don't know what I know. Well, what I think I know.'

Callum brushed past Alice. 'I'm wiping that memory now,' he said.

'What do you know, Nell?' Martin asked. 'Come on, love, let it out, then you can stop thinking about it.'

Alice stiffened as she waited for the answer.

'I...' Nellie's voice faded. 'Something bad. Something so bad I buried it years ago in the back of my mind. And you can try to prise it out with a crowbar, but you won't find it.'

Alice bowed her head. Things were getting really bad if the otherness was affecting her beloved big sister. 'Callum, will you bugger off?' she screamed, unable to stop herself.

The two men looked at each other. 'What's that about?' Martin mouthed silently.

Dan shrugged. His wife's otherness could be embarrassing at times.

'Shall we eat?' Martin asked.

'You can do what you damned well like,' was Nellie's answer. 'I'm going home.' She marched out of the room, down the hall, and through the front door, which she slammed in her wake.

'Go after her, Martin,' Dan suggested.

But Martin joined his brother-in-law at the table. His wife's fear and fury had moved him, and he would support her. But there was something he had to do before he went after her. 'No, I'll say my piece first.' He took a deep breath. 'Elsie bloody

287

Hard-Face ruined my Nell's life. I take responsibility for some of that, because I buggered off to Manchester thinking Nellie would get rid of her. She didn't. I kept in touch with the Turners for a while, so I knew Elsie was still there. Then the girls went, and your bloody mother took over the shop and made a show of my wife, called her stupid in front of customers, moved herself into our daughters' bedroom. Meanwhile I lived in a bedsit, and I saved and saved so I could pay off the mortgage on the shop. We owe next to nothing, and I still had enough left to open a business for my girls and their families.

'I was working in Woolworth's when I got word that Janet and Claire were married. Later on, I was told that they had a baby each. So I gave notice and came home. I threw the bitch out, and the applause from Smithdown Road could be heard down the Pier Head.'

He shook his head gravely. 'And you expect me and Nellie to come for a cuppa after Sunday dinner?' He glared at Alice. 'I hope you know what you're doing, girl, but leave us out of it. My wife's happy. Let's keep it that way, because it's what she deserves. All I want is for my wife, my daughters and their families to be safe and contented.'

Alice opened her mouth to speak, but Martin rose and walked to the door. 'You are welcome to visit us any time. If you bring the old bag with you, your names will join hers on my list of poisons.' He left abruptly.

Dan stared at his wife. 'Bloody hell with custard – what have you started now, eh?'

She shook her head.

'And you're missing your second period, so you're definitely carrying our child. Once Elsie digs her claws into you, there'll be no peace, and you could lose that baby.'

'I won't.'

'How do you know? Is the ghost only you can see a bloody fortune-teller?'

'In a way, he is. I stopped him frightening Muth, because she has to be here on my birthday.'

'Why?'

'It's part of his plan.' She paused. 'He made a mistake, scaring her. I thought ghosts wouldn't make mistakes.'

'I'm still human,' Callum whispered in her ear.

'No, you're not,' Alice yelled. 'Show yourself to Dan and prove I'm not crackers.'

The kitchen window suddenly turned to stained glass.

'Can you see that?' she asked her husband.

'Yes,' he whispered.

'That's my uncle,' she said. 'My dad's older brother. Don't be afraid.'

'I'm not.'

'Good. Because we're staying in this house until after my birthday no matter what happens.'

The colours faded before reappearing at the table. Dan began to shake, and Alice screamed, 'Leave him alone.'

Callum disappeared.

'I'm all right,' Dan said softly. 'Go and get our food. Seeing what you see has given me an appetite.'

'Right.' She walked to the other end of the kitchen and picked up two plates of salad. Turning to walk back, she stopped before taking a step. The salad landed on the floor among shards of broken crockery. 'Dan?' She rushed to his side. 'Be careful, please.'

'Hello, love.' He was upright, steady and without crutches. 'He did a miracle,' Dan whispered.

She couldn't answer. Tears poured down her face like a miniature waterfall in a hurry. Her Dan could walk again.

Callum spoke, and they both heard him. 'The miracle's nothing to do with me; it's from a power above and beyond. Walk, Dan. Enjoy yourself.'

Twelve

'Daniel Quigley, will you get in this bed immediately if not sooner?' Alice snapped. 'You won't forget in your sleep. The walking isn't going to disappear while you're unconscious.' She threw up her arms in a gesture of despair. 'Keep still; you're making me dizzy.' He was like a soldier on parade – straight of spine, heavy of foot, head held high.

He paused in his travels. 'How do you know?'

'How do I know what?'

'That I'll still be able to walk in the morning.'

She sighed heavily. 'Because it's a miracle. When Jesus turned that water into wine for the wedding, it didn't go back to being water.'

'How do you know?' Dan repeated. 'Were you there?'

Alice rolled her eyes to the ceiling. 'No, I was at home cleaning my front step, you clown, and my name wasn't on the guest list. Oh, God help me.' Dan hadn't sat for more than a few minutes all night, pacing up and down the bedroom, the hall, the kitchen, his own recovery room and the bathroom. 'Stop it,' she ordered yet again. 'And use your walking sticks, at least, for Olga and Peter's party. I'm not having you taking the shine off their celebration. Either that, or tell everybody before we go.' She spoke to the dog. 'Frank, don't walk with him – you're egging him on.'

Dan left the room and returned yet again with a very tired boxer in his wake. The dog, already talented when it came to looking sad or confused, stared blankly at his master. This was all a terrible shock for a canine. The master couldn't walk, but now he could. And he wouldn't stop. Frank had had enough. He yawned, turned his back on both owners and went to find his basket in Dan's recovery room. He scrabbled about, rearranged his cushions, then dropped like a stone into an exhausted heap. His guardians had not made much sense today, so rest would be a welcome change and an escape from guarding two very strange people. Within seconds, he was snoring.

'Even my muscles work,' Dan said, noticing a twinkle in the corner of the room. 'He's here, Alice. He's over there near that chest of drawers with your dad's photo on top. Does he never sleep?'

She sighed. 'He's dead, you loony. Just shut up and get into bed.'

'I had muscle wastage, didn't I?'

'I know. Callum – tell him, will you? He's getting on my bloody nerves here.' She nodded before addressing her husband. 'He says get in your hospital bed or he'll fix you so you can't walk tomorrow. This baby and I need to get a proper night's sleep, so get lost. And he didn't do the miracle; God did it.'

Dan glared at her. 'I didn't hear Callum saying anything.'

'No. It's usually just me he talks to.'

'How do I know you're telling the truth? How do I know you're not acting the giddy kipper?'

'You don't. But I'm hoping you'll do the sensible thing and get some rest, because I'm going to have the baby confirmed this week.'

He grinned knowingly. 'It's not even been baptized.'

Alice narrowed her eyes, telling herself inwardly that she'd been right all along, and men were definitely stupid. They had no common sense, a lack of imagination, and they were loud.

He interrupted her moment of private thought. 'I know – you mean the pregnancy confirmed by the doctor.' Holding up a hand, he backed away towards the door. 'I'm going, I'm going. I'll sleep in my own room.' He left. Alice listened while he placed himself in the bed next door. 'And stay there,' she yelled, 'unless you need the bathroom.'

'Yes, your majesty,' was his quick reply.

She snuggled down in the bed. How to explain a miracle to family and friends? 'Well, we have this rainbow in the house, you see. It's a bit like stained glass, all different colours, and it drifts

292

round the rooms. So does my dad's tobacco smoke. A baby cries, but not as often as it used to. The rainbow or stained glass is my uncle Callum, and he got God to do a miracle, because he's been promoted at work – he's an angel and God made Dan walk again.' It would sound bloody pathetic, and she might well end up in the madhouse in a back-to-front coat and on tablets. 'Still, it would be a rest, I suppose,' she murmured.

Alice sat up and inflicted grievous bodily harm on an innocent pillow; she would achieve some comfort even if it took further assault and battery on linen and feathers. Ah, he was snoring. Callum had probably made that happen. 'Give me a few more awake minutes,' she begged her now invisible companion. 'I need to think.'

She thought. With just one clear day between now and the wedding reception, Dan would be forced to rush around tomorrow telling everyone about the sudden improvement in his health. Otherwise, he would need to play to the gathering on Saturday with crutches, sticks, wheelchair... He should definitely not be the centre of attention at the celebration. 'You got it wrong again, Uncle Callum. Your timing's rubbish.'

Callum was back yet again. He chuckled. 'The best wedding gift you could offer to your friends would be Dan's God-granted ability to walk.'

'We got them some velvet cushions and a crystal vase.'

'I know. They'd rather see Dan's crutches on the rubbish heap. Learn to play life by ear, sweetheart. Write your own music, live in the moment and enjoy the good bits. You can't always follow the score of other composers, you see. Life happens, and sometimes you have to go along with your flow. Stop worrying. Stop trying to control everything. And go to sleep.'

She heard no more, though the dream she experienced that night would stay with her forever.

'I baptize thee Callum Daniel in the name of the Father, the Son and the Holy Ghost.' The priest wore happy vestments. A gold and white maniple hung from his left arm, while the chasuble glistened with strands of precious metal thread. Gold meant Eastertide or Christmas. Or did it mean baptism? Alice couldn't see the baby, as he was in the arms of Nellie's Claire, his godmother.

The scene faded, though priest and church remained the same. She looked down at her dress; it was cream with long sleeves, and the skirt rested on beige shoes in good leather. She turned to her right and saw Harry. He was very smart: dark grey suit and a cream shirt with a tie in a slightly darker shade. In his buttonhole sat a yellow rose. The man looked wonderful, yet she felt sad, because Dan was dead.

When the priest had finished speaking of consanguinity, affinity or spiritual relationship, bride and groom had nothing to confess. A small congregation was asked to declare any reason why the couple should not be joined, and a whirlwind travelled up the aisle. It brought with it an icy draught, and Alice shook in her new shoes. She felt cold and afraid.

'There is no Callum,' the whirlwind shrieked before placing itself in the front pew to the left of the bride. It was Muth, of course.

Stained glass behind the altar was suddenly brighter. In its centre, a figure stood out, arms raised to heaven, beautiful wings unfolding and spreading outward. Muth was wrong; there were two Callums, one Alice's baby, the other a dead uncle who was part angel, part comedian and part crazy magician.

But the priest's garments had changed. He wore purple. Alice's cream dress became a dark suit, and a coffin stood on a bier at the foot of altar steps. Who was in the coffin? Was it Dan?

She woke at ten minutes past one, wet with sweat. Her first thought was for her unborn child; her second for her husband. She slipped out of bed and went into the next room. The dream had been in the wrong order – it should have been baptism, funeral, then wedding – but dreams were seldom sensible.

'So it's all right for you to wander about in the night,' grumbled the man in the bed. 'Whereas I have to do as I'm told by my bossy wife.'

'I'm borrowing your bathroom. There's a baby growing above my bladder, so I go more often these days.'

Dan yawned. 'Leave the money on the shelf above the sink,' he ordered before falling asleep again very suddenly.

In the bathroom, Alice soothed her heated face with cold water. Callum was up to mischief again. Had he sent the dream; was it some kind of warning about the future? No. Everyone had dreams, and not all dreams were sent by angels.

'Nothing to do with me,' Callum said. 'I was concentrating too hard on Mr Atherton's poker.

Ten pounds he won tonight. The dream was your own, dear Alice. I know what it was, because it remains in your mind, but don't be afraid. As I told you earlier, life has its ebb and flow. Ride the waves, because you can't stop the moon's phases, nor the water's rhythm.'

Alice shook her head. 'You talk in riddles,' she accused him.

'Do I?'

She sighed. 'What's poor Olga doing while her new husband's playing cards for money he doesn't need?'

Callum chuckled. 'She's playing, too. The other two fellows have no chance. Fascinating to watch; nobody smiled.'

Alice shook her head sadly. Gambling was a crime, and the country was going to the dogs. Mind, if the dogs were anything like her Frank and Olga's Leo, there would surely be a chance of recovery. Recovery. Her Dan could walk again, and that was a recovery that should be truly appreciated. But she still worried, because he would probably go too far, too fast, and wear himself out. Worn out herself, she returned to bed, placed herself in the hands of her guardian angel and slept till morning.

Homing pigeons, they were supposed to be, but they didn't know north from south, east from west, tail feathers from beak, and he was fed up with them, because they seemed to be educationally subnormal. Blue Lady was safe, caged with others at her new place where all she had to do was look pretty for Liverpool's pigeon folk who visited in droves. Or were they in flocks? A few of these birds were ... confused, Harry supposed. They'd had too many moves, and he should feel sorry for them, but what could he do? And he was supposed to be taking Vera on holiday–

'Psst.' His train of thought did an emergency stop at the buffers, while his heart went into overdrive. It was just gone eight o'clock in the morning, and he hadn't yet had so much as a cup of Horniman's, but Alice was here, peering over the wall that separated the houses. She was mouthing at him.

He stepped to the wall. 'What?'

'Dan can walk,' she said bluntly. 'It was Callum's doing.' With the exception of her husband, Harry and Olga were the only ones she trusted completely to believe in her. 'Happened last night,' she said. 'I had a job trying to get him to stop. But the fact is, he's mobile again.'

'I see.' What he saw was a sweet little face with tendrils of blonde hair acting like tiny dancers in the light, summer breeze. Clear blue eyes were wide and solemn, while her mouth continued to look extremely kissable. 'So?' he asked. 'I'm glad he's back on his feet, but why are you acting all mysterious?'

'So he can walk. We can't do any more meetings by accident when I take Frank out for exercise.'

'But we only talk, queen. We've not done anything wrong since ... since you made my front room curtains. Even then, we didn't do much.'

'I know; I was there, if you remember.'

'Where is Dan now?'

'He's gone up to see Olga and Peter so he can

297

prepare them before the reception.' She paused. 'I know what'll happen, Harry.'

'What?'

'He'll go all busy and wear himself out dashing here, there and everywhere. Course, now that I want a word with Uncle Callum, he's keeping a low profile.'

Harry nodded pensively. 'Look, Alice, you didn't want Dan struggling up and down Penny Lane on crutches or sticks for the rest of his life, surely? In the time he's got left, let him live. By living I mean having a choice, a laugh, a pint down the pub. He can go to the pictures, the football, have a game of arrows or dominoes. It's a freedom he probably never expected.'

She nodded her agreement. 'I suppose you're right.' She changed the subject. 'When are you going to get rid of that loft?'

'When the birds stop coming back to it. They're creatures of habit.'

'I know,' she snapped. 'Bad habits. One of their bad habits is all over my sheets and towels. They're filthy little devils.'

'They're birds, love. Shit happens.'

'Don't be crude, and draw them a map. Show them where they should be and where they shouldn't.'

'It doesn't work that way, and well you know it. They'll learn in time.'

She bridled, her chin held high and arms crossed on top of the wall. 'It doesn't work at all. They've dumped stuff on Vera's blouse, the one she was supposed to be wearing this weekend for posh. She's only had it on once. Your feathered

298

friends' offerings bleached the colour out. She had a mad screaming fit in the middle of a play on the wireless. A woman was having trouble with her twins and ... stop grinning, cos it's not funny. These twins were going bad ways, then Vera found her ruined blouse, so she missed the end. She'll never find out what happened, will she?'

Harry sighed resignedly. 'I'd best buy my ticket for Australia, then.' Vera in a bad mood was not something he looked forward to. 'She'll be round here any minute screaming and ranting.'

'No, she won't.' Alice's chin thrust itself forward, and she folded her arms on top of the wall. 'She'll be here, at my house. I made the blouse, and I've enough material left to replace the back where the pigeon left its deposit. Get bloody rid, Harry.'

'It might have been a wild bird – any bird.' He could tell she wasn't going to back down. 'OK. I'll get rid; I'll poison them.' He waited; his statement had finally shut her up. Or down.

'You can't be doing that,' she cried.

'I can. There's only four regulars left, anyway. The rest have had the sense to move on.' He kept his face as straight as possible. 'I'll get rid of them for you.'

She gulped. 'Will it hurt them?'

'How the pigging hell should I know? I'm not a pigeon, and I've never been poisoned. Well, not so far.' This was one of the aspects of Alice that he adored. She was mouthy, obstinate, fierce, proud and ridiculous. Oh, and she was beautiful with it.

'Aw, but–'

He turned away so that he could no longer see her; she was flustered. When flustered, she was something else, and the Yanks called it cute, or so he believed. He didn't want Dan to die, but how long would he have to wait before keeping Alice in a permanent state of flustered?

'You can't do that,' Alice repeated. Emotion sat in her throat, causing her voice to wobble slightly. 'It's cruel,' she concluded.

He gave her his full attention. 'Then shut up and put up. What can't be cured must be endured. Or poisoned.'

Their eyes locked in the small space that separated them. 'You won't, will you?'

'Of course I won't, you soft girl. I'm just acting as daft as you.' His mouth spread in a wide grin. 'Don't ever change, Alice.'

'Into what? Clean knickers?'

'Please yourself when it comes to underwear. What I mean is don't turn reasonable, predictable and boring. And I'll take the loft down and they can follow the rest to their new home. That doesn't mean they won't dump on your washing, because they might do a fly-past or a lap of honour before moving on.' He lowered his tone. 'I love you, Alice.'

'Do you?'

'You know I do.'

Her face coloured slightly, emphasizing fine cheekbones in a face whose underlying structure was nearly perfect.

'You should be a film star,' he whispered, 'but I'm glad you're not. If you were in Hollywood, I wouldn't be able to keep an eye on you.'

300

'Shut up.'

He shut up for a short time. This relationship – if such it might be termed – was unusual, to put it mildly. He was waiting for the death of a man he admired, for a woman who was probably pregnant with the child of that man, and there was no time frame. This situation might well continue for years, and Alice was determinedly monogamous. But he hated to upset her. 'Are you going to tell the doctor who said Dan was worse? Will Dan go to see him?'

Her blush deepened. 'I lied,' she admitted. She could tell him now, surely? Because he knew about Callum, believed in Callum, and believed in her. 'It wasn't the doc, Harry. You knew about my otherness, but I wasn't sure you were ready to accept the idea of a haunted house. Callum told me. He's never wrong. He's daft, but accurate. Sorry.'

Harry shook his head slowly. 'He's good with paintwork, too. Don't lie to me ever again, Alice. Love between a man and a woman has to be honest. It's not like parents and children, because that sort of love forgives no matter what.'

She blinked. 'I'm sorry.' He looked so hurt, so crestfallen. 'It's wrong of me to expect you to wait. Take your own advice – go and live, meet a nice girl who doesn't tell lies.' She turned to step down from the chair on which she had been standing.

'Jesus Christ,' Harry exclaimed.

Alice righted herself, staying where she was and looking at Harry's garden. The grass was covered in a blanket of split light, one huge rainbow with each colour merging with its neighbours. 'That's Callum,' she whispered. 'He's come to tell you what he told me. It's all right, only you and I can see it.' She waited. 'Has he spoken to you? Have you been visited by the ghost from next door?'

'Yes, I have.'

'And?'

'He said we'll be married, but I have to be patient. Then he said I'll need to continue patient if I'm going to live with you because you'd drive a saint mad.'

'I told you he was daft.'

'No, he's dead right. You're more trouble than a box of monkeys.'

The rainbow disappeared, only to be replaced by Vera, who entered the scene via Alice's back gate. 'Have you told him about these last few birds?' she demanded to know, her thumb jerking in Harry's direction.

'I have.'

'I'll poison the beggars,' Harry told the newcomer.

Vera's head moved to look at Alice, then at Harry, then back to Alice. 'He can't do that, can he?'

'He can,' was Alice's reply.

Vera's fists were on her slender hips. 'He'll be had up by the RPSC hay.'

'Did you hear that, Harry?' The tremble in Alice's tone betrayed her barely contained laughter.

'I did.'

The visitor closed the gate. 'That is unexactable behaviour,' she cried. 'Poor bloody pigeons.'

Harry stroked his chin thoughtfully. 'I could strangle them instead. Then you could make pigeon pie. That's what we did during the war, though they were mostly wood pigeons; they're also called collared doves, I think. In fact, we're shipping some in from America so they won't die out completely. We seem to have eaten most of them.'

Vera's mouth closed with a snap. The old teeth had loosened somewhat during her time in hospital, but her new ones fitted nicely. 'You are not killing no pigeons,' she spat.

'OK.' He stepped back. 'I've had my instructions from two members of the superior sex, so I'll go in and make myself a cup of tea. Good luck with the sewing, Alice. See you later, Vera.' He went into the house, closed the rear door and placed his forehead against it. If he started laughing, he would never stop. So he didn't bother to start.

Toothy Tommy gazed into the area that had housed lion cubs.

Nigel winked at his wife; Tommy was perplexed.

'They're not the same as lions, are they?' This rhetorical question was delivered by the Irishman.

'Well, they're Asian for a start,' Marie said. 'And striped. There are people who live among lions and get accepted by a pride. Tigers don't negotiate. I think they're missing the sense of humour gene that lions have. But too many tigers have been killed by people with guns and an odd sense of fun. We have to save some before they become as extinct as dinosaurs. There are only a few thousand Bengals left.'

'And their mammy's dead?'

'Yes, Tommy.'

'That's sad, so it is. But tell me – how do we feed these snarling babies?'

Marie shrugged before walking back to the kitchen. She returned with two enormous feeding bottles, placing them where the cubs could see them through the bars. 'Don't worry, Tommy – they'll be gone in days.'

'Don't they scratch?' Tommy stood fascinated while his employers helped each other don back-to-front coats in what looked like thick leather. 'Straitjackets?' he asked.

'And gloves,' Nigel answered. 'They don't go for faces. Yet.'

At that moment, the larger of the cubs approached the gate and stared at Tommy, who was transfixed for several seconds. When he retrieved his senses, he blessed himself in the good old-fashioned Catholic way, though he continued to stare at the animal.

'Tommy?' Marie stared at him.

'The great decider,' he whispered.

'What?' the other two asked almost simultaneously.

'If God had a face, He would look like this. If I'd had no faith, I would have found it today. There's a poem – something about fearful symmetry, I think. Would you ever take a look at that? It's magnificent. An architect was involved here. This thorough killing machine was made to God's design. I never in my whole life saw anything so beautiful. It's the embodiment of anger.'

'Well, we're going to wean them,' Marie said. 'It'll be a short stay.'

Nigel agreed. 'That's the truth. We have to get them from milk to meat, because the Jersey folk are too busy. So we're doing this, but we're trying not to let them come in contact with human blood in case they develop a taste for it. They hunt singly and with dreadful intent. Tigers can kill humans.'

'And if they do kill people?' Tommy asked.

'We shoot them. There's nothing else to be done. Come on, Marie.'

Tommy stayed on the safe side of the bars. The animals were not as large as Hercules and Jason had been, but they were a great deal more furious. Yet he still saw God when he looked upon their mind-numbing beauty. Huge padlocks would keep these creatures contained until Chester found a special out-of-the-way place for them at the zoo. But they would not become exhibits – oh, no. The pair would go to India and learn to hunt. Like God, they were deciders between life and death; like God, they were mighty and beautiful. Tommy decided to steer clear. If blood might be spilt, it wouldn't be Irish.

Later that day, he found the poem in his collection. Blake asked questions about hammers, anvils, furnaces and forges, yet he echoed Tommy's feelings. Something as beautiful and deadly as a tiger was proof that a designer existed. On Sunday, Tommy would go to Mass.

For the first time in her adult life, Vera Corcoran was living with a gentleman. Yuri was kind.

Although he had spent many years imprisoned in Siberia, he was no criminal. An excellent gardener and a meticulous cleaner of windows, he was already appreciated by his clients in the Penny Lane area.

At home, he mucked in with the rest of the family, clearing out grates, making fires, fetching in coal, cooking occasionally, washing dishes, polishing shoes, laughing and joking with the boys. He also helped Vera with her English, guiding her away from her usual malapropisms and teaching her the words she ought to be using.

She bought a little hard-backed notebook and wrote down what she was learning, breaking up long words into syllables and practising them when she had time. A foreigner was helping her with her own language; that was amusing, but she accepted the strange situation, because Yuri was clever.

Vera had begun to take an interest in herself, accepting at last that she was as good as anybody else in these parts. Underneath her wig, little curls had started to grow, but she decided that she wouldn't show her new hair until it reached a decent length. Sporting her wig and a decent frock, she made several trips to the dentist and was provided with dentures that fitted instead of clattering about and whistling whenever she said a word that contained an s or two.

Of course, her efforts were noticed and discussed, especially by females in the area. 'It's ever since that funny little Russian bloke moved in' and 'Is she setting her cap at a Communist?' found a niche in many a conversation in shops or over cups of tea in kitchens. It was only fair; the general consensus among women was that Vera had gossiped about everyone and everything, and it was now her turn to be scrutinized.

She knew. She knew they were jangling on about her, calling her a tart – had they forgotten already that she'd been in a coma, that she'd almost died after being attacked by a drunken lunatic? Some people had very short memories. And anyway, Yuri was her lodger, a good man and a very helpful friend. Every home needed a Yuri, and she was keeping hers; if the gossips were jealous, they should find their own Russians.

So it was a happy Vera who picked up an official-looking envelope on the day of the Athertons' belated wedding reception. 'Bills, bills, bills,' she grumbled to herself as she placed the offending item on the dresser. How long had she been waiting for a sideboard to replace this item of her mother's? The dresser filled one wall and was deep enough to cover almost a third of the floor space. A nice little Utility sideboard would have been appreciated, but Jimmy had always poured half his wages down his– She paused mid-thought. The back of the envelope displayed a solicitor's name and address. 'Bugger,' she snapped, 'is he still tormenting me from beyond the grave? What the hell did he get up to during the last weeks of his life?'

But when she slit the flap and pulled out the single sheet, her heart went mad, beating like a drum performing in the Orange parade. She flew to the front door and flung it open, only to find Yuri standing there, bucket in one hand, letter in the other. 'Postman handed it to me,' he cried.

'Olga is giving me her shop.'

'And me five thousand pounds. I can buy the house, Yuri. No more rent. A sideboard, new beds, a nice suite for the front room.'

They went into Vera's parlour.

'Vera?'

'What?' She still couldn't believe what was written in black and white.

'She gives me flat above her shop, too.' He watched Vera's expression as it changed. She would rather he remained here, he thought. 'Not yet, because the money must come from America.' He decided that his landlady didn't look happy. 'You will work with me in the shop?' he asked.

She nodded. 'Course I will.'

'And we shall live here? This is my home now. I live here just a short time, but am happy. The flat we can rent to someone who needs it.'

'Good idea.' Vera wiped her eyes on the sleeve of her cardigan.

Yuri stared at the page in his hand. 'We say nothing, Vera – nothing at all. Olga has made gifts to you and to me, but we don't know if she has done the same for other friends.' He stared hard at her. 'Don't tell anyone.'

'I won't.'

'Shall we sit?'

Vera nodded, and they both perched on clean but battered armchairs.

'We trust each other, then?'

She agreed.

'You see, I was given some beatings when in prison. I am not man any more.'

'Oh? Well, I've never seen you in a skirt and

blouse, and you've not asked to borrow my wig.'

He almost laughed. 'My man parts do not work any more. But I want to stay here, in Liverpool, in England, so will you consider marriage with me? I can care for you, and you do same for me. We can share bed, talk, and we can hold each other.'

Vera stared hard at her lodger. Had she heard him right? 'You are a man,' she said eventually. 'You're the best man I know, good with my boys, helping in the house, working hard and not too much drinking. I'll have to talk to Tony and Neil, because they're young men now, but–'

'But yes if they say yes?'

'Yes.'

'Thank you for this, Vera. I am honoured.'

She sniffed back a sob. 'No, I'm the honoured one, Yuri, living with a man who doesn't scare me. Another thing that frightened the daylights out of me was knowing that Tony would have killed Jimmy sooner or later. He would, you know. He plays the big man who doesn't care, but he loves me. They both do.'

'As do I. For your generosity, your wrong words, for making me smile. We will be man and wife except for making love.'

She grinned. 'I'd sooner have fish and chips anyway.'

'With the mushy peas?'

'I can take or leave the mushy stuff, love.' She frowned. 'I'll have a Russian name.'

He shrugged. 'And this is a problem?'

The frown changed into a grin. 'No. I like confusing people.'

He gazed round the room. 'I will make your house pretty.'

'No; our house, Yuri. This will be our house.'

Alice was sweeping the front path when Dan returned from his visit to Olga and Peter. 'You look exhausted,' she scolded. 'You should take it easy. Short walks to start with. I know it's a miracle, but you have to get used to walking again.' She awarded him a stern stare.

'Has the postman been?' he asked breathlessly.

'Post's on the little table in the hall. Why do you want to–' She didn't finish her question. He had entered the house. Grumbling under her breath, Alice pursued her now mobile husband. She found him ripping open an envelope. 'What's the hurry?' she asked. 'It's only another bill.'

He scanned the page.

'Dan?'

He gave her his attention at last. 'Once the emeralds and diamonds are in the hands of the American collector, and when what they call proof of provenance is validated, we get money.'

Alice blinked stupidly. 'Money? What money?'

'From Olga and Peter.'

'But ... but why?'

'Come in here. I need to sit down.'

She followed her husband into their bedroom and perched next to him on an ottoman at the foot of the bed. 'What's going on?' she asked.

He gave her the full story. Olga and Peter would have too much money. Had they made wills, they would have been denied the pleasure of distributing their gifts, so they were doing it now. 'They don't want anything going to the government when they die, you see,' he said. 'They've no children, and they won't be having any, and so,' he shrugged, 'we're rich.'

'Rich? I don't think I know how to do rich.'

'We stay as we are and stash the money for the baby.'

'Good idea.'

He went on to tell her about a donation to Chester Zoo via Nigel and Marie, about Yuri and Vera, Harry, and the new business belonging to Martin and Nellie's family. 'Then there's some going to orphans and domestic pets and research into illnesses. They're givers, Olga and Peter.'

Alice pondered. 'So they're leaving the shop, giving it to Yuri?'

'They are.'

'Where will Olga and Peter live?' She didn't want to lose her friends.

'Menlove Avenue, so round the corner, more or less. They're getting a car, too. Oh, and a cottage in Wales or somewhere – they've not decided yet. Why are you smiling?'

'Because it's so Olga-ish. Like you said, she's a sharer. Whatever she gets, she'll give away half of it.'

'Not in this case, love. That set of jewellery is the last valuable remains of a great royal dynasty. Americans collect stuff like that. They love looking at what they've never had and never will have. Anything King George has breathed on would be worth quite a few dollars. Olga will have plenty left, believe me.'

Alice smiled broadly. 'Then they can live well,

311

Olga and Peter. They might even visit Moscow one day, just as she's always longed to.'

'Don't you want to know how much she's giving us?'

'No, not yet. It's not ours; it's for baby Callum.'

Nellie was crying. 'Happy tears,' she sobbed. 'Lovely woman, lovely woman.'

Martin put an arm round his wife's quaking shoulders. 'Hey, come on now, or you'll make it rain.' He read the letter again. 'Well, with Kevin and Paul turning into good carpenters, this will help them to buy nice wood and better tools.'

'And we can move nearer to them.' Nellie dried her eyes. 'Let the flat over our shop and get a little house up Crosby or Waterloo.'

'Good idea, love. Now, I'll feed these two starving babies while you go and tell our daughters the good news. And don't start crying – nobody's died. Send one of the girls to tell the boys – they're in the workshop today.'

When Nellie had gone, Martin shook his head in mock despair. His beloved wife was very emotional of late, a situation for which she blamed something called 'the change'. 'It's her hormones,' he told the babies as he spooned mushy food into their hungry mouths. 'Your grandmother doesn't know whether she's coming, going, or having a breakdown. I think I'll send her down to your dads' garage for a refit, an oil change and a good look at her gaskets. What do you think?'

'Goo,' Simon replied.

'Exactly. Carrots with mashed spud and gravy all over your bib.'

Once fed and orange-juiced, the babies were taken through to the back for changing. Simon settled into a cot, while Keith sucked his thumb and stretched out in the twin pram. Martin grinned at them; they were easy now, but God help everybody in another twelve months when they'd be running about like a pair of pups looking for trouble. He returned to the shop to find the nappy bag.

Trouble? Trouble was here, standing across the road and staring at the premises formerly designated Turner's Ice Cream Parlour and Milk Bar, now known as Myers and Holden, Furniture Restorers. He opened the outer door, but he couldn't march across the road to tell Elsie Stewart where to go, because he couldn't leave the babies. She gazed at him. He glared back at her.

What followed would be forgotten by very few who were shopping along Smithdown Road on that day. Like a bolt from a crossbow, Nellie Browne sped over to the opposite pavement. In her hands she held the long pole whose purpose in life was to raise and lower blinds over the Brownes' shop window. She brandished this weapon in the manner of a knight preparing to unseat a mounted rival.

'Oh, stop it,' Elsie screamed.

'Stop it?' was Nellie's loud response. 'Stop it? I've not bloody started yet, you miserable old cow.'

Doors flew open, spilling shopkeepers and customers onto the pavement.

Martin chose the lesser of two evils and left the babies. 'She'll kill her,' he muttered under his breath as he swerved to avoid the coalman's stationary horse. 'Nellie!' he called. 'Put that bloody thing down.'

She seemed to have gone deaf, because she didn't even look at him. Nellie had her mother pinned against a plate glass window, the business end of the implement pressing into the older woman's belly. Nellie's mouth was moving, though no one heard her words until Martin reached her side. 'I will,' she was saying. 'I will kill you.'

Elsie blinked, though she seemed unafraid. Nellie was the quiet one, the ugly daughter, the girl who'd never given any trouble. 'No you won't, Nellie.'

Martin wrenched the canopy tool out of his wife's hands. He stumbled back, so tight had been his wife's grip on the pole. By the time he had righted himself and thrown down the makeshift battering ram, she had her mother in a stranglehold. 'Nellie, for God's sake—'

But he needn't have bothered, because Collins the greengrocer dashed up the road and threw a bucket of water over both women. Ian Collins sniffed. 'Well, that's what I do when I see two bitches in a scrap – what's the difference?'

'You're all witnesses,' Elsie yelled.

'And we all know what you are,' said the greengrocer.

The small crowd hummed its agreement, while Nellie appeared not to notice her dripping hair and clothes.

'Let me go!' Elsie's nails drew blood on Nellie's neck.

Martin separated the two females and hung

314

onto his soggy wife. When he spoke to his mother-in-law, he did not raise his voice. 'You stay away from us and ours. If you don't, the books go to an accountant and a lawyer.'

The older woman's jaw dropped.

'Theft and fraud,' he continued. 'You took a good ten to fifteen bob a week out of that till.'

'She what?' Nellie's face was red with anger. 'You bloody, stinking old bag. What sort of mother and grandmother steals from her own family? How many times did you beat the living daylights out of Marie and Theresa? You never even mourned when Constance, Judith and Sheila got wiped out by a bomb. Twisted, that's what you are' She pointed a finger at her mother. 'Yes, I was the quiet one who caused no trouble, but no more, no bloody more.'

Martin understood. Nellie now had daughters, grandsons and a share in two thriving businesses, so she was discovering a degree of confidence. A born matriarch, she'd protect her dependants for as long as she could and, when necessary, this new ferocity would be allowed to boil. On a level not too far from the surface, Martin Browne admired the woman he loved; she had recreated herself, losing weight and inhibitions in a matter of weeks. Alice had played her part, of course... 'Go and see to the babies, love. They're asleep in the back, but I had to leave them to save you from yourself.'

When Nellie had gone, Martin turned on the hateful woman who had poisoned the lives of the Browne family for years. 'I hoped she'd find the guts to kick you out when I left, but you kept her where you'd always shoved her – at the bottom of the pile. I should have stayed, if only to stop you seeing off our daughters, and I regret doing what I did. But we're happy now. Leave us alone, or you'll get done for fraud.'

There was no answer to that, so she snapped closed her mouth, which had hung open since Nellie's attempt to strangle her. She turned and fought her way through the audience that circled the scene. As she walked away, boos and jeers could be heard above hand clapping.

'And don't come back,' Ian Collins advised loudly.

Seething and dripping wet, Elsie Stewart made her way down towards town. She couldn't get a bus, not while her clothes were soaked, and being saturated at her age was not a good thing.

It was him, she decided. It was Martin Browne who'd got Nellie all riled up. 'Will I still be going to Alice's a week on Sunday?' she muttered under her breath. Alice was very protective of her eldest sister. And could people really keep Elsie Stewart away from Smithdown Road? Of course they could.

Oh yes, it was him. What could she do about him? If she so much as breathed near Martin Browne, he'd have her sued for fraud. All she'd come for was to look at Myers and Holden, Furniture Restorers, because they'd advertised in the paper, with a photograph of Martin, who fronted the shop, while her grandsons-in-law were in charge of the restoring side of the business.

'A pound to a penny, I bet Janet and Claire are running Browne's,' she mumbled. Oh yes, it was all happy families for them, for Marie and for

Alice, too. While she, who had reared them, was taking a long walk in wet clothes. Yes, she'd been a firm mother – firm, but fair. The further she walked, the angrier she became while filling in the past with her own colours. She had never hit them hard, had never kept them tied to the house for too long. Perhaps she'd lost her rag once or twice, but who wouldn't? The raising of seven daughters had been no mean feat, especially with a husband who'd started off useless and ended up dead.

As she neared her so-called home, she slowed down a bit. Her clothes weren't as wet as they had been, but she kept off the beaten track as best she could, because defeat at the hands of Nellie and Martin hurt. She wanted as few people as possible to see her in this state of disorder.

'I'll find a means of slowing the buggers down a bit,' she whispered to herself. In her seventies, she remained alert in the brain department, and that was the main thing. Also, there was no hurry. She must give them time to come to terms with today's events. Then she would strike back.

Thirteen

The clothes dried quickly enough, though Elsie Stewart's anger continued to ooze until it contaminated every drop of blood, every cell, in her slight, furious body. Ian Collins, a fellow trader during Elsie's years on Smithdown Road, had

317

tried to drown her like some feral alley cat. Madam Helen Browne would be all right, because Madam-usually-Nellie was younger, fitter – especially just lately – and she lived close by, but...

What had happened to the other Nellie, the quiet, stupid Nellie, who today had turned into a virago reminiscent of Marie and Alice, those two beautiful, impossible daughters so full of cheek, disobedience, and sheer bloody-mindedness? Damn them. 'I might have been better off if they'd all copped it with that bomb, all seven of them.' She'd been a waitress, an usherette in a cinema, a cleaner. She had toiled to feed and clothe the younger ones after Chippy's death, and she had worked her fingers through to the bone. 'Mostly for the special one,' she muttered, 'the ungrateful little bitch.'

Elsie threw her soggy shopping basket across the room. 'Martin bloody Browne,' she hissed. She would have to be especially cunning, because damaging him was one thing, but Nellie, too, knew about the so-called fraud, which meant that direct action was out of the question. How, then? How was she going to administer punishment?

Sideways, she decided. A different target in a different place... The kettle boiled. While dunking biscuits and drinking a welcome cup of tea, Elsie began to formulate her plans. The three musketeers were inseparable. Hurt one, hurt all. Today hadn't been the end of something, oh no. It was just the beginning.

Frank, after stealing and eating Alice's ice cream cone, was now running about with what looked like half a tree. His owner sat on a bench and watched her dog and his antics, her mind still filled by the almost incredible knowledge that her husband could walk again. He had gone to town with Peter; he wanted a new shirt and tie for the reception this evening. And he was doing too much by far.

'Hello, beautiful.'

She looked up at Harry; he was the beautiful one. 'Oh, it's you.'

'What a miserable way to say hello. Shall I go away?' he asked.

She sighed dramatically. 'Just don't get too friendly. Any one of our neighbours might come along and I don't want to–'

'Don't want to be the talk of the bagwash?'

'Something like that.'

He placed himself at the opposite end of the bench. Her mad dog was dashing about with the bough of a tree, while Alice was looking gorgeous as usual. 'Did the doctor confirm your pregnancy?'

'A gentleman wouldn't ask that sort of question,' was her swift reply.

'I've never claimed to be a gentleman. You were getting the results today.'

Slowly, she turned her head and stared at him. 'True. And yes, I'm expecting a baby boy next spring. I have to call him Callum.'

'Who says?'

'Callum, of course. Our ghost, my father's older brother. You have met him – remember? Harry?'

'That's me.'

'Dan's dashing about too much. He could have

319

another stroke if he doesn't watch out.'

Harry thought about that for a few seconds before delivering his opinion. 'He's probably excited, Alice. I'm sure he'll slow down sooner rather than later. It's his life, so let him live it. What else can you do? Lock him up?'

She burst out laughing, raised a hand and pointed. Her puzzled boxer was trying to walk between two trees, but the timber he was carrying proved larger than the space available. 'Mad husband, mad dog,' was her delivered judgement. 'I suppose they make a good pair. I just wish my Dan would slow down.'

'I don't want him to die,' Harry said quietly. 'I've got used to him. He's a good bloke and an ace poker player, damn him. Two quid he's had out of me so far. Mind, he's got Peter coaching him. Pete's teaching Olga now, and she is bloody lethal. In fact, if she went to Monte Carlo, we'd have to contact all the casinos with a warning – "the Russians are coming".'

'She will be a devil at poker,' Alice laughed. 'I wonder if her name means grim determination in Russian? She doesn't do anything by halves – it's all or nothing.'

'Good marriage, that one,' he said. 'Why are you still giggling?'

'Oh, Harry you don't know the half of it.'

'Tell me.'

She turned and looked at him; he was a handsome devil. 'Don't go jangling to anybody. If you do, I'll get Callum to put a curse on you.'

'Trust me. Well, trust me unless you're up a ladder hanging curtains.'

Alice took a deep breath. 'Before they were engaged, she talked to me, asked me would I buy a hat or a pair of shoes without trying them on for size. So I told her I wouldn't. Then she said she was going to try on Peter.'

'For size?'

She shrugged. 'He was her first, and she's forty-seven. She probably gave him marks out of ten. Anyway, she told me he was all right, so she was going to marry him. The butcher was after her, you know.'

'With a meat cleaver?'

'No, you daft beggar. With two pork chops and a few sausages. Bribery.' Alice scanned the field for her dog. Frank must have turned sideways to get his branch through the row of trees, but he was now imprisoned and trying to get back out without turning sideways. 'Go and get the damned fool for me, Harry. He's stuck again.'

'OK.'

Alice watched as the man who might well become her second husband strode across the grass. Loose grey slacks and blue shirt failed to disguise toned muscle that expanded and contracted as he moved. Oh, and he had a very good bum. This was a sin, she advised herself inwardly. Was she willing Dan to die, or was she simply admiring the scenery? Well, a cat could look at a king, and Harry was no king. He was a plumber.

He returned with dog and tree part. 'I grabbed it off him, but he went back for it. I think he's for taking it home. Don't worry – I'll see to it when he gets fed up with it. I'm dismantling the loft, so what's one more tree on top of that lot?'

321

She chuckled. 'Vera's face when you said you were going to poison them.'

'Your face was the same when I told you.'

'Told me what?'

'That I was going to do away with the pigeons.'

'All right, all right.' She changed the subject. 'Olga's giving her money away before she's got it.'

'I know.'

'Are you on her list?'

'I am.' He lowered his voice. 'You have a lovely face.'

'And you've got good muscles. I was watching you when you went for Frank. And I'm wondering is it just lust, or do I love two men? Then there's this baby, and—'

'And I'll be there if and when ... well, I'll be there. Dan's asked me to look after you if anything happens to him. Alice, it was love at first sight for me. Or maybe first sound, when you spoke to me. I can't lose you.'

'Don't talk soft – I'm going nowhere.'

Frank stood by with his treasure at his feet. He was taking it home and would brook no argument.

A breathless Neil arrived on the scene. He threw himself at the bench and sat between the woman who had helped Mam come back to life and the man who had found apprenticeships for him and his brother.

'Are you all right?' Alice asked.

He shook his head and waited for his breathing to settle. 'I went for spuds and cabbage,' he managed after a few seconds. 'Cheaper down

Smithy Road. And she had the wotsit – that thing you use to pull the cover down over the window when the sun shines.' He gulped more air.

'Who did?' Harry asked.

'Mrs Quigley's sister.'

'My sister? Our Nellie?' Alice was flummoxed. Nellie with a weapon?

'Calm down, Alice – let him speak.'

She glared at Harry. 'Shut up.'

Neil picked up his thread. 'Yes – Mrs Browne from the paper shop. And she shoved the end with the hook against this thin old woman – I think it was your mother. It was frightening; I nearly dropped the spuds.'

Alice closed her eyes for a few moments. Old Elsie wasn't flavour of the month in Nellie's book these days.

'Take it easy,' Harry advised her.

'I'm all right,' she snapped. 'Sorry, Harry. I will be OK.'

Neil continued with his story. 'Somebody took the pole thing off her, then she had her fingers round the old woman's throat, and the old woman was scratching her. Anyway, somebody chucked a bucket of water over them and the old woman went away.'

The colour drained from Alice's face. 'When?' she asked.

'Er ... about half an hour ago. When it had all stopped, I took the shopping to Mam, then knocked at yours, but there was nobody in, and Frank didn't bark, so I thought I'd try here.'

'Bugger,' Alice breathed. 'You two go home. Take Frank and his tree. I'll have to go and check

323

our Nellie.' What the hell was going on now? She nursed the strong suspicion that it was her own fault for inviting Muth to Sunday dinner.

Leaving the pair to look after Frank and his sacred wood, Alice made her way up Penny Lane, turning when she reached Smithdown Road. In the newsagent shop, she found Claire, but no Janet. Janet had gone to tell their husbands that Olga would be putting money into the business. 'It all kicked off,' Claire told her. 'Our Janet only missed it by a few minutes, but she left through the back door, so she saw nothing. Mam used the awning pole from here, from this shop. She came to tell us about Olga's money, and then–'

'Where's your mother now?'

'She ran in when it was all over, got dried and changed upstairs because somebody threw–'

'I know about the water, love.'

'She'll be with Dad and the babies.'

'The other shop?'

'Yes. Mam's upset.'

'Don't you worry, love.'

'I'll try, Auntie Alice.'

Alice took herself down to the new shop. Just before she reached it, Callum spoke. 'I told you it would be better if I kept her away. I was right.'

'Bog off,' she whispered from the corner of her mouth. He had better leave everything alone until April, because she had a developing baby to think about as well as a daft husband. Dan probably had delusions of immortality after the miracle performed by God via Uncle Callum, while she needed to be calm and ... normal. Normal? Living in a haunted house? That wasn't going to help

324

towards calm, was it?

She walked into the new shop. Nellie was seated on a dining chair, one of a refurbished set on sale, while her husband stood behind a small counter. 'Hello, Alice,' he said.

Nellie waved a finger. 'This is your fault,' she told her sister.

'I never told Muth to come here, Nellie. She's having her Sunday dinner with us next week, that's all.'

'Go away,' Nellie whispered. 'Go before I get that pole again.'

Alice straightened her stance. 'So you want to kill my baby, do you?'

The older woman's jaw dropped. 'I didn't–'

'You didn't know? Do you deserve to know? Because you are turning into Muth. Remember the strap and the slipper? What's the difference between them and an awning pole, eh? What's the difference between my baby and whatever's going on in the stomach of a seventy-odd-year-old woman?'

'Hang on,' Martin shouted. 'Don't be saying stuff like that to her – she's had enough stress for one day, thanks.'

'No, I won't hang on. Muth could have cancer, an ulcerated bowel – anything. Bodies start to wear out after nearly three-quarters of a bloody century. Don't be surprised if she has you up in court over this, because she was walking down a public street, a shopping area, and you saw red. I don't like her, but Nellie committed a crime by assaulting her.'

'She was standing and staring,' Martin managed to say. 'Giving us the evil eye, she was. And she won't sue, because I told her I knew she stole from the till for years.'

Alice put her hands on her hips. 'What do you want? To sell tickets? To charge people for standing and looking in shop windows? Because you'll be bloody lucky to get that past Parliament.' She returned her attention to Nellie. 'Why didn't you see red when she made your family's life hell, eh? Can you only see red when you have a man to guard your back?'

Nellie, stunned by her little sister's ire, offered no reply.

Martin came to stand beside his wife. 'It's nothing to do with having me here. Nellie's got a cob on because she's a grandma who doesn't want your evil mother coming near the babies. Elsie got rid of our daughters, and we had to find them. We missed the first part of our little grandsons' lives. And you expected us to say yes to your invitation? Did you really think we'd sit all nice and tidy after dinner drinking tea with a witch?'

Alice had no more to say. She turned on her heel and marched out of the shop. Dashing tears from her cheeks, she walked homeward.

'Alice?' Callum whispered.

'And you can piss off,' she mouthed. Until the eighth of April next year, she needed to keep Muth onside. That was when Callum planned to do the big reveal, after which everything would get back to normal. She wondered about normal. Was normal shy, unassuming Nellie making war on Smithdown Road? Was it Marie having baby lions in the house and a llama in the back garden?

She entered her own house, closed the door and leaned on it. 'Or is it me with a ghost, Dad's tobacco smoke, and a husband who suddenly jumped to his feet as if Jesus had told him to take up his bed and walk?' And Harry, who occupied too much space in her head, especially when she was asleep. 'Hormones,' she told the empty house.

It wasn't empty for long. As soon as the kettle was on, Vera arrived. 'Did our Neil tell you? I wish I'd gone for me own veg now.'

Frank and Harry arrived.

'Where's his tree?' Alice asked.

'My garden. It'll do for firewood when he's fed up with it.'

Vera was keen to get to the bottom of things, but she couldn't be heard, because Frank was barking.

'He says he wants his timber in his own garden,' Alice said.

'What happened and why?' Vera asked when the noise stopped.

Harry took Vera to one side while Alice brewed tea. 'Don't ask, love. Look at her face – she's been crying. Nellie lost her rag with their mother. Leave it.'

So it was an awkward trio sitting at the table drinking tea. 'Your blouse is on our bed, Vera.'

'Thanks, love. Harry, you never poisoned them pigeons, did you?'

'No.' A heavy silence descended on the kitchen. Harry stood up. 'I'd better leave you two to get painted and decorated for tonight. I've a spare tin of undercoat if you need it.'

'You cheeky devil,' Vera said. 'We're natural beauties, me and Alice. Aren't we, love?'

Alice nodded.

'Course, there's me wig and me teeth, I suppose.' Vera grinned and left, picking up her blouse on the way. 'See yous later,' was her parting shot.

They were alone. He pulled a chair towards her and sat down again. Folding her in his arms, he licked the evidence of tears from her face before kissing her gently on the mouth. 'My girl,' he whispered, 'my beautiful girl.'

Alice shivered. The cleaning of her face had provided some of the most intimate seconds in her whole life. She wanted more, of something for which she found few words. Dan was a wonderful man, though she was beginning to realize that he lacked something in the imagination department. The way Harry looked at her, the words he used in rare moments like this one, his smile, the tiny corner missing from an incisor ever since, as a young boy, he had pinched a bike and crashed. She swallowed.

'All right?' he asked.

She wasn't. She wanted him, and she couldn't have him, because Dan's baby was in her belly and ... and she wouldn't allow herself to become adulterous. Catholicism was a heavy burden to carry. 'I wish...'

'You wish what, angel?'

'That I had no morals. That Moses had never found the ten commandments up that mountain.'

Harry's smile was rueful. 'No. I wouldn't change a thing about you. Even if we're still waiting in our dotage, there'll be nobody else for me. I love you just as you are, stubborn, too pretty for words, funny, unpredictable and a good cook. What more could a man ask for in a beloved neighbour?'

She giggled. 'You only want me for my scouse, right?'

He nodded.

'The secret is to use lean mince with your stewing steak.'

They both jumped when Callum spoke. 'Go now, Harry. Back door, quick as you can.'

As the back door closed, the front opened to admit Dan and Peter. Sometimes, though not often, a ghost could be useful, Alice thought. Now she had to tell her husband and Olga's about Nellie and Muth.

A clatter in the rear garden announced the arrival of Frank's dead piece of tree; Harry must have heaved it over the wall. Alice opened the kitchen door, allowing the dog to be reunited with the current object of his affections. No doubt he would reduce the fallen limb to sawdust, which would probably be spread the length and breadth of her beautifully kept home.

Dan and Peter entered the kitchen, and she began to tell the tale all over again. 'With the mood our Nellie's in, she might not be at the reception tonight, Peter, and I don't think Martin would come without her.'

Sawdust, Harry and Nellie had made for a very odd day, but Alice would cope. When it came to coping, women had precious little choice...

'They've only known one another for five minutes,' a surprised Peter told his wife when he returned from his outing with Dan. 'Vera and Yuri? Never in this world.'

'She told me herself, Peter. We were same, you and I. Just weeks we knew each other when we married. How did Dan manage with the walking?'

He sat down. 'He's OK; had the sense to take a stick with him. I thought Vera would steer clear of marriage after what she went through with that husband of hers.'

'They will live in house with boys and run the shop together. I made sure they carry on with Christmas book for customers.'

'And leave this flat empty?'

'They letting it to somebody of good character who will be caretaker when shop is closed. Oh, and engagement is a secret until after tonight is finishing. She says this our party, not hers and Yuri's.'

'Right.' Peter was quiet for a moment. 'Have they got something to hide?'

Olga shrugged. 'Vera is saying he not a full quid in the trousers. Does that mean what I am thinking?'

He shook his head. 'Depends what you're thinking.' After watching the blush painting itself along her cheek-bones, he smiled grimly. 'I think I know what you're thinking. And we keep that to ourselves, too. Bloody Siberia, I'll bet. Whippings and beatings and kickings. Poor Yuri.'

She agreed. 'I believe Vera will be happy at last, because her first husband was bad man. He hurt her many times. Perhaps he forced her when he came home angry. Yuri will look after her, and she will care for him, too. After many years of starving, he now has good food, comfortable house and nice neighbours.'

'And she'll get a good bloke who'll appreciate her. I'm glad, then, Olga. OK. Now I'd better tell you about Nellie.' So the tale was related yet again.

Olga was not surprised. 'This is bad mother. She pushed Nellie to the edge, and Nellie jumped, but this time, she jumped where she stood instead of running away. She fight for husband, for daughters, for grandchildren. Shall I go there? Shall I go down the road and tell Nellie and Martin they would be missed at the party? It would be sad if they did not come, and Marie might be upset, because it's in her house.'

'Well, I'm not going to say no, love, because you should do what you want to do, but I wouldn't interfere. She may be hoping that none of us knows about it or at least that we're not discussing what happened. But it's up to you.'

Olga paced about for a few seconds. 'I do not want to make it worse. You are right, Peter. I stay here, get ready for party. Oh, so much happening, and poor Marie and Nigel just back from Jersey.'

'They're off to Africa in a few weeks, and I wouldn't bet money on them coming back. It's their hearts' home. He says somebody's got to start saving big cats. There's folk out there doing just that already, but he's determined to join in.'

'Alice will miss Marie.'

'I know, Olga. She's already worried about Nellie, I bet. Now, calm down and start getting ready for our party. We can't mend everybody's troubles, can we? Anyway, I'm going for Frank; Leo needs company. They can play together in the yard.'

Agreeing with every word, the bride went to bathe and wash her hair. It promised to be a long night, and she would need all her strength to function well in the midst of so much tension. Poor Alice, poor Nellie – and Martin, too. But it was very much a case of carrying on no matter what. They would be celebrating Mr and Mrs Atherton's marriage and she, as Mrs Atherton, intended to be radiant.

'Nellie, it's none of Marie's doing, and you know that – and she's the hostess. And what about Olga and Peter? This is their wedding reception, not just some night out in a pub. Olga's sold all that jewellery belonging to her mam, and she's giving us some money to buy a better life for us and our girls and the babies!'

Nellie shrugged. 'I know, Martin. It's just that I–'

'It's just that you, Marie and Alice are the three musketeers. You've always stood by one another through thick and thin. Why weaken that link, love? I'd miss them, too, with having no family of my own!'

'I know,' she repeated.

'Our girls have got the other two grandmas to babysit, so Janet and Claire will wonder where we are tonight. You've got to let this drop, Nell.'

Her mouth was set in a hard, thin line, as if drawn on by an infant in his first week of school.

'Talk to me,' Martin begged.

She stared at the floor for several seconds before speaking. 'It's our Alice,' she stated. 'And something else, something I used to remember, but it's gone out of my head. Our Alice knows Muth's evil, but she's invited her round for Sunday dinner a week tomorrow, and she asked us to call in, didn't she? That was when I lost my rag. You know our Alice has always hated Muth more than I did, more than Marie did. Now, she's going to break bread with the twin sister of Judas. Talk about two-faced...'

'There'll be a reason. Alice Quigley does nothing without a reason, as you very well know, queen!'

'Then I want the reason,' she snapped.

'Shall I go and ask?'

Nellie wasn't going to hide behind her husband; hadn't she recently been accused of doing just that? She was fifty-three years of age, head of a family if everybody discounted Muth. Elsie Stewart had never been a mother, so it was time for Nellie to step up. 'Can you mind the shop and two babies at the same time?' she asked.

'Course I can.'

'Right.' She nodded. 'Well, I'm going to have this out with my sister before it grows bigger than the pair of us. I'll be back.'

She went to pick up her summer-weight jacket from the flat over the other shop, stopping only to tell her daughters where she was going. Leaving through the back of the building, Nellie began the

333

walk to Penny Lane. She wanted answers.

Alice wasn't in. 'She's gone to buy some stockings,' Dan told her visitor. 'She said her old ones have ladders big enough for Jacob, whoever he is. Come in. I'm in the downstairs bedroom, but there's a couple of chairs in there now. Are you all right, Nellie? I believe you haven't had the best of days, thanks to old Elsie, as per usual!'

'You've heard, then?'

He paused momentarily; he could see she was upset. Nevertheless, he chose to speak the truth. 'I've heard? I think the whole of Liverpool has the story by now. What the bloody hell happened to you? It's not like our Nellie to go marching about with an awning pole.'

'And you walking again,' she said quickly. 'I reckon the North Pole knows about that, never mind an awning pole. I'm really happy for you, Dan.'

'You don't look happy.'

She sank into one of the chairs while Dan used the other. 'I'm not, love, not really. I mean, how do you feel about Muth coming here for her Sunday dinner? Do you really want to sit down and eat with her?'

He offered no immediate reply.

'Do you?' Nellie persisted.

Dan shrugged. 'Put it this way, Nellie, if the chip shop opened on Sundays, I'd be in the park eating with my fingers. It's something to do with Alice's ghost, Callum, I think.'

Nellie blinked several times. 'You believe in him?'

'He made me walk again. I think – I'm not completely sure – but he might have been tormenting old Elsie. Something's going to happen on Alice's birthday next year, so she's softening her mother up, because the old cow has to be here.'

'It's her birthday, too. Alice was born on Muth's fortieth, and it was ... it was terrible. Stuff happened – weird stuff, I mean. I can't remember now, because somebody climbed into my head and rubbed it out.'

'Callum. He will have had his reasons for making you forget, Nellie.'

'What are you on about now?'

'You have to trust your sister. Alice is different and sometimes difficult, but she's honest to the core. You were the one who worried about Elsie being out in the world on her own as an elderly person. Alice didn't know you'd flip your lid when she suggested coming round after Sunday dinner.'

Nellie walked to the window and stood at the side of the bay that gave her a view up the lane. There was no sign yet of Alice. How long did it take to buy a pair of stockings? Without turning to face her audience of one, she delivered again the reason for her change of heart over Muth's isolation. 'I lost the girls. Martin left in the hope that I'd come to my senses and throw my mother out, but she robbed me of all power. She has a way with her, and she made me feel stupid. Martin found out about the babies. We had missed months of their lives. That was when my real hatred for Muth was born. And yes, before you

335

ask, I did want to kill her. I just lost my common sense in a street filled with people.'

'And if Elsie goes to the cops, or a solicitor?'

She raised her shoulders. 'Apparently she fiddled the books and stole money from the shop. We have her over a barrel, as Martin put it. Oh, Alice is coming now.'

'Right. I'll go into my recovery room and leave you to it. It's better if the two of you sort this out. You put the kettle on, love. And good luck.'

Nellie watched as her brother-in-law walked away. He looked as if he'd never had anything wrong with him, so perhaps Callum really was a worker of miracles. What the hell was she going to say to their Alice? Sorry? Was she sorry? Yes, she was.

She walked through the hall and into the long kitchen. This was a smashing room, with a place for dining furniture at the end nearest the hall, and with the business area close to the back door, the two parts separated by open shelving where ornaments and best crockery were displayed artistically. She had a good eye, their Alice. Compared to the Brownes' flat on Smithdown Road, this place was luxury.

As she set the kettle to boil, she heard the front door opening. With a straightened spine, Nellie turned to face her baby sister, the one who'd been born on Muth's fortieth birthday ... there'd been towels, sheets, a pillow. Blood, a lot of blood. As for the rest of it, Nellie couldn't remember.

'Hiya, Nellie.'

'Hello, Alice.' That was supposed to be what people called the ice-breaker, though both women wondered whether the greeting might be little more than the bell at the start of a boxing match. 'I'm sorry,' Nellie said.

'Me, too. It's hormones with both of us, I think. You on the change and me pregnant.'

Was it really going to be this easy, they wondered simultaneously?

'Why did you do it, Alice?'

'Make that brew and I'll tell you.' The younger sister flopped onto a dining chair. 'Where's Dan?'

'In the back room.'

'Give him a cup first, Nellie.'

When both women were at the dining table, Nellie asked, 'Why, love? Why feed her?'

'Because she'll take months to feel easy with me and Dan. I need her sweet as sugar by our birthday.'

Nellie cleared her throat. 'Sweet as arsenic would be more likely.'

'You think I don't know that? I'm not daft, sis.'

'So why are you bothering?'

Alice shrugged. 'I'm under orders. Well, not completely, because I can override him.'

'Who?'

Seconds ticked by. 'Wait a minute, and don't get frightened!'

'Eh? What do you mean?'

'Just sit there and relax. He won't hurt you.'

Nellie frowned. 'Frank? He wouldn't hurt a fly.'

'Not Frank. Frank's visiting Leo, anyway; Peter took him up earlier. He'll be back soon, because Olga will be doing herself up for tonight. Just keep quiet a minute.' She sat back, arms folded. 'Callum?' she shouted.

The air shimmered, as if the rainbow needed to be thin in order to cover the whole room. It wasn't vivid. Alice looked at her sister. 'Can you see that?'

Almost paralysed by fear, Nellie whispered, 'Yes.'

'That's Callum, Dad's older brother. He was haunting Muth, so I stopped him. He's playful, daft and Irish in spite of the surname Stewart. It's Scottish, from the time when the Scots and the Irish changed places or something. Think of him as a mentally unstable guardian angel.'

The shimmer brightened.

'You can stop that before you start,' Alice chided. To her sister, she said, 'He thinks he's a bloody magician working the halls and clubs. Now, he says we'll know everything come April next year. Muth has to be there, so I'm buttering her up.'

'Margarine would do for her,' Callum said. 'Hello, Nellie. Don't be afraid, I'm not dangerous. Yet.'

Nellie's jaw dropped.

'So you hear him, then. You are honoured. He helped to make Dan walk. He introduced himself to Harry, too. And he wanted to keep Muth away from all of us till next year, so he started messing about like a poltergeist.'

'I didn't.'

'You did. So I stopped him,' she told Nellie. 'Callum, shut up for a few minutes, will you?'

The senior sister closed her gaping mouth. 'So you have power over him?'

'Some. He works through me. After all, I'm the

338

seventh child. When we moved back into this house, my otherness got stronger. That was his doing. You can go now,' she shouted, her words directed at the pale rainbow. 'And don't go messing about in my sewing room.' Alice turned to her big sister. 'He hides my tailor's chalk when he's sulking. Like an overgrown kid, he is.'

Nellie was calmer by this time. 'So you treat him like you treat everybody else? Even though he's dead?'

Alice chuckled. 'Dead? No, he's on the move all the while, can be in several places at once, and he makes us so-called alive folk look dozy. Now look, Nellie. To get back to what's been happening between me, you and Muth, let's just stick it on one side and ignore it. I won't have her here every Sunday, but I'll let you know when she's coming.'

'Can't you leave it for a while? Like till the end of this year? That would still give you three clear months.'

'No.' Alice shook her head. 'I've got to get her used to being here, so that when it's our birthday she'll come for a party – just me, her and Dan. Only there'll be one or two more here, witnesses for Callum's final show. A gallery for him to play to. When it's over, he'll disappear, and this house will get some peace.'

Nellie burst into tears. 'She's our mother,' she sobbed. 'That night when you were born, she was screaming. Dad stayed with her till the midwife came. I remember that bit, but the rest is gone. I had to take towels and things off Dad, but there was more to it than blood and screaming.' She dried her eyes. 'Dad was never the same after it was over. Neither was Muth, because she got nastier and nastier until she turned herself into the creature we know and don't love today.'

Alice thought about that. 'I think she's always been nasty. She has three brothers and three sisters, all abroad, and she never hears from them. Muth was the baby, the seventh child – wouldn't you think the others would have kept in touch?'

'Does she write to them?'

'What do you think, Nell? Has she ever given a thought to anything beyond her own comfort? Anyway – enough. Are you wearing that blue dress I made for you? It brings out the colour of your eyes.'

Nellie managed a feeble smile. 'I am, love. I got a very near match – bag and shoes, then a turquoise necklace and earrings. You were right – turquoise and navy look great together.'

Alice giggled. 'I'm always right. Had you not noticed?'

Elsie had made a friend among the residents; well, Phyllis was a friend of sorts, she supposed. They drank tea together occasionally, played dominoes, talked about the weather or the price of fish, and Phyllis would babysit the house sometimes, occupying Elsie's quarters on a Friday or Saturday night, thus allowing Elsie to go out to the pictures.

But on this particular Saturday, the caretaker was in no mood for a visit to the cinema. After being attacked by her own daughter in broad daylight, and having been soaked by Ian Collins, she was still simmering, and she knew it wouldn't take much for her to return to boiling point. Phyllis agreed to sit in and listen to Elsie's wireless, so Elsie was out of the door like a bullet from a gun. Was Marie back from Jersey? If she could manage to hurt Marie, the other two musketeers would feel her pain, as it was one for all and all for one ... oh yes, they took good care of each other.

Walking was good. Being active made her feel positive, as if she were moving towards something rather than running away like a half-drowned rat. She knew where she was heading. Marie, the second daughter, had turned into a jumped-up middle-class do-gooder with a wealthy husband and the only house in this part of the world with a couple of acres and a menagerie. There were animals aplenty, and Marie Stanton, wife of re-nowned veterinary surgeon Nigel, was one of the darlings of various charity groups, a must-have at dinners and party nights.

Elsie stopped and stared hard at the mock Tudor building. Tonight, Nigel and Marie were host and hostess. Near the front window, a massive wedding cake took up space, though familiar faces passed by at each side of the large white confection. Well, this was a bit different, as was the music, whose volume travelled through open windows all the way to the opposite side of the road. Elsie frowned. It was an unusual sound, Eastern European – was it Russian, or Hungarian maybe?

Whatever it was or wasn't, Elsie needed to get away from here, because Alice had a habit of homing in on her, so she retraced her steps and

341

began the journey homeward. She hadn't caught sight of her youngest daughter, but there was never a show without Punch – or, in this case, Judy – was there? And the party would probably continue until the early hours of the morning.

When she judged herself to be at a safe distance, Elsie slowed down. They were holding a wedding reception in Marie's house. She imagined caviar and smoked salmon, pretty little finger foods, game pie and some wonderful desserts. The Stantons probably hadn't suffered much even during the war; rationing remained in force to this day, but not for them. Oh no, people of standing in the community never did without much, did they?

She placed herself on the wall opposite the house for which she was responsible, her body taut, her mind breaking the sound barrier. Phyllis would wonder why she'd returned so quickly. They'd all be drunk down at Marie's place. A game of dominoes with Phyllis might be called for. The party wouldn't be over till well gone midnight; Marie and Nigel would be enjoying the sleep of the inebriated. All for one and one for all. Tonight was the night.

After crossing the road, she took the keys from her pocket. It was time for dominoes, just for an hour or so...

At half past one on Sunday morning, Elsie Stewart positioned herself opposite Marie's house, making sure she was hidden by the trunk of one of a pair of enormous oaks. Her intention was clear and simple; she wanted to allow the outside animals to escape. To achieve that aim, she needed to open a gate at the rear corner of the house. She would be visible from the kitchen, but who would be in the kitchen at this hour?

The landing lights were on, but they always were after dark. Other than this feeble illumination at the top of the stairs, the house was completely dark and still. But Elsie's heart was in overdrive, its quickening beat thrumming inside her ears and making her feel sick and exhausted. Was it worth risking a heart attack? Chippy had died of one of those, and the doctor had said he'd hardly felt a thing, because his heart had stopped before he'd hit the floor – something about bruising or lack of it...

'I'd be no use dead,' she whispered, 'but the three witches aren't getting away with what happened today.' Or yesterday, she supposed. Nellie adored her two remaining sisters, and all hell would be let loose alongside the animals.

Remaining invisible while crossing a road was not easy. People in the Twin Oaks flats, though at some distance from the main pavement, would perhaps catch sight of a small, thin woman, and might speak up once the morning brought chaos to the upmarket area. 'But I'm a caretaker, and I never left my post,' she murmured. 'I am asleep in my bed.' Nonetheless, those in the flats could be going to the bathroom, might be insomniac, or shift workers like nurses or firemen, or even policemen.

Elsie made her way down the side of the house. It had changed. A single storey addition was tacked on to the kitchen, so she would not be visible from the main window under the kitchen sink, since it overlooked the rear garden and the new extension would block the view of Elsie's position. But beyond the extension, and fixed to it, she found a huge cage. It was built around a door, an open door that implied that the new building might be a laundry area, as she could make out the shape of two huge, ceramic sinks. Strange? Yes, it certainly was, an empty cage fastened to a house. Still, some folk moved in mysterious ways, especially when they were lovers of animals.

An open padlock hung helplessly from the cage gate, and she lifted it out of its keeper bar. How careless, she mused. Anyone and everyone could access the house, with or without keys. Perhaps she could release all the inside animals as well – she might gain access through the new laundry room if push came to shove.

She stepped in, pushing the gate into its closed position behind her. And they appeared as if from nowhere, two huge cats illuminated only by the frail light of a half moon. Claws tore at her clothing, finally finding flesh to rip. They rolled her about like a doll, playing with her, tossing her about the cage as if she were weightless.

At last, they stepped back and stared at her. Santa and Claus were used to humans who brought meat and drink, but this one carried neither. After judging her as useless, they wandered back into the laundry room. They had little time and utter contempt for bipeds who carried no food.

Elsie dragged herself to the gate through which she had entered, using metal bars to help herself

344

stand. There was no sign of the padlock – had she left it inside? 'Come on, girl,' she muttered breathlessly, 'it's a long walk home.' She turned once more to look at the cage; the padlock was in place and closed. How? Had she been having a dream? Was the pain a nightmare? 'Come on, soft girl,' she ordered herself in a whisper, 'get walking.'

It was, indeed, quite a distance. Standing upright was difficult, and life was not improved when blood began to gel and stick to bits of torn clothing. Thank goodness there was no one about, she told herself as she made her way back to Brighton-le-Sands.

By the time she reached the large, grey house, it was quarter to three. Quietly, she opened the front door, then her own. After drinking a cup of water, she began the business of removing her clothes. Arms and legs were covered in scrapes, and bruising was beginning to develop. Her coat was ruined, as were cardigan and blouse. Scratches on her back had begun to heal; because of her clothing, they weren't deep, but they stuck to material as she slowly peeled off her bloodied blouse.

Her face looked all right, so she'd better be grateful for small mercies. As she looked in the mirror, she finally realized that she had been attacked by tigers or leopards or cheetahs. Bloody Nigel. Damn him and damn Chester Zoo. No padlock on the bloody cage – he shouldn't be allowed the responsibility for dangerous wild things.

She ran a bath and poured in two capfuls of

Dettol. There was no point in titty-fal-lalling about, so she immersed herself as quickly as she could manage, her mouth closed tightly against a rising scream of pain. 'Control,' she mouthed. 'Don't give in, Elsie.'

'I failed,' she continued when the pain lessened in intensity. 'No horses and donkeys will be stopping traffic and causing accidents today. And I'll be staggering round like a cripple.' Still, Phyllis would call in after church. Elsie's explanation for her condition had already taken root in her mind. She'd heard noises outside during the night, had gone out and fallen badly. No, she didn't need a doctor, but Phyllis could perhaps clean the hallways and stairs.

Elsie climbed out of the bath and, resourceful as ever, tied clean lint to the head of a long-handled brush intended for scrubbing her back. With this improvised tool, she smeared antiseptic cream over the shallow wounds at each side of her spine. 'Damn bloody Nigel to hell,' she mumbled, 'and damn the lot of them at the same time.'

Forced to sleep on her front, and covered by blankets up to the waist only, one disgruntled old woman dozed fitfully. And the nightmare was back, though this time, it was about tigers, and she didn't wake screaming. That padlock. How had it...?

By dawn, she was up and about. She wore lisle stockings to cover the bruises on her legs, while a long-sleeved blouse camouflaged her upper limbs. 'I'll live,' she whispered. 'But there has to be a way of paying them back...'

When Nigel rose, he found Tommy and his teeth already making inroads on the piles of dishes that needed washing. 'I fed the devils,' the Irishmen said. 'Borrowed your suit of armour, I did.' He stopped scrubbing and turned to look at the boss. 'It was very strange. There was blood in the cage, but they hadn't been fighting.'

'And the padlock was on?' Nigel asked.

'Of course it was. The laundry door was open, but. It gives them somewhere to lie if the weather turns!'

Neither man noticed the arc of colour in the sky. Had they seen it, they would have been surprised. There had been no rain...

Fourteen

Dear Callum,

You kicked me hard yesterday, son. Don't ask me how I always knew you were a boy – I just did. Some people are odd like that. I joked with Daddy and said you are probably going to be a hockey player, and you're bringing your stick with you! You are kicking me now, but more gently, so I suppose you ate the stick at half time. Well, never mind – we all get hungry while we're growing fast. Anyway, do keep shifting about, because that shows us you're healthy and happy.

Daddy has felt you moving and he cried tears of joy the first time you wriggled under his hand. He's building your cot and getting mad because it's not easy. I just ignore him, or I'd laugh. He keeps finding new bits and saying there are too many pieces or not enough screws. I told him to leave it and to let your uncles Kevin and Paul make you a cot, because they are becoming successful producers of furniture, but no. Daddy said he has to make his own son's cot, and there you have it – he's as stubborn as a mule, but likeable with it. I know he'll go all soppy the first time he sees and holds you.

I try to imagine you in my arms, your little face, your eyes, your ten tiny fingers and ten tiny toes. But I can't see you yet – it will be almost five more months until you're old enough to come out and face the world. This letter is for you to read when you're a bit older. Your dad and I want you to know that you were loved from the very first day we learned that you were growing inside me. Dad's the one who lies with his head next to my belly and talks to you. I wanted to tell you that the cow didn't jump over the moon, and dishes and spoons can't run, but you'll know that by the time you read this. Sometimes, I wake in the night, and Daddy's halfway down the bed talking or singing to you.

I must apologize for his terrible singing voice. He really can't help sounding like a dog with a sore throat. Speaking of dogs, our Frank already knows you. He stands very close and sniffs as if he's asking are you OK in there. Frank's a character – you will love him. He's a boxer with a friend called Leo – also a boxer – and a pet pigeon. I'll tell you more about the pigeon later.

Today, Daddy and I are going to a wedding so you may hear some decent singing though I'm not promising. It's Yuri and Vera's wedding this time. They live next door on one side, and Harry lives at the other side of us. Your aunties Nellie and Marie will be there today, with uncles Martin and Nigel. There will be photographs to look at when you're here, in the outside world.

Right, let's go back to Frank and his pigeon. Harry next door built a loft for pigeons, but he gave them away to someone who knows more about them. Three or four kept coming back, and Oscar was the one that decided to stay forever. I went in the garden one day in the summer to peg my washing on the line, and I found Frank sitting on the grass with a pigeon on his head. I got pigeon food from Harry and fed Oscar, and this has been going on for a while now. They are very comical when they play. Seeing a dog with a bird perched on his head is enough to make the Pope chuckle.

Harry and Daddy built a kennel for Frank and put a little house inside for Oscar. Frank still sleeps inside our house at night, though he goes in the kennel with Oscar when it rains during the day. We have to lift out the little bird house to clean it, but they are such good friends – it's worth it. The pigeon comes on walks with us and Frank. People stared at first, but they're used to us now. I will put the cuttings from newspapers in the back of this journal. There are photographs, too.

I must go now and beautify myself for Vera and Yuri's nuptials. Vera fell out with the Catholic church when the priest wouldn't talk to her first husband, who was cruel. So we're going to the church of St Barnabas, which is C of E. It's not far – just across the road from the Penny Lane barber shop. I am supposed to ask permission of Father Shaw in order to attend a service in a non-Catholic church, but that's a step too far for me. I give myself permission in matters of faith. God

349

will look after me no matter what.
I will write some more very soon.
All my love,
Alice (Mummy)

Yuri had spent the night before the wedding at Harry's house. Harry was best man, and he had taken Yuri, Peter, Tony, Neil and Dan out on the town for a meal during the groom's last evening of freedom. Poor Yuri had ended up rather inebriated and padlocked to some railings near the Pier Head. After police involvement and a telling off for Harry, Dan, Peter and Vera's boys, poor Yuri was released and brought back to Penny Lane. 'Why?' he asked the next morning. 'Why did you do to me this terrible deed last night?'

'Tradition,' was Harry's swift reply. 'It's what we do – an English thing, like Morris dancing and winning wars.'

'I was cold,' Yuri complained. 'Where were you?'

'Hiding behind parked buses.'

'Why?' Yuri asked again.

'Tradition,' Harry repeated. 'This is Liverpool, England, so get used to it.'

Yuri blew out his cheeks and puffed. 'I do tradition. I can do fish and chips, I can sell firewood and tools, but being fastened to rails is not my idea of England.'

'Tell me your idea of England.'

The Russian pondered. 'Green fields, rain, pretty houses and some lakes and mountains; beautiful women. I looked at picture books in Olga's little library when we were young. And freedom; it means freedom, which is not being

350

locked up in Siberia, or stuck to railings near Mersey. A place called Yorkshire I would like to visit. It looks wild. London I have seen. Many people, but lonely place.'

'Apologies for what we did. Trouble was, we never thought about your past, and I'm sorry we did that on your stag night.'

Yuri grinned ruefully. 'I had enough of prison in Siberia, and did not expect to be chained in England. But it was a good meal. So thank you, but don't fasten me to anything ever again.'

They finished breakfast and went upstairs to get dressed.

'These coats and hats are strange,' Yuri complained. 'I am not looking right in the things. They are from some old silent film.'

'Tradition,' Harry told him for the third time. 'Vera's never had anything special in her life. She was married to the lowest of the low, and this is probably the best time for her so far. Top hat and tails, she wants, so that's what she'll get. Nothing's too good for her, so do as you're told. We've hired them, and we'd better keep them clean. They have to go back on Monday, and the shop folk won't be happy if we cover them in gravy and ale.'

Yuri laughed. 'In Liverpool, you are bossy people. Always laughing, talking, sometimes weeping. Emotional is the word, yes, for people who feel things deeply?'

'Yes, it is. We look after one another. So shut up and get the suit on.'

Dressed as gentlemen from an earlier century, they walked to the church of St Barnabas to

351

await the bride. She would be given away by her two sons. As they entered the church, groom and best man were surprised to find it packed; there was standing room only. Penny Lane, with its many adjoining streets and roads, had come out for Vera. 'They care,' Harry whispered to his companion. 'They're happy for both of you.'

Vera entered with a son at each side of her. She wore a full length ice blue gown with a small birdcage veil covering her newly sprouted curls. A happier woman these days, she had gained a healthy covering of flesh and a sparkle in her eyes. With new teeth and prettier spectacles, she looked happy and relaxed as she approached her second husband to the strains of 'Love Divine'. Her fiancé cut quite a figure in his tailcoat.

Yuri turned to gaze at her. She looked wonderful, as did her boys and Mrs Alice Quigley, Matron of Honour. Halfway up the narrow aisle, the bride stopped. 'Right,' she said, her voice as shrill as ever, 'there's not room for the three of us. You two back off a bit. Alice, come here and walk with me.' The hymn seemed to have died out. 'You can carry on now,' Vera announced to the vicar. 'I was just sorting my boys out. They were standing on me frock.'

A corporate giggle trickled through the church.

Alice smiled. This was how it would always be with Vera; she would invariably let the words roll from her tongue before allowing the world to continue rotating on its axis. Harry was staring, his eyes almost boring into Alice. She loved him, wanted to stand with him, but she was Dan's wife. It was, so far, just a sin of thought, but it was enough to make her worry. Loving more than one man was weird.

She ignored Harry studiously. The shoes were killing her, but she soldiered on in her sapphire blue dress with its cummerbund that echoed the bride's ice blue. Her bulge preceded her, and she had made no attempt to conceal it when designing her gown; she was pregnant and proud.

'Will you stop bumping into me?' These words, spoken loudly by the bride, were directed at her sons. The singing died again. Row by row, the congregation stood and applauded. This was Vera, their Vera. She had been there when some were born, had laid out their nearest and dearest, and had been halfway to a bloody death at the hands of Jimmy Corcoran. Vera must never change. She *was* Penny Lane; her foundations were deep, her eyes were everybody's windows. This gossip-monger was probably capable of writing an account of the area, its history and its residents, all the way back to the early years of the twentieth century.

The bride dug her elbow into the ribs of her matron of honour. 'Do one of your whistles, Alice. Go on. It's better than this poor vicar having to sound off and make them all behave. Showing me up, they are.'

Alice complied, and delivered a noise shrill enough to shatter crystal.

The congregation, which might be better termed audience, shuffled, sat, and spoke in whispers to each other. A confused organist turned, assessed the situation, and started playing a bit of Bach, no singing required. The vicar peered over the top of rimless glasses. He hadn't enjoyed himself so much since VE Day.

When he asked 'Who gives this woman?' Tony and Neil shoved her forward as if trying to get rid as quickly as possible, and chorused 'We do,' rather forcibly. Alice swallowed a giggle; the bride needed no help to show herself up.

Yuri started to laugh, and the vicar joined him. Like a disease fiercer than the plague, glee passed through the gathered crowd until all were laughing noisily. The celebrant leaned forward and begged Alice to do another one of those whistles. When quiet was almost achieved, he announced, 'This is more like a football match than a wedding, what with applause, laughter and a referee with a very good whistle. Shall we continue?'

In the front row on the groom's side, Olga smacked her husband's hand. 'You did not laugh.'

'I've got a headache.'

'Is overhang,' she whispered.

'Hangover,' he replied.

Olga rolled her eyes heavenward. Her husband had arrived home in the early hours and collapsed on the sofa, where he had remained until this morning. He had sworn on the Romanov Bible never to get so drunk again, and she was still struggling to believe him.

Yuri and Vera made their vows, and Olga walked up the aisle to stand with the newly wed pair. With no accompaniment, she delivered a Russian hymn in a beautiful contralto voice. Nobody but herself and Yuri understood a word, though all appreciated the delivery. When new applause died, bride and groom went off to sign the register.

354

It was over. The crowd followed members of the wedding party into the chill autumnal air, and the main players climbed into a charabanc provided by Nigel and Marie. They were waved off by the crowd and by people standing at their front doors or gates. The bride, unable to pronounce her married name, was practising Ivanovski under her breath. Her husband was easy to live with, but difficult to say.

'No matter,' Yuri whispered, 'We learn this at home. Plenty time to get it right.'

'Well, you don't need to learn it, cos you've been stuck with it forever.'

'Shorten it to Ivan,' he suggested.

'Yuri Ivan,' Vera whispered. 'It doesn't sound right.'

'Ivanov?'

She tried that, and it seemed to fit. 'That'll do. Hey, I hope we get trifle.'

Yuri pretended to be sorry. 'We will get dogs, cats, horses, donkeys and a llama. Trifle? Perhaps no.' He grinned. 'Sorry, I am pulling leg. Alice has made trifle with no jelly and lots of sherry. The wedding cake has had so much brandy poured into it for weeks that it will walk to us.'

'Stagger,' Vera said. 'Drink makes walking hard.' She closed her eyes and thought of Jimmy. But Jimmy was gone, and she had a new, decent husband. She had her own business, which belonged to Yuri too, and a shop was a great place for picking up gossip. They were both members of the Penny Lane Traders' Association, and that made her proud. Her beautiful dress made her proud, as did her lovely, gentle husband, as did her reformed and hardworking sons. 'I'm happy,' she told Yuri.

'As am I, Vera. Yes, very happy.'

It will be bonfire night soon, little Callum.

You will both be with us in four months. Now, I must say hello to your sister. She will be Danielle, but we'll call her Ellie, I think. What a surprise, Ellie. The doctor has found two heartbeats, and I feel sure that you two are one of each. I will get twice the joy, twice the love, and twice the trouble, I suppose, but I am so happy to be expecting twins.

'Didn't you believe me, then?' Angel Callum asked. 'I told you about the twins.'

'Of course I believed you. But I had to write something sensible, didn't I?'

'She'll be tiny, blonde and beautiful like you. Callum's going to look like his dad, so he'll be handsome.'

'Good. Now, go away, because I'm writing to my children. And you are harassing me again.'

'All right, I'm going. But I was the one who told you about Ellie – not the doctor.'

She finished her message and sat chewing her pen. What did Angel Callum expect? The idea of her children reading about a ghost delivering messages was not a good one. It was better to say that the doctor had told her. Twins. She would go to see the doctor soon and ask him to listen for two heartbeats. Fortunately, he was getting used to what he called her feyness.

After walking upstairs, she looked into the front bedroom which was still a parlour and sewing room. Everything needed to be swapped back again. The back bedroom would become a nursery for the twins, and she would have to tell Dan that a second cot would be required. 'Jeez,' she whispered. 'I'm not telling him till the doctor does find the second heartbeat. All that banging and cursing – I've had enough of him and his woodwork.'

Dan had a job. The doctor, shocked and delighted by the patient's sudden, unexpected recovery, had given Dan permission to work. He was helping to front the furniture shop, since Martin now travelled about taking orders for bespoke items. Kevin and Paul, formerly Royal Air Force engineers, had turned themselves into carpenters and were doing very well. Nellie was still looking after babies who were now mobile, and she travelled to north Liverpool almost every day to chase and catch crawling infants in order to feed and clean them. She was a busy woman.

Alice, too, was busy. While Kevin and Paul made furniture, she produced soft furnishings for the firm. Fortunately, her advancing pregnancy meant an end to morning sickness, though she was aware that she wouldn't be able to work indefinitely; she was carrying two babies, and was beginning to look like a barrel on legs. Once the doctor had found the second beating heart, Alice knew that her real job would be to make sure that her twins remained healthy; she would cease working after Christmas, though she might continue with a little dressmaking.

Muth came for Sunday dinner twice a month, and was behaving herself for a change. She professed to being happy about her youngest daughter's pregnancy, yet sometimes Alice thought she caught an expression on the older woman's face as if she might be planning something or other. It was hormones, of course. Pregnancy had its drawbacks.

The cover provided by the longer nights of autumn and winter was a boon to Elsie Stewart. At last, she knew where everybody was. She had found the house shared by Nellie's daughters and their families, discovered the workshop behind the garage from which the husbands had meant to make their money, and she'd already known where Marie and Alice lived.

Her relationship with the youngest of her daughters was working quite well, though Dan contributed only infrequently to conversations. But Elsie knew something about Alice; the scene she had witnessed was burnt into her brain, and it made her smile, because Alice had another man. He lived next door, and was a handsome chap...

Harry Thompson had been holding the pigeon. The dog was wagging his rump wildly and making small noises; the bird had wriggled and Harry had laughed. 'They're like lovers, but without the contact,' he had said. 'They're like us.'

Elsie had stayed hidden; she was looking at them through the gap Alice had left in the back door. If her daughter didn't want to be spied on she should learn to close it properly, shouldn't she?

'Loving two men isn't easy,' Alice had told him,

'so yes, I suppose we are like Frank and Oscar, together but separate.'

'But at least we're the same species,' Thompson had said, chuckling.

Alice had taken the bird from him and placed it on the dog's head. Elsie had seen bird and dog together before, but never the two mice playing while the cat was away. It had looked like what people call real love, though it was hard to tell these days, with so many war widows snapping up returning soldiers and sailors and air force men.

Elsie had backed silently away from the door, turned and walked quietly out of the house.

The job continued to be all right. Everyone paid rent on time, and there was no trouble, little noise, and a lack of drunken marauders. Phyllis continued to visit occasionally, but Phyllis was very boring. The good side of boring was a tendency to be biddable, so Elsie allowed the relationship to continue, though the two women came together only once or twice a week.

A few days before bonfire night, Phyllis knocked on Elsie's door. She was tearful when she confessed to the caretaker that her grandson had not been working abroad; he was out of prison today, was staying in a halfway house, and wanted to visit his grandmother. 'Oh, I'm not sure,' Elsie replied. 'It'll be my fault if anything happens.'

'Nothing's going to happen, Elsie. My Lawrence is a good lad who fell in with a bad crowd, and he was in the wrong place at the wrong time. Four of them were sent down, but Lawrie never done nothing. Me son and his wife were as much use as a concrete couch, so it's no surprise that Lawrence joined up with that crowd of scallies.'

Elsie folded her arms. 'He can come in daylight for half an hour, and you will both sit in here with me. That way, I won't be letting any criminal–' she raised a hand when she saw Phyllis open her mouth to protest. 'I know you say he's innocent, love, but he still has a record. I can't let him in any of the bedsits. The boss would have my guts for Christmas decorations and my head on a pole down Crosby beach. Look at me, Phyllis. We're not young, you and I. We need a roof, food, heating and lighting, so we have to hang on here. At least it's cheap.'

'All right – thanks, Elsie. I'll go and see him tomorrow and tell him what you said. I mean, how's he going to get a job while he has a prison record? He could end up living on the streets, and his mam and dad don't give a hoot. He sent me a letter to say he was coming out, and I should have been there to meet him at the gates, but I thought I might show him up by crying. But it meant there was nobody waiting for him when he got out. Like I said before, I'm not proud of my son and the bitch he married.'

Elsie nodded. 'Don't talk to me about families. My lot's useless, too.'

'But you get your Sunday dinner sometimes, don't you?'

'I do. But my son-in-law hates me, so I'm not comfortable. I eat what I can and end up with indigestion every time. You go and see your Lawrence, eh? Tell him I'll get some little cakes tomorrow, and explain that I daren't lose my job

360

by letting him loose in the rest of the house. Try not to worry. We'll play cards and stretch his first half-hour to most of the afternoon.'

Phyllis sniffed. 'You're a good woman, Elsie Stewart.' She left with a handkerchief held to her damp face.

Elsie shook her head. She knew all about damp. She knew all about dripping wet, and she would neither forget nor forgive anyone involved in the incident on Smithdown Road. Sitting in a comfortable chair, she began to think about Phyllis's grandson. Would he be up for earning a few quid? Or was he going to be too scared of prison to risk his freedom all over again? 'I'd have to get him on his own,' she mouthed. Better still, she might find the halfway house and keep an eye on its inhabitants...

She clung to one solid fact; if she hurt Nellie, all three sisters would be bruised emotionally. Marie? Hell, no, because she and her fool of a husband sometimes took in dangerous animals. As for Alice – well, she was the only one who was making an effort to mend fences. If Alice stopped being amenable, Elsie already held a weapon, and its name was Harry Thompson.

It was time to get real, and Lawrence Rigby might well be the means to a perfect end. As long as no one got caught, she mused. If arrested, Phyllis's grandson might well give them the name of the woman who'd paid him to – to what? She hadn't worked that out yet. 'Hurt one, hurt all three.' She whispered her mantra to the empty living room. It had to be Nellie's lot. Marie was untouchable, and Alice was pleasant. And that

361

bucket of water had been Nellie's fault. Oh, and Lawrence was a bad idea except for the fact that there would be others in the house for newly released criminals.

My dear Callum and Danielle,
It will be Christmas next month, the final Christ-mas Daddy and I will have without you. Next year will be all teddy bears and noisy rattles, I suppose. You will be nine months old, so possibly crawling and getting into mischief, but I can't wait.
Ellie, your father managed a lot better when building your cot. He didn't have pieces left over, and there were enough screws. Don't worry about your cot, Callum. I had Uncle Paul give it the once-over, and he says it's strong and sturdy, so that's another weight off my mind.

'Alice?'
She didn't even turn her head. 'Not now, Angel Callum.'
'Yes, now. It's important.'
Alice slammed down her pen. 'You are harassing me,' she accused him.
'So get a solicitor and sue me.'
'Go away. I'm writing to my babies.' Picking up her pen, she suddenly became aware that the room's walls were brightly coloured. He was serious, then. 'OK, you win.' This angel in his current state would not be ignored. She laid the pen down again. 'What's the problem?'
'Your mother. You have no idea what that woman is capable of.'
'And you do?'

'Oh yes, I most certainly do. So does your dad – you'll be seeing him in April.'

'On my birthday.'

'And Elsie's. Alice, she's up to no good.'

She pondered, a hand resting on her swollen belly. 'Go on.' After several months of living with Callum, she knew when he was fooling and when he was not. He had shown himself to Dan and to Harry, so if she refused to listen, he would probably start mithering one or both of the men in her life. 'I'm ready,' she sighed.

He began by reminding her of the day Nellie had attacked her mother with the awning pole. 'I tell you, even if she lived for three hundred years, Elsie would keep that occasion at the front of her mind, as fresh as a daisy, as infuriating as a mosquito. Well, that night I had to tidy up after she was attacked by Nigel's two baby tigers – remember them? He got the pair of them onto solids and moved them on.'

'Was she hurt?'

'Do you care?'

Alice pondered. 'I'm not sure. Why would she go near Marie's house, anyway? Nellie was the one who started the kerfuffle, so what was Muth doing round at our Marie's?'

'It's hurt one and hurt all three, isn't it? It's been like that since you lost four of your sisters and there were just three of you left. Then Marie escaped. You joined her and married Dan. Nellie was treated as if she lacked brainpower, so you've all looked after each other. Your mother meant to let all the Stantons' outside animals go. You see? Punish Marie and Nigel Stanton, and the other two sisters would have been collateral damage – job done. Anyway, I took charge of a certain padlock, and she was mauled.'

Alice kept quiet while absorbing this information. She remembered Muth walking awkwardly because her back was hurting, supposedly the result of a fall outside the house that contained her little flat.

'Yes,' Callum said, 'you're right – it was tigers, not a fall.'

'Get out of my head, please.'

'Listen to me, young lady–'

'Don't call me a lady – I'm a woman.'

Callum chuckled, and colours on walls shivered. 'Woman, then. It's Guy Fawkes soon, isn't it? Lots of bonfires. One extra behind a row of businesses may not get noticed.'

'You what?'

He explained. Elsie had followed a young man to a place that housed recently released prisoners. 'She was clever enough not to use him, because she knows his grandmother, but she hung round yesterday until she found a hard man. He's going to burn down Kevin and Paul's workshop. Your mother intends to pay him to commit arson on the fifth of November. We need to move fast.'

Alice snapped her mouth into the closed position, and blinked several times. 'Just another bonfire,' she mumbled.

'Yes. Behind petrol containers that may be almost empty, but could do harm if the fire spreads. It has to be stopped, but not by me.'

She remained seated. 'We could warn the police.'

'Yes, and your mother would be in jail.'

Alice jumped to her feet. 'Isn't that what she deserves?'

'Of course. But she also deserves to be here on her birthday and yours. After that night you won't be bothered by her again for the rest of your lives. That I can promise you, and angels don't lie.'

She walked to the window and stared out at nothing in particular. 'I suppose you could force yourself to stop her, Callum.'

'We want her here next April. I can stop her by wiping it out of her mind. But I have a better plan, one that will make her think before she leaps in future. Two plans, actually. One, you could go round and tell her that everyone knows what she's planning, because the criminal community is spreading the word.'

'And plan number two? Because I don't know any criminals.'

'Right – let's move to idea the second. Tell her the police know about a plan to commit arson at the woodwork shop.'

'I don't know any policemen.'

'Use your imagination, Alice.'

'I am all out of imagination and full of two babies instead. Leave me out of it. None of this is fair on a woman who's pregnant. Twice.'

'An anonymous letter might do the trick.'

'Fingerprints,' she reminded him. 'And there are handwriting experts.' The room shimmered. 'You're smiling,' she accused him. 'I don't know what you find so funny.'

'You're funny. Alice, I leave no prints, and no

one will recognize my writing. Anyway, your mother isn't foolish enough to show the authorities a letter that charges her with planning an arson attack.'

'Oh, I see – I never thought.'

'Exactly – you're pregnant, so cloudy-minded. I'll even deliver it, cut out the postman. She won't know who sent it, and there'll be no prints, no evidence. Yes, it will be done by me, but she'll think it's the work of an earthling.'

'Shall I get you some paper?'

'No. You have fingerprints. I could remove them, but I want you, above all, to be safe. I'll get what I need elsewhere. Trust me? Trust between the two of us is vital.'

'Do I have an option?'

He laughed again. 'No, although you reached the right conclusion anyway. With my help, of course.'

'But you make all the decisions. You pretend to ask.'

Colours faded. 'I'll go now, Alice. The letter will be on her doormat before tomorrow morning. There's no need to involve the family – you know how nervous Nellie gets. Claire and Janet will worry, too, and the men would probably break the necks of Muth and the hired arsonist. So say nothing.'

'Have faith in me, Callum.'

A brief flash of light touched her arm. 'I have. I love you, Alice.'

She tutted and muttered something about not wanting three men – life was bad enough with two. But when he'd gone, she felt the wet rolling down her face. She wept because she loved him, and she wasn't sure why. 'I suppose I'll miss him,' she told herself. 'Well, you miss earache when it stops, don't you?'

Callum never left her completely. Inside her head his voice whispered, 'I heard that.'

'Oh, go and write your letter!'

'It's done.'

'Quick worker, aren't you?'

'Different time zone. In fact, we go beyond time to a new dimension.'

She had to ask. 'What's He like?'

Callum chuckled. 'God is hard to describe in terms of the five senses awarded to humans. Imagine a white light so bright that your eyes would need shielding. Or music so beautiful that it fills your very soul until it brims with joy. He is faith, hope and love and He's everywhere. He loves you, too. In fact, He loves everyone, sinners as well.'

Well, that was good to know. 'Callum?'

He seemed to be keeping quiet; was he up to mischief somewhere? She smiled, remembering his magic tricks. 'Callum?'

'Shut up, I'm praying.'

Alice shrugged. 'Typical,' she snapped, picking up her pen. 'Now, where was I?'

Transfixed almost to the hem of paralysis, Elsie scanned the letter. It was like looking at an old religious tract, so perfect was the calligraphy. What the hell could she do?

She found her feet and began to pace about. The letter told her thou shalt not kill, though that was the only biblical reference. Nevertheless, it

367

read like something delivered from a pulpit on a Sunday morning, possibly by a hellfire preacher from one of the more basic branches of Christianity.

What the hell should she do?

A cup of tea. Yes, a hot drink might wake up her dead brain. As she set the kettle to boil, she noticed that her hands had begun to tremble uncontrollably. What was his name? How could she stop him? He had half the money now, and expected the rest after ... afterwards. 'Ian,' she said aloud. His nickname was Lofty, because he was well over six feet in height. She must go down Brighton Road and wait for him to emerge from that shabby house.

Another thought crashed into her skull. The men in that place weren't allowed out during the hours of darkness, so Lofty would have primed them to cover for him while he did the job. He might have told them details. The tea was still almost boiling, yet she drank it quickly. Lofty must be found soon, and she dressed hastily in the first garments that came to hand. She was almost out of the house before noticing that she wore one black shoe and one brown.

After rectifying the situation, she sat for a few minutes. The suspicion that she was being manipulated hovered at the front of her mind. But what might she do about that? Must she go to the police station and show a letter that accused her of plotting an arson attack? God, no.

Someone must have spilled the beans. Who knew? Only the men in the halfway house... Yet Elsie felt sure that this beautifully written missive

368

had been penned by an educated person. But clever criminals did exist, so she had better be on her way. Like the original Gunpowder Plot, this one must be foiled. It had seemed almost foolproof, just one more fire among thousands throughout a country that celebrated the failure of the original treason.

'Pull yourself together, Elsie. You haven't time to be sitting here.' Wearing shoes that matched, heavy coat, woollen hat, warm gloves and scarf, she set out with one thought in mind – she must save herself.

The SSS was formed by Marie and Alice, who had put their heads together a few days after Vera's wedding. It was all well and good for male lunatics to make a 'final' break for it on a stag night, but women? Shopping, cleaning and laundry came higher on the list. They were also nursemaids, cooks, first-aiders, teachers and general dogsbodies. It was time to have a little fun, wasn't it?

Their beloved partners, having achieved a mess on the stag night, continued to make a break for freedom once or twice a week. They had poker nights, darts matches, or we're-just-going-for-a-pint evenings. So retaliation was declared, and the Seven Sisters Society was formed. Since four of the original Stewart girls were no longer available, their places would be taken by Olga, Vera, and Nellie's two daughters.

The two founding members of the women's party decided to have the SSS meetings at Marie's house, which was the largest by far. They chose Thursday evenings, since that was the day Nigel did an evening shift at the zoo, performing small operations and inoculations while the zoo was closed. He promised to go straight upstairs on his return, as he wished not to interrupt his wife's social arrangements.

On the first occasion, they all contributed food and drink. Having never visited a public house or a restaurant unless on the arm of a man, each woman was happier in a domestic setting. This inaugural meeting was happening because they needed to form a plan. 'Being in each other's houses will still be giving in,' Alice said. 'As soon as a baby cries or a button drops off a shirt, we'd be on duty. So we stick to the rule that on the third Thursday of each month, the husbands are housewives.'

Marie had something to say. 'Visit any city and see the truth – men-only clubs,' she announced. 'Especially in London, where there are places where women are only let in to clean. We may have the vote, but many of us are still just lackeys. One day, we should form a women-only club in Liverpool. Isn't it time? No men allowed except to perform menial tasks like decorating.'

'I know a good plumber,' Alice said.

Nellie laughed. 'How well do you know him, love?'

Alice blushed to the roots of her hair, and her jaw dropped.

Everyone present knew that Nellie seldom noticed anything beyond her own immediate family of husband, two daughters and two grandsons; if Nellie had spotted the attraction between

Alice and Harry, what about the rest?

Claire directed a shushing sound at her mother. Most here had seen it – the stolen glances, the don't-look-at-me games, those attempts to avoid standing or walking too closely to each other. Auntie Alice would never cheat on Uncle Dan – Claire was almost sure of that. She glared at her mother. Nellie Browne often tripped over her own tongue, since she didn't always think before speaking. When Alice left to visit the bathroom, Claire spoke. 'Don't you dare do that to her again, Mam. Didn't you know she's carrying twins? Her doctor found two heartbeats.'

Nellie burst into tears.

'Stop that before you start,' Marie snapped. 'See? This is why we have to grab some freedom, but that freedom will be worth nothing if we start getting personal. I have no children and that makes me sad, but who births them? Women do. Who stays at home and rears them, feeds them, cleans their bums? Who's their first teacher? No matter how good a job he has, remember that your husband was taught by a woman how to use cutlery, fasten shoes and wipe his backside.'

'But not all three simultaneously,' Vera said, and was bemused by the ensuing laughter.

Janet spoke up. 'In our case, Mam does the baby-minding while we keep the businesses going, but what you say is right. Women do a lot.'

'So we stick together. Nellie, dry your eyes,' Marie said. She waited until the youngest sister reappeared. 'Right. We can't buy a club for women, but we can use my house once a month. There are seven of us. That's enough.'

'We'll decide menus and who brings what,' Alice added, now cool as the proverbial cucumber. 'You lot might have wine and spirits, but I can have just a small Guinness. Iron for the babies.' She rose to her feet again.

'Where are you going now?' Vera asked.

Alice left the room again after mumbling something about two babies playing football with her bladder.

Marie followed her. 'What's up?' she asked. 'Did Nellie upset you?'

'No comment. Muth's just walked past with a giant of a man. I need a few minutes on my own, that's all.' She left Marie and climbed the stairs to the posher bathroom. 'Callum?' she whispered. 'Is it fixed?' He was a pest. When needed, he was absent; when unwelcome, he inevitably turned up.

'I know you can hear me.' Her tone was accusatory.

'She's on her own now,' he said. 'Hiding behind the oak on the left, she is. Seeing you all together will annoy her.'

Alice sighed heavily. 'No fire?'

'No fire. But it still cost her the full price. Go back and close the curtains; we don't want her riled any more than usual.'

For once, Alice Quigley did as she was told. Sometimes, she couldn't be bothered to argue with an angel.

Fifteen

1947

Several things of importance – not all good – took place in the first two months of the year 1947.

The weekly meat ration was reduced to one shilling's worth per head, the coal industry was nationalized, and Lord Louis Mountbatten took up the position of last Viceroy of India, which country's independent status would supposedly be achieved by the middle of the following year. In Britain, troops were deployed to move food from one place to another, since transport workers were on strike, and, on the twentieth day of February, Alicia Marguerite Quigley gave birth to twins on a very valuable silk rug during a meeting of the SSS in Marie Stanton's house.

The seven members of the club had been discussing ideas connected to corned beef, because everyone was going to be allowed an extra two-pence-worth of that imported meat, but recipes were scrubbed from the agenda when the rug got soaked during an exciting lecture on how to jazz up corned beef hash with tomatoes and mouse-trap cheese.

It was chaos, as the expected were unexpected at this stage of pregnancy. 'They're early,' screamed the mother as her waters broke. 'There's still a

373

fortnight to go. What have I done wrong? Is it my fault?' She dropped her cup of tea, as if trying to make worse the damage she had already inflicted on her sister's perfect décor.

'Babies don't have calendars or diaries,' Nellie muttered as she ushered dogs and cats out of the room. 'They just come when they're cooked. Mine were both ten days late. I was thinking of charging them rent for their lodgings.'

Most of the exclusively female audience gabbled about fetching doctor and midwife, but Vera rolled up her sleeves. 'Stop flapping, you lot,' she yelled. 'They'll be all right – twins often turn up early. Marie, go upstairs with Claire and empty a couple of drawers. Stick a flock pillow – no feathers – in each one and bring clean towels for blankets. Janet, find string and big scissors. The scissors need to be sterilized in boiling water. Olga, stop swearing in Russian, love – you're getting on me nerves. I hear enough of that at home with Yuri.' She made Alice lie down so that the patient's underwear could be removed. 'Alice?'

'What?'

'How long have you been pushing, girl? You shouldn't push yet, cos you might burst your periwotsit.'

'No, I haven't been pushing. It's just happening without pushing.'

'Any pains in your belly, then? Or in your back?'

'Some. Things keep tightening then stopping. It feels wrong.'

'Oh, so the pains are not too bad?'

'No, they're not as bad as I thought they'd be.'

374

Then she heard an angel whispering inside her head. 'Here comes Danielle,' Callum said. 'It will be easy. I'm with you. I've been with you since the day you were born, and I'm staying here while you get through this.' She would be fine, she decided. Her dad's older brother was watching over her. Lying down on an old, clean tablecloth at the dry end of the rug, she waited for events to unfold. She wasn't in charge of her body – it was weird.

The baby made much of her first screaming exhalation before she was fully out of the birth canal. 'Not much wrong with this one,' Vera announced. 'Don't know whether it's a boy or a girl, but crying fit to bust already.'

'It's probably Danielle – Ellie,' the mother told her unqualified but experienced midwife. 'I've never liked standing in a queue, and I'll bet she's just like ... ooh, that was a big squeeze. Is she out?'

Vera grinned from ear to ear. 'Perfect, love. She's so gorgeous, if I didn't know different, I'd think she was a Caesariant.'

No one laughed at Vera's murder of the language; it was part of her.

'String and big scissors,' she shouted. 'Cool the scissor handles if you can, but not the blades.'

Baby Callum slid out as if he'd been rolled in butter. Vera blinked away her tears. She had never before witnessed a birth so quick and so nearly pain-free. Both babies screamed healthily. 'Nellie – get some warm water and a bit of soap. You wash these babies, but steer clear of the navels when I've tied off – I've some belly button

375

powder at home. I have to see to the afterbirth stuff. The rest of you get out of the way and sit down with your corned beef. By the way, they're about six pounds each. No wonder Alice looked so fat that we thought we'd need Big Bertha to shift her.'

'Shut up,' Alice ordered. 'I've been pregnant, not fat.'

'Who is the big Bertha?' Olga asked. 'Does she live in the Penny Lane area? Is she the large lady with metal curlers under the scarf?'

'She's a crane on the docks,' Claire said as she arrived with the infants' makeshift beds. 'We've got some nice, soft towels. Oh, God – they're here already. You're a quick worker, Auntie Alice. I took ten hours, and our Janet took going on fifteen.'

'Why big Bertha?' Olga persisted.

'Because she's big and some daft sod called her Bertha.'

Olga decided not to pursue the matter. Liverpool did strange things for strange reasons – this she had learned since arriving many years earlier. She'd given up trying to find out what kind of birds were Livers and why they sat the way they did, one looking inland, the other seaward.

'You can call the doctor now,' Vera conceded. 'Just to make sure I've got everything out of Alice. And I don't mean there's another baby, but we need to ensure I've got rid of the other stuff. What the hell are you doing now?' she asked her charge.

The new mother was shuffling along towards the fireplace where the babies, after a quick wipe-down, were wrapped in and snuggled under soft towels in a couple of drawers from Marie and Nigel's bedroom. 'I'm going to try to feed them myself,' she said, 'but in case I can't, I've got bottles and National Dried at home.' She stared down at two tiny people. 'Beautiful,' was her expressed opinion as she assessed her children. 'Is there any petrol in your little car, Marie?'

'Yes, there is.'

Alice turned to face her sister. 'Will you go and get Dan?'

'I've gone.' Marie dashed from the house, picking up her car keys from a hook in the hall.

'If you feel well enough, try feeding them now,' Vera advised. 'Your milk won't be in just yet, but they need the colostrium. It's yellowish stuff.'

'Colostrum,' Alice said with a grin. 'It helps babies not to get ill, because the mother's lifelong ability to fight disease is in it. Even if I bottle-feed them, it will give them a good start. I read about it.' She smiled at Vera. 'Thank you from Callum and Ellie, and from me. You did a great job.'

'You did the work, Alice. If you'd gone the full forty weeks, they'd have been eight pounders, and you might have called it a launching, not a birthing.'

The mother of twins chuckled. 'There wasn't much pain. But look at our Marie's best rug. I've buggered it. That thing cost a fortune. They bought it in North Africa and had it shipped across.'

'Then we buy another,' Olga said. 'We have the money, no? We can all give some to replace it. Or perhaps it can be cleaned?'

377

Nellie had been quiet since washing the twins. Her daughters stood at either side of her, each holding one of her hands. 'Stop crying, Mum,' Janet begged.

Nellie broke her silence. 'Don't let her near them, Alice.'

Alice, trying to feed her little boy, glanced up. 'Why, Nell?'

'I can't remember. I used to remember, but it just went out of my head like chalk wiped off a blackboard.' She recalled Muth's screaming coming from the front bedroom, towels, sheets, a pillowcase and blood. A bundle ... she'd carried downstairs a bundle of bloody washing before returning to sit on the top step of the stairs until the midwife arrived. Alice had been born screaming like these two precious babies, yet... Yet? Yet what? Dad had stamped about a lot, and he'd started working longer hours soon after the birth of the seventh daughter. In fact, truth be told, the lovely man went into a decline and never recovered.

The new mother whispered into her son's dark, downy hair. 'That would be Callum, your namesake. He's cleared Auntie Nellie's mind and wiped paintwork in Harry's house as well. Very handy, he is – for a lunatic. He's my uncle and your greatuncle, and he's dead. God gave him a ticket, and he's come back to mind us. He loves us.' Should she be talking about a ghost? Baby Callum wouldn't understand a word, she decided.

When the little boy was asleep, she picked up his twin. 'Hello, blondie. You're going to need eyebrow pencil when you grow up. A real little platinum, eh?' There wasn't much hair on Ellie's head, but the damp clumps were light brown, while eyebrows and lashes were white. 'Oh, my word, you are pretty.'

As soon as the doctor arrived, Vera dragged him into the kitchen. 'It's all in here.' She showed him a bowl. 'Two sacs, both looked all right and all there, as if she delivered a couple of footballs. They've flattened a bit now, but I'm sure I got the lot. Will you have a good look at her, make sure she didn't get ripped?'

He adjusted his spectacles. 'Of course, and well done. Now, can you clear that room of everyone except the mother and the babies?'

'I will.' She went to obey the doctor's orders, then stood back while the man examined the patient for damage or heavy bleeding. Satisfied that the mother was fine, he took Ellie from her. 'Lovely,' he pronounced. 'About six pounds and fighting fit. And yes, she's taking the colostrum – she's dribbled a bit.' He examined Callum. 'Right, a job well done, I'd say. If you feel worried or ill, get your own doctor out.' He turned and shook Vera's hand. 'Glad you were here. I was told the delivery was swift. She's not losing too much blood.'

'It was quick,' Vera told him. 'Thanks for coming to check on them. Sorry to get you out in the evening, like.'

On his way out, the medic almost collided with Dan and Marie, who were on their way in. Alice's husband was attached to her sister, as she was holding fast to his left ear. 'That, Daniel Quigley, is the last time you sneak out on a Thursday night while we're in a Seven Sisters Society meeting.

See the two drawers from my tallboy? Your son's in one, and your daughter's in the other. The woman on the floor is your wife. You'll be baby-sitting on Thursdays, all right?' She spoke to Alice. 'I'll get you something clean to wear and run you a bath with a bit of salt in it.'

With the ear released from his sister-in-law's grip, Dan looked at his children. They were lovely, and he said so, his voice shaky and pitched at a higher than normal level. 'Your Marie didn't tell me what had happened, though I guessed.' He rubbed his ear. For a small, slender woman, Marie Stanton had one hell of a grip. 'They're perfect,' he managed.

Alice laughed. 'With a handsome dad and a beautiful mum, they're made of good stuff.'

He managed a smile. 'They're not creased. Don't they usually look as if they need dipping in starch and ironing?'

Having disposed of the bowl's contents, Vera returned. 'Sit down, Dad,' she ordered. 'Marie says you were out playing poker. Men? They're kids.'

He sat and waited while his next door neighbour, an expert in her field of work, scooped up the twins and placed them in his arms. Dan's tears flowed. 'I knew he'd kick off,' Alice said. 'He's been a bit daft since we found out we were expecting.'

Vera grinned broadly. 'Well, they're having their baptism of tears. Perhaps you won't need to take them to church.'

Marie and Nellie came to help Alice upstairs for a warm salt bath, leaving Janet, Claire, Vera and Olga to join Dan in a game of pass the parcel with two new babies swaddled in soft towels. He spoke to his wife before she left the room. 'Thanks, love.'

'I've ruined Marie's rug,' was her reply. 'It was so beautiful, but look at it now.'

Marie, in the doorway with Nellie, tutted her disapproval. 'Shut up about the flaming rug. It's replaceable. Babies aren't.'

The whole company heard the break in Marie's voice in her final two words. Everyone knew that she would have given a hundred silk rugs in exchange for a baby of her own. Dan waited until he knew Alice and her two sisters had reached the bathroom. 'Cruel world,' he whispered, no longer trying to hide the emotion that flooded down his face. 'Just one would have been enough for Marie, God love her. And here we are with two. Cruel world,' he repeated.

Alice Quigley was, for the most part, a sensible and pragmatic woman. A stickler where housework was concerned, she attacked dust and mess as soon as it appeared, cleaned brasses once a week, kept paths, windowsills and doors polished, scrubbed the kitchen floor on hands and knees twice a week, and kept everything in its rightful place.

Suddenly, she had two babies and a husband who was now working full time and overtime. One baby kept waking the other and– 'Alice? You there?'

And the endless stream of visitors woke both infants. 'Where else would I be?' was her reply when Vera walked in. 'I was trying to have a doze on the sofa. The twins don't share a timetable, and there's always one awake.' She would need to start locking the front door during the day as well. The only person who really helped her always came in the back way when he wasn't out on a plumbing job. Harry was brilliant with the babies, which was unexpected, since he'd never been a dad or a hands-on uncle, as his siblings and their families had moved south. Dan, on the other hand, wasn't coping with parenthood... Dan was emotionally shallow, possibly weakened and spoilt during his illnesses.

'You do look tired, love,' Vera pronounced. 'I've left Yuri running the shop. Do you need any help? Washing, ironing, shopping – I'm having an hour or more off, so I can give you a hand.'

'I've got to find my own way, Vee. I think having two at once makes more than twice the trouble.'

Vera nodded sagely. 'I don't know which is worse, Alice, twins or what I had – one at the walking stage, but still with no sense, and the other brand new in my arms. I'd the toddler yelling his head off because he'd fell out of the back door hole, and the little baby screaming hungry. I'd be running to pick Tony up off the path, and our Neil would be crying all over me frock because he wanted feeding and needed a clean nappy. No walk in the park, eh?'

Alice shook her head in agreement. 'Speaking of walks in the park, will you take Frank out for me? He got a bit confused when we brought the living room down here again and took the bedroom back upstairs, and he's been sulking in the kitchen ever since. He hates change. I've had him

out with the babies, but he shows his teeth if anybody comes near the pram, carries on like he's
guarding Buckingham Palace. He's too protective of our new arrivals. Try to give him a run,
please.'

Vera chuckled. 'Course I will.' She left the room
to get the boxer. 'Come on, Churchill,' she said,
because she always swore she could see the
likeness.

Alice closed her eyes and settled on the sofa in
a seated position. Where was Callum now, when
she needed a bit of magic? He'd not shown himself since the day of the twins' birth – even then,
he'd been just a pale streak on the ceiling and a
few words in her brain. Was Harry at home?
Harry had taken to honorary unclehood like the
proverbial duck to water, whereas Dan ... she let
the recurring thought drift away.

'See you later,' Vera yelled as she dragged a
reluctant Frank through the hallway. 'Behave,'
she told the dog. 'Alice, if I'm not back by five
o'clock, get the police out. Come on – buck up,
you lazy hound.'

The front door closed. Alice sighed and sent a
silent thank you to God; the twins had remained
asleep for almost an hour. Even Vera's shrill tones
hadn't managed to disturb them. The new mother
didn't need to open her eyes, because she already
knew that her house wasn't up to scratch. She was
heavily engaged on a daily basis in the boiling of
nappies, the preparation of bottles, and the washing of tiny clothes. The rest of her time seemed to
be spent in comforting, feeding and cleaning two
new babies, which chores left little time and no

energy for her usual jobs.

She sighed heavily. Dan was almost useless. He'd taken a close interest for the first few days, but once he'd realized that crying infants kept him awake and that meals were often late or thrown together in haste, he'd begun to back off. Backing off meant longer working hours, eating out or scrounging off Nellie and Martin – oh, and a tendency towards enjoying pub life in the evenings.

'Thank God for Harry,' she whispered. When he visited, Alice always fastened the front door properly, explaining to her locked-out and exasperated husband that a woman with two babies needed to feel safe in the evenings. When they heard Dan at the door, Harry did a quick disappearing act through the rear garden while she admitted the husband from whom she now felt estranged.

Harry told her she was even more beautiful since she had become a mum. She had filled out slightly, especially in what Harry called the upper storey or the balcony, and this made her laugh every time he referred to it. Her face was slightly fuller, too, 'especially the gob,' he said, meaning her lips. He was her comfort, her joy, her dirty secret, and her love for him grew exponentially alongside the increasing disappointment she felt towards her husband. She also experienced guilt, though nothing would ever entice her away from Harry's kisses – of that she felt very sure. Kissing was all she allowed.

'Why?' Harry asked repeatedly, his eyes directed at the balcony. He had joined Alice, Ellie and

Baby Callum as soon as Vera had left.

'Stop it.'

'Stop what?'

'Looking at me like that.'

He groaned and sat down. 'Where is he, Alice? How can he bear to stay away from you and these two little diamonds?'

The pair of gems lay on the rug in front of the fire. Dancing flames, clearly visible through the guard, seemed to fascinate the infants. They gurgled and blew bubbles. This was the quietest they'd been all day; Harry seemed to have a positive effect on their mood.

Alice shrugged. She had no idea where Dan was, and she said so, her tone implying that she couldn't care less. Her husband was becoming another chore – or another child, one who got under her feet.

Harry tried not to jump when a voice whispered in his ear. Callum Senior had arrived at last, but he seemed unwilling to talk to Alice. 'He's with a barmaid in the Brook – that pub near Marie's house,' the disembodied voice said. 'Go home in a few minutes and stay there. I think Nigel will deal with it. Look after her, Harry.'

'Harry?' Alice's eyebrows were raised.

'Sorry. I was just in a world of my own.' He joined her on the sofa, placing an arm across her shoulders. 'I don't understand Dan,' he told her for the umpteenth time. 'A beautiful missus, two lovely babies, and where is he?'

Alice stared at her companion. 'I don't know. It's probably because there are two babies. He can only manage one thing at a time, so he's buggered off to find some peace.'

'Or a piece of some tart in a pub. Sorry, I shouldn't have said that.'

'Why not? I've thought it often enough.'

'Have you?'

Alice nodded. 'Of course. He wants female company, not babies.'

'He was the one worried about dying and leaving you on your own.'

'I know.'

'Like a dog with two tails when you got pregnant.'

'I know.'

'You repeating the words "I" and "know" gets on my nerves.'

'I know.'

'What am I going to do with you, Alice?'

'Is it all right if I say I don't know?'

He kissed her until they were both breathless, then he went home. Experiencing a strong urge to kill Dan Quigley, he distracted himself by listening to some light music on the wireless while polishing his best shoes. When the footwear shone like black glass, he sat and tried not to hate Alice's husband, but it wasn't easy. And how would Nigel deal with the soft lad and his barmaid? Animal tranquilizers, poisoned dart, a kick up the back passage? Alice. How could any man cheat on her?

A car's brakes screamed. Harry strode to the front window and watched while Nigel and a man he didn't recognize dragged Dan out of the vehicle. When they hammered on Alice's front door, Harry decided to push open his window.

'Hello, Nigel. She keeps the bolt on because she's left alone a lot. But Vera's out with Frank, so Dan should be able to get in.'

'We're knocking to be polite to Alice. This is serious business.' Nigel Stanton seemed to speak while scarcely moving his lips.

Harry decided that Dan's nose had been bleeding.

Alice noticed the same when she pulled her front door inward. 'Yes?'

The other man, finally recognizable as the landlord from the Brook, dug his elbow into Dan's ribs. 'Tell her, or we tell the whole neighbourhood,' he growled. 'We'll get them all out and let them know about your carryings-on.'

'I'll tell her inside.'

'Too easy,' Nigel growled.

Alice folded her arms. 'What's happened?' she demanded.

'When your wife hears the truth, you'll be lucky to cross the threshold,' Nigel said, his tone acidic.

Seconds ticked by. The landlord cleared his throat. 'Molly Evans,' he shouted. 'This worthless bugger's been up to no good with one of our part-time barmaids. At it in the back yard at dinner time, they were, till my missus went to get something out of the shed. And I'm the one who smashed his nose.'

Alice, apparently unimpressed, simply closed the door and bolted it. Her outward calm was followed a minute or so later by the opening of the front bedroom window, from which gap rained down shirts, socks, shoes, trousers and underwear. 'Nigel?' Her tone was quiet. She threw down a suitcase.

'Yes, love?'

'Take him to our Nellie's. He can sleep in her spare bedroom until he finds somewhere else.' At last, she looked at the man she had married, adored, visited in hospital, nursed, spoon-fed and spoilt. 'You're not as ill as you were, and you don't need me, don't want our children. That's fine. The Catholic Church and I have been on a slippery slope for a while now. So I'll sue for adultery and get a divorce.'

'We'll back you up,' Nigel said.

'We will,' the landlord.

'I love you,' Dan wailed.

Alice closed the window, drew the curtains and signalled that she had left the bedroom by switching off the centre light as she walked out to the landing. Dan knew what was going on and why, because she'd hammered home her feelings about betrayal. 'One hour spent with one other woman, and you'll be burnt toast,' she'd told him often enough.

When she reached the ground floor, the babies were asleep in their day cribs and Harry was back and using a large drill on the back door. 'More bolts,' he explained.

'Thank you.' She sat in a straight-backed chair. 'We must be very careful now, or he'll counter-sue naming you.'

'Wouldn't bother me,' he replied.

'You're not a mother of two babies, love. It's different for me, because I have to protect them.' She sighed. 'And he's going to die. So I might do better if I let him come back until ... until then.

He could sleep in his recovery room, because he won't be sharing my bed. I just don't want Ellie and Callum to be the children of divorce. Better to wait till Dan...' She couldn't say it again. 'I know it all sounds cold, but I've always felt I could bear everything except betrayal, so he knows it's over. And he won't force himself on me, so don't be worrying.'

'Worrying about you's my full-time job.'

'What about plumbing?'

'A drop in the ocean, sweetheart.' He winked and returned to the job in hand.

Vera arrived and begged to be admitted by hammering on the door. When Alice let her in, the neighbour was grumbling about the bolted door, and Frank looked cheesed off. He walked away from the humans and settled in his bed. There was something going on and he couldn't be bothered.

'He doesn't like walking in the dark,' Vera said. 'I think we've had no more than about four hours of daylight today, what with the rain and black cloud. Never mind – soon be spring.'

Alice apologized profusely for locking out her good neighbour.

Vera stepped further into the hall and stood with the other two. 'What was all that about?' She jerked a thumb towards the street. 'I seen it from the bottom end of the lane. It looked a right battle, too. Folk across the way were staring.'

Harry, security supervisor, shrugged – he would leave Alice to explain.

'He's got a girlfriend,' Alice replied bluntly. 'She's a barmaid – well, she was – in that nice pub near our Marie's. I've told him time and again

389

that another woman would finish us, and it has.'

'Blood and bullets,' Vera hissed. 'What happened to sense, eh? What happened to love for his wife and kiddies?' She burst into tears. They were all bastards apart from her Yuri. 'God love you,' she sobbed, 'he'll not find another one like you, because the mould got broke.'

'We'll look after her, Vee.' Harry's voice was choked as he pulled the famous gossip into his arms. 'She's got loads of friends round here, and then there's Nellie and Martin and Marie and Nigel.'

'I'll kill him,' Vera whispered. 'Like I should have killed mine.'

'You and whose army?' Harry managed, his voice still rusty.

Vera smiled through her tears. 'Who needs an army when we've got our Olga? She's better than a Sherman tank, that one.' She pulled herself out of Harry's embrace and dried her tears. 'What are you going to do, queen?'

Alice's shrug was designed to be determinedly carefree. 'He can live in his recovery room. He'll go and see his tart, but he'll stay away from me. It's just to keep things looking right for the twins' sake.'

'But what if he...?' Vera's words died a natural death.

Alice's eyes were riveted to Harry's. They shared the near-knowledge that Dan was not long for this world. 'We'll manage, Vera, for two reasons,' Alice stated. 'One, I warned him that if he was unfaithful, we'd be done. And two, there's a lot of disease about since the war.'

'Ooh, I never thought.' Vera's eyes were wide, and her specs were slipping – a sure sign that she was flustered. She blushed. 'Yuri can now,' she informed them apropos of nothing at all. 'He won't have no diseases cos he couldn't do it for a long while.'

Harry smiled for the first time since the start of the conversation. 'I'm pleased for you, Vera. He's a good man.'

'The best.' Her cheeks displayed a deeper blush. 'With ... the other one, I felt as if he was ... you know ... forcing me.'

'Jimmy knew no different,' Harry said, 'and no, I'm not defending him. His was a rough family, and he followed in his father's footsteps. His mam was so thin, you couldn't see her if she stood sideways next to a lamp post. Best thing Jimmy ever did for you and the lads was to hang himself.'

Vera sniffed. 'Right, I'd best get back to the shop. With doing long hours, we've wotsnamed – we've increased turnover by fifteen per cent. That's what Olga's accountant said, any road. Ta-ra.'

Alone once more with his beloved, Harry begged, 'Don't have him back, Alice.'

'He'll be a lodger, no more. If he wants to be a dad, I won't stop him, but no way does that man have a wife. I'm engaged to you.'

'Aren't you going to try me on the way Olga did with Peter?'

'No, but I'll test your nappy-changing skills.'

'Shit.'

'Yes, that as well.'

The trouble with women, Harry decided, was that they had an answer for everything.

Sixteen

8 APRIL 1947

Alice Quigley stood before a small audience in her bedroom.

Her children, over six weeks old and fighting fit, were next door with Vera, Olga and Yuri, as was Frank, the family dog. For the first time in over thirty years, Alice was about to lead carefully chosen people into an otherness. 'I know you'd rather not be here, Muth, but this has to be done.' She smiled at Peter, whose chair was blocking access to the door. 'Thank you,' she mouthed in his direction.

Elsie Stewart was frightened, fidgety and in a very bad mood. This was her birthday; it was Alice's, too. Elsie had been fooled into coming up here to the bedroom for a birthday gift, a dress made by her youngest daughter, and she'd found Peter Atherton, Harry Thompson, Martin Browne and her second daughter, Marie Stanton, waiting for her. Yes, she'd been given a dress; she'd also received the shock of her life, since she was forced to stay in the room.

The youngest of seven daughters continued to speak to her. 'Mother, I have suffered otherness for as long as I can remember. I was diagnosed years ago as having petit mal followed by a question mark, but it's not epilepsy and it never was, so we can scrub that off the page. You wanted me to tell the future but, until recently, I saw only events that had already happened or, occasionally, the present time in another place. And then we moved here, into the house where all seven of us were born, and I began to see and hear more.

'I heard a baby crying, children playing, and a man speaking; I saw Olga Konstantinov's family being murdered in Russia. In this very room, as well as downstairs, I saw my dad's tobacco smoke hanging in the air – I could even smell it. Frank used to share the otherness with me, but he got an honourable discharge and I was suddenly alone except for disembodied voices. Dan experienced nothing until quite recently, when he was–'

'What about your boyfriend?' Elsie asked, her voice unsteady.

Alice would not be distracted. 'Harry saw, too. It's all right, Mother. In love and war, all's fair. Dan has his own arrangement. May I continue?'

Elsie, having fired the only bullet in her armoury, sat back. When would that bloody man move away from the door? She needed to escape this madness before it killed her.

'The name Callum fell into my head and out of my mouth. It was totally unexpected, of course.'

Elsie squirmed. Callum had been her husband's older brother in Ireland, so what the hell was he doing here? Was it possible that...? No, surely not. She closed her eyes for a moment. Charlie hadn't... God, she was shivering. But this was only the beginning for her. When she opened her eyes, she screamed loudly enough for all

393

Liverpool to hear.

Charlie 'Chippy' Stewart stood beside his Alice. He had adored the youngest child, and he had now placed himself at the right hand of his gifted, difficult daughter. 'Hello, Elsie,' he said as if he'd just stepped off the bus from town. 'Yes, I did. I did all I could for him. I know who and what you're thinking about.'

The mother of seven girls lost her ability to speak; she opened her mouth, but not one syllable came forth.

'This is our dad,' Alice announced, tears flowing freely down her cheeks. 'He was the loveliest, kindest man, and his wife mithered him to death, didn't you, Mother?'

Elsie, stiff as a board, made no further effort to speak. Mother. It was clear that Alice Quigley meant business, and when she meant business, Alice was as keen as mustard.

Marie, also moved to tears, was being cuddled and comforted by Harry. Alice, his precious neighbour, nodded her approval. Harry was almost family; his behaviour with Marie was natural. Dan seldom came home, so this beloved man was always welcome in Alice's house. He was affectionate, helpful and generous. He was also hers.

'Back in a minute,' Charlie said before fading away near Alice's dismantled bed. His voice remained. 'Here's Callum.'

Callum made a show of himself as usual, throwing colours at walls, singing 'Abide With Me', finally shaping himself into an enormous stained glass angel with every colour of the rainbow expressed in the panels. Alice dried her tears and said, almost apologetically, 'He never grew up.'

Angel Callum fixed his gaze on Elsie. 'There have been three of us, Elsie. The oldest Callum died many of Earth's years ago, and the youngest is currently next door being cared for by Alice's friends. I am the one in the middle. Surely you remember me?'

Elsie emitted a sound reminiscent of someone being strangled or garrotted. 'Go away,' she managed when her breath returned.

He moved and shone his lights on Alice. 'It is unusual, though not unheard of, for a twin to give birth to twins. You did just that, sister.'

Confused, Alice blinked several times before sinking to the floor. There were three Callums; there was the uncle, the new baby and a ... brother? Her brother, her twin brother? Her twin was an angel.

'I am the seventh child; you are my twin sister and the eighth born. Since I lived for just a few minutes, I have worked through you, because we grew together in the womb of that terrible woman. Here's Dad.'

This time, Charlie's face showed anger that verged on fury. 'He breathed, Elsie. You passed him to me and told me to kill "it". It.' Charlie shook an index finger. 'I baptized him Callum after my brother. I'm sure you know that in the absence of clergy anyone may baptize, even with tap water or rainwater. My son got Lourdes water, bless him. Cleansed of mankind's original sin, he went straight to the Lord and is now an angel.

'When you said something might be done about his open spine, I foolishly passed him back to you and went to fetch the midwife, but our Marie had already gone for her. When I came back to this room, you still had the pillow pressed over his whole little body, including his face. You murdered our only son. He is now standing beside me.'

Elsie screamed, 'You buried him! You put him under a flag in the yard. I'm not the only one who did wrong.'

'Yes, I did bury him. I did it because I didn't want my girls to be labelled as children of a criminal who committed infanticide. I know he might have needed help, a wheelchair, some nursing. But he had the right to life. And he wants his baby bones left where they are, don't you, son?'

For answer, Angel Callum spread himself out until the whole room was multicoloured. 'Stand up,' he ordered his twin sister. 'I know you're a shrimp, but walk as tall as you can.'

'So a midwife delivered me?' Alice whispered as she rose to her feet.

'Yes,' Charlie replied. 'While Callum's body lay cooling under the bed.'

Peter shifted slightly when someone tried to open the door. 'Who's there?' he called.

'It's me – Nellie. I remember, I remember – it's all come back to me.'

When Peter opened the door to admit Nellie, Elsie tried to make a break for freedom, but she was dragged back in by her oldest daughter and the man who had guarded the door. 'Sit,' Peter snapped.

The new arrival acted as if she saw her dead father and Angel Callum every day; there was not the slightest sign of nervousness. 'Two babies,' she announced. 'Muth told me that our Alice had stopped crying and started up again, but it was two different cries.' She turned on her mother. 'The midwife delivered Alice. So either Alice was born twice, or we were missing one baby. Did you kill our little sister's twin? Did you?' She turned to her father, who looked very solid for a ghost. 'Did she, Dad?'

'She did,' Charlie replied. 'His legs were likely to be paralysed, so he wasn't whole in your mother's eyes. Once he was dead, she wiped him out of her mind and made Alice the seventh child. But it didn't work out your way, Elsie, did it? Because the perfect soul of a murdered child went straight into God's care and became an angel. Look what you lost, what you smothered. He's bright, funny, beautiful and good. This is the man he would have been, crippled or not. His loyalty to his family, especially to Alice, is boundless.'

Nellie addressed the mother she loathed. 'The best thing you can do is bugger off as far as you can from Liverpool. None of us can forgive you for killing our little brother. We wanted a boy, and we would have looked after him. But no. You were too bothered about what people might say when you birthed a child who was less than perfect. Have you any idea how much I want to break your neck, how badly our Alice wants you gone? She was nice to you for a reason, and that reason is today, isn't it?'

'Yes,' Alice replied. She was taken aback somewhat by this display of strength on the part of her oldest sister, who was known to be hesitant and edgy when facing the unusual. Nellie had found her backbone, so something good had come out of this difficult evening. 'You'd better go, Mother. Pack up and clear out before I change my mind and get that flag lifted.'

'Your dad buried it, not me.'

'Yes, and Dad's dead. You're not, so you'll cop for the lot.' Alice raised her head higher – it had been bowed and buried in thought for long enough. 'Would you mind leaving – all of you? I want to say goodbye to my brother, my other half.'

Elsie fled like a bat out of hell while Marie and Nellie waited for a minute or two to drink in the impossible vision of their two dead male relatives. Then, hand in hand, they left.

Alone at last with Charlie and Callum, Alice listened intently to their advice. 'Dan's not a bad man,' Charlie said.

Callum agreed. 'He's weak rather than bad. The reality of the twins scared him, and he turned to that woman because she's as stupid as he is. This will sound odd, but he still loves you. He's in awe of you, Alice. He knows you're a lot cleverer than he is.'

'Long spells in hospital made him used to being waited on.' Charlie smiled. 'So losing your attention to the twins is too much for a spoilt child to endure. You're looking after him and the babies as best you can – treating him like the brother who was stolen from you. We have to go now, love.'

Alice panicked. 'Will I never see you again?'

Callum laughed. 'Perhaps not, but you'll know we're nearby.'

'Thank you.' Her tone was sad, because she would surely miss Callum and his tricks. As for Dad ... she blinked away new tears.

'It's easier for us,' Charlie Stewart said. 'We don't measure time. Just live your life and be happy, Alice. You don't need a divorce; Dan knows he's doing wrong, and Purgatory will be his first destination.'

And they were gone in the blink of an eye. In their wake, Callum's voice, quieter now, reminded her that he was number seven, while she was the eighth child. She felt abandoned and lonely, but she had no right to such emotions. 'I have my twins and Harry,' she mused aloud, 'and my sisters, plus some very good friends. Yes. I'm a very wealthy woman.'

She walked to one of a pair of windows and looked down on Penny Lane. So much had changed, but the lane, like Old Man River, remained the same. 'No more Callum,' she whispered, 'no more fooling about and making me laugh.' Other changes had occurred, of course. Olga and Peter now lived on Menlove Avenue, Vera was married to Yuri, Dan was drinking too heavily, Harry acted as father to Ellie and Callum.

She missed Dan, the daft Dan who had chased her through Blackpool, through most of Liverpool and all the way to an altar. She still fed him, washed and ironed his clothes, had conversations with him. Deep inside, she knew when her marriage had gone wrong, so she took herself to that point. It had been about pregnancy, no more than that, but it had been too clinical for her, while twins had been one too many for him to cope with. 'And enter Harry stage right,' she murmured. He was right, right for her and for the twins. 'I am now guilty of adultery.' She wiped the silly smile off her face.

A black car stopped outside and two men stepped out of it and towards her path. Before leaving her post at the window, she knew who they were and why they were here. 'Ta-ra, Dan,' she whispered. Her heart leapt about for a few seconds, finally resting in her chest like a lump of lead.

Voices climbed the stairs, but the words were unclear.

The bedroom door opened. 'You all right, queen?' Nellie asked.

'Not bad, love. What's going on?'

The oldest Stewart sister arrived at the side of the youngest. 'Muth's gone. She said she's catching a train in the morning, and we won't see her again.'

Alice turned. 'Not interested in her, Nellie. Tell me about the men downstairs – are they plain clothes coppers?' She waited. 'Well?'

A few slow seconds strolled by. 'It's not good news. Dan's had a heart attack in the Liver pub up Waterloo way.'

'Is he in hospital?'

Nellie sniffed. 'He was. But he's in the morgue now, love. Martin says he'll go with you to identify his body. I mean, they know who he is … who he was, but they need to do things properly.

Don't cry, love. You've shed enough tears for one day. Harry's waiting for you downstairs with the policemen.'

'Nellie?'

'What?'

'Go next door and explain to Vera, Olga and Yuri. And yes, I'll borrow your Martin.'

'They said tomorrow would do, but I think you should get it over and done with, Alice.'

The younger woman straightened. 'So do I, Nellie. So do I.'

Thus ended Alice Quigley's thirty-fourth birthday. It had begun with gifts and cards, but now it was ending with the loss of Dad, Callum, Dan and Muth. Alice would go with Martin to confirm her husband's death, as it would seem strange to take Harry. She set her shoulders firmly. 'Come on, Nellie. I have to tidy poor Dan away.' She thanked God for Harry before setting out to close a chapter. Soon, a new story could begin.

Seventeen

JUNE 1953

My dear, beautiful children,

Callum and Ellie, I thank you for behaving so nicely through the coronation of our new Queen. Daddy says he will get a television set soon, and we won't need to go to Auntie Olga and Uncle Peter's house to watch important events. Of course, I missed the Vivat Regina

401

bit, as our Kristina – please remember she's younger than you twins are – had one of her famous tantrums and I had to take her out into the garden.

Alice grinned. Kristina's tantrums were spectacular, though she was almost three. At just two, about a year ago, she had decided that making a fuss was fun, that Daddy or Mummy might read to her in order to calm her down, and that being in charge was great. Kristina – one of Olga's given names – was a character. Reading a few weeks before her third birthday, the young Kristina was also a capable child. Alice picked up her pen.

We had a lovely coronation party, didn't we? Ellie and Kristina, you were so beautiful in the frocks I made. Callum, you were in your first grown-up suit, also tailored by me. Daddy looked posh enough to be waiting at table for the Queen, the Duke and their children, and I didn't look bad for my age. You will always remember where you were when Queen Elizabeth was crowned. It was wonderful.

Olga had seemed a little sad, Alice thought. The Romanovs had been related to the Windsors, probably via Queen Victoria's brood, though Alice wasn't sure. The pomp and circumstance meant a lot to a Russian whose family had been royal, and Olga had wept through 'Zadok the Priest', the coronation anthem. 'Hello, Frank,' Alice said. He was older, slower, but as gentle and sweet as ever.

Kristina, it will be your birthday in sixteen days. Ellie and Callum, at six years of age, you have already ventured out into the world of school, and I am so proud of you, as is Daddy. I'm glad it didn't rain when we took flowers to Daddy Dan's grave.

Poor Dan. Poor Molly, too. The girl had been destroyed by the loss. Alice's twins were Dan's, and Kristina was Harry's, but all three called Harry Daddy, and Dan was Daddy in heaven. Everything was explained in one of Alice's letters, though details were few, and there was no mention of her mother or her deceased twin brother.

Frank lay at her feet. Every time she thought about losing him, her heart hurt. They'd been through a lot together, first living as tenant and guard dog in the Sefton Park flat, later here, on Penny Lane. Now, another move was on the cards because Marie and Nigel were going to live their dream out in Africa. There they would care for young, orphaned or abandoned lions with the intention of returning them to the wild once they grew strong enough.

'Don't worry, Frank. Larry the llama has settled down at last, and you like Marie's dogs and cats, don't you?'

The boxer raised an eyebrow.

She laughed at him. 'Don't you believe me? Honestly, Larry's much better. And you love donkeys and horses. Harry will be back soon, and he'll take you for a wander down the lane.' Frank's tame pigeon had disappeared years ago; perhaps he would feel better when surrounded by Nigel's miniature zoo. 'Leo will visit, too. You'll be fine – just you wait and see.' He had better be fine; Alice adored her old boxer.

Harry's house was already tenanted, as he had moved in with Alice and the twins after the wedding. Alice's place was now advertised for rental, since she, Harry and their children were moving into Chesterfields, which was too valuable a house to be left empty for years. Nigel had sold the veterinary practice, while poor old Toothy Tommy was too frail to care for the house, the grounds and the animals without help. 'I'll miss Penny Lane, Frank. It's not just you – I'm used to living here, too!'

She stared through the window near which she always sat to write her journal. Mrs Wolstenholme was out donkey-stoning her step. Her skirt had ridden up, so Alice had a good view of huge tea-rose pantaloons with elastic at the knees. The old lady was as deaf as a post, so there was no point in trying to shout about the enormous knickers.

Vera was sweeping, glasses slipping down her nose as usual. Alice giggled. Her neighbour did a better job than the corporation when it came to the cleaning of this section of Penny Lane. 'What will it be like, Frank, living in a detached house? We've always had neighbours, haven't we?'

Frank snored while his owner complained about his lack of interest in their new situation. She returned her attention to her letter.

So I'm sitting here looking out at the lane. Kristina, you're visiting Auntie Nellie in Blundellsands. Auntie Nellie and Uncle Martin sold their shop and bought a house in Crosby to be near their grandchildren. Your cousins Claire, Janet, Kevin and Paul run a big factory that makes wonderful furniture, and their child-

404

ren are lovely. Callum and Ellie, you are at school. I want you to read this when you are adults, so that even the smallest details of our happy lives might be relived and enjoyed by you.

Harry marched in, shoeless and covered in dust. 'Don't ask,' he said, raising a hand. 'Don't mention cellars, rats – including drowned ones – gas pipes or drains.'

'I wasn't going to. Go and clean yourself up a bit; you look like nobody owns you.'

He winked. 'You own me, angel.'

'We own each other,' she replied, 'but don't come any nearer. I'm not sure I want to know a bloke who's been up to his eyes in drowned rats.'

'My fair-weather bride,' he teased.

'It rained the day we got married,' she reminded him.

'And what did I say at the time?' Harry asked, teasing her.

'Erm ... I do?'

'What else?'

She stood up and hugged him. 'Did the rats have fleas?'

'That's not what I said on our wedding day.'

She gave in, just as she always did. 'A French proverb, but in English. You said, "Rainy wedding day means a happy household."'

'And I was right.'

'Yes. You always are.'

This Large Print Book for the partially sighted, who cannot read normal print, is published under the auspices of

THE ULVERSCROFT FOUNDATION